DIFFERENT RAINBOWS

GAY MEN'S PRESS

Different Rainbows

edited by Peter Drucker

First published 2000 by Millivres Ltd,
part of the Millivres Prowler Group,
Worldwide House, 116-134 Bayham St,
London NW1 0BA

World Copyright © 2000 Peter Drucker and contributors

A CIP catalogue record for this book is available
from the British Library

ISBN 1 902852 10 9

Distributed in Europe by Central Books,
99 Wallis Rd, London E9 5LN

Distributed in North America by InBook/LPC Group,
1436 West Randolph, Chicago, IL 60607

Distributed in Australia by Bulldog Books,
P O Box 300, Beaconsfield, NSW 2014

Printed and bound in the EU by WS Bookwell, Finland

Preface

This book is the result of many people's efforts over too many years. A few words of acknowledgement do not by any means do justice to the extent of the contributions all these people have made.

Thanks are due above all to the authors, not only for their own articles but for their helpful comments on each others' work as well as on mine. Writing is difficult and time-consuming enough without sharing in editing tasks as well, yet several of the authors took me up on my invitation to do so, and the book is undoubtedly better for it. Very special thanks go to Margaret Randall and Mark Gevisser for their myriad forms of help, advice, criticism and encouragement—I doubt I would have made it without them. Thanks also to the translators, César Ayala and Raghu Krishnan.

Different Rainbows would definitely never have seen the light of day without Salah Jaber, who first encouraged me to begin research on the topic, or David Fernbach of Gay Men's Press, whose contributions were countless: getting my first article on the topic published, offering to publish a book on it, showing endless patience and generosity, giving me the benefit of his own thinking, and persevering with the project after every deadline had passed and through every kind of adversity. My employers and colleagues at the International Institute for Research and Education have been generous in allowing me time to work on this topic and this book.

For help in finding authors, thanks to Kwame Anthony Appiah, Daniel Boyarin, Lingfang Cheng, Paul Crook, Heather Dashner, Ken Davis, Shivananda Khan, Saleemur Rahman Kidwai, Gary Kinsman, Michiel Odijk, Aly Remtulla, Glen Retief, B. Skanthakumar, Noel Valencia, Alan Wald, Nancy Wechsler, Iden Wetherall and Sergio Yahni. Paul Crook also helped me with his knowledge of China, as Ken Davis did with his knowledge of Africa.

I would also like to thank the people who submitted draft articles that for one reason or another did not ultimately make it into the book. In every case their work and their thinking have been valuable, even if they or I decided in the end that this book was not the place to publish it.

Thanks to Arthur Bruls, Paul Crook, Mirka Negroni of the International Gay and Lesbian Human Rights Commission, B. Skanthakumar, the staff of the Documentatie Centrum Homostudies and especially Torvald Patterson for help in assembling useful information.

Thanks to Tom Boellstorff, Gary Kinsman and Michael Tan as well as several of the authors for their extensive comments on the introduction and conclusion.

And as always thanks and love to Christopher Beck, who did his best to make my prose readable and keep me halfway sane throughout it all.

Peter Drucker
Amsterdam, August 1999

Introduction: remapping sexual identities

Peter Drucker

The Third World, the part of the world that shares a colonial past and an economically dependent present,[1] has been part of the global lesbian/gay community for a long time. Lesbian/gay politics emerged in a few major countries of Latin America early in the 1970s, very soon after the modern lesbian/gay liberation movement took off in 1968-69 with the May 1968 events in Paris, the Binnenhof protest in Holland and the Stonewall rebellion in New York. In most of the Third World—much of Latin America, the Caribbean, Southern Africa, South and Southeast Asia—movements have emerged later, in the late 1980s and 1990s, but spread rapidly. The Third World is also a steadily bigger part of the lesbian/gay world. Gay commercial scenes are spreading there; immigrants and tourists are travelling back and forth; and in a few Third World countries lesbian/gay scholars are even publishing books about their communities as well as reading them. At the same time anthropologists have paid increasing attention to same-sex sexualities in parts of the world where lesbian/gay politics and even open commercial scenes have so far emerged barely or not at all, such as the Arab world and much of sub-Saharan Africa.

But the fact that the Third World is such a large and increasing part of the lesbian/gay world does not mean that it is taken enough into account. The whole body of writing on Third World communities has grown up *after* many 'classics' of lesbian/gay liberation and lesbian/gay studies were already written. By the time people in the 'First World' started noticing the Third World, some of their basic political and scholarly assumptions were well established. These assumptions were based largely on middle-class experience in advanced capitalist countries. More recent European, North American and Australian innovations and debates, which have been more or less simultaneous with the rise of Third World movements and studies, have usually been disconnected from developments in Latin America, Africa and Asia.

This is unfortunate. Movements and writings in the Third World do not just extend activism and thinking into new areas, they raise issues for lesbian/gay movements worldwide and for the whole field of lesbian/gay studies. Sexual identities and concepts of oppression and liberation are historical, social, cultural, and differentiated by period, region, class, and nationality. Applying identities and concepts to new social layers and countries has to involve questioning, challenging and enriching them. The much-needed process of overcoming Euro- and US-centrism could help transform lesbian/gay movements and studies globally. *Different Rainbows* aims, first, to give a sample of some of the most interesting work being done in or on different Third World countries, and second, to raise some of the fundamental issues posed for scholars and activists.

In the introduction and conclusion, I highlight some questions that come up in many of the contributions to the book, about the reality of lesbian, gay, bisexual and transgendered communities and the strategies of lesbian/gay movements. What are these communities like in the Third World? What is their place in a globalized world which is also a world of increasing social inequality? Does 'lesbian/gay liberation' mean the same thing in the South as in the North or something different? In responding to these questions I put forward elements of an overarching framework, in the hope that this can not only help illuminate the different articles but also be of use for those working in or on countries not focussed on here.

But the introduction and conclusion are individual products, written by one individual editor. They have benefitted from comments by other contributors, as all the articles have; but they do not define an analysis or a politics for the book as a whole. The other authors are not part of any single current or collective and do not necessarily share my analysis or politics. Nor should my analysis or politics be seen as a kind of 'master narrative' into which the other articles are incorporated. The authors of this book have also commented to some extent on each others' work as the book took shape. The other authors also refer to examples from each others' countries, showing that there is a certain spontaneous Third World identity. All the articles, including the introduction and conclusion, should be read as different voices in an ongoing dialogue.

In this dialogue I have in a sense been at a disadvantage relative to the others in not having lived experience or even in-depth study of any particular Third World region. All my thoughts in the introduction and conclusion are based on others' work. Like Dennis Altman 'I see myself as co-researcher, ultimately dependent on both the goodwill and self-interest' of people in the Third World. This is not an ideal situation. It is to be hoped that people in the Third World, writing on the basis of their own personal experience, activism and research, will themselves take over the discussion in the years to come.

The obstacles to Third World people's taking charge themselves of studying the Third World should not be underestimated, however, especially when it comes to attempting syntheses that look at the Third World as a whole. We live in a world where dialogue and collaboration among different Third World regions is difficult, for crude material reasons. Third World organizations have much smaller budgets and staffs; libraries and universities in the Third World have much less funding; languages indigenous to the Third World are little used as languages of international politics or scholarship; and even flying from Latin America to or from Africa or Asia is often more difficult and expensive than flying from New York or Paris.[2] I expect and trust that people in the Third World will reject or drastically amend much of what I propose. But I think it would be false solidarity on my part to hang back from attempting any kind of synthesis, albeit initial and tentative, until they are ready to tackle it themselves. I have at least tried in the introduction and conclusion to foreground what unites *Different Rainbows*' authors.

Social construction without Eurocentrism

The Third World raises significant questions for the dominant 'social constructionist' current in lesbian/gay studies, which maintains that subcultures of self-identified gay men and lesbians are a historically recent phenomenon that emerged only in the nineteenth century in Western Europe and North America. The questions raised from the Third World are not so much about *whether* sexuality is socially constructed. The 'essentialist' argument that lesbians and gay men have existed everywhere throughout human history remains a minority position, including in the Third World. Despite continual media uproar, it has not been very much rehabilitated by attempts to find genetic causes of homosexuality. Most studies agree on the historical and geographical uniqueness of modern lesbian/gay identity. As David Fernbach concluded nearly twenty years ago, 'it is only relatively recently [and in certain parts of the world] that the space has emerged for a gay way of life'.[3]

Studying the Third World in fact adds new evidence to the case for social constructionism. On the one hand, it shows how different the Third World's indigenous sexualities are (or were) from lesbian/gay identity as it exists in contemporary Western Europe, North America or Australia. The overwhelming majority of same-sex sexualities in past cultures were in some demonstrable way different from what Europeans, North Americans and Australians now see as lesbian/gay identity.[4] Today as well, many Third World people who have same-sex sexual relationships do not define themselves at all as a particular kind of person ('a homosexual'). Many others do; but their identities in their particular cultures do not necessarily match up with European or North American lesbian/gay identity.

• In some cultures people have same-sex sexual relationships with one other without being seen as a particular kind of person: in gathering-and-hunting cultures when men are together on hunting trips, for instance. Afro-Surinamese women who call themselves each others' *mati* have long-term, intense, often open sexual relationships with each other in between or along with their sexual relationships with men, but a *mati* is not a distinctive kind of woman equivalent to 'lesbian'.[5]

• Some cultures have same-sex relationships that are 'transgenerational' (where for example boys may perform oral sex on adult men but not vice versa) or status-defined (where for example servants may be penetrated sexually but masters may not). But in these cases the two sexual partners do not share a 'gay' identity.

• In many cultures same-sex sexualities are 'transgenderal'. They involve assigning a gender identity to one sex partner different from his or her biological sex, while the other partner is considered a 'real man' or 'real woman'. Often in these cultures, for example, a man who penetrates other men sexually is still considered a 'masculine' man, and may often be expected to marry a woman and have children. A man who is penetrated sexually, however, is no longer considered masculine and becomes a person of the 'other gender' or a 'third gender'—a 'transgendered' person.

There are many words in use in the Third World that put gender identity in question in various ways: 'marimacha' (for females) and 'loca' (for males) in much of Latin America, 'bicha' (for males) in Brazil, 'moffie' (for males) in South Africa, 'hijra' (for hermaphrodites and males) in India, 'tomboi' (for females) and 'waria' (for males) in Indonesia, 'bakla' in the Philippines, etc. All these words for 'transgendered people', which almost always refer to only one partner in a same-sex relationship or encounter, are used instead of or alongside 'bisexual' (which might sometimes be used for the non-transgendered partner), 'gay' and 'lesbian' (which do not necessarily put men's 'masculinity' or women's 'femininity' in question). In many Third World countries the terms 'lesbian' and 'gay' exclude not only many people who have same-sex sex—in the US and Europe too, many married men who have sex with men do not identify as gay—but also many of the transgendered people who have same-sex identities. Only an awkward, portmanteau expression like lesbian/gay/bisexual/transgendered (LGBT) is reasonably inclusive.[6]

In all these different cultures, people engage in same-sex sex, and some of them have acquired specific identities, but clearly not all of them can be called 'gay'.

On the other hand, identities and communities that clearly *are* lesbian and gay *have* been emerging in one Third World country after another. It seems that their social construction keeps on happening. Similar causes lead to similar effects, even in different countries or cultures. Each of the different, to a large extent complementary, variants of social constructionist thinking can now draw on Third World evidence to make its case. The Marxist-feminist analysis that sees the development of capitalism, urbanization and changing family forms as causes of the rise of a lesbian/gay identity is bolstered by the fact that capitalist development in the Third World is accompanied by the emergence of lesbian/gay communities there. Michel Foucault's emphasis on the role of science, medicine and police surveillance and queer theorists' attention to popular culture are also largely vindicated by the role of science, medicine, the police and popular culture in redefining sexuality in the contemporary Third World.[7]

Studying the Third World does raise questions about *how* sexuality is constructed. If sexuality is contructed socially, then clearly it is not constructed in isolation but as part of society constantly in (re-)construction. It is linked to gender, class, nation and ethnicity. Theorists and activists in advanced capitalist countries have not always looked for the full complexity of these links. In the Third World there is no escaping them. Taking into account the complexity and diversity of the construction of gayness can help LGBT people respond to three major challenges that haunt them in the Third World.

One challenge, the most immediate and threatening in practice, comes from Third World nationalists and fundamentalists who condemn all same-sex sexualities as 'Western'. These people either deny that Third World LGBTs exist at all, or reject them as aliens cut off from their countries' own cultures. Intellectually, this challenge is easy to refute. The most elementary historical research exposes the extreme claims of the Third World's anti-same-sex ideologues as groundless. No serious scholar denies that, even if modern lesbian/gay identity is a historically recent phenomenon, evidence of same-sex eroticism can be found throughout human history and on every continent.[8]

A wealth of evidence shows that the first European colonizers used same-sex sexuality in the Americas, Africa and Asia as evidence of their inhabitants' 'savagery', and that both pre- and post-independence rulers have been kept busy trying to stamp it out ever since.[9] The writers in this book provide still more evidence. Max Mejía notes pre-Hispanic influences that are still at work in Mexico today. Mark Gevisser points out that for Zimbabwean President Robert Mugabe 'to sustain his lie that homosexuality is un-African, he has to intimidate black gays into invisibility'. John Mburu adds more evidence of how pervasive and how false this lie is in Africa. Sherry Joseph and Pawan Dhall cite very ancient references to same-sex sexuality in India, both male and female. Chou Wah-shan draws on same-sex erotic literature of the Chinese Ming dynasty (14th to 17th centuries).

A second challenge comes from gays in advanced capitalist countries who see New York's Christopher Street and San Francisco's Castro Street as defining 'gayness' for the rest of the world. The implication is that Third World lesbians and gays are simply latecomers, adopting identities wholesale that had already achieved their finished form in Western Europe and North America. If they don't quite fit in on Castro Street now, this logic suggests, they will sooner or later. 'Progress' is inevitable.

This one-sided picture of lesbian/gay identity does not stand up under examination either. The extreme reading of social constructionism asserting that before the nineteenth century there were only same-sex acts, but no same-sex identities, cannot survive even a superficial examination of pre-colonial Asian or African cultures. Many non-European languages have centuries-old words for people who habitually engage in same-sex sex, not just for particular sex acts. Nor are the identities expressed by these words, identities in many cases claimed by Third World people today, inherently 'primitive' or 'backward'. There is no reason to assume that Third World people are doomed to shuck off these identities completely in order to take on 'modern' ones.[10]

The third challenge comes from some Third World LGBTs themselves, who dream of returning to a happy, mythical, pre-colonial past when their sexualities were authentic and accepted. Attempts to portray pre-colonial Asia, Africa and the Americas as paradises for same-sexers do not stand up to serious scholarship any better than attempts to portray them as immaculately heterosexual, however. Mejía rightly warns in his article on Mexico against superficial deductions 'from the repeated references to "sodomy" which fill the documents, reports and testimonies written in colonial times'. Gevisser and Mburu point out in their articles that homosexuality has traditionally been taboo in many African cultures.[11]

The idea that Third World LGBT identities are *purely* indigenous or *entirely* different from European or North American ones is also problematic. Colonialism happened; its legacy has not been wiped out by formal independence. Economic dependence on the advanced capitalist countries and cultural globalization are still at work today, in fact more than ever. Capitalism is a global system with far-reaching social and cultural consequences, more powerful in the world since 1989 than any system has ever been in human history. In these circumstances, the idea of absolutely pure, authentic, superior Third World same-sex identities is just as untenable as a false universalism.[12]

At least one change now under way in Third World same-sex patterns is surely a positive development. *Public affirmation* of a same-sex identity was virtually never a feature of indigenous traditions. The local *loca* may have been known to everyone in a Central American village, the *kathoeys* may have had well-developed communities in Thailand, but they did not make collective demands, hold marches, or found formal social organizations, let alone political movements. In this specific sense, lesbian/gay identity began to emerge in Europe only in the 1890s, and in the United States only after the Second World War; in this specific sense, it is emerging in many parts of the Third World today. There are still tensions between many traditional ways of living with same-sex sexuality—which as Gevisser says find 'ways of accommodating it and not talking about it'—and the choice to live an openly 'gay' life. Joseph and Dhall make a similar point about India: same-sex behaviour '"on the side of" or "parallel to" marriage, procreation and family ... does not raise very many eyebrows', but repression begins 'as soon as it confronts any of these institutions in the form of homosexual identity'.

Given that same-sex sexualities and identities have a long, rich history in many Third World cultures, then, and given that public affirmation of a lesbian/gay identity in the Third World is a development of the last few decades, *when* and *why* do Third World LGBTs adopt lesbian/gay identities, as supplements or replacements for their own indigenous patterns?

One possible explanation would be that there is a process of 'globalization' of lesbian/gay identities at work, functioning by analogy to economic globalization. The problem with this explanation is that social and sexual identities travel more slowly, and change more as they travel, than products or capital. Coca-Cola has been for sale for decades now in villages which are not even accessible by dirt roads but only over paths through the forest. Automobile parts can be manufactured almost anywhere the world where transport is available to import raw materials and machines and export the parts. Anyone in the Third World with a computer, a modem, reliable electricity and phone lines and enough money can buy and sell stocks on Wall Street. But in many Third World areas where people can watch the BBC and MTV, the emergence of lesbian/gay identities is far from straightforward. For example:

• In Sri Lanka, where British-imposed laws prohibiting 'sodomy' are still on the books, their repeal has been opposed by cabinet ministers whose homosexuality is widely rumoured.

• In Cairo and Karachi, metropolises with millions of inhabitants where many natives and tourists know where to go for male-male sex, there is not a single gay bar or club and hardly an identifiable gay couple.

• In Beijing and Shanghai, where there *are* gay clubs, those who go to them do not always call themselves gay, let alone march for lesbian/gay rights. While the word 'gay' is increasingly used, the word '*tongzhi*' ('comrade') is at least as common. As Song points out in Chou's article, this word appropriates 'the most sacred political label of the mainstream world'.

• In Johannesburg, where there *are* Lesbian/Gay Pride Marches, the 1992 march was led not by white lesbians or gays, nor by Zulu transgendered '*skesanas*' from the black townships, but by the *skesanas*' butch '*injonga*' boyfriends—who were not considered gay.[13]

Looking for logic or trends in the kaleidoscope of identities is no small undertaking. In order to grasp the progress and limits of lesbian/gay identity in different Third World countries, and the extraordinarily varied forms it takes, the authors of *Different Rainbows* refer largely to four different factors:

i) The pre-existence of very diverse same-sex identities in indigenous Third World cultures;

ii) Rapid economic and social change in their societies, largely resulting from their common, increasing, dependent insertion into the global capitalist economy;

iii) Cultural influences from regions, particularly North America and Western Europe, where lesbian/gay identity is already well established; and

iv) Major political developments in some of their countries.

If we want a term that can sum up this whole array of causes, we can paraphrase the Marxist concept of 'combined and uneven development' and talk about 'combined and uneven social construction'. This term has the significant advantage that it avoids any implication of a uniform process moving more or less quickly in a single direction, which the idea of 'globalization' seems to suggest. The idea of 'combined and uneven social construction', by contrast, can help us understand how different indigenous starting points, different relationships to the world economy, and different cultural and political contexts can combine to produce very different results—while still producing identifiable common elements of lesbian/gay identity in one country after another. It can help us understand how some indigenous forms of sexuality can be preserved within a global economy and culture, changing to a certain extent their forms or functions; how new forms can emerge; and how indigenous and new forms can be combined.[14]

This approach leaves room for discussion about which of the four factors—indigenous sexualities, economic and social development, cultural globalization, and political change—have the most weight. I—and probably other *Different Rainbows* authors—would at least raise the question whether cultural globalization is the least essential factor. The basic possibility of attraction and affection between people of the same sex, deep-going social processes like urbanization, and a minimum of political space to organize a community all seem to be central to lesbian/gay identity formation. Whether access to European magazines and Hollywood movies is equally central is not clear to me. Even when Third World LGBTs do read European magazines or watch Hollywood movies, it by no means follows that the magazines or movies either create or define their identities. Cultural borrowings are no proof of influence, let alone causation.[15]

'Third World' is in any event not a cultural category equivalent to 'non-Western'. Argentina, for example, is no less 'Western' or European-influenced than the US and Canada, and more European-influenced than Japan, an advanced capitalist country which is not part of the Third World. Of the countries discussed in this book, Brazil and obviously South Africa have undergone major African cultural influences (as has the US)—and have major LGBT communities. India and much of Southeast Asia as well as China have maintained their own, non-European, cultural continuity to a greater extent than other countries discussed in this book—but few Third World countries have stronger LGBT communities than Thailand or Indonesia.

If I am right about this, it makes for a strong case that new or changed LGBT identities that have grown up in the Third World are not cultural imports—at least, no more than factories or police forces are. Very few of those who plead for purely African or Asian sexualities—whether they mean stamping out all same-sex sexualities or preserving culturally pure forms of same-sex sexuality—call for complete deindustrialization of their countries, breaking up all big cities, returning to purely traditional medicine, or dissolving all police forces. Yet these very developments—industrialization, urbanization, medicine, police—foster the rise of lesbian/gay identity. The effects of European and North American cultural influence are admittedly hard to disentangle from those of domestic capitalist development and modernization. But one could hypothesize—through an improbable thought experiment—that even if outside cultural influence were zero, economic development, modernization and political openings might lead to the rise of lesbian/gay identity anyway. A Marxist analysis would even suggest that Third World dependence on Western Europe and North America, by helping to hold back and distort economic growth and modernization, has *delayed* the emergence of lesbian/gay communities.

This introduction draws in part on the other articles in *Different Rainbows* to suggest how lesbian/gay politics and studies might be transformed in response to issues arising in the Third World. It looks at the conditions of emergence or non-emergence of LGBT identities and communities and at the forms that these emerging identities and communities take: indigenous or 'globalized', politicized or not. First it looks at the consequences of economic development for identity formation, testing the Marxist emphasis on the role of capitalism. Then it examines cultural factors, including the rise of police and medicine emphasized by Foucault, popular culture foregrounded in recent queer theory, and religion, which is particularly important in the Third World. Third, it focusses on an autonomous political dimension that has perhaps been the most neglected factor in the rise of Third World LGBT communities.

Capitalist development and lesbian/gay identity

Involvement in a market economy and a certain minimum income level seem essential in allowing people to become part of lesbian/gay communities in the Third World. In South American cities, for example, same-sex scenes grew up in Argentina and Brazil before the First World War, as industrialization and urbanization gathered speed.[16] In poorer countries like Paraguay and Bolivia, LGBT scenes emerged more recently and slowly. Gay subcultures have grown up in recent years in Turkey's major cities, but not in other major cities of the Islamic world like Cairo or Karachi. This is probably the result to some extent of a degree of economic development greater than the Middle Eastern average; per capita GDP in Turkey is about four times what it is in Egypt and eight times what it is in Pakistan. Economic development alone is not always enough, however; Saudi Arabia and other Gulf states are richer than Turkey, but intense repression has effectively driven same-sex activity deep underground.

Economic ups and downs often seem to speed up or slow down community formation. Lesbian/gay movements in Latin America, the earliest and to begin with by far the strongest in the Third World, retreated in almost every country in the aftermath of the 1982 debt crisis and the 'lost decade' that followed. James Green in his article mentions the hard times the Brazilian movement went through in the wake of the 1981-82 recession, and the same could be said of Mexico. LGBT communities in Southeast Asia by contrast grew during the period of prosperity there in the late 1980s and early 1990s.

Economics can also help explain why lesbian communities are smaller than gay male ones; women participate less in the waged work force and earn lower wages when they do.[17] When lesbian organizing does emerge, it seems to a large extent to happen in regions where women are entering the waged work force and thus achieving a measure of economic independence—in East and Southeast Asia in the late 1980s and 1990s, for instance.

Our analysis can go deeper than mere hunches and comparisons. Beginning in the 1970s, socialist feminists have analyzed sexuality as rooted in the ways a labour force is reproduced in capitalist economies, via the family system and male and female gender roles. To start with, it can be useful to lay out how the emergence of lesbian/gay identities and communities in Western Europe and North America fits into this analysis. Then we can see how the analysis needs to be drastically revised in order to make sense of the Third World. Three phases of the process can be marked out: the commodification of same-sex sexualities; the initial formation of public communities; and the rise of large-scale lesbian/gay ghettos.

1. Commodification. Beginning with the spread of market relationships and the growth of cities in medieval and early modern Europe, a new form of same-sex sexuality arose. Like many other forms of same-sex sexuality past and present around the world, it was transgenderal: it involved assigning a gender identity to one sex partner different from his or her biological sex, but not to the other partner. But in crucial ways it was different from most forms of transgenderal sexuality.

Transgendered people in medieval and early modern Europe seem to have lived mostly in cities, while transgendered people in other cultures often lived in the villages where most human beings in history have lived. They were cut off to a large extent from their families, while many traditional forms of transgenderal sexuality have fit transgendered people into elaborate kinship networks. They were more or less involved in prostitution for money, whereas transgendered people in many cultures have had stable marriages to people of the same sex; particularly in this sense same-sex sex was treated as something to be bought and sold, something 'commodified'. And while transgendered people in many cultures have had well-defined roles in traditional religions, for example as shamans, in medieval Europe transgendered people were condemned and persecuted by the Christian church as well as by the civil authorities. Their subculture was therefore covert and hidden.[18]

It also seems to have been exclusively male. The restrictions on women's travelling and trading apparently prevented transgendered women from appearing in any significant numbers. Although there were certainly female prostitutes in medieval and early modern Europe, we do not know that they had any female clients. There were perhaps cases, then as later, of individual 'passing women' who disguised themselves as men and married women, but the cases that have come to light are individual and exceptional.

2. Public community formation. The Protestant Reformation and bourgeois revolutions changed this situation, beginning with a change in the character of the family, as production increasingly took place outside the home and women's tasks shifted from domestic production to housekeeping and emotional nurturing. Relationships between husbands and wives, parents and children in middle-class families were increasingly seen as based not only on religion and natural male authority but also on affection. In nineteenth-century Europe and North America these ideas also gained ground in the working class as women entered the waged work force. They took hold even more as women moved into the universities and professions. By the beginning of the twentieth century 'sex reform' movements were urging attention to wives' sexual satisfaction and the right to birth control.

As Chou points out in his article, popularization of ideas of romantic love made marriage more painful for those whose strongest sexual and emotional bonds were with people of the same sex and who were therefore pressured to 'pretend' in a new way. Men who may have earlier gone to transgendered men for sex began looking for romance and even longer-term relationships with men as well, while lesbian romance and relationships began to be possible alternatives to heterosexual marriage for women. The rise of wage labour and the resulting individual economic independence made new institutions and relationships possible outside prescribed family and religious patterns.[19] By the late nineteenth century in Europe and the early twentieth century in the US, particular bars in big cities became associated with lesbians and gay men, men organized underground drag balls, and lesbian couples (generally discreet) became more common. Scientists 'discovered homosexuality'—and in the process invented the concept of heterosexuality. One of these sexologists was the German Magnus Hirschfeld, himself gay, who in 1897 founded the first organization advocating gay rights, the Scientific-Humanitarian Committee.

While it was not meant to be a gay group, the Scientific-Humanitarian Committee's founding can be considered as the emergence of a lesbian/gay community onto the public stage. But the lesbian/gay identity it was associated with was still somewhere in between late medieval transgenderal identities and late-twentieth-century lesbian/gay identities. Hirschfeld described himself and the people he was studying and defending as members of a 'third sex'.

3. *Gay ghettos and identities.* With the development of mass consumer society, beginning in the mid-twentieth century in the US and later in other advanced capitalist countries, gay ghettos arose as mass phenomena. In the US, the uprooting of millions of men and women by the Second World War contributed to the emergence of lesbian/gay communities. In some European countries lesbian/gay communities that existed before the war converged over the decades with the emerging North American pattern. By the 1960s, more working-class men and women than ever before had a degree of economic security and independence that enabled them to lead lesbian/gay lives. The transgenderal pattern of sexuality, polarized between 'masculine' and 'feminine' partners, gave way to less polarized relationships in more inclusive communities. Reciprocal relationships between self-identified lesbian women or between self-identified gay men, in which 'masculine' and 'feminine' roles do not necessarily determine sexual identity, became the norm in advanced capitalist countries. 'The homosexual displaced the [transgendered] "fairy" in middle-class culture several generations earlier than in working-class culture; but in each class culture each category persisted, standing in uneasy, contested, and disruptive relation to the other.' By the 1970s, in any event, a gay commercial world emerged that was fully a part of mass consumer culture and central to lesbian/gay communities.[20]

This very schematic outline gives a sense of steady upward progress towards a predetermined objective which does not however correspond to the reality. The development of capitalist societies was accompanied by periodic crises, which in turn were often accompanied by 'moral panics' and waves of persecution. These crises and persecutions were as important to shaping lesbian/gay communities as the spread of market relationships and wage labour. Late medieval transgenderal subcultures were driven deep underground by persecutions that were part of the general fourteenth-to-seventeenth-century witchhunts.[21] More recently the 'long depression' of the last quarter of the nineteenth century saw persecutions that included the trial of Oscar Wilde, an immediate impetus for the founding of the German Scientific-Humanitarian Committee. The feminist and sex-reform movements of the early twentieth century were mostly crushed by fascism, Stalinism, and a generally more conservative social climate that reigned from the 1930s to the 1950s.

Markets without affluence

If the process of lesbian/gay community formation was rocky and irregular in Europe and North America, it is many times more so in the Third World. Just as Mexico City and Kinshasha occupy a very different position in the global economy than New York or Amsterdam, the connection between wage labour, economic security and participation in a community is much less straightforward in the Third World. For most Third World LGBTs the combination of spreading markets and enduring poverty is crucial.

1. *Commodification.* The capitalist market was imposed on the Third World from the outside. African villagers were forced to pay colonial taxes and Indian villagers were obliged to buy British textiles long before they themselves were involved in wage labour. Even when Third World people were recruited to work in mines and factories, they were often expected to return to their villages when they were not needed, thus preserving traditional authority structures and means of subsistence that were convenient for colonial and neocolonial governments. Their traditional families and sexualities seemed to endure, even if beneath the surface they were adapting to changed circumstances.

Where it has taken place, industrialization in the Third World has been both late and dependent. This has usually meant low productivity, low wages, low employment levels, and cities swollen with impoverished migrant families. Urbanization and industrialization have nonetheless changed Third World families and sexualities. This happened first in Latin America, the part of the Third World where colonization began first and went deepest. Large-scale urbanization in the Southern Cone of South America fostered the growth of transgenderal subcultures similar to those that existed in Europe and North America.[22] A world of tranvestite balls and prostitution sprang up in Buenos Aires, and there were well-known cruising areas in Rio de Janeiro.

In Southeast Asia, indigenous transgenderal sexualities existed before colonization (Thai *kathoeys*, Indonesian *waria*, Philippine *bakla*—roughly analogous to South Asia's transgendered *hijras*). With urbanization and industrialization in the twentieth century, Southeast Asian transgenderal subcultures were commodified in ways similar to what already existed in Europe and the Americas. Transvestite beauty contests and brothels were probably not part of Asian traditions, for example, but they are often important parts of transgendered people's lives in Asia today.[23]

Limits to industrialization have sometimes meant that women, massively pulled into the waged work force in many capitalist countries, have been excluded from it in much of the Third World, including most of South Asia, the Middle East and Africa (except South Africa). When women have gone out to work in industry, they have often faced extreme exploitation and controls on their sexuality and reproduction. When they have stayed at home, economic development has sometimes increased rather than decreased their economic and sexual dependence on men. Household production has often declined, but this has simply decreased the value of women's contribution to the family rather than making them valued as nurturers. In India, for example, women of lower castes, whose parents traditionally received bride price when their daughters married, are now undesirable unless they come with a substantial dowry and can suffer gruesome consequences if they do not.[24] Arranged marriage, or marriage under pressure of circumstances, has often remained the rule. Women may still dream of romantic love, encouraged by movies and novels, but it often has little to do with their real family and sexual lives.

In these circumstances, particularly in the Arab world and South Asia, acknowledged lesbian sexual relationships of any kind seem to be beyond women's reach. As Adrienne Rich has said, many of the ways in which men oppress women can also serve specifically to repress lesbianism: 'men's ability to deny women sexuality or force it upon them; to command or exploit their labor to control their produce; to control or rob them of their children; to confine them physically and prevent their movement'; even genital mutilation in some parts of the Islamic world.[25] In those parts of the Third World where women are most dependent on men, lesbian relationships may grow up only in unnoticed corners of households and villages, where women segregated away from men bond more or less invisibly with each other, perhaps even including unnamed, unspoken sexual bonding.

In Egypt 'in a rural village you would not find a lesbian if you want to define lesbianism the way it is defined in the West'. If women do make love to one another they do not talk about it, and in fact everyday Egyptian Arabic has no words to name it.[26] People in many cultures resist the idea that 'sex' can happen among women at all, particularly where male penetration or ejaculation is the criterion for 'sex'. (Not so long ago in Europe and North America, straight people would routinely ask about lesbians, 'But what do they *do*?') In some cultures deep kissing or even cunnilingus between women may not be seen as sex.

This does not mean that lesbianism is impossible in all sexist societies, however; far from it.[27] According to one estimate, three out of four working-class Afro-Surinamese women have committed sexual relationships with women at some point in their lives. Women open about sexual relationships with other women do not seem to be discriminated against in poor urban neighbourhoods in Jakarta. For a significant layer of working-class women, economic development has made possible transgenderal lesbianism, in which one woman partner takes on a male identity, from Lima to Jakarta to Soweto. Their milieus are sometimes reminiscent of the 'butch/femme' subcultures of 1950s North America and Europe.[28]

Even where transgendered people had traditionally been accepted, however, colonial laws have often driven them underground. There are many examples of persecution of indigenous American transgendered people by the colonizing Spanish and Portuguese and by the US as it expanded westward. Laws against sex between males on the books in much of Africa and Asia today are copies of an old British law repealed in Britain in 1967. For example, Joseph and Dhall point out in their article that the British were responsible for criminalizing 'sodomy' in India in 1833. Mburu shows how widespread persecution of indigenous sexualities was in Britain's African colonies. The US has carried on the imposition of puritanical legislation. In Latin America, once Ecuador's Constitutional Tribunal overturned the country's 'sodomy' law in 1997 and Chile repealed its law in 1998, Nicaragua and Puerto Rico were the only countries left with such laws. Puerto Rico had copied its law directly from California after it came under US rule in 1898, while Nicaragua adopted its law only after US-backed forces came to power in 1990 after a decade-long war.

Commodified, covert same-sex sexualities in the Third World have been further shaped by the global economy through the domestic sex trade and international sex tourism, both of which are of course predominantly heterosexual. Altman traces same-sex sex tourism back to rich European gay tourists in North Africa in the 1890s and Bali in the 1920s. Sex tourism from the US, Japan and Europe has grown since then to be a major industry in the Caribbean, Brazil, North Africa and Southeast Asia, while the domestic sex trade is important in countries in South Asia where sex tourism is proportionally less important. Chou's interview with sex worker 'Peter' in Shanghai shows how the recent spread of market relations in China has also fostered the phenomenon there. The sex trade's customers are usually mostly Third World people themselves, and crackdowns usually victimize sex workers more than tourists. Altman rightly warns in his article against the 'danger of both moral indignation and over-romanticization'. It is ironic that same-sex sexualities in the Third World, commodified and driven underground by European colonialism, are being further stigmatized today by European sex tourism, which in many if not all cases is very exploitative and even coercive.

2. Public community formation. While many factors that led to the rise of transgenderal subcultures in Europe—urbanization, commodification, weakening of traditional authority—have arrived in many parts of the Third World, factors that led to the rise of reciprocal lesbian/gay identities in Europe—mass consumption, women's economic independence, and a welfare state supplanting many family functions—have arrived much later, if at all. LGBTs have less opportunity for sexual autonomy from their families even in the Third World's biggest cities. Transgenderal patterns have persisted among LGBTs in many Third World countries.

Yet at the same time, in many of the same countries, people have increasingly looked for romance and long-term relationships, formed communities and even movements. Taken as a whole, the combination is unique to the contemporary Third World. By contrast with the 'butch/femme' subcultures of 1950s North America and Europe, for example, black lesbians in Johannesburg and Cape Town townships helped build a lesbian/gay movement and link it to the anti-apartheid struggle. Nicaraguan lesbians and gays in San Francisco organized in support of the Sandinistas in the 1970s. This was a rather different way of relating to the world than transgendered people had in Renaissance Italy or eighteenth-century London.

Altman has a point when he says in his article that 'to see transvestism as a particular characteristic of Asian [or other Third World] cultures is to miss the role of drag in all its perverse and varied manifestations in Western theatre, entertainment and commercial sex'. But a feature common to different cultures can still be qualitatively more prominent in some than in others. The prominence of transgendered people among working-class Thais or Filipinos, or for that matter Brazilians or South Africans, may be more comparable today to the working-class world in New York about 1940 than to New York today. As in late nineteenth-century Germany, the Third World's first open same-sex communities have often consisted in large part of transgendered people. The association between lesbian/gay identity and reciprocal sexuality, which has become characteristic of advanced capitalist countries since the Second World War, is not as characteristic of the Third World.

Why do LGBT public communities emerge in some countries and not in others? Urbanization is important; 'civil society' has developed in Third World metropolises like Manila and São Paulo, while in rural villages nonconformity can make life very uncomfortable if not impossible. But urbanization alone is not enough to produce LGBT communities. It cannot explain why LGBT communities have emerged in Johannesburg, including its black townships, but apparently not in Kinshasha, a metropolitan area with roughly twice as many people. Nor does it account for the hunted, covert lives that Mburu describes LGBT people living in Nairobi, another city with over a million inhabitants.

The difference is probably in the *kind* of urbanization. Even if there is terribly high unemployment in South African townships, a high proportion of their inhabitants came for and found jobs in the country's modern industry, in some cases passing through the modern mining work force along the way. Nairobi's population is further towards the periphery of the world market. This difference has many social, cultural and sexual consequences. Though blacks in South African townships are poor, they are still nowhere near as poor as the poor in Nairobi; this means they have more access to commercial gathering places and mass media. Together with the disruption of family and community life caused by apartheid, it means that family and village structures arrived more intact in Nairobi than in Soweto.

Any LGBT communities that do arise in the Third World are vulnerable to economic crises, which hit harder and deeper in the Third World, and their social and political fallout. Communities' fragility helps explain why the first wave of Latin American LGBT movements—beginning in Argentina in 1969, Mexico in 1971 and Puerto Rico in 1974—proved so vulnerable. Those movements that were not destroyed by dictatorships (as in Argentina after 1976) suffered when the debt crisis hit in 1982. Latin American communities did weather the storm and rebuild their movements in the 1980s and 1990s. In countries where LGBT communities are less well established, fundamentalist and nationalist upheavals can drive them further underground, as in Iran.

3. *Gay ghettos and identities.* Consumer society in the Third World is

restricted to much narrower social layers than in advanced capitalist countries. Women in particular, but also most GBTs, usually have incomes too low to spend much on housing or going out. Even the most prosperous Third World countries, like South Korea, have less developed welfare states than Western Europe, Canada or Australia. But many, even very poor, Third World countries have developed large middle classes in recent years. Countries like South Africa and Brazil have had prosperous middle classes, with incomes many times their countries' average, for decades; in both countries class is linked to 'race', though in very different ways. Other poor countries whose income distribution used to be less inequitable have converged in recent years with a global pattern of growing social inequality. Millions of middle-class people in poor countries are now able to buy consumer goods and services at something approaching the average levels of rich countries.

This has made it possible for gay ghettos of a sort to emerge in the Third World, with discos and clubs that do their best to imitate Paris or San Francisco. They may not be actual gay neighbourhoods, but gay neighbourhoods are a North American specialty, rare even in Europe. They are more likely than in advanced capitalist countries to be middle-class preserves, since Third World working-class lesbians and gays can rarely afford to go to discos or fancy bars. But their existence can have an impact on LGBT culture in general. Tastes and trends can trickle down from them to people who cannot often afford to set foot in them. The results can be contradictory.

Many LGBT people in the Third World do seem to be increasingly giving up the traditional sexual distinctions. In some cases role playing that has become unfashionable may persist covertly. In many other cases people were clearly straying from the old roles covertly before, but ashamed to admit it openly. There is even a Mexican word, *hechizos,* for 'real men' who have become open to reciprocal sex.[29] The reasons why they are adopting a lesbian/gay identity are not limited to cultural shifts, but consist in large part of economic and/or political factors indigenous to their own societies. The greater numbers of people who can afford to live gay lives make it possible in more countries to define a broad, inclusive LGBT community; and in an inclusive community who plays what role in sex tends gradually to be seen as less significant.

There is no easy way to distinguish between slippage towards more reciprocal roles, on the one hand, and the distance that exists in every culture between ideology and reality, on the other. An Indian who did research on 'these big truckers [who] picked up these little guys in saris' (*hijras*) commented, 'Picture our shock when we found out that a lot of these guys in saris weren't castrated after all, and were fucking the truckers!' The same kind of role reversal may be common among contemporary Philippine *bakla* and their 'non-gay' sex partners. Even in Egypt, where men who identify as gay are still a small minority of those who have same-sex sex, some men talk about 'face-to-face' sex, meaning that anal sex is completely avoided in order to evade the issue of who is the inserter and who is the insertee.[30]

Nor is it easy to be sure just how closely aligned differences between transgenderal and reciprocal identities are with class differences. Mejía says in his article on Mexico that 'apparently in the upper class the difference between heterosexuality and homosexuality is more clearly delimited'. In Indonesia, gay communities are in some areas virtually segregated from transgendered *waria* and *tombois*, more or less along class lines.[31] The point is not that working-class and poor people never develop reciprocal identities. Individuals' life histories and psychologies may have everything to do with the sexual identities they adopt. But working-class and poor people as a group, if not as individuals, do seem to develop reciprocal identities later than middle-class people and to abandon other, more traditional same-sex identities more slowly.

Police roundups and queer videos

Alongside economic factors such as urbanization, commodification, the spread of wage labour and the accessibility of consumer goods, cultural factors such as scientific, medical and police classification and images in popular literature contribute to the rise of lesbian/gay identity, in the Third World as in the First. Norma Mogrovejo talks in her article about the prevalence of police raids and roundups through much of Latin America, usually on the basis of vague laws about 'immoral and indecent behaviour' since not many laws against homosexuality exist. The goal of such attacks—besides collecting easy bribes— is presumably to discourage LGBTs from gathering. But the effect can sometimes be to label people in lasting ways that foster a sense of community.

Medical and psychiatric 'treatment of homosexuality' has taken place in the Third World as it has in Europe and North America, as early as the 1930s in Brazil and the 1940s in Thailand. Chou's article points out that it has been used in China, Taiwan and Hong Kong too, especially in the 1970s and 1980s. Foucault and others have shown how such stigmatizing 'science' can at the same time propagate same-sex identities and make them better known.

By far the most important intersection of medicine and same-sex sexuality in the Third World has been around the AIDS epidemic. Altman points out in his article how European and US epidemiologists and anthropologists have used it as an opportunity to track sexual behaviour. Measures by health authorities in response to AIDS have helped consolidate LGBT communities. In Costa Rica, for example, the health ministry's raids on gay bars and mandatory testing policies gave rise to a wave of protest in 1987 and the founding of the country's first lesbian/gay groups.[32] AIDS also prompted the formation of groups in Guatemala, Malaysia, Singapore and Thailand in the late 1980s which, while not strictly speaking gay, were in fact their countries' first tolerated, largely-LGBT public organizations. Pink Triangle in Malaysia has even received government aid, even though not only same-sex sex but 'promoting homosexuality' is illegal there. Vietnam and Kenya are two of the most recent examples of countries where AIDS prevention has given the first impetus to gay organizing, though Mburu reports that political pressures have forced the Kenyan group to break up.

Wherever communities are formed, they come together around cultural forms that acknowledge their existence, since most of the culture surrounding them does not. The role of beauty contests among drag queens has already been mentioned; it is a common feature of transgendered life today in Latin America, South Africa and Southeast Asia. Sport is a binding element among lesbians in the Third World as in the First, with soccer in particular being a favourite butch pastime from Lima to Soweto. Joseph and Dhall mention the importance of theatre, music, dance and fiction in Indian LGBT communities, and Mejía comments on the growing importance of LGBT cultural groups in Mexico.

This kind of homemade LGBT culture is valued, but in the Third World as in the past in the First, even a little validation from the mass media can be enormously important. A single movie can make a big difference to a country's community, like *Strawberry and Chocolate* in Cuba (which played to packed houses) or the Chinese movie *East Palace, West Palace* mentioned by Chou (which was not publicly released domestically but circulates as a video). In recent years LGBTs have even broken through on TV in many Third World countries. Gevisser mentions the importance of TV talkshows in South Africa; Joseph and Dhall talk about India's TV serials; and there are now LGBT characters on Brazilian *telenovelas*. The 16-segment daytime soap opera on Cuban TV with a lesbian couple as protagonists may have had even more influence than *Strawberry and Chocolate*. Some of these products get exported from one corner of the Third World to another.

All these are examples of indigenous Third World cultural production. Countries like Brazil and India have very large culture industries, including export industries, so there is no economic reason why they should not be able to meet the demand for LGBT images. But where domestically produced images are not plentiful or positive enough LGBTs are bound to go looking for foreign ones, and sometimes they find foreign images more appealing even when local ones do exist. 'Foreign TV channels, cable networks, e-mail and Internet have become accessible even in the smaller towns' in India, say Joseph and Dhall, and 'have been instrumental in creating significant lifestyle changes, especially in the younger generation'. Altman too mentions the role of rock videos and Internet in Southeast Asia. He describes the focus on US and French posters, magazines and films in a Manila gay club with an almost exclusively Filipino clientele.

In poorer or less tolerant countries where there is less access to videos and Internet, even importing a foreign book or magazine can make an enormous difference. Zimbabwe's International Book Fair has been a central moment for the LGBT community there year after year. President Mugabe's decision to ban Gays and Lesbians of Zimbabwe from the August 1995 fair led to its membership reportedly doubling over the next several months—and shifting from white to black over the next few years. The ban led to global repercussions and built-in confrontations in subsequent years.

Analyzing the role of cultural imports requires great care. It is all too easy to conclude that because people read a European book, watch a US video, or wear the same kind of leather jacket you could see in a Sydney bar, their identities and lives are the same. Even as a US immigrant living in Holland I am often struck by how superficial the borrowed imagery is and how different the mentalities behind it can be. In Nicaragua the LGBT community chooses to celebrate Gay Pride on the day that commemorates their own struggle against repression, rather than on the anniversary of Stonewall. Local and global imagery and identities are in constant, sometimes contradictory, sometimes complementary interaction.

This kind of ambiguity can be seen in the very words people use—the adoption of the word 'gay' in many different countries and languages, for example. Chou says that the same Chinese who call themselves '*tongzhi*' in some contexts can use the word 'gay' in others, particularly when they are identifying in some way with international lesbian/gay culture. The Hindi word *sakhi* has a comparable ambivalent and complementary relationship to the English word 'lesbian'.[33] Altman mentions that 'some Filipinos who belong to gay groups might also see themselves in particular contexts as *bakla*.' The word 'gay' and 'lesbian' and various indigenous words in different languages are usually neither mutually exclusive nor completely clear in their connotations. Both borrowed and indigenous words are tools of cultures that continue to change over time and are not sealed off from the rest of the world.

Santería and secularization

Religion plays a crucial role in structuring most Third World societies. It is not just a way of meeting people's spirtual needs and making sense of good and evil, life and death—though many people in advanced capitalist countries, including in gay ghettos, seem to find this dimension lacking in their lives. It is also the foundation of identity, family life and customs. But it is not socially or politically neutral. Religion in the Third World has always been political, from the Conquistadors to the Iranian revolution to the Pope's visit to Cuba.

Though lesbians and gays in the Americas and Europe who have wrestled with Christian homophobia might not credit it, the effect of religion on LGBT identity formation is not always negative. Buddhism as a religion has traditionally been more or less neutral towards same-sex sexuality. Some indigenous African religions even provide ways of expressing same-sex identity, through the idea of possession by deities of the other sex. Transgenderal sexuality reflected in West Africa's Dahomeyan and Yoruba religions has survived among African slaves' descendants in the Caribbean and Brazil and persisted underground in Christian-dominated cultures. Many LGBTs in Haiti find a degree of acceptance in the *voudun* religion, as Brazilians do in *candomblé* and Cubans in *santería*.[34] The Cuban regime's encouragement of *santería* as a counterweight to Catholicism has given a curious boost to LGBT identity there.

Not even all Christian denominations in the Third World are closed to recognizing LGBT identity. The most striking example is the spread of the Universal Fellowship of Metropolitan Community Churches (MCC), as in

Johannesburg's Hope and Unity MCC and other MCCs as far-flung as Buenos Aires and the Philippines. Gevisser notes the positive role of the Anglican church under Archbishop Desmond Tutu in promoting acceptance of LGBTs in South Africa. In Buenos Aires even Catholic monks and nuns have joined a local coalition for tolerance and against police attacks.

Still, most major religions in the Third World, specifically including Christianity, Islam and Hinduism, have clearly helped hold back the development of LGBT identity. The negative role of the Catholic Church is hard to overlook for LGBTs anywhere in Latin America or in the Philippines. Mejía speaks of the Church's 'long history of anti-gay hostility' in Mexico; so do the Nicaraguan lesbians interviewed by Randall. Even Catholicism's liberation theology wing can act as a brake on LGBT progress, as noted by Green in the Brazilian Workers Party's internal debates. Nor are Third World Protestant churches more pro-gay on the whole than Catholics. Mburu's article shows how central anti-gay attitudes have been to East African Protestantism over the past century and still are today. US Baptists were observed by Gevisser as isolated dissenters at Johannesburg Lesbian and Gay Pride, and the Protestant fundamentalist African Christian Democratic Party was the only party to oppose gay rights in the South African constituent assembly. Protestant evangelicals have been gaining ground in Latin America, including in Brazil and inside the Workers Party, where according to Green they align with Catholics in opposing gay rights.

LGBT identities are still exceptionally weak in Muslim countries generally today, despite the lack in Islam of the sex-negativism present in early Christian scriptures,[35] the richness of same-sex traditions in Islamic cultures, and widespread male-male sex by all accounts today. While transgenerational sex between men and boys is traditionally the 'idealized form' of male-male sex in Arab culture—and even today in many Arab countries male adolescents can play a passive role in sex with men without suffering lasting disgrace[36]—adult men who do not marry or persist in playing a passive role are transgendered and stigmatized. There are common words in many Muslim countries for such adult transgendered men: *hassas* in Morocco, *köçek* in Turkey, *khanith* in Oman, *khusra* in Pakistan, etc. Mburu describes the persistence of same-sex traditions among the Muslim Swahili peoples of the East African coast. Gevisser sees Muslim influence by way of Indonesians brought to the Cape under Dutch rule in the transgenderal 'moffie' traditions of South Africa's Cape region. The existence, even ubiquity, of male-male sex in the Islamic world is often accompanied by fierce repression. In a number of Middle Eastern countries today, such as Saudi Arabia, Iran and Afghanistan, 'sodomy' is a capital crime. One scholar was dismissed from her professorial chair at Kuwait University in 1997 merely for suggesting that lesbianism was common among students.

The fact that most major religions condemn same-sex sexuality is compounded by the way virtually all religions have historically reflected and reinforced women's social and sexual subordination. Countries that accept religious diversity also seem more more open to sexual diversity.[37] In most Third World societies, therefore, some degree of secularization is a major stimulus, even a precondition, for LGBT identity. The fact that secularization has been slower in the Third World than in advanced capitalist countries has limited the emergence of LGBT communities there, though the political power of Protestant fundamentalists in the US and the Catholic Church in Latin Europe shows that secularization has its limits in core capitalist countries too.

The example of Turkish cities like Istanbul, Ankara and Izmir shows the importance of secularization to the rise of lesbian/gay identity. The lesbian/gay commercial scenes and organizing efforts there have no parallel in any Arab or Muslim Middle Eastern country, even in major metropolises like Cairo and Karachi, which like Istanbul have populations of between five and seven million.[38] Economic differences probably account for the difference to some extent. But the cultural and religious factors at work are much more complex and striking.

The idea that Turkey is 'partly in Europe' or 'closer to Europe' or 'more European' is of dubious relevance here. Egypt and Pakistan both experienced colonial rule (by Britain), which Turkey escaped, and the European influences have been great, at least on their ruling elites. The extent of European settlement in an Egyptian city like Alexandria was as great or greater than in any Turkish city. Nor are Turks any less likely to be Muslim; the Christian minority in Egypt is proportionally far larger than in Turkey, and its attitudes towards same-sex sexuality are no different than the Muslim majority's. But paradoxically, British rule in Egypt and Pakistan left Islamic social hegemony unaffected or even strengthened, while Turkey went through a profound process of secularization in the process of defending itself from European colonization after the First World War. The strength of secular values in Turkey is unequalled in any other Muslim-majority country west of Indonesia. It can hardly be a coincidence that Turkey is, along with Indonesia, the Muslim-majority country where LGBT communities are strongest.

India, whose decolonization was ultimately negotiated with Britain rather than won by force as in Turkey and Indonesia, did establish a secular political order. But in hindsight secularization in India did not penetrate the society very deeply. The enduring social hegemony of Hinduism and to a lesser degree Islam has been unconducive to the development of lesbian/gay identity, as the rise of communalism in the 1990s has made clear. Joseph and Dhall say in their article that the current government's talk of enacting a Uniform Civil Code is unlikely in the short run to help LGBTs win basic civil rights or repeal of colonial-era criminal laws. The attacks in 1998 by the ruling party-linked, Hindu fundamentalist Shiv Sena on more than a dozen movie theatres across the nation, which intimidated managers into suspending showings of the lesbian-themed film *Fire,* unfortunately lends credence to Joseph and Dhall's pessimism.

The political dimension

Politics has been one of the most neglected factors in accounts of the emergence of LGBT identities. Mere party politics may have relatively little influence on the development of lesbian/gay identities, but the political climate and culture and major social-political movements certainly do. This is true in both advanced capitalist countries and the Third World.

The vision of male 'comradeship' in Walt Whitman's poetry, clearly influenced by the democratic ideology of the Civil War-era United States, played an important role in shaping many gay men's first self-images. Particularly through Whitman's influence on Edward Carpenter, this vision, cross-pollinating with the ideas of the early labour and socialist movement, influenced the vision of gay love in Britain.[39] In Germany, home of the world's first enduring gay political movement, varying politics were intertwined with varying forms of gay identity. The women and men drawn to Hirschfeld's Scientific-Humanitarian Committee came under the influence of his 'third sex' theories as well as his Social-Democratic political leanings; those who came together in and around the Community of the Special celebrated an often self-consciously aristocratic ideal of male-male friendship. The contrast may be related to a tendency of working- and lower-class people to be involved at a historically later period in transgenderal relationships, and of middle- and upper-class people to move earlier towards more reciprocal patterns. Certainly political alignments in Wilhelmine and Weimar Germany were particularly associated with class affiliation.[40]

While the influence of politics is most important for the minority of LGBTs who actively engage in it, it can spread more widely when community gathering places become bases for political mobilization. This is what happened in San Francisco by the early 1960s, for example.[41] New York's Stonewall bar, a gay gathering place that seemed anything but political, was the birthplace of US lesbian/gay liberation in 1969. The political worldview that prevails among activists can be important for the self-conception of other LGBTs who mix with activists in the community's gathering places or are influenced in far more indirect ways.

In the Third World, as Altman comments, a certain degree of economic development is a crucial but not exclusive factor in the development of a commercial gay world. The fact that 'it appears to be bigger in Manila than Singapore is due to a number of factors of which comparative political tolerance seems to me perhaps the most essential'. Among the poorest Latin American countries, the strongest lesbian/gay movement seems to be in Nicaragua. After wage labour and mass consumption, deep-going popular mobilizations are a factor that seems important in fostering lesbian/gay identity.

The contrast between Turkey, on the one hand, and Egypt and Pakistan has already been mentioned. Turkey is not only a less poor and more secular country, it is also one with a somewhat greater margin for independent and radical political organizations. Two of its progressive parties, the Radical Democratic

Green Party and the Freedom and Solidarity Party (ÖDP), have played important roles in supporting its very embattled LGBT community.

Among the political factors important in the emergence of LGBT communities, links to feminism and black movements seem particularly important for LGBT communities. Mogrovejo's article explores the development of Latin American lesbian feminism in depth in the context of Latin American women's movements generally. Lesbian networking at the 1983 Latin American Feminist Gathering, the 1985 UN women's conference in Nairobi and the 1986 International Lesbian Information Secretariat conference all contributed to making possible the first Latin American and Caribbean Lesbian Gathering in 1987 and the first Asian Lesbian Network conference in 1990.[42] These international gatherings sometimes inspired women to found the first lesbian groups in their own countries after they returned home, for example in El Salvador. They were also forerunners of the first Caribbean lesbian/gay conference in 1996 (with fourteen countries represented) and the thousand-strong founding conference of the international Latino-Latina Lesbian and Gay Organization in 1997. Altman observes that in Asia too lesbian movements have often spun off from feminism, as in Thailand and the Philippines, and are not necessarily linked to gay male activism.

Green's article mentions the importance not only of feminism but of black consciousness for early LGBT organizing in Brazil. The links between LGBT organizing and black struggles against apartheid in South Africa are striking.

For lesbian/gay, women's and black movements, the impact of the New Left and youth revolts in 1968 and after was as crucial in parts of Latin America as in Europe and North America. The 1969 Stonewall rebellion can hardly be understood without taking into account everything else that was happening in the US in the late 1960s. Mejía says that the Mexican lesbian/gay liberation movement's 'presence under the banner of solidarity with other oppressed groups— political prisoners, workers, peasants—earned support and sympathy for their cause'. Green too links 1968 with the first Argentinian and Mexican lesbian/ gay groups.

In later years, as lesbian/gay movements grew more quickly in Europe and North America, influences from diasporas there, for instance from US Latinos, became a stimulus to community formation in the Third World. This was all the more important for regions where LGBT communities had not emerged in the 1970s. Joseph and Dhall mention the impetus provided by the emergence of South Asian LGBT groups in North America and Europe in the mid-1980s, and Altman mentions the influence on Asian LGBTs in general of Asian LGBT groups in North America, Australia and Britain. China in particular has been influenced by *tongzhi* organizing in Hong Kong and the US. Perhaps North American- and European-based networking among Arabs and Muslims will eventually have an impact on the Islamic world.

While feminist, black, youth and immigrant movements have a generally positive influence on lesbian/gay ones, nationalism seems to have a generally negative influence. Nationalist movements often have a particular interest in controlling women's sexuality, since women are supposed to reproduce the nation both physically by bearing children and culturally by raising them. In general, tolerance for sexual deviation seems greater where ethnic diversity and multiculturalism are valued, and much less where conformity is imposed in the name of nationalism.[43] At the same time, greater freedom for a previously repressed or despised national culture can be accompanied by greater freedom for women and gays, as has been the case in Quebec, Catalonia and the Basque country.

Probably most important of all in facilitating the emergence of LGBT communities is the existence of a minimal democratic space in which social organizing is possible. This was rare in the Third World twenty years ago, when open or veiled dictatorships ruled the great majority of Third World countries. For Latin Americans in particular, the link between dictatorship and anti-gay repression was clear. Green mentions the fierceness of the military dictatorship's attacks on LGBTs in Brazil after it took power in 1964, which choked off the first stirrings of community formation that were happening before then. LGBTs were also among the thousands who disappeared during the 'dirty war' waged by Argentina's military dictatorship in 1976-83, which wiped out one of Latin America's first and strongest LGBT movements. In Africa, Mburu points out, despite many formal transitions to multi-party systems in the 1990s, LGBTs still suffer under the strength of the ideology that individual rights in general are 'un-African and deleterious'.

Dictatorships' weakening hold on power did not always immediately work to LGBTs' advantage in the 1980s and 1990s. Insecure regimes have sometimes turned to anti-gay prejudice in attempts to regain waning popular support. Death squads have targetted LGBTs as well as union and peasant organizers in Latin America, killing hundreds of LGBTs who were neither political, nor activist, nor leftist in what has been called 'social cleanups'. The use of anti-gay prejudice to shore up shaky regimes is described by Gevisser in Uganda, Zimbabwe, Namibia and Swaziland. Former Zimbabwean president Canaan Banana has claimed that indecent assault charges against him were fabricated following rumors that he was planning a political challenge to Mugabe's rule. In any event Banana's trial in 1998-99 was accompanied by a public campaign to increase punishments for same-sex sex acts.

But while the decline of dictatorships can create obstacles to LGBT community formation, their actual fall and subsequent democratic openings are moments of great opportunity. Green's article describes how the fall of the Brazilian dictatorship in the late 1970s and early 1980s went hand in hand with the rise of LGBT communities and movements. The fall of Argentina's dictatorship in 1982 made possible the refounding in 1984 of its lesbian/gay movement, which took off in the early 1990s.[44] Some of the fruits of community organizing were harvested when Buenos Aires banned discrimination based on sexual orientation after winning municipal home rule in 1996. Mogrovejo's article describes how the fall of the Pinochet dictatorship created space for the rise of a lesbian community in Chile.

Gevisser's article captures a similar feeling of liberation with the fall of apartheid in South Africa, which spilled over to increase support for freedom for LGBTs. Along with international lesbian/gay solidarity with gay African National Congress member Simon Nkoli when he was on trial, Gevisser mentions social-democratic influence on ANC exiles during their years in Scandinavia, Canada and Australia as a source of post-apartheid tolerance. The first Johannesburg Lesbian and Gay Pride celebration took place in 1990, he notes— the same year that Nelson Mandela was released and the ANC unbanned.

The weakening of authoritarian Southeast Asian regimes since the outbreak of the economic crisis in 1997 also brings new dangers as well as new possibilities for LGBT communities. In 1998 for example, a People's Anti-Homosexual Voluntary Movement was formed in Malaysia by prominent members of the ruling party. They denied that their organizing had anything to do with the fall a month earlier of deputy prime minister Anwar Ibrahim, who has been charged with same-sex offences.

Similar dangers may exist in neighbouring Indonesia. Yet so far the possibilities are more visible than the dangers. Dédé Oetomo, founder of Indonesia's Gaya Nusantara in the 1980s under the Suharto dictatorship, has described it himself as 'a rather mild social service-oriented movement' to begin with. But he adds that the LGBT and democratic movements 'have always gone hand in hand'. Sex workers, 'especially the female sex workers, face repression from state ideology and from the armed forces who run the sex business areas,' he says. 'With the general radicalisation of the urban poor and working class, they will join in political activity. Sex workers took part in demonstrations and rallies in May [1998 that brought down Suharto] and against the Habibie regime in November.'[45]

Another link between lesbian/gay and broader democratic movements can be seen in Burma. Aung Myo Min, director of the Thailand-based Campaign for Lesbigay Rights in Burma founded in mid-1996, is also director of the Human Rights Documentation Unit of the Burmese government-in-exile formed after the military junta refused to accept the results of the 1990 elections. He organizes confidential workshops with gay Burmese activists who manage to go regularly to Thailand.

The left's unhappy marriage with LGBTs

Since many Third World dictatorships were backed by the US in the Cold War years in order to defend 'free enterprise', movements for democracy often included strong currents that saw global capitalism as the ultimate enemy. These currents often influenced LGBT communities and movements which shared the desire for democracy. In this sense the progress of LGBT communities was sometimes felt to be bound up with the progress of the socialist left. This was true particularly in Latin America in the 1970s. It was less the case in Southeast Asia in the 1980s, where rapid economic growth was fostering the emergence of LGBT communities. In Indonesia, Malaysia and Singapore, repression limited open expression of radical sympathies. In Thailand and the Philippines, where the left was more visible, Maoist predominance within it made it difficult for openly lesbian/gay activists to link up with it.

The connection between creating space for LGBT communities and challenging capitalism has come to seem less plausible. Few LGBTs today remember the days in the 1920s when not only Communists but the bulk of activists in the world's 'sex reform' movements viewed Soviet Russia as a beacon of enlightened policies, thanks in particular to its decriminalization of same-sex sex and its active participation in the World League for Sex Reform. Not only has socialism lost credibility since the 1989 fall of the Berlin Wall, LGBTs are increasingly aware that the record of anti-capitalist movements and regimes in the twentieth century on sexual issues has at best been very mixed.

Bolshevik policies of inconsistent toleration came to an end in 1934 with the consolidation of Stalinism.[46] From the 1930s to the 1980s, the Stalinist, Maoist and Castroist currents that dominated the international anti-capitalist left fostered anti-gay prejudice rather than lesbian/gay identity. No self-organization of women or LGBTs was allowed in their ranks or under their rule.[47] Both China and Cuba, whose regimes had great prestige in the Third World, had harsh anti-gay policies. In the Cuban revolution's first years the Soviet-linked Popular Socialist Party actively promoted prejudice. At the same time the US recruited gays for a counter-revolutionary underground, which ensured that 'private space was invaded as never before'. The consignment of LGBTs to the notorious UMAP camps in the mid-1960s was the height of Cuban repression.[48]

Against this backdrop, the influence of Stalinism, Castroism and Maoism throughout the Third World in the second half of the twentieth century has been a barrier to lesbian/gay identity, as several articles in this book attest. Green mentions the attitude of the Brazilian Communist Party that homosexuality was a form of 'bourgeois decadence'. Joseph and Dhall mention the example of a women's organization affiliated to the Communist Party of India condemning a conference for South Asian gay men in 1994 as an 'invasion of India by decadent Western cultures'.

Yet development, secularization and education have had effects on lesbian/gay identity in China and Cuba themselves that the Chinese and Cuban regimes presumably neither foresaw nor wanted. As the Nicaraguan lesbian Hazel recalls her visit to Cuba in Randall's interview, 'It's contradictory, because ... in Cuba I found a *massive* community. An enormous parallel world. I'd never seen so many lesbians and gay men in my life.' The Cuban regime has grown more tolerant since the 1980s, making possible a more visible lesbian/gay community and even (since 1994) attempts at organizing an openly gay group. In 1999 the gala opening of a lesbian Women's Centre was attended by an estimated 1200 people. 'Just frame your argument in Marxist orthodoxy, and you can get away with anything', commented director Lupia Castro in an interview.[49]

In China, open gay organizing is still repressed. Just knowing that feminists and lesbians would attend the 1995 Beijing women's conference led the government to isolate it far away from the urban centre, forbid Chinese women university students from attending, and arrest gay activists who tried to make contact with delegates. But the growth of civil society, due in part to economic development and in part to market reforms, has created more room for AIDS work with gay men (funded from abroad) and for debates over classifying homosexuality as a mental illness.

Since the 1980s, and particularly since the collapse of the Soviet Union in 1991, Stalinist hegemony over the international left has ended and space has opened for more democratic anti-capitalist currents, whose growth can foster rather than hold back the rise of lesbian/gay identity. This drama was first played out on the small stage of Nicaragua, as the Nicaraguan lesbians interviewed by Randall in this book recount. At the beginning 'lesbian rights didn't seem to even be a part of the horizon'. But as Ana V. says, 'The Sandinista revolution opened up a space that maybe didn't transform things completely but it certainly didn't close off the possibility'—witness the LGBT community's growing strength and openness in the regime's last years. International lesbian/gay solidarity, particularly from San Francisco's lesbian/gay Victoria Mercado Brigade, played a role in this turnaround.

During the same years in the 1980s new connections were being built between the socialist left and LGBT communities on a small scale in Mexico, with Trotskyists like Mejía of the Revolutionary Workers Party, and on a larger scale in Brazil with the Workers Party, a story told in this book by Green. The Workers Party had the advantage of being a newly founded party that did not include the older, more anti-LGBT currents of the Communist Party and Maoists. As Green explains, its relationship with LGBT communities has been sustained and deepened over the last twenty years.

Today, with the Asian economic crisis, similar links between the left and LGBT communities are beginning to take shape in Southeast Asia, notably in Indonesia and the Philippines. As the Indonesian LGBT and democratic movements draw closer, ties seem to be forming in particular with the democratic movement's most radical wing. Oetomo of Gaya Nusantara has remarked that so far only the leftist People's Democratic Party has supported and worked with his movement.[50] In the future, as in the early twentieth century, the growth of a refounded left may help foster LGBT community formation, as the growth of secular, feminist, black and democratic movements have over the past century.

Third-Worldifying the queering

The picture of the 'combined and uneven social construction' of lesbian/ gay identities that I have sketched out in this introduction has different emphases and a different overall angle of approach, I think, than most recent lesbian/gay academic or political writings do. My feeling is that this is not just the outcome of my own predispositions, but something that is natural, necessary and in a sense even inevitable when looking at the Third World. Perhaps a greater focus on the Third World in years to come could help change lesbian/ gay politics and studies as a whole. I see four shifts in emphasis that could be helpful in LGBTs' understanding the world better and in making it a better world for us:

—Reacting against crude forms of economic determinism and class-centred politics, feminists in the 1970s and queer theorists and activists in the '80s and '90s have tended to stress the importance of ideology and culture. To some extent they have helped right a balance that needed righting. But looking at the Third World requires us to acknowledge and analyze more the crucial role of a minimal level of living standards and social protections in making LGBT lives and freedom possible. The experience of the last quarter-century suggests that LGBTs cannot take these basic necessities for granted in advanced capitalist countries either.

—Among cultural factors, queer theorists have in recent years mainly studied the influence and challenged the prejudices of scientists, doctors, police and producers of popular culture. In the Third World there is no way of avoiding the crucial cultural significance of religion as well. Many LGBTs in advanced capitalist countries have also been coming together as Protestants, Catholics, Jews and Muslims. The discourses and power structures of these religions merit more systematic attention.

—LGBT activists around the world have been challenging discriminatory laws and policies for decades now. But scholars have not paid much attention to the place of LGBTs in their countries' overall political climate and order, and LGBT movements have been less likely recently to see themselves as part of broader efforts for political change. In the Third World the need for LGBTs to be part of processes of democratizing their countries is becoming steadily clearer. LGBTs in advanced capitalist countries should debate more whether 'actually existing liberal democracy' should be the limit of their historical and political horizon.

—Third World evidence raises questions about recent queer theory's emphasis on the diffuseness of power and its questioning of the systemic coherence of structures underlying LGBT oppression. In Third World countries, whether under open dictatorships or superficial democracies under the thumb of the International Monetary Fund, power does not seem all that diffuse. Nor is there anything diffuse about men's power over women in countries where female genital mutilation or dowry death are commonplace.[51] Frontal, systemic challenges have often seemed to LGBTs like an appropriate response to structures like the Catholic Church, military dictatorships or apartheid. Measured by Third World standards, Altman's charge that 'American "queer theory" remains as relentlessly Atlantic-centric in its view of the world as the mainstream culture it critiques' seems valid.[52] In advanced capitalist countries too, postmodern questioning of the coherence of power structures may play into the ideological camouflage practised by the power structures themselves.

Some queer theorists might respond by challenging any attempt at a systemic conception of LGBT oppression and liberation as essentially Eurocentric.

Does a systemic account of LGBT identity in fact have to mean imposing 'modern, Western' categories on other cultures or epochs? Take the cases of precolonial Mesoamerica and the Andes, where there is evidence that the Aztecs and Incas suppressed forms of same-sex sexuality that were tolerated and even celebrated among peoples that they conquered.[53] Is it inherently Eurocentric to see this as oppression, or to see the resistance of conquered peoples as resistance to oppression? Similarly today, in the conflict between Robert Mugabe and LGBT Zimbabweans, is it Eurocentric to recognize Mugabe's oppressive policies for what they are, or Afrocentric to dismiss LGBT Zimbabweans' fight for sexual freedom?

The approach of this introduction, and I think of *Different Rainbows* as a whole, is to say no. We can see that LGBTs in the world today, in all our enormous diversity, have converged enough to have a certain real commonality of identity. This constitutes an objective basis for solidarity in our oppression and in our struggles, past and present, and an objective claim on the solidarity of others.

[1] This includes all the countries discussed in this book (with the partial exception of China, a vast country which held its own against Europe until the early nineteenth century, was never fully colonized, cut its links to the world market in 1949 and has only partially restored them in the past two decades). 'Third World' is an unsatisfactory term for these countries. But I have preferred it to euphemisms such as 'developing' or 'less developed', or ideologically laden (though more accurate) ones such as 'dominated' or 'dependent'.

[2] Edward Said has pointed out how woefully underdeveloped 'Middle Eastern Studies'— not to mention 'European Studies' or 'American Studies'—are in the Middle East itself (*Orientalism,* New York: Random House, 1978, pp. 204, 322-24).

[3] David Fernbach, *The Spiral Path: A Gay Contribution to Human Survival,* Boston/London: Alyson/GMP, 1981, p. 82. For an insightful overview of the 'gay gene' debate and its political implications, see David Fernbach, 'Biology and gay identity', *New Left Review* no. 228 (Mar.-Apr. 1998).

[4] See above all the detailed examination in David F. Greenberg, *The Construction of Homosexuality,* Chicago: Univ. of Chicago Press, 1988.

[5] Gloria Wekker, '"What's identity got to do with it?": rethinking identity in light of the *mati* work in Suriname', in Evelyn Blackwood and Saskia E. Wieringa eds., *Female Desires: Same-Sex Relations and Transgender Practices across Cultures,* New York: Columbia Univ. Press, 1999, p. 120.

[6] For this reason, despite the unfortunate awkwardness, I use both the terms 'lesbian/gay' and 'LGBT' in the introduction and conclusion, as appropriate in different contexts. I avoid the word 'homosexual', which evades or confuses too many issues.

[7] John D'Emilio, 'Capitalism and gay identity', in Ann Snitow et al. eds., *Powers of Desire: The Politics of Sexuality,* New York: Monthly Review Press, 1983, was an early Marxist-feminist analysis. See also Michel Foucault, *The History of Sexuality, Volume 1: An Introduction,* New York: Random House, 1978.

[8] Clellan S. Ford and Frank A. Beach, *Patterns of Sexual Behavior,* New York: Harper &

Row, 1951, p. 130, notes that in 49 out of 76 societies studied some form of same-sex sexual behaviour (male and/or female) was not only known but socially accepted.

[9] Rudi C. Bleys, *The Geography of Perversion: Male-to-Male Sexual Behaviour Outside the West and the Ethnographic Imagination, 1750-1918,* New York: New York Univ. Press, 1995, recounts medieval European Christian stories of non-Christians' 'sodomitical' practices; nineteenth-century European racists' 'scientific' explanations that 'inferior races' were prone to 'pathological' forms of sexuality; and many other ways in which non-European same-sex eroticism was incorporated into European discourses over the centuries.

[10] As Will Roscoe and Stephen Murray say, no version of social constructionism is tenable that sees the 'history of homosexuality as a progressive, even teleological, evolution from pre-modern repression and silence to modern visibility and social freedom' ('Introduction', in Murray and Roscoe eds., *Islamic Homosexualities: Culture, History and Literature,* New York, New York Univ. Press, 1997, p. 5).

[11] Admitting that intolerance existed in indigenous cultures does not mean granting 'the West' a patent on tolerance. On the contrary, the extreme forms of persecution in late medieval Europe and Nazi Germany have not been surpassed in any other culture.

[12] Neil Garcia argues convincingly against the idea that 'cultures are by nature circumscribed by impermeable boundaries' (*Philippine Gay Culture: The Last Thirty Years,* Diliman: Univ. of the Philippines Press, 1996, pp. xvii-xviii).

[13] Hugh McLean and Linda Ngcobo, 'Abangibhamayo bathi ngimnandi (Those who fuck me say I'm tasty): gay sexuality in Reef townships', in Mark Gevisser & Edwin Cameron eds., *Defiant Desire: Gay and Lesbian Lives in South Africa,* Johannesburg: Ravan Press, 1994, pp. 164-65.

[14] For an initial attempt to apply the idea of 'combined and uneven development' to same-sex sexualities, see Peter Drucker, '"In the tropics there is no sin": sexuality and gay-lesbian movements in the Third World', *New Left Review* no. 218 (July-Aug. 1996).

[15] Barry Adam, Jan Willem Duyvendak and André Krouwel point out that even 'similar cultural practices have quite different meanings' in different cultures ('Gay and lesbian movements beyond borders?: national imprints of a worldwide movement', in Adam, Duyvendak & Krouwel eds., *The Global Emergence of Gay and Lesbian Politics: National Imprints of a Worldwide Movement,* Philadelphia: Temple Univ. Press, 1999, p. 348).

[16] Daniel Bao, 'Invertidos sexuales, tortilleras, and maricas machos: the construction of homosexuality in Buenos Aires, Argentina, 1900-1950', *Journal of Homosexuality* (Chicago) vol. 24 no. 3/4 (1993), pp. 192, 208.

[17] John D'Emilio has put forward this explanation for the US ('Capitalism and gay identity', pp. 105-06).

[18] Evidence of communities of trangendered men has been found for northern Italy as early as the fourteenth century, in France as early as the fifteenth, and in England and Holland as early as the seventeenth (Ellen Ross & Rayna Rapp, 'Sex and society: a research note from social history and anthropology', *Powers of Desire,* p. 65; Greenberg, *Construction of Homosexuality,* pp. 330-31).

[19] See Dennis Altman, *The Homosexualization of America, The Americanization of the Homosexual,* New York: St. Martin's Press, 1982, pp. 47-48.

[20] George Chauncey, *Gay New York: Gender, Urban Culture, and the Making of the Gay Male World, 1890-1940,* New York: Basic Books, 1994, p. 27. Altman's *Homosexualization of America,* pp. 79-97, has explored and analyzed gay consumer culture in depth.

[21] See John Boswell, *Christianity, Social Tolerance, and Homosexuality: Gay People in Western Europe from the Beginning of the Christian Era to the Fourteenth Century*, Chicago: Univ. of Chicago Press, 1980, ch. 10, 'Social change: Making enemies'.

[22] Daniel Bao, 'Invertidos sexuales, tortilleras, and maricas machos', pp. 192, 208.

[23] See e.g. Peter A. Jackson, *Male Homosexuality in Thailand: An Interpretation of Contemporary Thai Sources*, Elmhurst (NY): Global Academic Publishers, 1989, p. 227. Transgendered people in Asia still sometimes fill a social niche at least as much as a sexual one; in Indonesia many people even assume that *waria* are asexual (Dédé Oetomo, 'Gender and sexual orientation in Indonesia', in Laurie J. Sears ed., *Fantasizing the Feminine in Indonesia*, Durham: Duke Univ. Press, 1996, p. 261).

[24] See Trupti Shah & Bina Srinivasan, 'India: the effect of capitalist development on gender violence: dowry and female feticide', in Penny Duggan & Heather Dashner eds., *Women's Lives in the New Global Economy*, Amsterdam: IIRE, 1994.

[25] Adrienne Rich, 'Compulsory heterosexuality and lesbian existence' (1980), in Snitow, *Powers of Desire*, pp. 183-85.

[26] Interview with Hind Khattab by Didi Khayatt (9 Mar. 1995), in Khayatt, 'The place of desire: where are the lesbians in Egypt?', unpublished ms.

[27] Blackwood, while agreeing that compulsory heterosexuality is characteristic of many societies, has challenged Rich's blanket theory, pointing to examples of non-compulsory, non-oppressive forms of sex among women in different cultures ('Breaking the mirror: the construction of lesbianism and the anthropological discourse on homosexuality', in Blackwood ed., *The Many Faces of Homosexuality: Anthropological Approaches to Homosexual Behavior*, New York: Harrington Park Press, 1986). But Rich's picture of repression faithfully reflects the situation in many Third World regions today.

[28] Wekker, '"What's identity got to do with it?"', p. 122; Alison J. Murray, 'Let them take ecstasy: class and Jakarta lesbians', in Blackwood and Wieringa, *Female Desires*, p. 151; Saskia Wieringa, 'An anthropological critique of constructionism: Berdaches and butches', in Dennis Altman et al. eds., *Homosexuality, Which Homosexuality?*, London: GMP, 1989, pp. 215, 217.

[29] Ian Lumsden, *Homosexuality, Society and the State in Mexico*, Toronto: Canadian Gay Archives/Solediciones, 1991, pp. 45-46.

[30] Garcia, *Philippine Gay Culture*, esp. pp. 134-61; Iwan van Grinsven, *Limits to Desire: Obstacles to Gay Male Identity and Subculture Formation in Cairo, Egypt* (Nijmegen: unpublished ms., 1997), p. 37.

[31] Oetomo, 'Gender and sexual orientation', p. 265. Oetomo says that *waria* 'are mainly working-class or lower-class, at least by origin, while most gay men hail from middle- or upper-class families or aspire to middle-class standing' (p. 268). Thomas Boellstorff, *The Gay Archipelago: Translocal Identity in Indonesia* (unpublished PhD., forthcoming 1999), confirms that *waria* are predominantly lower-class, but shows that gay-identified men can be lower-class too; 90 per cent make less than US $60 a month, which is low even by Indonesian standards. Alison Murray says that lower-class lesbians 'are excluded from the global movement by the lack of two essentials: money and the English language'. Far from all lower-class lesbians fit into butch-femme roles, however, and even Sumatran *tombois* who see themselves as men will sometimes define themselves as lesbians in certain contexts ('Let them take ecstasy', pp. 140, 148).

[32] Jacob Schifter Sikora, *La Formación de una Contracultura: Homosexualismo y Sida en Costa Rica*, San José: Ediciones Guayacán, 1989.

[33] Giti Thadani, 'The politics of identities and languages: Lesbian desire in ancient and

modern India', in Blackwood and Wieringa, *Female Desires*, p. 86.

[34] Murray describes transgender roles in Hausa possession cults and mentions Dahomeyan and Yoruba counterparts in 'Gender-defined homosexual roles in Sub-Saharan African Islamic cultures', *Islamic Homosexualities*, pp. 222-24. A fascinating account of the consequences of African-derived religion for same-sex identity in Suriname is found in Gloria Wekker, *Ik ben een gouden munt: Subjectiviteit en seksualiteit van Creoolse volksklasse vrouwen in Paramaribo*, Amsterdam: VITA, 1994, forthcoming in English from Univ. of Cambridge Press. See also Murray, 'Haiti', in Wayne R. Dynes ed., *Encyclopedia of Homosexuality*, New York/London: Garland Publishing, 1990, p. 516; João S. Trevisan, *Perverts in Paradise*, London: GMP, 1986, pp. 171-74; and Lourdes Arguelles and B. Ruby Rich, 'Homosexuality, homophobia and revolution: notes toward an understanding of the Cuban lesbian and gay male experience', in Martin Duberman et al. eds., *Hidden from History: Reclaiming the Gay and Lesbian Past*, New York: New American Library, 1990, p. 445.

[35] The Islamic scriptures do include condemnations of male-male sexuality, however. One English translation of the Koran quotes Lot, seen as a Jewish prophet and forerunner of Muhammad, as saying, 'Are you blind that you should commit indecency, lustfully seeking men instead of women?' and, 'Will you fornicate with males and leave your wives, whom Allah has created for you? Surely you are great transgressors.' (*The Koran*, N.J. Dawood trans., Baltimore: Penguin, 1968, pp. 84 (27:56), 203 (26:165-66)). Omar Nahas of the Dutch Yoesuf Foundation on Islam and (Homo)sexuality says that the original Arabic text specifically condemns anal intercourse and not egalitarian, voluntary, adult homosexuality (Stichting Yoesuf, *Homoseksualiteit en de barmhartigheid van Allah*, Utrecht: Stichting Yoesuf, 1999, p. 12).

[36] Murray and Roscoe, 'Conclusion', in *Islamic Homosexualities*, p. 302.

[37] Adam, Duyvendak & Krouwel, 'Gay and lesbian movements beyond borders?', pp. 353-54.

[38] Van Grinsven says, 'Gay organizations do not exist' in Cairo, nor are there '"gay bars" or any other commercial institutions serving gays'(*Limits to Desire*, p. 15). Badruddin Khan, 'Not-so-gay life in Pakistan in the 1980s and 1990s', in *Islamic Homosexualities*, says flatly, 'There is no "gay life" in Karachi, in the Western sense of the word: no bars, no newspapers, and few instances of lovers living together' (p. 275).

[39] See Sheila Rowbotham & Jeffrey Weeks, *Socialism and the New Life: The Personal and Sexual Politics of Edward Carpenter and Havelock Ellis*, London: Pluto Press, 1977.

[40] See Manfred Herzer, 'Communists, Social Democrats, and the homosexual movement in the Weimar Republic', in Gert Hekma et al. eds., *Gay Men and the Sexual History of the Political Left*, New York: Haworth Press, 1995, and Peter Drucker, 'Gays and the left: scratching the surface', *Against the Current* no. 68 (May/June 1997).

[41] John D'Emilio, *Sexual Politics, Sexual Communities: The Making of a Homosexual Minority in the United States, 1940-1970*, Chicago: Univ. of Chicago Press, 1983, esp. ch. 10: 'The movement and the subculture converge: San Francisco during the early 1960s'.

[42] Sylvia Borren, 'Lesbians in Nairobi', in *Second ILGA Pink Book: A Global View of Lesbian and Gay Liberation and Oppression*, Utrecht: Interfacultaire Werkgroep Homostudies, 1988, pp. 60-65, gives a particularly inspiring picture of how international solidarity helped African lesbians affirm their identity and make themselves visible.

[43] Adam et al., *Global Emergence*, esp. Adam, 'Moral regulation and the disintegrating Canadian state', p. 18; Geoffrey Woolcock and Dennis Altman, 'The largest street

party in the world: the gay and lesbian movement in Australia', p. 328; Scott Long, 'Gay and lesbian movements in Eastern Europe: Romania, Hungary and the Czech republic', pp. 244.

[44] Stephen Brown, 'Democracy and sexual difference: the lesbian and gay movement in Argentina', in Adam et al., *Global Emergence*, p. 112.

[45] Dédé Oetomo (interviewed by Jill Hickson), 'The struggle for lesbian and gay rights', *Green Left Weekly* no. 351, 3 Mar. 1999.

[46] John Lauritsen and David Thorstad, *The Early Homosexual Rights Movement (1864-1935)*, revised edition, Ojai (CA): Times Change Press, 1995.

[47] Randall raises the 'question of whether a women's movement not led by women can make real inroads against sexism and women's oppression'. This should lead us to question Song's statement in Chou's article, that for the Chinese 'equality of the sexes is natural, not something achieved through the feminist struggle'.

[48] Arguelles and Rich, 'Homosexuality, homophobia and revolution', pp. 447-48. By far the best overview of Cuba's lesbian/gay community, its history and situation is Ian Lumsden, *Machos, Maricones and Gays: Cuba and Homosexuality*, Philadelphia: Temple Univ. Press, 1996.

[49] James Balducci, 'Dyke Revolucionaria has an attitude, a brain and a vision', *Bay Area Reporter* (23 Apr. 1999).

[50] Oetomo, 'The struggle for lesbian and gay rights'.

[51] Wieringa and Blackwood say that 'the term "queer" does not allow for recognition of gender hierarchies and women's oppression. A term lumping together lesbians and gays denies that lesbians are differently located within their societies.' ('Introduction', in Blackwood and Wieringa eds., *Female Desires*, p. 210).

[52] Kendall points out that queer theory 'privileges both nonconformity and the visible' ('Women in Lesotho and the (Western) construction of homophobia', in Blackwood and Wieringa, *Female Desires*, p. 173). Neil Garcia does rely heavily on postmodern literary theories in his book *Philippine Gay Culture* and draws on Judith Butler's and Eve Kosofsky Sedgwick's writings on 'queer theory'. Perhaps this is due in part to the fact that much of his book is devoted to literary criticism, though he interweaves it in stimulating ways with political reflections.

[53] Mejía, for example, makes a contrast between the relatively intolerant Aztecs and the relatively tolerant Zapotecs in precolonial Mesoamerica. There is in fact considerable controversy about the Aztecs' toleration or persecution of same-sex sexuality. Greenberg's *Construction of Homosexuality* mentions Spanish reports of transgenderal, religious prostitution among the Aztecs (pp. 164-65), but these seem unreliable. Geoffrey Kimball, 'Aztec homosexuality: the textual evidence', *Journal of Homosexuality* (Chicago) vol. 26 no. 1 (1993), concludes that the Aztecs disapproved of same-sex eroticism but did not repress it by force (p. 20).

Mexican pink

Max Mejía

> 'SODOMITE, WHORE— ... Effeminate. Pretends to be a woman. Deserves to be burnt, deserves to be scorched, deserves to be put in the fire...' In *Human Body and Ideology: The Views of the Ancient Nahuas.*[1]

Buggers, damned and divine

Mexicans' perceptions of homosexuality today include noticeable cultural influences from the contemporary globalized world. But they also include noticeable influences from remote cultures, inherited from pre-Hispanic times, with their particular understanding of homosexuality, as well as noticeable influences from the Christianity brought by the conquerors, with its vision of 'the infamous sin'.

All kinds of deductions have been made about pre-Hispanic cultures and homosexuality. Some of them go very far, such as the assumption that homosexuality was widespread in pre-Hispanic cultures and was widely accepted. This supposedly evoked the conquerors' moral outrage to such a degree that they turned sodomy into a *casus belli* against the conquered peoples.

These are superficial deductions, however, from the repeated references to 'sodomy' which fill the documents, reports and testimonies written in colonial times. Despite the writers' preoccupation with sodomy, it does not necessarily follow that homosexuality was a widespread practice in the communities, nor that it enjoyed wide acceptance among pre-Hispanic peoples. At most, what can be inferred from these allusions is a recognition of sodomy's existence from the moment it began to be punished, under more or less harsh rules according to the particular community.

In the Aztec culture of pre-Hispanic Mexico, the dominant culture at the time the Spanish arrived, the treatment of sodomy was not exactly favourable. On the contrary, the Aztecs had very harsh laws against it, punishing the practice severely with public execution for those who were caught. Punishment affected mainly males, but women were not exempt.

One example of the Aztecs' harshness was the city of Texcoco under king Nezahualcoyotzin, where 'the infamous sin was punished with immense rigour, since the individual, tied to a stick, was covered by all the boys of the city with ash, so that he was buried in it, while his entrails were removed through the sexual area, and then he was buried in the ash'.[2]

These harsh laws were probably motivated by the rigid distribution of social roles between the sexes for reasons linked to the imperatives of reproduction, as well as to the value attributed to masculinity. Both were matters of

primary importance to the Aztecs, an eminently imperialistic and martial people. 'Sodomy', in that context, could only be a serious transgression of the
established gender norms, which prescribed not only a sexual model aimed at
reproduction, but also ways of behaving and dressing according to gender. It is
no accident that the punishment for sodomy was meted out mostly to men or
women who cross-dressed. According to friar Bartolomé de las Casas, 'The
man who dressed as a woman, or the woman found dressed with men's clothes,
died because of this.' Friar Bernardino de Sahagún adds: 'in everything he
shows himself woman-like or effeminate in his way of walking or of talking; for
all of this he deserves to be burned.'[3]

However, there were exceptions to the Aztecs' rules against homosexuality. Most historians agree that the practice was tolerated when it took place in
religious rituals. The members of the spiritual elite, the priests, escaped punishment because of their divine ordination and their relationship to the gods.
Observe the following statement of Las Casas: 'among so many ancient nations
there were some and many that offered ignominious sacrifice to their gods by
exposing their venal bodies, not in the interest of the infamous trade, but only
to render agreeable sacrifice...'[4]

One must add that the Aztecs ruled over a vast array of peoples, who had
different cultural histories. Several of these did not necessarily share the Aztecs'
vision of homosexuality and its practice. Some even showed signs of singular
tolerance towards it in their communities. One of these was the Zapotec culture, derived from the Mayans and located in what is now the state of Oaxaca.
Although the Zapotecs' tolerant vision has been investigated very little, it is
notable even at present among peoples and cities of Zapotec origin.

This writer was able to observe in trips to the cities and towns of the
isthmus of Oaxaca, where one of the Zapotec groups is concentrated, that
people's attitude towards gay men there does not parallel that in other parts of
Mexico. They refer to gays as 'mampos', a descriptive term which lacks the
pejorative connotations of the words in common use in Mexico: 'puto', 'joto',
'maricón'. 'Mampos', though clearly identified by their delicate manners, con-
tralto voices and neat appearance or transvestite dress, are part of the landscape
of the life of the people. Women's accepting attitude towards them is striking,
as is everyone's tolerance for the frequent sexual contacts that young men, or
even adolescent boys, have with them.

It is easy to be astonished at such spontaneous tolerance for homosexuality. An example was my experience in the town of Barranca Colorada, twenty
kilometres from Juchitán. I was drawn there by stories I had heard from many
people. I arrived in the appropriate mood, following the advice of some friends
of mine who frequently visited a gay man in that town, Migue, and his family.
That is to say, I was so extraverted when I arrived that nobody could have any
doubt that I was a mampo.

I think I may have overdone my role a little, because in my zeal for con-
firming the inhabitants' open attitude, I did not neglect any occasion to indicate my identity. This encouraged spontaneous approaches by young men,

and—surprise!—a virtual siege by thirteen- and fourteen-year-old boys. The situation became absurd at a party in the town that I attended with Migue and his younger brothers.

As is usual in the Zapotec tradition, the women were dancing among themselves, while one group of women who were not dancing demonstrated their friendliness by sending us a case of beer, which we reciprocated by sending them another. Meanwhile, the boys were stalking our table. Finally I got up to go to the bathroom outside, and the boys followed me like a flock of birds. Smiling, they invited me to go with them, making offers in Spanish for my benefit while they carried on in Zapotec among themselves. They did not care that the adults were listening. 'And so what?', two of them answered in unison when I pointed this out. Meanwhile I was blushing like the shyest of provincial *mampos*. Finally an older lady appeared and calmed them down. 'Stop annoying the señor,' she said, adding to me, 'Excuse them, they're so impertinent.' At the table, I commented on the event to Migue. He answered: 'It's just that they're young and full of desire, but who is going to get involved with them while there are so many older boys in the town?'

The next day I asked the owner of the only beer store in town if a *mampo* would have problems as a result of getting involved with a minor. He answered, 'Why should he? In any event the problem would be theirs for annoying you when you're not interested.'

I do not want to romanticize homosexuality in Zapotec culture. The homosexual male enjoys wide social tolerance, especially in the sexual arena; but at the same time this tolerance is reserved for the prototype of the traditional homosexual, with a sexually passive role and effeminate behaviour. Deviating from this model and especially departing from the passive role can lead to conflict and aggression against gays. During my same holiday a pair of gay men from Juchitán had to flee Barranca Colorada in their car, chased from the party by a group of young men. The motive for their annoyance, Migue explained to me later, was that these gay men had wanted to play the active role. True enough, the gay pair chased out of town told me afterwards in Juchitán. Although both were indigenous Juchitecos, it was evident that they identified with the modern gay lifestyle. They attended university and were activists in the gay liberation movement, and they complained bitterly about their countrymen's machismo and traditional attitudes towards homosexuality.

There are those who suggest that the Zapotecs' tolerant posture has its origin in ancestral Mayan culture. Researchers have paid little attention to Mayan culture's attitudes about homosexuality. Nevertheless, some bibliographical references, sculptures and paintings suggest that, compared with the Aztecs, the Mayans had a more favourable view of diversity within the community, which suggests greater tolerance of homosexuality, above all when it concerned religious rituals and artistic practices.

Whatever the case, what I am trying to show is that in pre-Hispanic Mexico, alongside the rigid Aztecs, there existed—and there exist still today—other, more flexible cultures more tolerant of homosexuality. The example of the Zapotecs of the isthmus of Oaxaca and other regions of that state, with their particular way of accepting homosexuality, is enough to prove it. This is confirmed even within Aztec culture itself, in that there was a double standard about homosexuality, characterized by severe punishment on the one hand yet tolerance within a religious framework on the other.

The same can undoubtedly not be said of the closed discourse of the Spanish conquerors. An absolutist discourse enveloped homosexuality in the concepts of 'infamous sin', 'sin against nature', corruption of the soul and alliance with the devil. They punished the practice without distinctions, among both lay people and clerics. Their strictures against homosexuality, dictated by otherworldly, metaphysical considerations, greatly exceeded the inflexibility of the Aztecs, whose rules, after all, corresponded to their social order with its ethos of male supremacy in the interests of a warrior people. If the Aztecs executed 'buggers' for transgressing sexual norms and gender prescriptions, the conquerors executed them for transgressing the rules of the afterworld, the divine order. Furthermore, the conquerors treated 'sodomy' as a special Indian sin and hunted it down and punished it as such on a grand scale. They orchestrated crusades like the Holy Inquisition, which began burning sodomites at the stake as a special occasion, as in the memorable auto-da-fé of San Lázaro in Mexico City. Salvador Novo, among others, writes about them in his book of chronicles.[5]

The letter 'J' and the number '41'

Aquí están los maricones
Muy chulos y coquetones

[Here are the faggots
very cute and flirtatious]

Los 41 maricones (1901)

The number '41' has magical power over Mexicans' spirits. From early childhood, Mexicans react nervously and joke when they write the number 41. In buga (straight) language it is called a 'bad luck number', but in gay language its meaning is the opposite: a 'good luck number'.

The magic of the number 41 derives from an episode during a legendary homosexual party in Mexico City in 1901, immortalized by the engraver Posada with images of men dressed in elegant feminine clothes dancing with other men. The fiesta ended with a police roundup, resulting in the arrest of 41 homosexuals and their deportation to forced labour camps in the southeast of the country. This was the time of the Porfirio Díaz dictatorship, a period of authoritarian politics and frenzied puritanism such as Mexico had not known in many years. The period ended with the outbreak of the Mexican revolution in 1910.

The aura around the letter 'J' has a similar origin, though its freight of anxiety is even stronger for Mexicans, since the popular term '*joto*', which designates the homosexual male, derives from it. Its origins can be traced to the cells in the prison Palacio Negro de Lecumberri in Mexico City. The 'J' cell at Lucumberri was used for gays who had committed some crime, before they were deported to the María Islands in the west of the country, where those considered 'special' criminals were sent.

In the 1930s and '40s, homosexuality as such was no longer considered a crime in Mexico, in accordance with the penal legislation after the revolution inspired by the Napoleonic Code. Homosexuality in any event was still treated as an aggravating factor in other offences, such as sex with minors or the rape of minors.

These were times of cultural ebullience in the country. On the radio the public heard the first song about love between men: 'Amor Perdido' ['Lost Love'] by the Mexican composer Pedro Flores, sung in the masculine gender by the singer María Luisa Landín. Of course, outside closed homosexual circles, nobody noticed that it was a gay love song. Nevertheless, it is clearly a song sung by one man to another.

At that time the poet Salvador Novo was already a well-known writer. He was part of a legendary group of Mexican writers who like him were openly homosexual. Los Contemporáneos brought together such renowned poets as Xavier Villaurrutia, Carlos Pellicer, Genaro Estrada, Elías Nandino and others. Painters and artists of the time also identified with the group.

The poem 'Recinto' ['Enclosure'] by Carlos Pellicer says, 'I know about the silence before the dark people/ about silencing this love because it is different.' *(Sé del silencio ante la gente oscura/ de callar este amor que es de otro modo.)*

To this group of writers we owe the first defense in Mexico of a gay sexual orientation. Mexican writer Carlos Monsiváis says that 'with Los Contemporáneos, gays emerge in the record of Mexico's social and intellectual life'.

This group's daring did not pass unnoticed. It elicited scandal and provoked anti-gay criticism from other artists and writers. Among Los Contemporáneos, Novo was the most attacked, but also the boldest and sharpest in answering the assaults. 'There he is, joining mockery with malevolence, a Wildean aesthete, a very refined snob in a gilded jacket with a honeyed expression of fastidiousness, with his hand on his hip', writes Monsiváis in his book *Amor Perdido*. He adds: 'He's gay, he never denies it, and he turns the fact into a daily provocation against the moral order.'[7]

The flavour of the Mexican tortilla: manfloras and lesbians

As is well known, the tortilla is consumed by all Mexicans. It is used to accompany other food, and it preceded the use of the fork, which has not been able to replace it. The tortilla was traditionally made by hand and by women. Women baked tortillas among themselves, and they were called *tortilleras*. With time, the term '*tortillera*' was applied to lesbians and to their practices: 'making tortillas'. *'Manflora'* is an equally popular term in Mexico used to designate lesbians. It may derive from 'man' and 'flower', though nobody knows its exact origin.

In the 1950s gay and lesbian life in Mexico was largely confined to big cities, in particular Mexico City. Gays and lesbians moved in circles of friends and around figures in artistic milieux. Lucha Reyes' voice was heard on the radio:

> Por una mujer ladina
> perdí la tranquilidad
> ella me clavó una espina
> que no me puedo arrancar.

> [For a Latina woman
> I lost my peace of mind;
> she pierced me with a thorn
> which I cannot pull out.]

> *'Mujer Ladina'*

Reyes, mother of the Mexican ballad, took advantage of the innocence of the Mexican tradition, which allows a woman to sing to another woman. Without using the male gender, she sang deliberately and full of feeling to another woman. The singer's repertoire was made up of traditional Mexican songs, but also of comic songs impregnated with Mexican camp humor.

'Bugas' and bicycles

In Mexican gay slang bisexuals are called 'bicycles' and heterosexuals are called *'bugas'*. 'Bicycle' simply sounds like 'bisexual'. The word *'buga'*, on the other hand, is heavy with irony. It implies incredulity about straights: *'bugas* are those people who claim not to be gay' would be the closest translation.

The truth is that Mexican gays have serious doubts about heterosexual men's sincerity. Their mistrust is not fortuitous; it is reinforced by hundreds of years of Mexican tradition, where the men have always been together, sharing public places, work, games and festivities, making sexual jokes and displaying physical affection. Mexican men, living in a culture they have dominated from the pre-Hispanic era through colonial times and up to the present, have freedoms and privileges that put them above women and at the same time separate them from women. Furthermore, *machista* behaviour, which traditionally has had women and gays as its victims, gives Mexican men rights of sexual access to both, provided they are the dominant partner: the penetrator, the sexually active.

It is worth dwelling on this point. Machismo, as opposed to homophobia of Anglo-Saxon origin, does not necessarily rule out homosexuality; machismo subordinates homosexuality to its rules, and uses a double discourse to refer to it. It fights against homosexuality in theory but accepts it in practice; rejects it in public but invokes it in private; despises it in daylight and procures it under cover of darkness.

It is only in recent years that people have begun to speak about how common bisexuality is among Mexicans. In 1987, in relation to the AIDS crisis, the official organization CONASIDA recognized that 'in Mexico there is a great incidence of bisexual practices, something which must be known by society'.[8] However, it is impossible to know how many bisexuals there are because, to start with, most of them do not consider themselves bisexual. Despite the greater information that now exists among Mexicans about homosexuality and bisexuality, most do not make much of having one or two or sporadic contacts with homosexuals. It is furthermore not customary to talk about these adventures, nor do they give rise to an identity conflict. They are simply things that happen.

Today in many regions of the country youth have encounters less clandestinely, even as they continue not to talk about them. I am referring mainly to youth from the middle class down, since apparently in the upper class the difference between heterosexuality and homosexuality is more clearly delimited.

And now, coming out of the closet: the sixties and seventies

Some say that Mexicans are made for theatre, because our most important conflicts always take place surrounded by spectacular choreography. In the 1960s, when president Gustavo Díaz Ordaz—the eleventh president in a row from the ruling Institutional Revolutionary Party—was offering the world sumptuous proof of our national progress with the spectacular 1968 Olympics, behind the thousands of balloons and hundreds of doves sweeping across the sky another reality was hidden: the massive student revolt denouncing authoritarian government and the lack of democracy, the slaughter of hundreds in the 'Plaza of the Three Cultures' in the ancient neighbourhood of Tlatelolco, and the explosion of the deepest political crisis since the Mexican revolution.

The demands of the '68 student movement included those of an entire generation of Mexican youth. Outstanding among the demands were political freedom and also sexual and personal freedom. Gays and lesbians were among the movement's activists and main leaders. The recently 'disappeared' actress and theatre director, Nancy Cárdenas, who was the first in the country to put forward a political defence of homosexuality, was in its ranks.

Young people's sexual discourse was fundamentally directed at dismantling traditional control over their lives by the government, family, and austere, stern paterfamilias. But it also expressed many women's desire for freedom, as well as gays' and lesbians'. Nancy Cárdenas commented that on certain occasions she and several friends attended demonstrations carrying their own signs with gay demands, which they disguised a little by writing them in English:

'Gay rights'.

As a result of the youth movement, gay life flourished in Mexico in the '70s. In the main cities, such as Mexico City, Guadalajara and Acapulco, gay clubs emerged and proliferated. There gays and lesbians could be themselves openly; the traditional semi-clandestine bar practically disappeared from the scene. In Mexico City the number of streets, cafeterias and meeting places for gays increased precipitously; and the Zona Rosa neighbourhood (literally, the Pink Zone) soon lived up to its name and became populated largely by gay people. In 1972 in that freewheeling atmosphere in the capital, Nancy Cárdenas organized the first Mexican gay group, the Gay Liberation Collective, which in spite of its short life laid the foundations for the battle for gay rights and foreshadowed the emergence of the gay movement six years later.

In 1978 the gay liberation movement emerged in Mexico City. Its fundamental driving forces were three groups, all of which sprang up spontaneously in the same year: the Lambda Gay Liberation Group, composed of men and women; the Gay Revolutionary Action Front (FHAR), made up of men; and OIKABETH, a lesbian group.

The public appearance of the gay liberation movement greatly surprised the country, particularly by the founders' boldness in appearing publicly and their brave indictment of the 'invisible' marginalization of Mexican gays and lesbians, who were subjected to isolation, police repression and violence experienced by no other group in the country. The effects of this indictment and the three groups' successive actions opened new horizons in national life. Their presence under the banner of solidarity with other oppressed people—political prisoners, workers, peasants—earned support and sympathy for their cause. Their daring behaviour and their repeated exposure of abuses gained them the support of the feminist movement and the left, changed the attitude of the traditional yellow press, and won over prominent intellectuals. Most important, they convinced a wide sector of society of the legitimacy of their demands.

The best summary of the period is: greater public visibility of Mexico's gays and lesbians; support for their exposure of police abuse from a broad sector of public opinion; legitimation of the struggle for civil rights; and the emergence, through the influence of their example, of other gay groups in several cities, most notably in Guadalajara and Tijuana.

The revelation of the extreme marginalization experienced by gays and the emphatic denunciation by gay groups of police abuses were factors that strengthened the gay liberation movement and quickly made broad public outreach possible, generating a strong base of support in the population and helping to make possible the first ventures into politics. For the first time the gay liberation movement was able to run candidates in the elections to the Chamber of Deputies, on the slate of the Revolutionary Workers' Party (PRT).

By the mid-1980s, after exhilarating experiences involving tens of thousands of gays and lesbians in Mexico City, the great holiday came to an end. The three pioneering groups were hit by internal crises provoked by the question, 'Now what?' This led to their collapse and consequently an extended impasse for the gay liberation movement. The achievements of the great odyssey were: overcoming the old perceptions in the national consciousness, which linked gays and lesbians to vice and crime; increased social tolerance; and the opening up of social space. But—what a paradox!—among the gay groups themselves, the holiday ended badly. There was a superficial glorification of the movement's achievements and a neglect of any concrete perspective for winning civil rights, with an extremely ideological approach as the pretext.

In other words, activists were caught off balance by the real limits of the changes achieved in society. Whether they liked it or not, these changes were limited to support for gays and lesbians insofar as they were victims of brutal marginalization and abuse, but they did not translate into support for gay people's personal orientation and lifestyle. In my very personal opinion, the importance and limits of this balance sheet showed the need for the gay liberation movement to shift from gay liberation to the struggle for civil rights. This observation is still valid today. If the first effort of the gay liberation movement was to convince society of the unjust character of repression against gays and of their inequality in terms of civil rights, its second effort must be to go deeper and persist in condemning every abuse, outrage and form of discrimination. I cannot imagine another way for Mexican gays to achieve changes which will really usher in a new deal for us.

On the trail of Mexican democracy

One wishes things were easier, but Mexican reality indicates that real advances for gay and lesbian rights can only be obtained in the context of substantial democratic changes in the country. As long as this has not happened, gay and AIDS activists will keep on swinging at the piñata without breaking it open. Worse yet, traditional problems of the law's indifference—the silence of the Mexican constitution on gays' and lesbians' right to benefit from its guarantees and on discrimination on the basis of sexual orientation—are compounded by the corruption of the authorities, the dead letter of such laws as the constitutional right to health care, and such puritanical and vague laws and police regulations as those in defense of 'morals and public decency'. All of this forms a dark passage from which one can see no exit.

As I noted above, we Mexicans are continuously caught up in drama. In 1988 Carlos Salinas de Gortari, the candidate of the party that has been in power for seventy years, had serious difficulties acceding to the presidency. His opponent, Cuauhtémoc Cárdenas, son of Lázaro Cárdenas, an ex-president dearly loved by Mexicans, was apparently the real winner of the elections. However, the events that followed did not allow the voters to ascertain who had won and who had lost, since the morning after the vote the official spokesman of the government announced something extraordinary: the collapse of the computer system counting the votes. That did not prevent Salinas de Gortari from being sworn in as president of Mexico or from governing as he pleased. Meanwhile, the protagonists of the collapse of the system, that is, the population that voted for Cárdenas, were as astounded as he was, full of historical amazement.

Cárdenas, grown more familar with the system's tricks, opted for building his own party, the Party of the Democratic Revolution (PRD). Today the PRD is an important political force in the country, in competition with the PRI and the conservative National Action Party (PAN). Cárdenas has taken a public stand in favour of gay rights; his party, the PRD, is the only major party that mentions gay rights in its statements.

Everything for everyone, nothing for us: the Zapatistas

In 1994 Salinas de Gortari announced with great fanfare Mexico's entry into the First World, as the North American Free Trade Agreement (NAFTA) took effect. Many Mexicans, amazed by his reiterated audacities, sincerely believed him. But the other Mexico, that of the Indians of the Lacandon jungle, rose in arms and announced at dawn on January 1st the truth of the situation: to millions of Mexicans, Mexico means marginalization and exclusion from social justice and democratic rights. Mexicans ran to their TVs and the whole country was moved. They believed in the Zapatistas and supported them in spite of Salinas. But Salinas continued to be president through a fast and furious sequence of political events including masterful political assassinations: first of his party's presidential candidate, Colosio, and then of the party president, Ruiz Massieu. Today Salinas's brother is confined to a high security prison, accused of participating in Ruiz Massieu's assassination, while the ex-president lives abroad.

The Zapatista Army of National Liberation (EZLN) is still entrenched in the Lacandon jungle. Its fate depends on democratic changes which have not yet materialized. The Zapatistas, in spite of being an armed movement, have not forgotten any sector of the population that is fighting for democracy, including the activists of the gay liberation movement. Gay liberation movement activists attended the Aguascalientes Convention, held in the heart of the jungle with the participation of hundreds of Mexico's political organizations and personalities, and their statements were included in the resolutions of the meeting.

Nevertheless, the struggle of gays and lesbians is teetering on a tightrope. Although the governing system has been considerably weakened by the PRI's internal crisis and its loss of important regional power centres, which have passed mainly under the control of the conservative PAN or the progressive PRD, the atmosphere of hostility against gays tends to worsen periodically. In all the municipalities where the PAN has won, it has unleashed puritanical vigilante campaigns which include shutting down gay bars, roundups in the streets and censorship of artistic expression. The PAN's excesses have reached the point of attempting to forbid women from wearing miniskirts in the city of Guadalajara. In Veracruz they banned the celebration of gay culture week, and in Monterey they closed all gay establishments.

The threat of an era of puritanism under the PAN is based on the great advances the party has made in recent years, but also on its strong links to the conservative hierarchy of the Catholic Church. The Church too has orchestrated some wide-ranging puritanical campaigns, such as the one unleashed in the state of Guanajuato against sex education in the public schools.

Clearly the Catholic Church has a long history of anti-gay hostility in Mexico. The Church was the real moral author, through its medieval understanding of homosexuality, of the oppressive atmosphere of the not very distant past—though this was a product of several factors including animosity and prejudice deeply rooted in the population—and of the anti-gay prejudices that accompanied the traditionally high value put on machismo. The state's written and unwritten rules aimed at safeguarding Mexicans' 'morals and public decency' were copied from the Church's teachings.

The cooperation between clergy and state to maintain the ban on abortion in Mexico must not be underestimated; and the Mexican state's moral presuppositions about homosexuality as well are wholly inspired by the Catholic Church. This creates an unfavourable situation for gays and lesbians, whose conflicts with the law or government are based by and large on censorship of a religious type and not on civil or secular regulations. One example is the legal foundations of the articles of Mexican law referring to 'shame', 'morality' and 'public decency'. These are the same criteria used in the famous roundup against the 41 in the period of dictator Porfirio Díaz, and the same criteria that govern the repression and censorship campaigns that the authorities are carrying out in some municipalities today.

In spite of all the threats, Mexican gays will not easily accept being set back twenty years. In fact, the achievements of the pioneers of the gay liberation movement are still apparent in the work of new gay and AIDS activists, as well as in progressive sectors of the country. The PAN's puritanical actions have frequently faced unexpected criticism from human rights groups, prominent intellectuals and politicians, as well as resistance from local gay and lesbian communities who no longer think of themselves as people without rights. The PAN's actions have provoked public discussion about homophobia on national television, featuring prominent intellectuals such as Carlos Monsiváis.

On the other hand, the ruling PRI, skillful in adapting to political changes, began to follow the PRD's lead in criticizing the PAN's puritanical postures in the fight for control over Mexico City. Since the July 1997 elections the PRD has a lesbian activist among its congresspeople.

Even though the exciting experience of the first years of Mexican gay activism are a thing of the past, most of the people who made that experience possible are still active in new projects and groupings. Many things have changed, and new problems have emerged which have modified in practice the emphases of the gay struggle. For example, the customary lack of protection for gay rights was compounded by the problem of AIDS, which amplified anti-gay prejudices, the rise of discrimination against people with HIV, and the lack of health care for people with AIDS. Reflecting these realities, new groups emerged, combining AIDS issues with gay rights issues. Veterans of the gay liberation movement converged with a new generation of activists. Projects emerged which focused on subjects that had never been dealt with before in Mexico: AIDS and human rights; AIDS and homosexuality; AIDS and sexual diversity; AIDS and homophobia; and gay communities along the Mexico-US border. The groups involved in these projects are the Social Research Group on AIDS (GISIDA) in Mexico City, the Tijuana AIDS organization in the state of Baja California, and the group Abrazo [Embrace] in the state of Nuevo León).

Alongside these, other groups emerged: the so-called 'cultural groups', devoted to the propagation of gay culture. They came together to organize cultural events, such as art exhibits, dance and theatre performances, discussion panels, etc. Their work is supported by people who do not belong to the gay community, such as artists and intellectuals—many of them well-respected— who have broad social support and are capable of outreach beyond the gay community. It is impossible today to talk about gay struggles in Mexico without mentioning the important work of groups such as the Gay Cultural Circle in Mexico City, the lesbian 'Patlatonalli' group in Guadalajara, or the Civil Culture Net in Tijuana. These groups' activities, represented mainly by annual art and culture festivals, have undoubtedly opened a new political space for the defense of homosexuality and lesbianism. At the same time they have become much more attractive for many gays and lesbians than (for example) the less and less well attended gay pride marches.

Clearly the current configuration of groups has very little to do with previous organizations of the gay liberation movement, which were more numerous but at the same time more messianic in their objectives. In any event, the framework today branches out into small groups, which have identified their fields of action and goals more precisely, and in this sense they hit the mark. This also describes lesbian groups, which have maintained more continuity with the past. Groups such as The Closet of Sor Juana in Mexico City have a better identified field of work today, while Patlatonalli has made a turn towards health programmes and cultural activities.

The weakest point in the current panorama is the limited interaction among different groups, which does not go beyond occasional, ad hoc coalitions around matters of common concern. This is a failing. But apparently the problem is more than the existing groups can deal with, since it requires taking major initiatives on issues that have an impact on all of Mexico's gays and lesbians; and frankly this work demands considerable intelligence and maturity. Particularly in current conditions formulating such initiatives is closely bound up with matters of complex political and legal importance: reforming the Mexican constitution, reordering the antiquated legal system, and the current process of democratic change in the country's political system.

translated by César Ayala

[1] Alfredo López Austin, *Cuerpo Humano e Ideología: Las concepciones de los antiguos nahuas*, Mexico City: UNAM/Instituto de Investigaciones Antropológicas, 1980.

[2] Fernando de Alva Ixtlixóchitl, *Obras Históricas*, Mexico City: UNAM/Instituto de Investigaciones Históricas, 1977.

[3] Bartolomé de las Casas, *Los indios de México y de Nueva España*, Mexico City: Editorial Porrúa, 1987; Bernardino de Sahagún, *Historia General de las cosas de Nueva España*, México: Editorial Porrúa, 1979.

[4] De las Casas, *Los indios de México*.

[5] Salvador Novo, *Las locas, el sexo y los burdeles*, Mexico City: Novaro, 1972.

[6] Carlos Montavais, *Amor Perdido*, Mexico City: Era Editorial, 1977.

[7] Ibid.

[8] Bernardo Sepulvera, *Prácticas bisexuales y uso de condones*, Mexico City: Secretaria de Salud/CONASIDA, 1994, cited in *La Jornada* and *Excelsior*, 16 July 1998.

[9] On these last three projects, see the cultural supplement 'Society and AIDS', founded by the 'disappeared' Francisco Galván; the cultural supplement 'Letra S' of the national newspaper *La Jornada*; and *Frontera Gay*, Tijuana, Baja California.

Desire and militancy: lesbians, gays and the Brazilian Workers Party

James N. Green

Over six hundred delegates and activists crowded into the ballroom of the Rio Palace Hotel in Rio de Janeiro in June 1995 for the opening ceremonies of the Seventeenth International Conference of the International Lesbian and Gay Association (ILGA). To thunderous applause, the keynote speaker, Marta Suplicy, a federal congresswoman from the Brazilian Workers Party, announced support for two national campaigns proposed by the recently-formed Brazilian Association of Gays, Lesbians and Transvestites. The first involved amending the federal constitution to prohibit discrimination based on sexual orientation. The second proposed the legal recognition of same-gendered relationships (*união civil*). Given the conservative composition of the Brazilian Congress, it seems unlikely that either measure will become law in the foreseeable future. Nevertheless, the fact that a politician from the Brazilian party most closely identified with the labour movement has been at the forefront of these congressional efforts symbolizes an important relationship which has developed over the last twenty years between the lesbian and gay movement and the Brazilian left.

There are, however, tensions in this relationship. In recent years, sectors of the progressive wing of the Catholic Church who are associated with liberation theology and support the labour movement have pressured the Workers Party to tone down certain political issues that contradict church teachings. As a result, during the 1994 presidential race, the Workers Party candidate, Luiz Ignácio da Silva, popularly known as Lula, retreated from the party's position on same-sex marriages and another platform plank in favor of legalizing abortions. Some leaders, rank and file members, and supporters of the Brazilian Workers Party have also questioned the organization's stand on these issues.

On the whole, however, significant sectors of the Brazilian left and several important labour unions have positioned themselves on the side of lesbians and gays fighting for equal rights. This association did not develop overnight. Rather it has been the result of a complicated process lasting over two decades. This article will trace the development of that relationship from the late 1970s— when the country's most important trade unions and other social movements entered the political arena to challenge both the military dictatorship which ruled the country at the time and other important specific aspects of Brazilian society—to the aftermath of the 1994 presidential elections and the recent campaign for domestic partner benefits.

The first wave of gay and lesbian liberation in Latin America

In 1968 student mobilizations swept through Latin America from Mexico City to Rio de Janeiro, confronting authoritarian regimes and demanding more political freedom. A year later, in a seemingly unrelated event which took place several months after the 1969 Stonewall Rebellion in New York City, a group of fourteen Argentine men met in a working-class suburb of Buenos Aires to form Nuestro Mundo [Our World], the country's first gay rights organization. By 1971 six divergent Argentine groups had come together to form the Frente de Liberación Homosexual de Argentina [Homosexual Liberation Front of Argentina].[1] That same year, a short-lived gay organization, the Frente de Liberación Homosexual, was founded in Mexico. A year later, theater director Nancy Cárdenas organized the 'Colectivo de Liberación Homosexual', marking the definitive establishment of a movement in that country.[2] In 1974, Puerto Rican lesbians and gays organized the Comunidad de Orgullo Gay [Gay Pride Community] and began publishing the newspaper Pa'Fuera on the island.[3]

During these tumultuous years of the early lesbian and gay rights movement in three of Latin America's more urban and industrialized countries, small groups debated ideas emanating from an emerging international movement and struggled to create authentic endogenous expressions of social and political action. Notably absent from this process was Brazil with its lively gay male subculture—most prominently expressed during Carnival—and its growing yet more clandestine manifestations of lesbian sociability. While incipient movements struggled to survive in Buenos Aires, Mexico City, and San Juan, Brazilian gays and lesbians were living under the most repressive years of the military dictatorship which ruled the country from 1964 to 1985. In December 1968, the governing generals closed down the Congress, suspended constitutionally-guaranteed rights, increased press censorship, and stepped up the arrest and torture of those who opposed military rule. Although homosexual men and women were not specifically targeted by the dictatorship, the increased numbers of military police in the street, the arbitrary rule of law, and the generalized clamp-down on artistic and literary expression all created a climate which discouraged the emergence of a Brazilian lesbian or gay rights movement in the early 1970s.

By the middle of the decade, however, the combination of economic difficulties and mounting opposition to the government by students, political figures, and a newly energized labour movement shifted the balance of power in the country. Facing the possibility of a social explosion, the ruling generals orchestrated a controlled political liberalization which in turn was accelerated by successive strike waves in São Paulo, the country's economic center. In this ebullient period of gradual political openings between 1977 and 1981, new social movements emerged, most notably the Movimento Negro Unificado [United Black Movement], which questioned the traditional portrayal of Brazil as a racial democracy; a feminist movement, which confronted the sexism of both the orthodox left and Brazilian society at large; and a lesbian and gay rights movement.

Autonomy v. alliances: An early debate splits the movement

Three elements combined to characterize the movement's formative years from 1977 to 1983—the public visibility of politicized lesbians and gay men, the first efforts at political activism, and sharp debates about how to work with other emerging social movements and the leftist opposition to the dictatorship. For the first time, a group of gay men, primarily intellectuals, came out as homosexuals in the press and emphasized the political nature of their self-declaration. A dozen prominent writers and intellectuals initiated this process in April 1978 when they launched the journal, Lampião da Esquina.[4] The monthly tabloid, which sold up to 20,000 copies nationwide during its three-year life span, was also the first forum for a small number of lesbians who were in the process of publicly coming out, and concurrently moving toward the feminist movement. Lampião sparked the formation of SOMOS: Grupo de Afirmação Homossexual [We Are: Group of Homosexual Affirmation], the country's first gay political organization which began as a consciousness-raising group in the city of São Paulo in 1978 and timidly moved toward political action. In turn, both Lampião and SOMOS inspired the founding of a dozen similar organizations in capital cities of some of Brazil's more important states between 1979 and 1982.[5]

In the first two years of the movement's life (1978-1980), SOMOS and other nascent groups moved from semi-clandestine operation to a more public profile and slowly began to take modest political initiatives. The editors of Lampião shaped the movement's agenda by arguing that the journal should be a vehicle for discussions on sexuality, racial discrimination, the arts, ecology, and machismo.[6] Following this approach, activists turned to the newly constituted feminist and black movements to offer their support based on the analysis that lesbians and gay men shared the same marginal status in Brazilian society. On 20 November 1979, for example, SOMOS members joined a protest march against racial discrimination and in celebration of the National Day of Black Consciousness. They distributed a leaflet that stated: 'The combativeness of Zumbí [an Afro-Brazilian who fought against slavery in the seventeenth century] is an example for all oppressed sectors of our society in the fight for freedom. Coming from our own discrimination as homosexuals, we show our solidarity with all blacks in their struggle against racism.'[7] The reaction by other protesters to SOMOS members' participation in the demonstration ranged from enthusiasm to indifference, which encouraged the gay and lesbian activists to consider assuming a more public profile in other political events.

Likewise, nascent groups like SOMOS made overtures to the recently-structured feminist movement. This initiative came not just from the growing number of lesbians who had joined groups that had been originally dominated by gay men, but also from a political conviction. Some of the leading male members of the movement shared with lesbian members a perspective in which feminism offered an important ideological critique of heterocentric normativity. While many feminists and members of black consciousness groups welcomed the alliance proposed by some *Lampião's* editors and leading gay and lesbian activists, these movements by no means universally embraced the recently formed gay and lesbian groups. Nevertheless, influential gay and lesbian spokespersons developed a binary 'we-they' approach, grouping together feminists, Afro-Brazilians, indigenous people, and ecologists in one camp, and the patriarchal and authoritarian Brazilian social structure in the other. Left-wing organizations were also included in the 'they' camp because they had a male-dominated leadership, conservative views on sexuality, and a rigid initial reaction to activists' questioning of dominant notions of race and gender. Ironically, even as the left led the opposition to the military dictatorship, it became the whipping boy of many feminist, black consciousness and homosexual activists.

Indeed, the first public event in which SOMOS members participated brought to the surface many of these controversies and debates regarding the Brazilian left. On 8 February 1979, a libertarian current within the student movement invited members of SOMOS and two *Lampião* editors to participate in a panel on homosexuality as part of a four-day series on 'minorities' held at the social science department of the University of São Paulo. The discussion period which followed their presentations reflected polarized viewpoints already held by many of the three hundred people attending the event. On one hand, student representatives from different semi-underground traditional leftist organizations argued that issues of sexuality and oppression were secondary questions. Rather, they insisted, activists should dedicate their energies to overthrowing the military dictatorship.[8] Representatives from SOMOS and *Lampião* countered that the left was homophobic and ignored important social issues that did not conform to what leftists understood to be the perspectives and values of the Brazilian working class. They insisted, moreover, that the lesbian and gay movement should operated autonomously without any connection to left-wing groups.[9]

Those gay and lesbian activists who had serious reservations about any tactical alliance with the left made a strong case. Their arguments were at times informed by gay liberationist, anarchistic, libertarian, and feminist discourses. They held that homosexuality per se subverted the entire social and gender system whereas the Brazilian left remained within the framework of traditional patriarchal and hierarchical understandings of sex roles and normative behaviour. Shunning the Leninist-influenced methods of internal party operations, they proposed alternative, decentralized and spontaneous organizational forms for the lesbian and gay movement.[10]

Some of the more articulate critics of the Brazilian left based their observations on concrete personal experience. Several of the leading editors of *Lampião* had been militants in different underground left-wing organizations which marginalized or expelled them when the parties' leaderships discovered that they were homosexual.[11] Moreover, the Brazilian Communist Party, which had spawned most of the other left-wing currents in the student and labour movement, held a traditional Stalinist position which considered homosexuality a product of bourgeois decadent behaviour.[12] At the time, no one clearly articulated a third political alternative, namely the possibility that the Brazilian left might be capable of integrating the issues of the lesbian and gay movement within its programmatic vision.

The absence of a Marxist-inspired pro-gay and lesbian perspective within the Brazilian movement would not last long. In early 1979, gay and lesbian members of Convergência Socialista, a Trotskyist organization with influence in the labour and student movements, formed an internal caucus with the objective of challenging traditional leftist positions on homosexuality as well as participating systematically in the budding gay and lesbian movement. That same year several members and supporters of the Socialist Convergence also began to play a more prominent role within SOMOS. Their activities sparked a discussion about the role of the left within the movement and the advisability of tactical alliances with the labour-based social movements which had exploded onto the political scene in 1978. By 1980, the members and supports of the Socialist Convergence within the gay and lesbian movement became the lightning rod which attracted all of the vehement anger that pro-libertarian forces within the movement retained against the entire left. A conflagration ensued shortly after the First National Gathering of the movement held in São Paulo in April 1980.

The three-day event took place during a prolonged general strike organized by São Paulo trade unionists in key industrial sectors which had the near-universal support of the growing public opposition to the military. Solidarity with the recently radicalized labour movement was so widespread that in the opening session of the First National Gathering of Homosexual Groups, the body unanimously endorsed a motion backing the goals of the general strike. However, a resolution presented the next day calling on the lesbian and gay movement to join a massive May Day solidarity march to be held in the industrial strike zone was narrowly defeated.[13]

Having lost the vote in the national gathering to endorse participation in the May Day rally, leftist-leaning SOMOS participants, who made up a majority of the group's active membership, decided to participate in the demonstration without forcing another polarizing vote. Organized as the Commission of Homosexuals in Favor of May 1st, fifty lesbians and gay men joined the march of over 100,000. They carried two banners proclaiming solidarity with the general strike and protesting discrimination against 'homosexual workers'. A leaflet distributed by the ad hoc commission linked the struggle of the strikers with that of the oppressed (blacks, women, and homosexuals), pointed to instances of job discrimination, and called on the unity of the working class to end such practices.[14]

Participation in the 1980 May Day protest marked the first concrete political interaction between lesbian and gay activists and left-wing unionists mobilized against the military dictatorship. While some activists had expected a degree of hostility from sectors of the working class, they were pleased at the positive reception from the crowd as they marched into the rally site of the day's event.[15] Those within SOMOS who opposed any participation in the May Day activities organized a picnic at the city zoo and split from SOMOS several weeks later alleging its domination by the left.[16]

Lampião editors joined those SOMOS dissidents in criticizing the apparent close relationship between Brazil's leading gay and lesbian rights organization and the Socialist Convergence.[17] Rather than pointing to the total absence of any programmatic support for the emerging movement by the Brazilian Communist Party and other leftist organizations with clearly homophobic positions, the monthly's most prolific editors focused on the only Brazilian left-wing group which defended gay and lesbian rights and portrayed that organization as the personification of the entire left. SOMOS members responded to Lampião editors' remarks by approving a statement of principles which held that while the organization was autonomous and 'would not affiliate with any political party, members of the organization were allowed to hold any political ideology and belong to any political party, and the group would participate in any political demonstration it saw fit to join'.[18]

The formation of the Brazilian Workers Party

In the late 1970s, the dictatorship faced mounting opposition from all sides. Fearing a defeat of pro-government candidates in the upcoming 1980 election, the military disbanded the two legally-sanctioned mainstream political parties and permitted a multi-party system. The generals hoped that this would split the opposition into warring camps and divide the electorate accordingly. In the process of political restructuring, opposition trade-union officials, headed by Luis 'Lula' Ignácio da Silva, the working-class leader of the 1978-80 strike wave, brought together diverse social movements, radicalized rank-and-file unionists, the progressive wing of the Catholic Church, Trotskyists, and other left-wing organizations to form the Partido dos Trabalhadores (PT), the Workers Party. The pro-Soviet Brazilian Communist Party, the pro-Albanian Communist Party of Brazil, the pro-Cuban October 8th Revolutionary Movement and other left-wing formations remained outside of the PT and aligned with the Party of the Brazilian Democratic Movement, a broad-based multi-class oppositional political party. Thus, from its inception, the Workers Party did not include significant sectors of the Marxist left which continued to maintain the traditional Stalinist position that homosexuality was 'a product of bourgeois decadent behaviour'. While this did not automatically create a guaranteed space for gays and lesbians within the ranks of the PT, the party largely attracted activists who positioned themselves on the left yet were critical of many of the policies and practices of traditional Brazilian Marxists.

Throughout 1980 and 1981, Workers Party activists carried out a grass-roots campaign to fulfill legalization requirements. At the same time, a small number of gay and lesbian activists began to approach the PT, seeing it as an umbrella opposition political party which might seriously support their demands. For example, during the 1981 May Day march, individual members of SOMOS and other gay men and lesbians joined together in an ad hoc committee, known as Homosexual Militants Building the PT. Marching as a contingent in this demonstration against the dictatorship, they carried a banner protesting job discrimination against gays and lesbians and another denouncing the undemocratic nature of the military regime.[19]

At the national convention of the Workers Party held in September 1981, the party's undisputed leader, Lula, set the tone for the party's attitude toward lesbian and gay activists within the PT. The labour leader stated that he supported 'the right of minorities to organize and defend their space', adding that 'we will not permit that homosexuality is treated as a sickness, and much less a case for the police, in our party. We will defend the respect that they deserve, calling on them to participate in the building of our society.'[20] Soon thereafter, psychiatrist João Batista Breda, a state assembly representative from the Workers Party in São Paulo, came out during a television programme, becoming the first openly gay elected offical in Brazilian history. However, he lost his mandate in the 1982 elections, a fact which he in part attributed to the public declaration of his sexual orientation and in part to the relatively poor showing by the Workers Party in its first election campaign as a new political party.[21]

Breda's electoral defeat was symbolic of the ebbing of the first wave of gay and lesbian activism in Brazil between 1982 and 1989. After 37 monthly issues, *Lampião* folded in June 1981. Plans that same year for a second national gathering of gays and lesbians scheduled to be held in Rio de Janeiro also fell through. Only three years later, in 1984, did five out of seven organizations still in existence manage to meet in the northeastern capital Salvador to exchange experiences and coordinate joint campaigns. Whereas in 1980 *Lampião* had published a directory listing 22 gay and lesbian groups in existence throughout Brazil, by 1985 only four organizations had survived. Moreover, fear and confusion surrounding the dramatic spread of AIDS in Brazil and the overwhelming tasks involved in responding to the disease further taxed the limited human and financial resources of the surviving gay groups. The waning of the movement coincided with the severe economic recession of 1981-82, the modest election gains of the Workers Party, and a temporary downturn in the labour movement. Many middle-class-based social movements also went into decline in the face of limited political successes. During this period, while most male-dominated gay groups folded, lesbian activists moved into the feminist movement and won a political space to address issues of sexism and homophobia.[22]

The movement's second wave and the Workers Party

After the return to civilian rule in 1985, a slow resurgence in movement activities took place, focusing on campaigns to enact provisions against legal discrimination, to respond to violence against gays, transvestites and lesbians, and to address the burgeoning AIDS epidemic. In February 1985, Luiz Mott, an anthropology professor and founder of Grupo Gay da Bahia (currently the oldest existing group in Brazil) achieved a long-term goal. He successfully steered the floundering movement through a campaign that convinced the Federal Council of Health to abolish the classification that categorized homosexuality as a treatable 'sexual deviance'.[23] Gay activists also entered electoral politics. In 1986, Herbert Daniel, a former member of a left-wing urban guerrilla organization in the 1970s who had came out while living in exile in France, ran for the state assembly on the Workers Party ticket. Although he failed to get elected, his campaign served as a model for future openly gay candidates and expanded the political space for lesbian and gay activism within the Workers Party.[24]

In the following year and a half, the Workers Party and other left groups supported lesbian and gay rights on an important political front. During 1987 and 1988 a national constituent assembly met to rewrite the Brazilian constitution. João Antônio S. Mascarenhas, a former editor of *Lampião* and founder of *Triangulo Rosa* (Pink Triangle) in Rio de Janeiro, organized a campaign to include a provision in the constitution prohibiting discrimination based on sexual orientation. On 28 January 1988, approximately 25 per cent of Constituent Assembly members voted in favor of a constitutional provision outlawing discrimination.[25] Twenty-five of the 33 evangelical pastors in the Assembly voted against the measure. All of the leftist Workers Party representatives backed the prohibition of discrimination based on sexual orientation. Interestingly enough, the representatives of the Brazilian Communist Party and the Communist Party of Brazil, while maintaining their long-standing characterization that homosexuality remained decadent bourgeois behaviour, voted for the amendment.[26]

Although activists failed to modify Brazil's constitution, the debate regarding the amendment led to the adoption of similar legislation in two states (Sergipe and Mato Grosso), the Brazilian capital (Brasília), important cities (Rio de Janeiro, Salvador, São Paulo) and over seventy other municipalities.[27] This did not necessarily mean that the movement managed to win widespread popular support for these anti-discrimination statutes. As long-time Workers Party gay activist William Aguiar has pointed out, in many cases local governments have the provision on the books because they copied the city of São Paulo's entire civil code which contained the anti-discrimination clause.[28] Nevertheless, the Constituent Assembly debate encouraged expanding legal protections against gays and lesbians and provided the basis for the recent campaign for domestic partnership rights spearheaded by Workers Party congresswoman, Marta Suplicy.

In 1989 Brazilians had the opportunity for the first time in almost thirty years to participate in direct presidential elections. In that race Workers Party presidential candidate, Luis Ignácio 'Lula' da Silva ran against Fernardo Collar de Melo, a former governor representing industrial and rural oligarchic interests. The Workers Party internal process of choosing Lula's vice-presidential running mate revealed the fact that while the party maintained a programmatic support for gay and lesbian rights, the battle to win the hearts and minds of many rank and file member as well as a sector of the leadership was still not over. A sector of the Workers Party nominated Fernando Gabeira for the number two spot. Gabeira, a former journalist and urban guerrilla fighter, had been involved in the kidnapping of the United States ambassador to Brazil in the early 1970s. Upon returning from exile in late 1979, he penned a series of books which criticized the traditional left's failure to address feminism, ecological issues, and gay and lesbian rights, among other questions. While Gabeira did not publicly state that he was gay, his flamboyant style, somewhat ambiguous sexual positioning, and articulate support for lesbian and gay rights fueled rumors that he was a 'faggot'. A behind-the-scenes campaign relying on a generalized perception that Gabeira was a 'citizen under suspicion' contributed to his failure to secure the nomination.[29]

While Lula lost the 1989 presidential bid by a slim margin, the subsequent massive mobilizations to impeach President Collar for alleged widespread corruption coincided with a significant increase in gay and lesbian activism in the early 1990s. Representatives of six groups traveled to the northeastern state of Aracajú in 1990 to attend the fourth national gay and lesbian gathering. Encouraged by the successful campaign of the hosting organization to get the city government to rename a street 'June 28th', Workers Party activists initiated a campaign calling on their elected officials to celebrate the Stonewall Rebellion and international pride events by proposing similar street name changes in other parts of Brazil.[30]

The fifth national gay and lesbian gathering held the subsequent year, while still bringing together only half a dozen organizations, marked the beginning of an expansion in the number of groups in the country. The next year members from a dozen groups met in Rio de Janeiro for the sixth national meeting which addressed the AIDS issue and proposed a series of campaigns. These included a systematic denunciation of violence against gays, lesbians and transvestites, further attempts at a constitutional amendment to prohibit discrimination based on sexual orientation, and the legislative proposal for domestic partner rights.[31]

That same year, on 11 June 1992, a handful of Workers Party militants met to found the Grupo de Homossexuais do PT [Homosexual Group of the PT] in São Paulo, the country's industrial center and the birthplace of the PT.[32] In one of the group's first achievements, Workers Party elected representatives in four different state legislatures guaranteed the passage of motions recognizing June 28th as International Gay Pride Day.[33] The group also participated in the 1992 electoral campaign by leafleting gay and lesbian bars in support of Workers Party candidates and addressing specific issues of the community.[34]

The growth in the number of gay and lesbian groups in Brazil dovetailed with the increased activities and influence of PT members and supporters within the movement. In 1993, 21 groups came together for the Seventh Brazilian Gathering of Lesbians and Homosexuals, held at a Workers Party Conference Center outside of the city of São Paulo. Among the significant aspects of this gathering were the increased participation of lesbians and the co-gendered leadership of the event, marking a shift away from a gay male-domi-

nated movement.[35] While those who attended the meeting continued to con-
cur with the position taken by SOMOS members in 1980s to build a gay and
lesbian movement autonomous from any political party, an informal survey of
the participants by this author indicated overwhelming personal support for
the Workers Party as the only electoral alternative in Brazil.

Electoral and domestic partnership

The 1994 presidential elections proved, however, to be a disappointment,
both for the left and for gay and lesbian activists who supported the Workers
Party. At the beginning of the year, the high rate of inflation and the significant
lead that Lula enjoyed in the polls seemed to indicate that the former labour
leader would be swept into office by the end of the year. However, significant
social sectors, including national and international monopoly enterprises, large
landowners and large portions of the middle class, rallied behind former fi-
nance minister Fernando Henrique Cardoso, who drastically cut inflation by
mid-year immediately prior to resigning his post for a presidential bid. Lula
and a sector of the party which dominated the campaign opted to distance
themselves from any issues which might undermine their slipping position.[36]
Of particular concern was waning support from 'progressive' sectors of the
Catholic Church's 'base communities'. The PT's stands on abortion and full
rights for gays and lesbians were among the programmatic points that suffered
in the wake of Lula's shift to the right in a desperate attempt to shore up his
campaign.

One of the first indications of this change involved the rediscussion of the
Workers Party 1994 Plan for Governing, a document widely discussed among
the party's rank and file. Long-time party leader Irma Passoni, with ties to the
Catholic Church-backed social movements, and Benedita da Silva, at the time
a state congresswoman and currently the first Afro-Brazilian senator, who has
links to Protestant groups in Rio de Janeiro, opposed the pro-choice plank and
another favoring full legal recognition of gay and lesbian domestic partnerships.[37] The press immediately picked up on this internal party conflict and
characterized the proposal for full legal rights as nothing more than support for
'homosexual marriages', a concept that gay and lesbian activists within the PT
had carefully avoided in order to win broader support for the platform plank.[38]
While the Gay and Lesbian Group within the Workers Party managed to keep
the legal protection wording in the party platform, campaign coordinators
blocked adequate distribution of election brochures directed toward the gay
and lesbian community by postponing their production until the last minute.[39]
In spite of behind-the-scenes maneuvering and a generalized programmatic
shift to more moderate positions on the part of the PT, Lula lost his election bid
by a wide margin. A strengthened currency, diminished inflation, and near
unanimous media support assured that Fernando Henrique Cardoso easily
won the presidential race.

While its tepid support for gay and lesbian rights discouraged some activists who had looked toward the Workers Party as an electoral alternative, the significant strengthening of the movement nationwide in 1995 propelled activists into closer relationships with this sector of the Brazilian left which continued to be the only political force willing to offer legislative alliance to the movement. In January 1995, representatives from 30 out of more than 50 gay and lesbian groups that had sprung up throughout the country met to form the Brazilian Association of Gays, Lesbians and Transvestites, a national organization designed to coordinate campaigns against human rights violations and in favor of full legal and social rights. Leading members of the group then proceeded to host the Seventeenth International Conference of the International Lesbian and Gay Association (ILGA) in Rio de Janeiro, marking the first time that the European-based organization had met in the southern hemisphere. The Conference's closing march resplendent with a 150-meter rainbow flag and over 2,000 participants symbolized a rejuvenation of the movement nationwide.

During the conference representatives from several groups met to plan running gay and lesbian candidates in the November 1996 municipal elections. Of the twenty-three individuals who ran in primaries, twelve received party nominations. Seven ran on the Workers Party ticket, one on the Green Party and another on the United Socialist Workers Party, the political heir to the Socialist Convergence. The highest vote-getter, Claudio Nascimento da Silva, an Afro-Brazilian activist and trade unionist from Rio de Janeiro, received over 3000 votes, a third of the number required to win a seat on the city council. In an election wrap-up, Nascimento, one of the main organizers of the 1995 ILGA conference in Rio de Janeiro, speculated that if the two other Workers Party members, a lesbian and a gay man, had not decided to join the race at the last minute, his campaign might have built the momentum needed to reach the 10,000 vote minimum required to elect a candidate.[40] Toni Reis, the co-secretary general of the Brazilian Association of Gay, Lesbians and Transvestites, who also ran on the Workers Party ticket in the southern city of Curitiba, fell only 600 votes short of an election victory. The only successful candidate was Katia Tapeti, a transvestite and city council representative from a small town in the impoverished northeastern state of Piauí, who had become popular locally for her efforts in 'getting things done'.[41] Her election remains an anomaly since she ran on the ticket of the most conservative party which has consistently voted against all civil and legal rights for gays, lesbians, and transvestites.

In the wake of the 1996 elections, the movement geared up for another campaign in support of congressional legislation granting civil rights to same-sex partners. The proposal, introduced by sexologist and Workers Party congresswoman Marta Suplicy in conjunction with leaders in the national gay and lesbian movement, guaranteed domestic partnership, including inheritance rights and access to health, retirement and social security benefits. The Brazilian National Congregation of Bishops carried out a systematic campaign against the legislation,[42] and a coalition of Catholic and evangelical churches coordinated a national petition drive. In response the Brazilian Association of Gays, Lesbians and Transvestites organized a nationwide lobbying and petition campaign to shift public and legislative support toward the bill. Wilson da Silva, one of the leaders of the Group of Gays and Lesbians of the United Socialist Workers Party[43] and a student activist, steered through a resolution at the 1997 Congress of the National Union of Students in favor the Suplicy Bill. Leaders of the Confederação Única dos Trabalhadores, the country's national labour federation, also come out in favor of the proposal. Despite this backing, however, conservatives still dominate the Brazilian Congress, and it seems that they will continue to block passage of the bill.

Conclusion

In the early years of the Brazilian gay and lesbian movement, before the military had returned to the barracks, the controversy around long-term strategies and the relationship to the left provoked heated debates and virulent polemics. In the years following a return to formal democracy in 1985, the issue has been rarely raised. In part this is because the question has been resolved in practice. In a society where economic and social polarization has widened in recent years and where the Catholic Church and growing Protestant evangelical movements openly opposed gay and lesbian rights, consistent opposition to the status quo remains concentrated in the left, and largely within the Workers Party. While homophobic attitudes still fester within that organization, it still provides the most viable political forum for legislative approaches to guaranteeing equal rights. The still-fragile Brazilian gay, lesbian, and transgendered movement has negotiated a cautious course between guaranteeing the autonomy of the movement from any organizational affiliation and political collaboration on specific issues with the Workers Party and other sectors of the Brazilian left.

---

[1] [Nestor Perlongher], 'Una historia del FLH Argentino', mimeo, Buenos Aires, 1977.

[2] Barry D. Adam, *The Rise of a Gay and Lesbian Movement*, Boston: Twayne, 1987, p. 89.

[3] Frances Negrón-Munaner, 'Echoing Stonewall and other dilemmas: the organizational beginnings of a gay and lesbian agenda in Puerto Rico, 1972-1977 (Part I)', *Centro de Estudios Puertoriqueños Bulletin* vol. 1 no. 1 (1991-92), p. 79.

[4] The name *Lampião da Esquina* had a double meaning: 'lamppost on the corner', in reference to gay street life, and Lampião, a Robin Hood-type bandit figure who roamed the Brazilian Northeast in the early twentieth century.

[5] For different interpretations of the Brazilian gay movement's early years, see James N. Green, 'The emergence of the Brazilian gay liberation movement, 1977-81', *Latin American Perspectives* vol. 21 no. 1 (winter 1994), pp. 38-55; Edward MacRae, 'Homosexual identities in transitional Brazilian politics', in *The Making of Social Movements in Latin America: Identity, Strategy and Democracy*, ed. Arturo Escobar and

Sonia E. Alvarez, Boulder: Westview Press, 1992, pp. 185-203; Miriam Martinho, 'Brazil', in *Unspoken Rules: Sexual Orientation and Women's Human Rights,* ed. Rachel Rosenbloom, San Francisco: International Gay and Lesbian Human Rights Commission, 1985; and João S. Trevisan, *Perverts in Paradise,* trans. Martin Foreman, London: GMP, 1986, pp. 133-154. For an overview from 1980s to the present, see Luiz Mott, 'The gay movement and human rights in Brazil', in *Latin American Male Homosexualities,* ed. Stephen O. Murray, Albuquerque: Univ. of New Mexico Press, 1995, pp. 221-30.

[6] Conselho Editorial, 'Saindo do Gueto', *Lampião da Esquina* no. 0 (April 1978), p. 2.

[7] 'Moção de apoio ao Movimento Negro Unificado contra a discriminação racial', mimeo, 20 Nov. 1979, my translation.

[8] At the time, among the underground left organizations which defended this position were the pro-Soviet Brazilian Communist Party, the pro-Albanian Communist Party of Brazil, and the pro-Cuban October 8th Revolutionary Movement.

[9] Eduardo Dantas, 'Negros, mulheres, homossexuais e índios nos debates da USP', *Lampião da Esquina* no. 10 (Mar. 1979), pp. 9-10.

[10] Trevisan, *Perverts in Paradise,* pp. 144-15.

[11] The best example was Aguinaldo Silva, the principal editor of *Lampião* who wrote about his experiences in the Brazilian Communist Party. See, for example, Aguinaldo Silva, 'Compromissos, queridinhas? Nem morta!', *Lampião da Esquina* no. 26 (July 1980), pp. 10-11.

[12] Hiro Okita, *Homossexuais: Da opressão a libertação,* São Paulo: Proposta, 1981, pp. 63-73.

[13] Francisco Bittencourt, 'Homossexuais: a nova força', *Lampião da Esquina* no. 24 (May), pp. 4-6.

[14] Comissão de Homossexuais Pro-1º de Maio, 'Contra a intervenção nos sindicatos de São Paulo, contra a discriminação do trabalhador/a homossexual', mimeo, São Paulo, 1980.

[15] Luis Amorim, interview by author, 11 September 1994, São Paulo, Brazil, tape recording. Luis Amorim was a member of the left wing of SOMOS from 1979 to 1981.

[16] Trevisan, *Perverts in Paradise,* pp. 147-48.

[17] Darcy Penteado, 'Convergindo: da Mesopotâmia a Richetti', *Lampião da Esquina* no. 31 (Dec. 1980), p. 14.

[18] 'Pontos do princípio do Grupo SOMOS', mimeo, June 1980, my translation.

[19] Vilma Maunder, Luiz Mott & Aroldo Asunção, 'Homossexuais e o 1º de Maio', *Em Tempo* (14-27 May 1981), p. 14.

[20] *Folha de São Paulo* (28 Sept. 1981), p. 6.

[21] João Batista Breda, interview by author, 5 Aug. 1995, São Paulo, Brazil, tape recording.

[22] Martinho, 'Brazil', p. 22.

[23] Mott, 'The gay movement and human rights in Brazil', p. 223.

[24] Veriano Terto, Jr., interview by author, 24 July 1995, Rio de Janeiro, Brazil, tape recording. Terto has been a gay and AIDS activist since the late 1970s.

[25] Only 461 of the 559 members of the Constituent Assembly voted on the measure. Of that number 130 voted in favor of the constitutional provision outlawing discrimination based on sexual orientation. João Antônio Mascarenhas, 'Quantificação do machismo no legislativo federal', Rio de Janeiro, unpublished, 1994.

[26] Ibid.

[27] Mott, 'The gay movement and human rights in Brazil', pp. 223-24.

[28] William Aguiar, 'Revisar para não discriminar', *Em Tempo* no. 266 (Apr. 1993), p. 16.

[29] Roberto de Oliveira Silva, interview by author, 19 July 1997, São Paulo, Brazil, tape recording. Roberto de Oliveira Silva is a leader of the Grupo de Gays e Lésbicas do PT in São Paulo.

[30] 'A história do "EBHO": Encontro Brasileiro de Homosexuais' (Continuação II), *Boletim do Grupo Gay da Bahia* vol. 13 no. 27 (Aug. 1993), p. 7.

[31] Ibid.

[32] '1ª Reunião do Grupo de Homossexuais do Partido dos Trabalhadores', mimeo, n.d.

[33] Huides Cunha, 'Na contra-mão', *Boletim Nacional do P.T.* no. 66 (Oct.-Nov. 1992), p. 2.

[34] William Aguiar, 'Grupo de Homossexuais do Partido dos Trabalhadores', mimeo, n.d.

[35] Rede de Informação Lésbica Um Outro Olhar, 'Registro e memória do VII Encontro Brasileiro de Lésbicas e Homossexuais de 4 a 7 de Setembro de 1993', São Paulo (Sept. 1994), pp. 2-3.

[36] For a comprehensive analysis of the Workers Party and the 1994 elections, see Jacob Gorender, 'The reinforcement of bourgeois hegemony: the Workers Party and the 1994 elections', *Latin American Perspectives* vol. 25 no. 1 (Jan. 1998), pp. 11-27.

[37] William Aguiar, 'Preconceito', *Boletim Nacional* no. 84 (Mar. 1994), p. 2.

[38] The proposal read: 'Initiatives toward guaranteeing social security benefits, property and inheritance rights for homosexual couples'. William Aguiar, 'Sobre questões "polêmicas"' (31 Mar. 1994).

[39] Letter from William Aguiar, Coordinator of the National Section of Gays and Lesbians, to the Coordination of the Lula for President Campaign, São Paulo, 5 Sept. 1994.

[40] Claudio Nascimento da Silva, interview by author, 1 July 1997, Rio de Janeiro, Brazil, tape recording. Claudio Nascimento da Silva has been an activist in the gay and lesbian movement since the early 1990s.

[41] Associação Brasileira de Gays, Lésbicas e Travestis, *Boletim Especial* (Feb. 1997), pp. 4-5.

[42] Ibid., p. 6.

[43] The *Grupo de Gays e Lésbicas do Partido Socialista dos Trabalhadores (Unificado)*—the Gay and Lesbian Group of the United Socialist Workers Party—is the organizational and political heir to the gay and lesbian group of the Socialist Convergence. It works within the gay and lesbian movement as well as in labour unions and student organizations, raising issues of homophobia and discrimination based on sexual orientation. Wilson H. da Silva, interview by author, 27 June 1997, São Paulo, Brazil, tape recording. Wilson H. da Silva is a leading member of the GGLPST(U).

* * *

This article is dedicated to the memory of Adauto Belamino Alves, who died of complications related to AIDS on 27 January 1997. A long-time activist, Adauto consistently fought to link the gay, lesbian and transgendered movement to struggles of the working class and other oppressed sectors of Brazilian society.

Lesbian visibility in Latin America: reclaiming our history

Norma Mogrovejo

Latin American lesbians have been around since the beginning of the gay and lesbian rights struggle. There are reports that Latina lesbians were very much involved in the Stonewall rebellion. The *Village Voice* reported the involvement of groups of young Puerto Rican women, transvestites, young Black Latinos, and more broadly of 'different', non-white groups. The police tried forcibly to remove a Latina lesbian who put up a big fight, preventing the police from putting her in their car. This heroic woman put up a phenomenal fight, according to the newspaper report.[1] One of those arrested at the time was an undocumented Argentinian, who threw himself out of a third-story window of a police station and was impaled through his neck on a iron railing. He was brought to a hospital where he died. This anonymous Argentinian gay man is the first martyr of the modern gay movement, whom one must assume no one has heard of since he was Latino. Lesbian and gay Latinos in the US see this as the most tragic example of their invisibility within the North American gay community, and add that if the martyr had been white there would be a monument to him today.[2]

The first demands of the gay liberation movement were aimed at decriminalizing homosexuality. The movement declared, 'It is not a crime; it is not an illness; it is not the product of emotional immaturity', in response to notions that the legal and medical professions had defended since the end of the eighteenth century.

The second wave of Latin American feminism[3] was also an inspiration for organizing lesbians and gays. It introduced the idea that interpreting sexuality was a democratic political exercise, challenging the imperative of reproduction and asserting the right to sexual pleasure.

Initially organizations were called 'gay', even though they had women members, who were referred to as 'gay women'. The influence of feminism soon led to a split within the lesbian/gay movement, since feminist lesbians were challenging the sexism of gay men. Thanks to the influence of feminism the specific label 'lesbian' was adopted, as was the idea of autonomy for lesbians. These lesbians addressed the role of sexuality in a male-dominated society that values female sexuality solely for its reproductive function and the fulfillment of (heterosexual) male desire.

The emergence of lesbian visibility in Latin America and the demand for sexual and emotional alternatives have gone through three historical stages. These stages correspond to three successive generations of theory put forward by the feminist movement.

First came the struggle for equality, for the recognition of civil and political rights. Tied in with socialist and feminist struggles, the slogan 'for a socialism without sexism' accurately reflects this initial stage.

Second came the struggle to assert difference. Lesbians described themselves as different and autonomous: from gay men, whose sexism and male chauvinism (*falocentrismo*, 'phallocentrism') were challenged; and from feminists, who in practice had only raised demands for heterosexual women and did not take differences in sexuality and erotic desire sufficiently into account when explaining the differences between women and men. This focus on difference led to the rise of a separatist current and a semi-clandestine, autonomous lesbian feminist movement that was primarily active in heterosexual feminist circles. For this current not only is man not the model for socialization, he simply doesn't exist. Separatists see this approach as a threat to male domination, making lesbianism in their view a subversive political alternative.

Finally, a third current is still in the process of emerging, complementing the two previous generations of theory by challenging the limits of the notion of 'gender' for understanding the lesbian question. This current argues for a radical theory of sexuality that analyzes the political persecution of different sexual dissident groups for their erotic nature: transvestites, the transgendered, prostitutes and consenting sadomasochists. This new analysis suggests that gays and lesbians should seek out new forms and strategies in their political struggles for social justice.[4]

In the lesbian movement, these three generations of theory that emerged as distinct feminist currents correspond to three forms of confrontation linked to three specific historic moments: first, the lesbian movement's relation to the gay movement; second, its relation to the feminist movement; and third, the building of an autonomous lesbian movement.[5]

Here we examine three case studies: Mexico, Chile and Nicaragua. These examples correspond to the beginnings of the lesbian, gay and feminist movements under three political regimes characteristic of Latin America: formal democracy, dictatorship, and a revolutionary government. Throughout, we will show the interaction between the three 'social subjects' at three points in time and in relation to three generations of theory. While belonging to three different points in time, the three generations of theory are not at odds with each other and are in fact complementary in as much as the debate remains unresolved.[6] This means that it is as possible to find the three historical moments coinciding as it is to find just one or two of them at any given time. We also examine the day-to-day dynamics of Latin American lesbian organization.

Mexico

The first gay organization, the Gay Liberation Front, emerged in Mexico in 1971 under a regime of 'formal democracy'.[7] Although the group's membership was largely made up of gay men, its public spokesperson was Nancy Cárdenas, a pioneer in the struggle for civil and political rights for lesbians and gay men.

A key event in the movement's history was Nancy Cárdenas's appearance on a television programme in 1973. She was interviewed by Jacobo Zabludowski on the show '24 Horas', at the time the programme with the largest audience in Mexico. The interview was organized in the context of allegations by a US citizen that the Nixon administration had dismissed him because of his sexual orientation. Cárdenas and Zabludowski spoke about the legal status of gays and lesbians, the systematic persecution and repression of gays in Mexico, and the distorted focus of psychoanalysis and psychiatry in relation to homosexuality. The interview had a tremendous impact across the country, particularly among gays and lesbians themselves, and led to the upsurge of the organized gay movement and its emergence on the public stage some years later.

The Gay Liberation Front brought together a significant number of 'gay women'. Nancy Cárdenas recalls initial attempts to organize lesbians as such and the atmosphere at the time. Alcohol, she says, was a way out for those women, who lived with guilt, fear, internalized lesbophobia and in so many internal and external closets:

> One group was organized in a restaurant, for women only since there had been problems with the men. It was my friends who were the boozers; they would arrive at meetings stone-drunk and totally fed up. We had a great time but this wasn't the best way to be spending my day off. Things weren't going too well, and then came the Zabludowski interview. It was a real shot in the arm, almost as if he had organized a national meeting for us...[8]

Nancy recounts how many lesbians felt their experience was substantially different from that of gay men. The presence or absence of a phallus creates a different cosmic vision of the world for heterosexuals, homosexuals and lesbians. For men the phallus is a symbol of day-to-day power and the only symbol of pleasure, whereas for lesbians this is not the case. This is the root of the difficulties lesbians have in their relations with heterosexual and gay men.

An important event in lesbian history was the Conference for the International Women's Year in 1975. At the conference an Australian student, Lauria Bewington, demanded an end to the marginalization of lesbians. 'I am proud to be a lesbian; I have not suffered from any form of physical or psychological disturbance and have freely chosen to be what I am', she declared.[9]

In the following days, the word 'lesbian' appeared in the press for the first time.[10] The 'incident' was described as the result of 'illness' or 'deviation' and as an airing of 'insignificant matters'. In response a group of lesbians organized around Cárdenas. The group read out a 'Declaration of Mexican Lesbians' at the conference, in which they said their feelings were natural, normal, dignified and just; that unfortunately they had been unable to establish a solid group; that as a result of their own self-hatred it was difficult to raise other lesbians' consciousness; that the law enabled judges to imprison lesbians for up to six years with no right to parole, for 'immorality' and 'vice'; and that this,

along with police abuses, made open organization nearly impossible. The declaration concluded by asserting that 'gay liberation is another form of social
liberation'.[11]

Mexican legislation does not penalize lesbianism or homosexuality as such,
but it uses 'morality' as a criterion in legal rulings to sow fear among lesbians
and gay men. Juan Jacobo Hernández says that the pioneers of the movement
interpreted the law in such a way as to find the judge guilty, by suggesting that
he had no moral authority to judge them.[12] The laws have not changed since
that time. The existence of the criterion 'morality', a the symbol of the existence of 'immorality', is invoked to hold lesbians and gay men in contempt and
used as a tool to repress them.

The first autonomous lesbian organization in Mexico, Lesbos, was founded
in 1977 in the context of two-fold repression: from the police and the feminist
movement. The experiences of Yan María Castro and Cristina in the Women's
Coalition[13] and of Luz María Medina in a discotheque sparked the lesbian
organizational initiative:

> In the Coalition I realized that the demands raised were necessary and
> correct, but that they were linked to the needs of heterosexual women.
> There were no lesbian demands. So when I said, 'I'm a lesbian', it was
> very shocking to them. Initially, they would say, 'In any case, we like
> you and appreciate you a lot.' Or, 'It's all right that you're like "that",
> since we respect all women here, but maybe it's best you not say so
> outside the movement.' I spoke with Cristina, another lesbian feminist,
> and both of us wanted to set up the first lesbian group, but we didn't
> know how to go about doing so. We didn't have any method to follow,
> were lacking a theoretical base, didn't know where to meet lesbians; we
> thought we were the only Mexican lesbians in the country.[14]
>
> I went to the Topo ('the Mole'), a gay bar that was near the
> monument to the Revolution; straight people would go there too.
> There was a raid at about 8 pm. The police were quite violent, and had
> brought along their paddy wagons. They hurled tear-gas canisters into
> the bar. Those of us near the exit managed to get away, but we stayed
> close enough to see what was happening. We saw how they beat
> people; they mostly arrested the men but also some lesbians and a few
> straight couples. Those of us outside raised our voices in protest, but
> since we were defenseless we decided to meet up at the Aguascalientes
> Sanborn's restaurant. We met there and talked; then the men returned
> to the bar and we women stayed to discuss what had happened.[15]

Lesbos's main point of reference was the feminist movement; they requested membership in it as a lesbian feminist group:

> We contacted other lesbians in the Women's Coalition, but they were
> not prepared to wage a struggle for lesbian rights; they didn't want to

join us because they didn't want people to know they were lesbians. We learned that often our worst enemies are closeted lesbian feminists, since they were the ones most hostile to us. One of the leaders of the Coalition is a known lesbian; she was the person most opposed to us and even theorized why it wasn't appropriate for a specifically lesbian group to be part of the Coalition. We had no information, no theoretical framework to formulate a political analysis that could form the basis of our activities; we were shut down. We almost felt guilty for having a lesbian group. Some people told us we shouldn't separate ourselves from the rest, that we should join with the other women. Others said it was a good thing we were together, since that way we kept away from them. Others saw our existence as a political threat, since we would inevitably want to be part of feminist organizations. We weren't allowed to join the Women's Coalition as a group and always remained separate and isolated.[16]

Since then, relations with the feminist movement have been tainted with internalized lesbophobia, as much from heterosexual feminists as from closeted lesbians. There has been a constant call by lesbians for recognition of their existence as lesbians within the feminist movement and for their demands to be recognized as feminist demands.

Lesbos, in its work towards self-awareness and self-affirmation, raised the need to 'come out of the closet', which has become one of the leitmotifs of the lesbian movement. This meant establishing a political identity which required members to come out and to give Lesbos a real public presence:

Luz María and I argued that Lesbos should open itself up and take its place on the public stage. No one wanted to; they were afraid of press attention. They didn't want to organize any public activities. Around that time, on 26 July 1978, the papers reported that a group of gays had marched in favour of Cuba. There were a number of articles in the press; it was a full-blown nation-wide scandal. Only gays had participated in the event. We quickly contacted the Gay Front for Revolutionary Action (FHAR)[17] and told the girls, 'The gays have come out of the closet, they weren't lynched, so we're going to come out too.' They told us they wouldn't come out. Since they weren't ready to come out in full public view, we broke with Lesbos.[18]

OIKABETH—from the Mayan 'Ollin Iskan Katuntat Bebeth Thot', which means 'movement of women warriors who blaze the trail and scatter flowers'— emerged as Lesbos's public face and joined FHAR, with which they soon broke due primarily to its gay members' misogyny:

We broke away and set up the group OIKABETH as part of the FHAR, but we only lasted four months. A gay member of the

Mariposas Negras (Black Butterflies) group assaulted us verbally: 'You stupid, useless butch dykes, thanks to laboratory reproductive techniques, we gay men don't need women, we can even wipe you off the face of the earth!' We were quite upset and Luz María said, 'We need to be an autonomous group.' So we broke away from the FHAR and set up OIKABETH as an autonomous lesbian group.

At about that time, the 'travelling women' began to arrive—many women, about 60, from Europe and the US. It was a movement of women that traveled all over the world, especially in the Third World, in the 1970s as part of the hippie experience. We gobbled up the ideas of European and American radical feminism that they brought with them. We decided to go autonomous; they had a major influence on us. In addition to being radical lesbians, they were also separatists. OIKABETH became a separatist group, and a very radical one at that.[19]

Separatism meant organizing as an autonomous lesbian group, neither in a common lesbian/gay group nor in a heterosexual feminist group.

Subsequently a large number of autonomous lesbian groups was formed. OIKABETH paved the way for 'Socialist Lesbians' and the 'Marxist-Leninist Seminar of Lesbian Feminists', both started up by Yan María Castro. Other groups were Comuna in Morelos, Patlatonalli in Guadalajara, the Group of Lesbian Mothers, Cuarto Creciente [First Quarter], MULA and Gestación, to name a few. It is worth mentioning the involvement of Claudia Hinojosa, the recognized leader of the mixed group 'Lambda de Liberación Homosexual' and a key figure in the feminist movement.

Lesbians played an important role in the gay movement, and their involvement at the same time in the feminist movement brought the question of gender into discussions with gay men. The original label 'Gay Liberation Movement' was changed to 'Lesbian/Gay Liberation Movement'.

The Latin American and Caribbean feminist gathering held every two years in different countries in the region was a space for an exchange of experiences and ideas and to coordinate the activities of the different lesbian groups in Latin America. This led to the idea of a Latin American lesbian gathering.

The first Latin American and Caribbean Lesbian Feminist Gathering (*Encuentro*) was held in Mexico in 1987, and the participants showed strong separatist tendencies. The establishment of a Latin American network led to the crystallization of a number of different political positions. One tendency sought to exclude lesbians organized with heterosexual feminists or with gay men, those who did not work exclusively with lesbians, and those who lived outside Latin America. Based on the need to assert a lesbian identity stripped of the qualifiers tacked on by gay men and heterosexual feminists, many women undertook a purist search for a kind of lesbian essence. The availability of financing for the establishment of a lesbian network led some to argue for a network which would be an autonomous space, not subsumed in the heterosexual feminist or gay male experience.

Although conflict-ridden, the first Latin American Lesbian Feminist Gathering was instructive. The emergence of two polarized groupings in the organization prevented Latin American lesbians from setting up viable spaces for carrying out strategic projects. A bloc of leaders emerged on the basis of political and romantic ties. With the institutional backing of organizations like the International Lesbian and Gay Association (ILGA), they came to form what would later be called the 'representative bureaucracies'.

The polarization of political positions stemming from the first gathering in Mexico led to the formation of the National Lesbian Coordination (CNL). Although it was formed in response to the possible setting up of a Latin American secretariat of the International Lesbian Information Service (ILIS) by 'the other side', the CNL managed to organize 13 groups in five states and Mexico City and two national gatherings, and it became a real and influential partner of the Mexico City Feminist Coordination. In 1990 this feminist grouping included free choice of sexuality as one of the basic requirements for membership.

In early 1997 there were about thirteen lesbian groups in Mexico. Nine of them have joined forces to set up a 'Lesbian Links' coalition (Enlace Lésbico) in order to strengthen the struggle against lesbophobia inside and outside the feminist movement.

The history of lesbian organizing in Mexico is highly diverse; about 30 groups have come and gone. Organized lesbians have had difficulties forming a strong movement with a real presence on the public stage and with reliable and ongoing financial backing. They have had difficulties being accepted as natural allies by the feminist movement. As a result they have been a marginal movement with little real impact, except perhaps on the feminist and gay movements.

Chile: Colectivo Ayuquelén

Following the second Latin American and Caribbean feminist gathering in Lima in 1983, a number of Chilean feminists returned to their country convinced that they were lesbians and that as such they had to struggle on their own behalf. The 'mini-workshop' on lesbianism at the feminist gathering had a good influence on some feminists, making them accept their lesbian identity and think about organizing autonomously once they returned to their countries. At the time lesbianism was a taboo subject, even for lesbians active in the heterosexual feminist movement.

'Ayuquelén' is a Mapuche expression meaning 'happiness'. The group was formed in 1984. That year, in full view on the Plaza Italia, an attractive blond woman was attacked with a cane and kicked by a heavy-set man yelling, 'Damned lesbian!' She died right there on the sidewalk under the shocked gaze of passers-by who didn't dare intervene. The only person who tried to defend her was a friend accompanying her that night, but to no avail. Monica's death induced sadness and fear in a circle of lesbians that met on a fairly regular basis. It accelerated the process leading to the formation of Ayuquelén.[20]

> I already knew Susana, Lili and some lesbians that hung out at a bar. In addition to being kicked out of a feminist group, I was affected by the killing of a friend who had been Susana's companion. She was a very daring woman; she was quite forthright in public with her lesbian identity and didn't give a damn that we were living under a dictatorship. A policeman beat her to death, but few people knew about the incident because her family kept things quiet. We heard about it firsthand. That day she had gone out for a drink with a friend. Since the curfew was on, people stayed at the bars and discotheques until six in the morning. The policeman was waiting for her. He had lost his girlfriend to Monica. When she left the bar with her friend, Monica was jumped and kicked. The friend tried to intervene but it was no use; she was hit a number of times, too. In the end he left Monica lying in the street and made it look like a car accident, as if she had been the victim of a hit and run. That was in 1983, under the dictatorship; the police freely abused their powers, and we had no organization ourselves. At the funeral, I told the many lesbians present that it was time to form a union. We all went to Susana's house, mourned Monica's death and decided that we needed to be organized. That's when the idea of Ayuquelén was born. We were a group of three persons in the main—the three founding members, Lilian Hinostrosa, Susana Peña and myself—but we had an ongoing periphery of about fifteen women.[21]

The main and closest reference point for Ayequelén was feminism, so they asked La Morada [The Abode] for space for their meetings. In 1987 they were interviewed in a left-wing magazine. For security reasons their names were changed. The article[22] provoked a conflict with the heterosexual feminist group. In a letter of clarification to the magazine the feminist group wrote that Ayuquelén was one of many groups that met in their space, and that the interviewees had treated the issues discussed in a superficial and sensationalist fashion that only served to reinforce existing prejudices. Ayequelén, they said, should have kept in mind the reprisals against La Morada that the interview might occasion.[23] This incident was seen as a kind of political judgement condemning Ayuquelén and its work. Paradoxically, the magazine was widely congratulated for bringing the question of lesbianism out into the open in Chile.

In 1987 we returned to La Morada, to hold meetings in a public place so more people could attend. A journalist contacted us for an interview. For the first time, lesbians were interviewed by a Chilean publication, the centre-left *APSI*. We still lacked a firm ideological foundation and had a rather eclectic approach. To top it off, the article was written in a highly sensationalist style with little attention paid to more serious issues. The journalist wrote that we were operating under the auspices of La Morada, which caused a major falling out with the people in charge there. What wasn't mentioned in the piece was that the then head of La Morada had tried to participate in the interview and that we had prevented her from doing so. Susana told her that since she wasn't a member of Ayuquelén, she had no business being there. In the end she said that we hadn't requested permission to hold the interview at La Morada. There was a kind of misunderstanding and manipulation, and they publicly attacked us at a plenary session of the feminist movement. They said the interview was worthless, lacking a theoretical foundation, superficial; in short, they wiped the floor with us. Letters to the editor appeared in *APSI*; the first was from them disclaiming all responsibility for the interview and saying that we weren't part of La Morada. We had never stated the contrary; it wasn't our fault that the journalist hadn't shown us the piece before going to print as we had requested. The whole incident created a major split, and we stopped meeting at La Morada.[24]

This type of conflict was repeated throughout Latin America. Lesbians didn't have their own space to do autonomous work and were therefore dependent on the feminist movement. This made them more vulnerable to the varying degrees of fear and lesbophobia of the different feminist groups:

The conflict erupted when the [Ayuquelén] women gave an interview to the opposition-controlled media (*APSI*), which by linking Ayuquelén and La Morada fostered the long-standing and deeply rooted belief among the general public that feminists are lesbians. La Morada's concern was keeping their space open to all women, since the majority of women do not understand that being a feminist doesn't necessarily mean being a lesbian, or that being a lesbian doesn't necessarily mean being a feminist. Not having given the subject much thought, they think that lesbianism is some kind of abnormality, deviation or crime.[25]

The fear that the feminist movement as a whole will be seen as a movement of lesbians is very present in the feminist movement. The above quotation is the only reference to Ayuquelén in a 256-page book on the subject of women in Chile from 1973 to 1990. The heterosexual feminist movement, even though many people in it are lesbians, continues to fear the public belief that lesbianism and homosexuality are abnormal, deviant and illegal.

The lesbian movement was institutionalized in Latin America by ILIS and ILGA (IGA at that time). These organizations claimed—and continue to claim—to represent the gay and lesbian population on an international level. One Dutch representative of ILIS was the source of a controversy at the first lesbian gathering in Cuernavaca. She had come to South America with financing from her government to train organized lesbians. ILIS was interested in establishing contacts in Latin America in order to expand its Latin American secretariat; so the Dutch woman had come in search of a Latin American leader:

> We held a kind of cadre school with two women from ILIS who had come to meet us. We worked through an interpreter, which they paid for, since neither of them spoke Spanish. In four days, they met with the three Latin American groups that were making the greatest progress: GALF in Brazil, Ayuquelén in Chile and GALF in Peru. We dealt primarily with organizational matters, on how to make our organization more effective. Great stress was also placed on our critical capacities, on being able to question ourselves, to function democratically. It is my understanding that the ILIS representative was looking to back someone to train her as a leader. The three of us from Ayequelén were interviewed. She never told us that she was looking for someone to train as a leader; we only learned this afterwards. It appears that she backed Rebeca. ILIS bought books for our library and financed our trip to the Mexican gathering in 1987.[26]

Although two Ayuquelén members remained in Mexico after the first Latin American and Caribbean Lesbian Feminist gathering—which was a real blow—the group was remarkably resilient. In spite of the dictatorship, clandestinity, the misogyny of gay men, the lesbophobia of the feminist movement itself and of the left, and the lack of financial backing, they were able to organize a national gathering and a number of workshops. They built up a regular periphery of about 30 lesbians.

A second generation of members emerged at the beginning of the 1990s and set up the shortlived lesbian group 'Punto G' ('G Spot'). Currently lesbians are organized in a 'Lesbian Coordination', which puts out the magazine *Amazonas*, organizes activities and collectively prepared a speech for the seventh Latin American and Caribbean Lesbian Feminist gathering, in which they expressed the need to maintain autonomous lesbian spaces.

Ayuquelén's experience with gay men and heterosexual feminists has strengthened the argument for organizing a specifically lesbian movement:

> We are the champions of autonomy. Ayuquelén doesn't want to be subjected to pressure from gay men or from feminists, even though we may be in sympathy with some feminist currents. Our experience is that these pressures divide lesbians when they try to organize themselves. When some women join the gay organization MOVILH, they become very hostile to us, even without knowing us, without having listened to what we have to say, all because of the things the gay men of MOVILH say about us. The feminists manipulate us around the

question of space. It's extremely difficult to find a neutral space for everyone.[27]

Divisions within the feminist movement have only served to divide the lesbian movement, whether the lesbians are feminists or not. Since we have no source of funds, we have no space to operate from. If we accept space from one side, the others hate us. When the side that originally gives us space changes its mind, the others refuse since they say we have already chosen sides. They're always screwing us around with this kind of thing.[28]

Thinking and growing on their own seems to be a necessity felt by lesbians throughout the region.

The illegality of homosexuality was a major theme for the Chilean gay and lesbian movement. The abrogation of article 365 of the penal code, which criminalizes sodomy, was the target of struggles in which lesbians participated even though the article doesn't specifically mention them. Some gay men sought to highlight 'lesbian guilt' instead of challenging the rules of the social and legal systems:

MOVILH has organized campaigns such as the one against article 365, and we participated in the initial stages. But they put out posters with the slogan 'Chilean gays are penalized and lesbians aren't, why?' This struck us as being a lack of respect so we withdrew. Then came the municipal elections and there were two candidates, including Rolando Jiménez, a founding member of MOVILH. There were a lot of problems with his candidacy, such as lesbophobia and the denial of access to transvestites. We didn't feel he represented the gay and lesbian community. Rolando withdrew from MOVILH, and they called us back for discussions. We went in the name of Ayuquelén and the Coordination, although the Coordination wasn't too enthusiastic about working with men. We all agreed that Rolando Jiménez couldn't be the candidate; we signed the MOVILH letter; but then I realized that, aside from the rejection of Rolando Jiménez, there wasn't much we could agree with. For Ayuquelén elections and negotiations aren't the way to go; Pinochet is always in the background watching with his finger on the trigger. This isn't the right political framework. We wrote a letter to the campaign saying that we were opposed to Rolando Jiménez and that furthermore we would not participate in the campaign to back a gay candidate, since this wasn't a guarantee of anything. MOVILH and Lambda—mostly men—decided to run a candidate parallel to Rolando Jiménez. Their candidate opposed Rolando Jiménez and genuinely represented diversity, including transvestites and others. We said that was great, that we wouldn't come out against their candidate, but that we wouldn't spend time and energy on something which we didn't believe in very strongly. We didn't participate, nor did we come out against.[29]

Lesbians initially encountered criticisms of the quest for legal status in statements from the left. The old debate over 'reformism versus revolution' has forced us to prioritize our demands. The debate now stems from the autonomous feminist current, which challenges the institutional manoeuvering of the so-called institutional feminist current that has declared itself representative of the feminist movement. The autonomous current has once again raised the need for structural changes, opposing all agreements that seek to reinforce the legitimacy of the state.

The struggle for legal status—which we will examine more closely further on—is a key issue in Latin America. Nicaragua and Puerto Rico are the only Latin American countries that still penalize homosexuality as such.[30] But in almost all countries police abuses, extortion, murder and even torture persist.

Nicaragua

The Nicaraguan experience is rich with lessons because it is an example of the lesbian/gay struggle under both a revolutionary government and a regime of formal democracy, and also because there was a coming together of lesbians, gay men and feminists in a struggle for a sexuality without prejudices.

Organizing began after the triumph of the revolution, following the expulsion in 1986 of lesbians and gays from the FSLN for their sexual orientation. This created serious doubts about the so-called 'political openness, freedom of expression and struggle against all forms of discrimination.'

> After the victory of the revolution, there was an ideological opening. A broad range of sectors of the Nicaraguan population was able to voice their opinions and organize themselves politically. This was a wake-up call for us, since we realized that while we lived in a system that declared a broad freedom of expression and where a struggle was being waged against different forms of discrimination, we still felt oppressed. We had been part of a long process of struggle, but we realized that we had to make a revolution within the revolution, that all was not well even within a supposedly open and discrimination-free political and social space.[31]

Lesbians and gay men began to meet in private homes, united by a socialist identity and the desire to struggle for gay rights. Unfortunately, this first organizing attempt foundered due to the intervention of state security through forms of direct repression such as arrests, phone tapping, threats and expulsions from jobs and political organizations. As a result, lesbians and gay men felt intimidated and did not come out of the closet:

> In 1986, I accepted myself as a lesbian and came out of the closet at

work and in the party. For no other infraction than that of being a lesbian, I was expelled from the party and from my job. That was the first time I began to understand that there was sexual discrimination in the FSLN, too.[32]

We had problems with state security, which harassed us and destroyed the organization we had taken such pains to build. We were called to state security headquarters; our fingerprints were taken; and we were photographed. I was arrested; there was a clear abuse of power. We defended ourselves in a dignified and political manner, whereas they took a voyeuristic, scandal-mongering approach. They asked for the names of people in our movement and of gay and lesbian revolutionary leaders. They gave us a 'friendly' reminder that the Revolution could not tolerate such organizations as it endeavoured to create 'new men and women'. Gay men and lesbians, they said, were simply not up to scratch. We decided not to talk about our visit to state security, since we were Sandinistas and such happenings could damage the FSLN. We didn't want to reveal anything that could be used against the FSLN.[33]

Confronted with the abuse of authority and the violation of human rights of lesbians and gay men, those interrogated and arrested by state security decided to 'hush up the story' in an act of party discipline and prioritization of demands.

Later, in the framework of AIDS prevention and safe sex work with the Health Ministry, the Collective of Popular Educators (CEP/SIDA) organized a number of important activities aimed at raising consciousness around sexuality within largely homosexual sectors of the population. This work was a boon for gay and lesbian organizing in Nicaragua. The first collective of lesbian feminists—'Nosotras' ('We Women')—was founded in 1989.

With the change of government in 1990, gay men and lesbians decided to come out of the closet with the goal of testing the establishment of 'real democracy' in the country. They organized two major marches for Gay Pride Day in 1991 and 1992, in which various grassroots groups—including heterosexual ones—participated. The response of the new political system was to reform the section of the Penal Code dealing with sexual crimes. The National Assembly voted to penalize 'sexual relations between people of the same sex and the promotion and publication of such relations'. This provoked a major mobilization by lesbians, gay men, feminists, NGOs and well-known heterosexual figures in a 'Campaign for a Sexuality Without Prejudices'. A constitutional challenge was also raised against the reform, in tandem with a number of activities that opened up the debate on sexuality and democratic freedoms in Nicaraguan society.

There was a strong response, and dozens of groups got together to set up the 'Committee for a Sexuality Without Prejudices' for the fight against the law. We collected thousands of signatures, authored a document explaining the unconstitutional nature of the law, got prominent heterosexual and gay figures to write opinion pieces in the daily press; we organized public meetings and lobbied the National Assembly without success. Amnesty International called on the president not to sign the legislation into law, arguing that consenting sex between adults and freedom of expression were not crimes. The minister to the Presidency (the president's son-in-law and current presidential candidate) told the president she shouldn't sign and should instead make a public statement against the law. He said, 'If homosexuality is legal at the Vatican, it should also be so in Nicaragua; it's time to enter the twentieth century.' Under pressure from the Church hierarchy, the president signed the legislation into law.

We appealed, citing the legislation's unconstitutionality. The formal request had to be made within 90 days of the day the legislation was approved. The workers at the official register of government legislation were on strike; when they returned to work they published all the laws that had come into force during the strike. We learned that the law had been published only one week before the 90-day deadline. We found 30 people to sign our appeal. The Supreme Court had 90 days to render its judgement, but we were still waiting a year and a half later. Finally, in 1994, the Supreme Court ruled in favour of the legislation. There wasn't a single legal argument in the decision, nor did they reply to our document; their position was solely 'moral' in nature. The decision was not published, we only heard about it by accident. By that time, we no longer had the energy to organize against the law. However, if anyone were to be arrested on that basis we would definitely organize.[34]

The legal defeat dealt a major blow to the movement, which was too exhausted and demobilized to respond anew. The 'democratic' political-legal system had achieved its repressive objective.

Conclusion

The democratization of Latin American countries that had been military dictatorships and political reforms in countries with formal democracy led to the emergence of a feminist movement that permeated civil society and the state. Nevertheless, no political system (democratic or otherwise) has respected gay and lesbian rights. Repression has been the norm, whether in the form of criminalization, the closing down of bars, firings from jobs, or intimidation by family members.

While homosexuality as such may not be illegal under Latin America's different political regimes, it continues to be tracked down and punished through other legal channels, such as 'corruption of minors' and 'immoral and indecent behaviour'. The law can be used in practice to legitimate or excuse the arbitrary persecution of gays and lesbians, especially those who are visible in public.

What type of political system would genuinely ensure democratic and political freedoms and freedom from persecution for gays and lesbians? What is the way forward for the struggle?

Questions such as these have revitalized the debate over 'reform or revolution' that was sparked by the autonomous (straight) feminist movement in response to the institutionalization of the feminist movement. The debate concerned relations with the state, international state institutions and financial agencies. The autonomous feminists argued that the feminist movement had become a conduit for the social system, since it played by and enforced the rules of the patriarchal system. They called for an ethical approach towards fund-raising.

> We can no longer accept funding policies that trammel our democratic methods of functioning and thought and that bind us to the system in an effort to co-opt each and every sign of rebellion. We refuse to negotiate with national and international institutions that are responsible for hunger and destitution, such as the World Bank and the International Monetary Fund.
>
> The involvement of the feminist movement with the whole array of women's labour organizations (which may have a clearly feminist focus) means that the political interests of the movement are being subsumed into the interests of those institutions and the professional aspirations of their leaders. Further, the leadership of the feminist movement is now concentrated in those institutions which [the Ministry of] Development Cooperation sees as the most 'efficient' and deserving of support. As a result, such institutions have more resources in order to provide 'services, activities, contacts and organizing space'. This has nothing to do with the goals of a subversive, radical movement and instead honours the criteria of efficiency, productivity and dialogue with the state laid down by the funding agencies.[35]

Autonomous feminists have criticized the passive acceptance of the rules of the game in a patriarchal and homophobic social system. They have also criticized the participation of feminists and lesbians in elections, which, they argue, strengthen the very system that excludes us. To accept the rules of the neo-liberal system—and to become an integral part of it—would make the movement a reformist force that abandons its subversive, counter-culture identity. The feminist movement is 'revolutionary' in the eyes of the autonomous feminists only insofar as it seeks to create a new vision of civilization, based on cooperation rather than domination, and to build collective awareness and support for this vision. For Margarita Pisano, a theoretician from the autonomous current, the feminist movement raises awareness and builds this awareness into a political alternative. She argues that cultural change cannot come from having women in a few positions of power, since this does not change the power relations that form the basis of patriarchy. She sees the need to build a movement that organizes women around ideas of social change tailored to women's needs, within a framework that brings together intimacy, private experience, and public life.[36]

Within such a perspective, elections are part of the reformist logic that legitimates the patriarchal system. However, there is a need to rethink the concept of social change. There is a historical need to reach some form of agreement with the political system—not as an end in itself, but as a means to raise awareness and mobilize, to strengthen autonomy in a framework of dialogue.

Like it or not, being a lesbian or a gay man is an intolerable threat in our continent. We are meant to be unseen and unheard. Lesbians have been cajoled into silence in both socialist and feminist struggles.

Social change has taken centre stage thanks to the new social movements based on the momentous events of everyday life.[37] Change begins in daily life. If marriage, family, inheritance, social security and the whole range of social and political rights denied to lesbians and gays are judged to be worthy and desirable for some segments of the population, then they should be available to anyone who wants them.

It is misguided to think such an approach is pointless, unethical or reformist. Such an attitude merely creates new closets hiding us from view and condemns gays and lesbians to a language that is not their own, to aspirations that are not their own.

Two clearly defined generations stand out in the history of the lesbian movement. The first called for equality and had a universalist approach. It identified with the social struggles of the left at the time and saw itself as a marginal sector that would win freedom along with the rest of society. Nicaragua is a telling example. From the beginning the organization of the Nicaraguan feminist movement—either from within or near the power structure—did not leave room for the emergence of any significant separate currents. This allowed lesbians, gay men and heterosexuals to work together. But it guaranteed neither real harmony nor the emergence of an organized gay and lesbian community. Most gay work today takes place under the guise of AIDS activism, creating a tremendous void for lesbians seeking concrete political and social alternatives.

The second historical generation of the lesbian movement—advocating difference and separatism—highlighted its specific differences with the gay and feminist movements. It asserted an identity grounded in the rejection of the masculine and phallocentric symbolic order and of the exclusively heterosexual character of the feminist movement's demands. This was the first step towards increased autonomy from both movements. The Mexican and Chilean experiences show clearly the importance of this assertion of difference with respect to the gay and feminist movements.

At the same time, in relating to power structures, as in the feminist movement, the lesbian movement has seen the emergence of a representative bureaucracy that constantly seeks and obtains dialogue with patriarchal institutions.

The lesbian movement's break with the gay movement was sharper than with the feminist movement. Like loyal daughters to their mothers, the lesbian movement has continued to fight for space as women and feminists within the feminist movement. However, the theoretical framework of feminism only helped lesbians to see their oppression as women, not as members of a sexual group persecuted and oppressed for its dissident sexuality. Feminist theory addresses gender oppression—that is, the differences and hierarchies that exist between men and women—but fails to analyze the social organization and basic power relations of sexuality. It falls short of understanding that lesbians, gay men, transvestites, sadomasochists and prostitutes have similar sociological profiles and, consequently, endure the same types of punishment at the hands of society. Lesbians are also oppressed as homosexuals and 'perverts' because of sexual stratification, not only stratification by gender.[38]

In a third historical phase, not yet clearly defined, the lesbian movement is re-evaluating the masculine figure—seen no longer solely as an opponent, but rather as a potential ally: gay men, transvestites, transexuals and the transgendered. The first exchanges between various types of dissident sexuality have been encouraging. Having understood the need to define an identity going beyond their oppression as women, lesbians are redefining themselves in concert with 'the others' based on the idea of sexual dissidence.

In the same way that the 'women question' could not be fully understood by Marxist analysis, the main criteria of feminist thinking do not allow for an appreciation of basic power relations in the field of sexuality. We cannot have a complete analysis of the lesbian condition if we only see ourselves as women with sexual differences solely in relation to men. This does not grasp the specific persecution of our dissident sexuality. I agree with Gayle Rubin when she argues that we have to develop a radical theory of sexual oppression that can enrich feminism, to work towards a feminism that takes on lesbian demands and towards a more well-rounded lesbian movement.

Of course, we cannot forget the specific features of Latin American society—an eminently traditional society, immersed in the narrow conceptions of Catholicism, with high levels of poverty, where discrimination on the basis of sexuality can take extreme forms such as homophobia- and lesbophobia-inspired murder. Theoretical work must therefore be subversive, seeking to wrench the lesbian movement out of all its closets, to link the issue of sexuality to the whole range of Latin America's problems.

This approach has renewed our common thinking with gay men and other sectors that are persecuted for their erotic desires.

translated by Raghu Krishnan

---

[1] Víctor Hugo Monje, 'Revolución Gay: Stonewall 1969', in *Confidencial* (Costa Rica) vol. 1 no. 9 (June 1991).

[2] Gonzalo Aburto, 'Abriendo caminos, nuestra contribución', *LLegó: Nuestra Herencia, Stonewall 25,* June 1994, pp. 4-5. Although the article uses the word 'white' as an expression of ethnocentrism, as referring to people who in the US are called WASPs (White Anglo-Saxon Protestants), this does not mean that the Argentinian was necessarily a Native American or Black. He was a Latino, which in US culture means that he was a person of colour.

[3] The resurgence of Latin American feminism beginning in the 1970s is referred to as 'second-wave feminism', to distinguish it from the earlier struggle for the right to vote.

[4] See Julieta Kristeva, 'Women's time', in *Signs: Journal of Women in Culture and Society* vol. 7 no. 1 (1981); Nattie Golubov, 'De lo colectivo a lo individual: la crisis de la identidad de la teoría literaria feminista', in *Los cuadernos del acordeón* vol. 5 no. 24 (1993); Toril Moi, 'Feminist, female, feminine', in *The Feminist Reader,* London: Macmillan, 1989; Gayle Rubin, 'Thinking sex: notes for a radical theory of the politics of sexuality', in Carole S. Vance ed., *Pleasure and Danger: Exploring Female Sexuality,* London: Pandora Press, 1989.

[5] See Norma Mogrovejo, *El Amor es bxh/2: Una propuesta de Analisis Historico-Metodologico del Movimiento Lésbico y sus Amores con los Movimientos Homosexual y Feminista en América Latina,* Mexico City: Ed. CDAHL, 1996.

[6] See Kristeva, 'Women's time', and Golubov, 'De lo colectivo a lo individual'.

[7] The first attempt at founding a gay organization in Latin America was Nuestro Mundo ('Our World') in 1969 in Argentina. In 1971 they joined with a group of intellectuals to found the Argentinan Gay Liberation Front (Frente de Liberacion Homosexual).

[8] Nancy Cárdenas, interview for 'Otra forma de ser mujer', Mexico City, 1990.

[9] Carmen Sarmiento, *La mujer: Una revolución en marcha,* Madrid: Ed. Sedmay, 1976.

[10] Claudia Hinojosa, 'El Tour del Corazón', in *Otro modo de ser: Mujeres mexicanas en movimiento,* Mexico City, 1991.

[11] 'Declaration of Mexican Lesbians', Mexico City, June 1975 (photocopy). This document was read publicly in the Forum on Lesbianism organized by the lesbians who took part in the World Conference for the International Women's Year.

[12] Interview with Juan Jacobo Hernández (18 Dec. 1995).

[13] The Women's Coalition (Coalición de Mujeres) was a coordinating body of various feminist groups in 1976-78.

[14] Interview with Yan María Castro (9 Feb. 1995).

[15] Interview with Luz María Medina (3 Dec. 1994).

[16] Interview with Yan María Castro (9 Feb. 1995).

[17] The Gay Front for Revolutionary Action (FHAR) was a majority-male group with anarchist tendencies.

[18] Interview with Yan María Castro (9 Feb. 1995).

[19] Interview with Yan María Castro (9 Feb. 1995).

[20] Mónica Silva, 'Para romper el ghetto', in *Página Abierta* (Santiago, Chile) no. 70 (July 1992).

[21] Cecilia Riquelme, former member of Ayuquelén, 1995.

[22] Milena Vodanovic & Colectivo Ayuquelén, 'Somos lesbianas de opción', *APSI* no. 206 (June 1987).

[23] *APSI* (29 July 1987), p. 63.

[24] Cecilia Riquelme, 1995.

[25] Edda Gabiola et al., *Una Historia Necesaria: Mujeres en Chile, 1973-1990,* Santiago, 1994.

[26] Cecilia Riquelme, 1995.

[27] Interview with Gabriela Jara, member of Ayuquelén (28 Nov. 1996).

[28] Marloré Morán (28 Nov. 1996).

[29] Interview with Gabriela Jara (28 Nov. 1996).

[30] Homosexuality was decriminalized in Ecuador in November 1997 and in Chile in December 1998.

[31] Lupita Siqueira, Grupo Nicone (Nov. 1994).

[32] Lupita Siqueira, Grupo Nicone (Nov. 1994).

[33] Rita Arauz in Margaret Randall, *Sandino's Daughters Revisited: Feminism in Nicaragua,* New Brunswick: Rutgers Univ. Press, 1994.

[34] Ammy Bank, Feminism(s) in Latin America Conference, Berkeley, Apr. 1996.

[35] Ximena Bedregal, 'Pensar de un modo nuevo', Presentation to the 7th Latin American and Caribbean Feminist Encuentro, Chile, 1996.

[36] Talks by Margarita Pisano posted on the Internet: 'Movimientos sociales y sus desafíos: Definiciones como espacios políticos' and 'Movimiento feminista: su historia y sus proyecciones' (28 May 1997).

[37] José Nun, 'La rebelión del coro', *Demos,* 1981.

[38] See Rubin, 'Thinking sex'.

To change our own reality and the world: a conversation with lesbians in Nicaragua[1]

Margaret Randall

I lived in Nicaragua from late 1979 through early 1984, during the decade of Sandinista government. I was a middle-aged and middle-class white woman from the United States and mother of four children (two of whom accompanied me to Managua). Through almost two decades in Mexico and then in Cuba, I had been in close touch with political movements to make change possible—for people and, increasingly as I began to understand my own feminism, for women. I had written a number of books of essays and oral history, often dealing with feminist issues. Several of these books focussed on women in Nicaragua.[2] At that time I called myself a socialist and a feminist. Today I am still a socialist, still a feminist, and a lesbian.

At the time of my move to Nicaragua, the FSLN[3] had recently taken power with a mixture of socialist, Christian, and indigenous concepts of how to bring about social change—and with enormous energy and a makeshift creativity unique to its particular history and culture. The United States was already doing everything possible to defeat this new experiment; everyone knew it, as the evidence of overt as well as covert warfare surfaced early on. But the mostly young men and women who had waged and won the recent war believed their magic would carry them through. Every problem was being addressed: land, the economy, education, health, housing, recreation and the arts, as well as freedom.

Freedom, to those who had lived through the Somoza years, often meant little more than being able to leave your house in the morning with some sense that you would return alive. Then there was the freedom to learn how to read and write, powerfully addressed by the 1980 literacy crusade. The freedom to own title to the land one worked. The freedom to hold a job, to be healthy and to have healthy children.

A number of gender issues found a receptive ear among the Sandinistas. One of the revolution's first decrees was against the use of women's bodies in commercial advertising. Irresponsible paternity—a man's fathering one or more children and then going off to leave the mother to care for them—was a widespread problem, and the new government established Women's Offices[4] to defend the economic needs of single or abandoned mothers. Fully a third of the victorious Sandinista army was female, and a number of women showed exceptional political and military leadership. We talked about the fact that among the Sandinistas, women struggled for equality in the ranks before taking power, rather than leaving the issue of sexism to be grappled with later.

León, the first city to be liberated completely so that it could house the provisional revolutionary government, had been won by a woman: Commander Dora María Téllez. Although no women were on the FSLN's nine-member National Directorate, at all succeeding levels women occupied positions of responsibility and power.[5] Still, in that Nicaragua of the early eighties, abortion was considered too dangerous an issue to tackle, violence against women was not discussed, and lesbian rights didn't seem to even be a part of the horizon.[6]

From shortly after the Sandinista victory, AMNLAE[7] was the mass women's organization. It was firmly controlled by the FSLN, acquiring and forfeiting degrees of autonomy but never really operating independently of the Front. The question of whether a women's movement not led by women can make real inroads against sexism and women's oppression is still being debated, in Nicaragua and elsewhere. AMNLAE defended many women's rights and opened ideological as well as material space in the struggle to better women's lives. But the organization ultimately did more to rally women around the revolution than to make women's issues a revolutionary priority.

For the first time since leaving Nicaragua early in 1984, I returned for a brief visit in October 1991. It was heartbreaking to see the changes, so typical of the underdevelopment and dependency suffered by the majority of Third World countries. Where before a monthly basket of essential goods—rice, beans, sugar, cooking oil, soap, and other necessities—had been government-subsidized to every family, now the markets were filled but at prices few could afford. Sex education and other progressive programs were no longer a part of public schooling. Headlines screamed of epidemic hospital deaths caused by the lack of antibiotics and other drugs.

For the most part I found Sandinista political cadre disoriented. The shock of the electoral loss, a year and a half before, lingered in the air like some lethargic cloud. US promises of generous economic aid had not materialized. In the midst of continued economic crisis, the chaos of new political divisions, ex-Contras and ex-Sandinistas in the rural areas renewing armed struggle as *Revueltos*,[8] and repressive legislation rolling back many of the last decade's gains, women now appeared to be the single most vibrant and active political force.

AMNLAE was going through a profound re-evaluation of its role. Issues such as abortion (illegal before, during, and since the Sandinista government) and domestic violence, once considered too 'feminist', were now the subjects of priority campaigns. But many revolutionary women felt that AMNLAE did not address their most important demands. These women were organizing outside what was once the single women's movement. Young women, calling themselves The 52% Majority, celebrated International Women's Day in 1991 with a large public program. Lesbian feminists, claiming these two words in how they speak about themselves, were also beginning to have a multifaceted presence.

Women from some of the more conservative women's groups had crossed political lines to meet with their revolutionary sisters. Shortly after my October visit (in January 1992), close to 800 women were to come together in Managua for an energetic gathering. Peasant women, professionals, women from within and outside of AMNLAE, feminists and lesbian feminists, religious women, and even the only woman to have had a seat on the Contras' high command, all shared experiences and ideas.

It was in this atmosphere—economically impoverished, desperate, shell-shocked, exhausted from years of superhuman work but bursting with questions that could no longer be shelved—that I asked to meet with a group of lesbians who might be willing to speak about their recent experience. I wanted to know how their movement had started; it had been quite invisible when I lived in Managua in the early eighties. I wanted to hear about how they conceived of their struggle, the responses they were getting from various quarters, and what their concerns and projects were.

We met on one of those hot wet nights typical of October in Managua. The rainy season. Where a group of women talked with one another in a circle of rattan rockers the lush leaves of large tropical plants dripped moisture onto the tile floor. Half inside, half out... like so many sitting rooms that become patios and then sitting rooms again in houses half hidden behind high walls.

*   *   *

These women see themselves as part of a lesbian, gay, and bisexual movement. Many if not most of those involved are Sandinista revolutionaries. Sandinism clearly opened a space for diverse freedoms even when it did not succeed in fully taking up their causes.[9] It's also worth noting that gay and lesbian organizing has been going on throughout Central and South America for the past eight to ten years. Regional gatherings of lesbians have been taking place in places like Mexico, Argentina and Costa Rica.

Ana, who is a founding member of Puntos de Encuentro [Common Ground], a feminist centre that works with young men and women, with gays and lesbians, and with women in the broad-based independent women's movement, had been able to contact several of the more active members of the Nicaraguan movement. And so, on this humid night, before some of these women had even completed their long workday, we engaged in a conversation aimed at providing me with history as well as some insight into the current state of a new but growing movement.

Ana R., in her late thirties, came to Nicaragua from France in 1973. She was nineteen years old then, married to a Nicaraguan and with a one-month old daughter in her arms. Tall, with light hair, she is now a Nicaraguan citizen. Hazel, shorter and darker, is a young woman with a frank smile. She is from Matagalpa, the city to the north from where, I'm told, a good number of the 'out' lesbians come. Much later she would remind me that she and my youngest daughter were in the same militia battalion when my daughter and I lived here in the early eighties. Carmen is from that part of northern Spain called Catalonia. She also came to work in Nicaragua out of her previous experience in the solidarity movement. Mary is a familiar face. I remember meeting her in the early days of the revolution. Ana V. is from Costa Rica. She works in the area of community health. Callie, also tall and blond, comes late. She is from the United States. And finally, Amy is also a North American woman. Our paths have crossed on several occasions. She and Callie have both lived here for six years.

It's Hazel and Amy who begin by offering a brief picture of the origins of this movement, each remembering the details slightly differently. This is a history still in the process of being compiled. I wanted to know when lesbians and gay men first began to come together in more than a social context. What follows is a partial transcription of our conversation:

*   *   *

Hazel: We called it a collective. Or, that's the way we talk about it now. It started in 1985, that's when the first few women and men came together...

MR: What was the collective called? Did it have a name?

Hazel: No, at least not back then. It was a group of women and men who began getting together out of the need to talk to one another, in the atmosphere of prejudice that existed.

Amy: It was a difficult situation. Towards the end of 1985 a small group of lesbians and gay men began meeting. There were seven in all, six women and a man. They all lived in the same neighborhood, or were friends of those who lived there. At first it was just to talk about the issues people had: relationships, problems in the family, that sort of thing. For quite a while it was all very informal. Towards the end of 1986, they decided that they wanted to organize and they began inviting friends. And a larger network emerged, because lots of people were still in the closet. People felt a terrible isolation...

MR: How did people find one another?

Amy: When I got to Nicaragua at the end of '85, I found this group of people who knew one another, they lived in the same neighborhood. As a matter of fact, two women lived across the street from each other, right across the street, and didn't even know it. People began coming together because one heard about another, rumors, that sort of thing, someone's reputation, old friendships.

In 1984 the Victoria Mercado Brigade came down from San Francisco. That's one of the first gay and lesbian brigades that came to build a community centre in Selim Shible.[10] Anyway, some of them looked up another North American woman who was working in that neighborhood, and she knew one of the women. From there on out, one got in touch with another.

It was still *very* informal. Very underground.

MR: We're still talking about 1986?

Amy: Yes, towards the end of 1986. There'd already been a year of very informal gatherings. When there were fifty or so people showing up for meetings, they elected a small coordinating committee, just to take minutes...

MR: Women and men...?

Amy: Women and men. A man and a woman were elected to co-coordinate the group. And they elected a treasurer to manage who knows what funds, because they never had any money; but in case they collected for something. And there was a woman who was an advisor. One of the early agreements was that you had to be politically involved. Most of these people were members of the FSLN, or of the Sandinista Youth Movement, or they were active in the communities or at least sympathized with the revolution.

In December of that year, or January 1987, a problem emerged. We were in a state of emergency[11] then, and everyone was on edge. Someone from State Security infiltrated the group, and we didn't figure it out until March 1987. Suddenly people began receiving summons, to come to the office of State Security. The first person called in was Rita, who was the advisor. Everyone kept quiet about all this, because it was a very dangerous time and no one wanted to make more problems for the FSLN than what they already had.

It was a mistake on the part of Security, but it was an act of repression. Security really broke the group up. They said the only reason they weren't coming down harder was because they knew that those involved were Sandinistas. But they said that in a state of siege this kind of group couldn't exist, in fact that it could never exist.

MR: What reasons did they give? Was it an issue of 'morality'...?

Amy: Yes. And they had their own morbid interest too. In the interviews they asked the women 'how you do it'. They asked a bunch of questions that really had nothing to do with politics.

MR: How long was Rita in prison?

Amy: Oh, just one day. For as long as the interrogation lasted. She wasn't tortured or anything, but they didn't treat her well. They didn't show her respect, they pressured her. And then they called all the rest of the group in and made them give declarations, sign papers, that sort of thing. It destroyed the group. And everyone took a vow of silence, because they felt that this could affect the international solidarity that was so badly needed. In many parts of the world solidarity with Nicaragua was headed by lesbians and gay men, and we knew that the reaction to what had happened could be terrible. It wasn't that we didn't want to act, but because of the political situation we felt that speaking out then could be worse for the movement we were building. We kept on working, silently, like an army of ants. The first time it was spoken about publicly was at the Gay and Lesbian Pride Celebration in June this year [1991], and later in *La boletina*.[12]

Anyway, at the end of 1987 people doing AIDS work came to one of the public health conferences. The Public Health Ministry wanted to educate around safe sex, and they held some workshops for gay men. The government was interested in launching a campaign against AIDS, but when they invited a few men to participate the men insisted that the invitations be formal so they could show them to State Security, given that they had been warned never to try to organize or participate in gay activities again. Look, they said, this is a government invitation. Is it all right if we go? And of course they said it was.

They held workshops in the neighborhood clinics, at the Public Health Ministry, in different places. And the same five guys went to all of them. Because there weren't that many who were willing to go out to public clinics, in the community, and submit themselves to workers saying: 'There goes the faggot...' Not many wanted to make themselves vulnerable to that. That was when one of the most active of the men said: 'There's got to be another way.'

So that's when Commander Dora María Téllez[13] called a meeting of all those who had been called in to State Security. She challenged them to do AIDS work within the lesbian and gay community. And they formed a popular education collective to fight AIDS, they distributed condoms, talked to people, mostly in the park in the centre of Managua where a lot of men come to cruise. The group did some excellent work. The collective grew, it acquired its own history, and that's how the Nimehuatzin Foundation got its start. We're talking about 1988...

MR: It's 1988 already?

Hazel: Well, the Foundation didn't really get off the ground until this year, 1991...

Amy: But its roots go back to 1988...

Hazel: There are so many versions, it would be interesting if we sat down one of these days and talked about all this, maybe even wrote it up...

MR: You're Nicaraguan. What part of the country are you from?

Hazel: I'm from Matagalpa. I came on the scene as a result of the AIDS education work that was being done. But by then the women decided that we wanted to meet on our own...

MR: Why was that?

Hazel: Because we felt that we had our own specific reality, as women. We wanted to analyze our condition as women. It was a period of conscious-ness raising. But we also continued our activities with the men. For exam-ple, on the tenth anniversary of the revolution we all went out with our T-shirts, men and women together. It was our way of telling the FSLN that after ten years of struggle we were there, we were Sandinistas and we were with them. That was our first public appearance, so to speak.

MR: What kind of a reaction did that get?

Hazel: Well, we all formed a line, right when the National Directorate passed by [in the parade]. We wanted to make sure that they saw us so we all stood in a row, with our black T-shirts with the pink triangles. They just looked at us. Some laughed, some were serious, no one really said anything. But for us it was important. It was our collective coming out, you might say.

Our next big event was the party we held to commemorate the third anniversary of the day that State Security called members of the gay com-munity in for interrogation. We invited the public, and the press. We showed the film called *Torch Song Trilogy,* and invited people to ask ques-tions, express whatever concerns or questions they might have...

MR: That's a beautiful film...

Hazel: Yes. And we wanted to provoke a discussion. It was our first public observation of Gay Pride. That's when the press took notice, and they published interviews with some of us...

MR: What was the general attitude in the press?

Hazel: Mostly very positive. And where it wasn't all that positive it wasn't so much a negative attitude about lesbians and homosexuals as an atmosphere of questions, a reflection of the level of disinformation there is, I mean in society as a whole. And there were some very positive articles, where they interviewed women and men...

MR: What was the date of this event?

Hazel: June 30th, 1988. Gay Pride Day. It was a Sunday. Around that time some of us, women and men, also went to Mexico, to Acapulco to participate in an international gathering of gays and lesbians. We went as a group, lesbians and gays together, not just the lesbians on our own. And that was something I noticed there, that outside of Nicaragua there's a lot of separation, lesbians working with lesbians and gay men working with other gay men, a lot of division between the two.

Also, it seemed to us that internationally the European model was more in evidence. So the Latin Americans there put out our need to get to know our own reality, do our own networking so we could become familiar with what was going on in the different countries and get to know each other, exchange information and get closer to one another. So we held an assembly and decided to form a network of our own. We named a provisional committee made up of twelve people, six delegates and six alternates, all from the countries of the Americas. We want to convoke a meeting of our own.

MR: What countries are represented among the delegates?

Hazel: Mexico, Peru, Puerto Rico, Nicaragua, Argentina, and the United States—that is, the Chicanos who live in the United States. Those are the delegates. The alternates are from Costa Rica, the Dominican Republic, Mexico, Argentina, and Brazil. Nicaragua holds the delegate seat for Central America, with the alternate being from Costa Rica. For now, what we're doing is sending a questionnaire out so we can find out who's out there, what the different groups are called. We want to invite them all to a meeting in 1993. That's where we're hoping to give birth to the future Latin American and Caribbean network.

We're just beginning to understand our realities. For example, in Acapulco some people had a very negative attitude towards the Latinos who live in the United States. They in turn often felt excluded, like the rest of us didn't consider them Latin Americans anymore, and are struggling to become accepted as Latinos who have lived for years in the United States, dealing with people who say they have all these advantages we don't have, more freedom and all that. We want to break with these prejudices, with the different walls that exist.

MR: I wanted to ask you something about your own history, Hazel. How is it, that growing up in a small town like Matagalpa, you came out of the closet?

Hazel: Well, it was a process. I considered myself heterosexual at first. I didn't know I was a lesbian. I began to understand that I was around 1981, but I didn't come out right away. I didn't even assume it fully. Around then I started living as a bisexual. And even that brought me problems, because I was a member of the FSLN and bisexuality was seen as political deviation.

They said that bisexuals and homosexuals could easily be bought by the enemy, utilized in ways that could hurt the revolution. It became an ideological conflict for me.

But my history is an interesting one, because I made a trip to Cuba about then. And you might say that's where I really began to accept myself as a lesbian. It's contradictory, because Cuba is a country where homosexuality has been heavily persecuted. Still, I grew a lot there. I began going around with other lesbians and gay men. Before that, in Nicaragua, even though I had a relationship with a woman I never really had a community. In Cuba I found a *massive* community. An enormous parallel world. I'd never seen so many lesbians and gay men in my life. You could go to *un lugar de ambiente*[14] and most people wouldn't have known that that's what it was. Except that everyone there was gay. So when I returned to Nicaragua from that first trip to Cuba, I began to identify as a lesbian. And then I returned to Cuba.

I went to study at the film school, and of course, in the world of artists, well it's even more accepted. I met students from all over Latin America, from Africa and Asia, and I got to know much more about lesbian and gay culture, what was happening on other continents, I met a lot more people. That's when I really came out. I learned to live my lesbianism much more completely. At the school there were no prejudices at all, we had complete freedom to do whatever we wanted, live together, whatever. So when I came back to Nicaragua in 1988 I began to meet with the lesbian group I mentioned. From then on, it's all been much easier.

[Carmen has been listening. Now it looks like she has something to say.]

Carmen: I come from the feminist movement in Spain. Actually, I came to Nicaragua as a heterosexual. It's here that I had my first relationship with a woman. I began working with the different women's groups.

When I fell in love with a Nicaraguan woman, that's when I decided to support the work being done by the lesbians. The group was already functioning, and in spite of the fact that I didn't have any prior experience, I thought: this is where I can put my efforts.

MR: When did you come to Nicaragua?

Carmen: In April 1989. So I was in on the beginnings of the group that started at the end of that year. And that became my main area of work. Although the group had its good and bad moments. But I was a part of that. I was a feminist and had always supported a person's right to their sexual preference, and obviously, from the moment I came out as a lesbian, that became more important to me. I'm a doctor and I also work in sex education. So I've been concerned about the degree of homophobia there is, in the population as a whole and even among some of the leadership cadre.

I don't know if you heard about the letter that was published a week ago. There's been a tendency here to call feminists lesbians, as a way of making them look bad, tarnishing their reputations. Our argument has been to insist that there are lesbians everywhere, market women, professionals, Sandinistas. That we're as responsible as anyone else, as serious, as hard-working. But we need to do a lot more work around this.

Ana V.: I'm from Costa Rica. But then, that's right next door. And, well, my history is a bit different. I came to Nicaragua as a lesbian, with my partner who was already living here. But I didn't join the group until about six months ago, maybe a year. I've always functioned in heterosexual society. Everyone where I worked knew I was a lesbian. I never felt any particular prejudice. My co-workers were men, they all knew it, and they accepted me fine.

MR: This was in Nicaragua?

Ana V.: Yes, in Nicaragua.

MR: Because I know there is a movement in Costa Rica as well. I've met Costa Rican lesbians who tell me they have gay bars in San José...

Ana V.: It's a different kind of movement there. Not as linked to politics, or to the idea of changing society. In Nicaragua it's very much a part of all that. In Costa Rica you have the homosexuals' struggle within the context of a struggle for human rights. Here it's much broader. It's the struggle to make society as a whole more comprehensive, more open. For that reason it's much more interesting. In Costa Rica you end up in a ghetto, something that hasn't happened here, at least not yet. Here we've wanted to push society, so it will make a place for us, not carve a place out which is only for lesbians and gay men. I think this makes for a stronger fight against homophobia in general.

Carmen: I'm interested in how we can do this work, fight against society's homophobia. Because it seems to me that the worst homophobia of all is inside the revolutionary movement itself. AMNLAE's attitude really affected me. It hurt me deeply. I wasn't that surprised, but it hurts to hear women labelling other women 'lesbian' as a way of denigrating them. And I know that as a foreigner it's not my job to lead this struggle. It's up to the Nicaraguan sisters to do that. But we need to intensify this work, in all the different sectors. Among the youth. In our sex education. Because the prejudices run very deep.

When I think about how the sisters and brothers who were repressed back in '87 were reduced to silence. Or they chose to be silent because they supported the revolution, some were members of the FSLN, their organization said that being gay was a deviancy and they were afraid of being separated from their militancy unless they stayed in the closet. That silence is a terrible thing. I think about how hard it's been, it's taken four years for that silence to be broken, and now AMNLAE comes out with that article...

MR: Four years of silence can be hard, a day of silence can be hard. On the other hand, four years isn't much, when you think about homophobia and heterosexism everywhere, how deeply rooted in society these prejudices are. I think what Ana said about the difference between a place like Nicaragua and other countries is interesting. In spite of the official repression, at one point, it seems to me there is more openness now. Maybe particularly now, since the elections, when the FSLN is no longer the party in power and all sorts of issues have come to light...

Ana V.: There are basic differences, especially in the ways that certain values are being changed, which permit this type of space, this type of discussion, these concerns. Because in capitalism the whole legal aspect, even the definition of morality, is more developed. The value structure is more defined, everything in neat little packages. In this sense, the Sandinista revolution opened up a space that maybe didn't transform things completely but it certainly didn't close off the possibility.

In spite of the official repression you had here at a particular moment in time, most people, I mean the general population, have a lot of questions about sexuality. And this makes it easier to talk about taboos. Among the youth, especially, we have the opportunity of talking about all sorts of things, including different sexual options.

MR: In the United States the word 'lesbian' continues to be an epithet, used by many against feminists, or against women who are political, whether or not they are gay. I was involved in an immigration case, for example, for five years, and I wasn't yet out as a lesbian. But frequently in the press or on the radio when someone wanted to insult me, they called me a lesbian. It seems to me that what's happening here is extraordinarily positive, in spite of the obstacles.

Hazel: One of the most successful things is the work being done by homosexuals in the struggle against AIDS. They work a lot among gay men who, you might say, live on the edge. Because in the poorer neighborhoods there are men who sell themselves in order to survive. And the brigades teach them safe sex, give them condoms.

Another thing we're trying to do now is to open up a place where people can come, not just for political work, but *un lugar de ambiente*, a place lesbians and gay men can get together socially. Although, you know, I heard something today that's got me worried. It seems that some of the

entrepreneurial folk who have come back from Miami are opening a club
over in El Carmen. That worries me. In the first place because they're going
to make a lot of money. But also because it's going to be run by those folks
that have come back from Miami, with their money mentality. I can
imagine what kind of a place it's going to be. And then people who support
the FSLN will have to open our own place in reaction to that. And it won't
be like the work we've been trying to do, creating a certain kind of consciousness, making it possible for us to understand ourselves, our own
reality, first, and then getting together more publicly. It's been a long and
hard process, and I don't like it that all of a sudden, because UNO [the
ruling party at the time] thinks of opening up a place like this, there are two
places, disconnected with what we've been doing.

Mary: I wanted to say something else. Inside the FSLN it hasn't just
been repression towards homosexuals. I'm a product of my own particular
history, of course, but my experience hasn't been anything like what you've
been talking about here. I'm a long-time member of the FSLN. My comrades have always known I'm a lesbian. No one's ever accused me of anything, and no one's ever refused me positions of responsibility because of my
sexuality. I've always had positions of responsibility.

In a Sandinista Assembly they've even said officially that no reprisals
would be taken against anyone because of his or her sexual preference. I'm
not saying that this policy has always been carried out, that there haven't
been people who have done what they wanted. But it's depended a lot on
who happens to be in charge, on what kind of a human being that person
is, their amplitude, their vision.

I'm not speaking only for myself. I know a lot of Sandinistas who are
gay, and who have never been expelled from the party because of that. Of
course it's been hard. We've had to fight to show that we are as good as
anyone else, like any group about which prejudice exists. I'm not denying
that. But it's also true that there are many of us who are known to be gay
and have been accepted.

This is something that's made an impression on people from other
places. For example, a Colombian comrade and I were talking once and she
told me how surprised she was that the Sandinista Front had known
homosexuals in its ranks. She said that couldn't happen in Colombia. That
comrade was also surprised that homosexuals were revolutionaries, not
rightists. And I think that most of us, here in Nicaragua, are progressive, or
we try to be revolutionaries, or we *are* revolutionaries.

And I think this is something that the movement here in Nicaragua
has given to the rest of Latin America, it's made others stop and think about
the fact that homosexuals can be revolutionaries, it's a small contribution
we've made. I think what Ana said about not creating ghettos is important.
We need to defend our place in society as a whole, make society respect us
for what we are, for what we do, for our work.

MR: I'm really interested in what you're saying about demanding social space. In the United States, at least in certain areas and in certain professions or trades, in our political life or as a writer or artist, we have come to the point where many of us can be out. We've struggled for that space, and to some extent we've won it. In my own case, I demand that my partner be recognized as such, at least as far as that's possible.

On the other hand, at least at this point in time, I don't think I'd feel comfortable going dancing with her at a mixed club. There's too much homophobia. It's too dangerous out there. We feel more comfortable, at least for now, going dancing where we know we're accepted. And that's among other lesbians, and sometimes gay men.

Hazel: Here there's some discussion around that. But I want to say that I disagree with Mary. Because the FSLN, as a party, *did* repress the group of gays and lesbians. It respected those who were gay but didn't make waves. If you stayed in the closet, that was fine. But when you started a group, a movement, it was something else. Although I agree that the revolution opened up the space that made it possible for us to wage this struggle. And our struggle has helped other gays feel socially accepted.

There are examples. There's a group of gay men in El Viejo, there must be 80 or 90 of them. And that's a peasant population, in banana country. These guys are all ages and they're accepted in their community. They have parties in the streets, street fairs, they participate in all sorts of events, and it hasn't been easy.

Hazel: There's also a difference between men and women. It's not the same for lesbians and gay men because there's always the matter of *machismo*. It's always easier for the men. Men exercise their male privilege even when they dance together. But if you're a woman dancing with another woman, right away some guy is going to come up and: 'What's this? Imagine...!' And he'll ask you to dance because it's impossible that you'd prefer a woman over him...

Several voices: ... Yeah... butting in and...

MR: I look at the last few years of Sandinista struggle, before the elections, and I think about how hard it must have been. All sorts of issues were sacrificed, abortion for instance, and in retrospect I think many of us agree that those sacrifices were mistakes. But at the time I wonder how much was due to homophobia and how much was simply the fear of going out on a limb at a time when defending the process itself demanded so much energy. I'm not excusing homophobia. I'm just wondering if we can expect so much in such difficult periods...

Hazel: There are plenty of homophobes in the FSLN, I can tell you...

MR: Everywhere...

Hazel: Sure, there are homophobes everywhere. But look, it's not that I expected the FSLN to make some kind of a pronouncement. It would have been enough if they'd have let us be. Because if you're going to let some be because they're in the closet, but come down on others because they're not, that's not right.

Mary: I'm not denying that there's been repression, at least against the group that started organizing. The thing you have to understand is that many of us weren't ourselves anymore. We stopped being ourselves in support of a cause. There were lots of things we pushed aside because we believed in that cause. In many cases we forgot about our personal life, about attending to our own personal issues.

When we lost the election, that's when I began to pay attention to my personal life, that's when I began to *have* a personal life. And this isn't just my story; it's a phenomenon shared by many of us. I'd say that a great many Nicaraguans are experiencing this, maybe the whole 40 per cent that voted for the FSLN. I think we need a more profound analysis of all this now...

Carmen: I think that all this has to do with the issue of feminism, too. Feminism is something that was always relegated to a secondary place here. I mean there was an official women's organization and all that, but the real feminist issues weren't addressed. Issues like abortion, sexuality, family planning... It doesn't do much good to stay in the past. We have to learn from our mistakes. Revolutionary struggle always has its contradictions. It couldn't be otherwise, because we are human beings and humans have our contradictions. We need to deal with the contradictions, but simultaneously, not try to pretend that some things must be done first and that the rest can wait.

I belong to a revolutionary organization too, and I think that the struggle around women's rights is just as important as the struggle for the economy, as the struggle for workers' rights, respect for sexual preference. Like Mary says, we have to learn from our history. We know there was a time when all that mattered was survival, but that's changed now. And I think we have to promote an educational process among militants... when I say militants I mean members of the Party.

Mary: I agree. But I ask myself, right now, how do we do this? If you think about it, there's a huge vacuum right now, and no one has yet found a way of dealing with that. Political life in this country is in pretty bad shape. We're lying if we say that any of us have a structured political life right now. Each of us has gotten behind some social flag or other: women's rights, community work, work with the farmers, whatever. But Party life, as such, just doesn't exist here now.

MR: What I've felt in the short time I've been back, is that an understanding of feminism, not an understanding of the need for a gay and lesbian movement but even an understanding of feminism itself, is not very prevalent among the FSLN leadership. I'm talking about feminism as an important ideology, a way of looking at the world, feminism in the broadest sense. It seems to me that there aren't very many among the highest level of leadership—maybe two or three at the most—who understand what feminism means. I was surprised...

Callie: I know that in different parts of the country there are women who are working hard, doing important work individually or in mixed groups. But sometimes I think that the struggle for women's rights—and I'm not talking about women having power, I'm talking about them simply having rights, the most elemental rights to their own reproduction, whatever—that's a struggle that's very incipient in the countryside.

MR: What kind of work do you do?

Callie: I work with promoters of public health and I travel around... in the mountains, beyond Jinotega.

MR: How long have you been doing that?

Callie: I've been with my current project for the past three years. But I've been working in the countryside here since 1985. Of course the Sixth Region[15] is one of the most backwards. Maybe in the Fourth Region things are better...

Ana V.: I think you're right. I work in Region One with a project for peasant women at the state level, where we begin with such primary discussions as children's sexuality. It's a project that deals with women's health. I couldn't agree more. The thing is, if we're going to talk about feminism in Nicaragua, at least for the moment, we're basically going to be talking about Managua. We're going to be talking about one small group of Association of Farm Workers women, who've been privy to an educational process that's by no means generalized.

But Mary said something I want to pick up on, which is that right now there really isn't such a thing as the FSLN. What there is, is a lot of different people in a lot of different political movements and, well, we're still fighting. That's important. And it's the result of a revolutionary process that's also been very important. The fact that a year after the kind of electoral defeat we've had you've got a whole society involved in this kind of a dynamic, concrete struggles, this says you've got a process that's still very much alive.

And on top of your own personal problem of how to put food on the table—because we've got to remember that in Nicaragua right now most people are just trying to survive—but beyond the struggle for survival, there's a movement of women talking about our rights. And that's more than you have in many other places.

MR: I can see that the revolution is very much alive. It's alive in the concrete struggles that continue, and it's also alive in people's consciousness. A consciousness has been created here that in many other Latin American countries has yet to be created... only in countries where political organization has been high, like Chile, Bolivia, countries like those. In the US we don't have the kind of generalized consciousness you have here. And this, for me, is a tangible product of ten years of revolution.

Hazel: There's something I want to say, and it's about peasant women, women in the countryside in Nicaragua. They might not know what the word feminism means, they might not use that word. But in their lives, in their everyday practice, in the way they express the need for change, they understand very well what feminism is. For example, I was involved in a study about women's mortality in childbirth. It was in the context of trying to legalize abortion, and what I found was that peasant women understood very well their need to stop having so many children. They don't want those huge families anymore. They may not know how to avoid them, what to use, but at the feeling level they're clear.

If you mention the word *abortion*, for example, you'll hear 'Ay, no, no, no, by the Holy Virgin!' But they'll try to abort all the same. The thing is, they'll go out on their own and try to solve the problem, because their objective conditions force them to. Or about their men: they won't talk about sexism, they won't use that word, but they'll talk about how their men make them pregnant and then move on to a younger woman across the way, leaving them to deal with the children, life, the works. Peasant women are tired of being treated like that, they don't want to go on that way.

And something else. This is something I was told, because I also worked with a group of midwives. They told me one of them got called to attend to a woman, and it turned out that the woman's husband showed up, he was drunk, he started beating up on his wife and she lost the baby. This happens a lot. And all those women together lynched that man. They all fell on him at once. So what I'm saying is that everyday life in the countryside teaches women about sexism, and they respond. They may not talk about it with the same words we use. But they're tired of it. They don't want to go on like they are.

The other day I was somewhere where they'd given out something like 1,000 *manzanas*.[16] It turned into an all-male cooperative. Something like six men ended up with most of the land. They only wanted to give three *manzanas* to the women. Well, the women planted some trees. And in one of their meetings the men began to attack them as stupid, what did they want to be planting trees for, who knows what all. But those trees proved nourishing to the cows, you know? So when the men began having trouble finding feed, they told the women: 'Give us what you planted and we'll give you three *manzanas* of land.'

The women said: 'No. Each of these trees is worth five pesos.' And the men tried to threaten them. But the women stood their ground. There are a lot more women than men, because there are a lot of women without husbands. The six men began calling them names, whores, crazy women, whatever. But the women are standing their ground. They're coming together, they're organizing, and they're dealing with the situation. So I think...

Callie: I think there's something else we have to understand. I don't know about other parts of the country, but in the Sixth Region we've got the influence of the church, the Catholic Church and the evangelical churches. I've seen things change.

Before women were more open about a lot of things, sex education, family planning, maybe not so much about abortion. But now it feels like we're going backwards. The church is everywhere, and I can see the change. The women go to mass, the kids go to their catechism classes, and I could see the difference in a sex education workshop we did. They start talking about religion. What the priests say and what we say produces a conflict in the women. Especially in the most remote areas...

* * *

It's getting late. We all acknowledge exhaustion as we say good night. I know that these women will rise early tomorrow to begin another day on whatever job faces them. Some will still return to offices or other meetings tonight. It's been a productive exchange, one in an ongoing series of such exchanges among women who are struggling to change our own reality and the world.

Afterword

In early April 1999 the first issue of a lesbian magazine appeared in Managua. *HUMANAS* was presented to the Nicaraguan public at a well-attended event, at which longtime Sandinista activist Dorotea Wilson gave an in-depth talk about that country's women—and lesbians. The magazine is an atttractive small-format quarterly; this first issue has 36 pages. Contents include first-person life accounts by local lesbians, a review of and protest against Nicaragua's anti-sodomy law, a piece on Nicaragua's participation in the Gay Games held in Amsterdam in 1998, an elegant detachable centrefold (a photograph of two lesbians making love), and the proverbial horoscope ('Lesboroscope' here!), among much else. In line with the progressive politics of most of Nicaragua's lesbian/gay/bisexual community, there is a report from Amnesty International and an article announcing the Fifth Latin American Lesbian Conference: moved from the Dominican Republic to Brazil because of difficulties arising from the first country's political situation. *HUMANAS* can be reached at Apartado Postal C-65, Centro Commercial Managua, Managua, Nicaragua; or at humanas@ibw.com.ni.

[1] First published in an earlier version in *Signs: Journal of Women in Culture and Society* (summer 1993).

[2] *Inside the Nicaraguan Revolution: The Story of Doris Maria Tijerino,* Vancouver: New Star Books, 1978; *Sandino's Daughters,* Vancouver: New Star Books, 1981; *Christians in the Nicaraguan Revolution,* Vancouver: New Star Books, 1983; *Risking a Somersault in the Air: Conversations with Nicaraguan Writers,* San Francisco: Solidarity Publications, 1984; *Gathering Rage: The Failure of Twentieth Century Revolutions to Develop a Feminist Agenda,* New York: Monthly Review, 1993; *Sandino's Daughters Revisited,* New Brunswick: Rutgers Univ. Press, 1994; and *Our Voices, Our Lives: Stories of Women from Central America and the Caribbean,* Monroe, Maine: Common Courage Press, 1995 (which included this article).

[3] Frente Sandinista de Liberacion Nacional [Sandinista National Liberation Front], the political and military organization that coordinated the Nicaraguan people's successful overthrow of the dictatorship of Anastasio Somoza in 1979. The FSLN was founded in 1961 by a handful of revolutionaries, who took their courage, some strategies, and their name from the earlier history of Augusto C. Sandino, the peasant leader who fought Somoza's father and the US Marines in the 1920s and '30s.

[4] Based on the early design that Magaly Pineda contributed to when she worked for the Nicaraguan Ministry of Public Welfare during the first months of the Sandinista revolution.

[5] The FSLN held its First Congress after its electoral defeat, in July 1991. At that time there was a strong movement to include at least one woman on the Directorate; Dora Maria Tellez was the obvious candidate. But once again the old boys' club prevailed, and Tellez was not elected to fill one of the two vacancies. In May 1994 the FSLN held what they called an extraordinary congress. There the National Directorate was expanded from nine to fifteen seats, and five women were included (as well as several men stepping down and others added). The new women members were Mónica Baltodano, Mirna Cunningham, Benigna Mendiola, Dora María Téllez and Dorotea Wilson.

[6] The women interviewed in these pages provide an overview of gay rights during and since the decade of Sandinista government. Since this was written, in June 1992, the governing UNO coalition introduced article 205 of the Penal Code, a tough anti-sodomy law. Although all Sandinista delegates voted against the article, the National Assembly passed it by a narrow margin, and President Violeta Barrios de Chamorro failed to exercise her veto. To date the law has not been utilized, and there has been a many-pronged movement against it, although Nicaragua's Supreme Court upheld the statute.

[7] Asociacion de mujeres nicaraguenses Luisa Amanda Espinosa [The Luisa Amanda Espinosa Association of Nicaraguan Women], a mass women's organization which had

its roots in the years of struggle themselves and evolved in different ways during the ten years of popular government. Luisa Amanda Espinosa was a working-class woman believed to have been the first female member of the FSLN to fall in battle. She was killed in April 1970.

[8] *Revueltos* translates as scrambled or mixed up; many of those who were up in arms with the US-sponsored counterrevolutionary forces and those who came out of the Sandinista tradition have joined together demanding land, work, survival. In the northern city of Ocotal, such a group of women only call themselves the Frente Nora Astorga [Nora Astorga Front]. In memory of a Sandinista heroine who died in 1989, they have organized and armed themselves. Their demands include work, reforestation, day care, women's clinics, and sewing machines.

[9] I was in Managua to attend a meeting of the international solidarity movement, called by the Sandinista National Liberation Front (FSLN) to discuss the results of its recent Congress and share prospects for further work. Particularly interested in what women are thinking and how they feel in the context of the changes that have taken place in their country, I met with as many as was feasible during the week I was there. This transcript comes from one of several conversations and is also informed by others.

[10] A Managua neighborhood, named after one of the early Sandinista martyrs, victim of the Somoza era.

[11] Because of the Contra war, the government decreed what was to be an ongoing state of siege.

[12] *La boletina: Un aporte a la comunicación entre mujeres* (The Bulletin: A Contribution to Women's Communication) is a small but vital publication, the first issue of which appeared in July 1991. It includes news and analysis about Nicaraguan women. Subscriptions are welcome and can be obtained by sending US $25.00 for one year to Puntos de Encuentro, Apartado Postal RP-39, Managua, Nicaragua.

[13] High-level Sandinista leader, Minister of Public Health at the time.

[14] A gay bar or gathering place.

[15] During the Sandinista government, the country was divided into regions.

[16] A *manzana* is a measurement of land.

Mandela's stepchildren: homosexual identity in post-apartheid South Africa

Mark Gevisser

Prologue

'I'm in the constitution!' a particularly edgy black drag queen howled to the crowds as the fifth annual Johannesburg Lesbian and Gay Pride Parade, 2000 strong, passed through the high-density flatland of Joubert Park. It was October 1994, just six months after South Africa's exhilarating passage to democracy, and the onlookers—ordinary black folk who live in the neighborhood—beamed back delight. 'Viva the *moffies!*' a young man shouted, appropriating a liberation chant: Long live the queers!

The first such event took place in 1990; not uncoincidentally in the year that Nelson Mandela was released and the African National Congress unbanned. That was the year of national euphoria, when prison cells were unlocked and marches were legalized and books could be read; anything seemed possible and everything seemed terrifying. That first year, march organizers provided participants with paper bags to wear over their heads if they wished; an utterly contradictory symbol for Pride, but one that offered a visible and tangible image of the closeted fear so many South Africans still felt in those first tentative months of 'freedom'.

Four short years later, there was a palpable sense of liberation in the air. On one level, the bonhomie of the onlookers was simply sheer ebullience at a South Africa which no longer compartmentalized and categorized and shut people off from each other; a South Africa where you could parade your identity, whatever it was. Where you could now *have* a parade. But there was something deeper in the crowd's clear—if sometimes bemused—approval of the event. 'No, I would not want to see my son or daughter marching there,' said one observer to me, a stolid and ample-hipped woman in one of those flowing floral dresses that working people reserve for church. 'But those people have the right to march. This is the New South Africa. When we were voting last April we weren't just voting for our own freedom, we were voting for everyone to be free with who they are...'

The only vocal dissidents were a group of American Baptist bible-punchers led by one Pastor Ron Sykes who, for five years, had faithfully harangued the marchers with his 'Turn or Burn' sign and his finger-wagging admonitions of Sodom. In 1994, Sykes told the Johannesburg *Sunday Times*: 'A lot of people consider us fantastic and freaks, but we hope to make these people realise that [what they do] is a wicked thing.' Here was a Christian fundamentalist, claiming to represent the moral majority, admitting that it is he and his troupe of naysayers who are generally considered to be 'fantastic and freaks'; acknowledging in effect that it was he—and not the gay marchers—who was marginal and out of step with the New South Africa.

Today, in 1999, five years into the new democracy, the Parade—now called a Mardi Gras—is escorted through downtown Johannesburg by a group of out-of-the-closet gay officers belonging to the South African Gay and Lesbian Policing Network. They are a little stiff, a little self-conscious, but beaming with pride. It takes your breath away when you remember how central the role of the police force was to apartheid repression, and how brutally it policed sexuality too.

1

Lebo Khumalo, a teenage girl from Soweto, is thrown out of her family home when she tells her parents she is a lesbian. Wandering the streets, she comes across Sis' Nongezo, a street-sweeper, proud that he is 'the only drag-queen in the employ of the Johannesburg Municipality'. The two are visited by the Spirits, a delightful trio of gay ancestors who sing and dance and recount their lives as gay men and women in the '50s. Lebo realizes that she has a place in the world and in the history of her people—that she is not a freak and that, in fact, even her grandfather was a homosexual—and is thus able to go home and reconcile herself with her family.

This, roughly sketched, is the plot of 'After Nines', a play about the black gay South African experience that deploys the burlesque musical theatre codes and the pastiche story-telling style of black protest theatre of the 1980s towards the new end of gay liberation. Performed in township community halls and at Johannesburg's Civic Theatre in August 1998, it is a remarkable piece of work, not only because of its representation of black gay experience and excavation of black gay history, but because the brilliant performers are five men and women in their early twenties who—just like their antecedents in protest theatre—have become involved in theatre because of a sense of mission and identity.

The highlight of 'After Nines' is the cast's campy rendition, led by Sis' Nongeza in full, stylish township-drag, of 'Nkosi Sikel' iAfrika', the black liberation hymn. Despite the sanctity of this anthem—this, after all, is what doughty church-matrons and angry young comrades have used, for close to a century, to sing themselves into freedom—the three men and two women on stage reclaim it with a playfulness that does not mask, for one moment, their deep-rooted sense of belonging in the new, democratic South Africa of which 'Nkosi Sikileli' is now the national anthem.

Indeed, in the very week their show began its run at the Civic, a far more momentous event was taking place just across the road in downtown Johannesburg, at the Constitutional Court—the highest court in the land. Here, the judges were hearing the very first test of the South African constitution's protection of gay and lesbian equality. The new constitution, passed in May 1996, is the first in the world to outlaw, explicitly, discrimination on the basis of sexual orientation. (Using the South African model, Ecuador became the second, in 1997.) Section 8(3) of Chapter Two of the South African Constitution reads: 'Neither the state nor any person may unfairly discriminate directly or indirectly against anyone on one or more grounds, including race, gender, sex, marital status, ethnic or social origin, colour, sexual orientation, age, disability, religion, conscience, belief, culture, language and birth.'

Following an application from the National Coalition of Gay and Lesbian Equality (NGCLE) and the Human Right Commission, a statutory body, a supreme court judge had ruled in May 1998 that all the laws that render sodomy still a crime—or that discriminated against homosexual practise (such as unequal ages of consent)—were unconstitutional and had to be scrapped. 'The expression of homosexuality,' wrote Judge Jonathan Heher of the Johannesburg Supreme Court, 'is as normal as that of its heterosexual equivalent, and is therefore entitled to equal tolerance and respect.' Heher's interpretation of the constitution was that sexual orientation cannot be a factor which influences 'the distribution of social goods and services and the award of social opportunities': in South Africa, homosexuals may longer be discriminated against— in the workplace, in medical aid schemes, in adoptions, even, theoretically, in access to marriage.

It was now the Constitutional Court's job to ratify Heher's ruling, and, at the very moment that the 'After Nines' cast was concluding its dress rehearsal at the Civic, it did so, unanimously: 'Once you take away prejudice, there is nothing left,' commented Judge Albie Sachs. 'All the justifications [for homophobic laws] are based on prejudice, the very thing the constitution is there to prevent.'

Now, in the aftermath of South Africa's second democratic elections, which took place in May 1999, the battle to implement the constitution's homosexual equality provision has begun in earnest. Already, there have been some milestone applications of the constitution: the National Defence Act prohibits discrimination in the military on the basis of sexual orientation, and the new labour legislation (the Basic Conditions of Employment Act and the Employment Equity Act) prohibits all workplace discrimination. Most significantly, in early 1998, a lesbian police officer, Inspector Jolande Langemaat, sued the police medical aid scheme, POLMED, for refusing to register her long-time companion, Beverley-Ann Myburgh, as a dependant. Langemaat claimed that this was unconstitutional—and won: 'Both [homosexual and heterosexual] types of union are demanding of respect and protection,' wrote Justice Roux of the Pretoria Supreme Court. 'If our law does not accord protection to [homosexual unions], then I suggest it is time it does so.'

A year later, in April 1999, the Pensions Fund Adjudicator—a statutory official set up by the pension fund industry to regulate it—used the constitution to rule that the exclusion of same-sex partners from the 'class of persons entitled to enjoyment of the spouse's pension' unfairly discriminated against lesbian and gay couples by denying them the same rights that heterosexual couples have. In late 1999, the Constitutional Court ruled that the state had acted unconstitutionally in regard to residency permits to foreign partners of homosexuals, and a state welfare agency used the constitution to justify its decision in allowing a gay couple to adopt a baby. With a speed that even South African gay activists did not expect, the country was, at the turn of the millenium, approaching a position where same-sex marriage existed in all but name.

2

In September 1999, Uganda's main newspaper, *New Vision,* ran a double-page pullout entitled 'Homosexuals increasing in Uganda. Who's responsible?' Homosexuals, the article disclosed, identify themselves on the streets of Kampala by wearing a 'unique perfume only worn by a "woman-man"'. Twenty-five students were recently suspended from the elite Ntare School for allegedly practising homosexuality, and this appears to have ignited a wave of moral panic in the country, where the vice, one school principal commented to the newspaper, has reached "unprecedented" levels. At girls' schools, lesbian students 'adopt carrots, eggplants and bananas for penises. Such fresh fruits are usually available in the first weeks of term... When they run out [the girls] resort to test-tubes.'

The article cites a psychiatrist—who believes that shock therapy might cure the deviants—enumerating the many dangers of homosexual sex, one of which is that 'because oral sex can be vigorous, it could fracture the jaw.' One might see the comedy in it all if it weren't for the fact that the Penal Code of Uganda, like that of most former British colonies in Africa, prohibits sodomy as 'carnal knowledge against the order of nature'.

The rule of Yoweri Museveni might have brought enlightenment to Uganda in other areas, but when Museveni's government rewrote the constitution and the penal code in 1990, the maximum penalty for 'unnatural' carnality was increased from fourteen years to life imprisonment. Indeed, Museveni pronounced in 1994 that his government would 'shoot at' anyone bringing the unnatural practise of homosexuality into his country; he reiterated, following the Ntare School scandal in 1999, that all homosexuals should be arrested and convicted.

He is by no means alone, on the African continent, in the extremity of his views. In 1995, Zimbabwean president Robert Mugabe declared that homosexuality "degrades human dignity. It is unnatural, and there is no question, ever, of allowing these people to behave worse than dogs and pigs. If dogs and pigs do not do it, why must human beings? We have our own culture, and we must rededicate ourselves to our traditional values that make us human beings.'

He made these statements after an international furore following the Zimbabwean government's refusal to allow a gay organization—the Gays and Lesbians of Zimbabwe (GALZ)—to exhibit at the high-profile Zimbabwe International Book Fair, even though the theme of that event was 'human rights'. The more protest there was, the more intractable he became, seeing each criticism as further proof of the fact that the West was trying to corrupt essential and pure African morality. When a group of American lawmakers, led by Maxine Waters and Barney Frank, wrote urging him 'to reexamine the issue and to follow the government of South Africa in respecting the human rights of all people', he shot back: 'Let the Americans keep their sodomy, bestiality, stupid and foolish ways to themselves!... What is human rights? Don't we have natural rights too?'

One of the leaders of his ruling party's Women's League, a Mrs Mangwe, who is a member of parliament, drew the terms of this debate more crudely when she was asked by a South African TV crew whether the Zimbabwean war of liberation wasn't meant to free *all* people. 'Oh my God, no!' she responded indignantly. 'Our war was to protect our culture. Not to destroy by allowing homosexuality to run rife in it. It's not in our black culture and we don't want it!'

The effects of Mugabe's attack were immediately felt: the day after his first speech at the Zimbabwe International Book Fair, one of GALZ's black officials was detained. Police went to his parents, who did not know he was gay, and showed them a photograph of him in a newspaper—he has been unable to return to his home township. While white gay Zimbabweans were relatively safe, black gay Zimbabweans stated that they feared for their lives, because for Mugabe to sustain his lie that homosexuality was un-African, he had to intimidate black gays into invisibility.

Mugabe's homophobia has provided other African leaders with a cue-sheet for how to rail against neo-colonialism. In the last few years, Kenya's Daniel Arap Moi has said that 'homosexuality is against African norms and traiditions,' and Zambia's Frederick Chiluba that 'homosexuality is the deepest level of depravity. It is unbiblical and abnormal. How do you expect my government to accept something that is abnormal?' In March 1997, following the formation of Gays and Lesbians of Swaziland (GALESWA), the Swazi king Mswati III declared that 'these people are sick'; at a meeting between the king and the country's religious leaders, the president of the Swaziland League of Churches, Isaac Dlamini, said, 'Your Majesty, such people hate God. According to the Bible, these are the people who were thrown into the dustbin. The Bible said they should be killed.' After having been detained briefly, the founder of Galeswa, Chief Mangosuthu Dlamini—a member of the royal family—wisely fled to South Africa.

Responding to the formation of a gay group called the Rainbow Coalition in Namibia, the country's president, Sam Nujoma, told a womens' conference in December 1996 that 'homosexuals must be condemned and rejected in our society.' He was backed up by an official statement, issued by the ruling South West African Peoples' Organization (SWAPO), that 'homosexuality deserves a severe contempt and disdain from the Namibian people and should be uprooted totally as a practice.' The statement called on Namibians to 'revitalize our inherent culture and its moral values which we have inherited for many centuries from our forefathers. We should not risk our people being identified with foreign immoral values.'

All the above deploy a contradictory arsenal of Christian fundamentalism and African nationalism: they claim that it did not exist in pre-colonial African society, and that it is a colonial depradation, a Western import—conveniently forgetting that it was the colonizer who brought both the bible and the penal code, with their censure of 'unnatural acts', to African soil. There is a clear relationship between the flagging fortunes of these African leaders, and their recourse to homophobia: gays become easy scapegoats and titillating distractions. Mugabe, who presides over a declining, corrupt and alienated state, unleashes his anti-gay rhetoric strategically to distract Zimbabweans from his government's failings: in the Mugabe world view, homophobia has become a way to rally his people around all that he thinks is wrong with 'Western' and 'liberal' society. Museveni became strident about homosexuals at exactly the time Ugandans were most critical of him for dragging their country into the Congo war; Chiluba did it when he faced a coup; Nujoma to distract attention from criticism against him for amending the constitution to serve a third term; King Mswati when he was facing massive internal strife from the pro-democracy trade unions.

In late 1999, succumbing to international donor pressure on his homophobia, Uganda's Museveni backtracked on his earlier extremism: if homosexuals 'did it quietly,' he was quoted as saying, they would be left alone: 'Homosexuals are the ones provoking us. They are upsetting society. We shall not allow these people to challenge society.' The message from Museveni, Mugabe and many of the others is clear: if homosexuals return to the old 'pre-gay' ways, they will be left alone.

Thus a difficult dialectic is emerging in contemporary African society: as gay organizations, heartened by the successes of the South African movement, are beginning to take root, state-sanctioned harrassment and discrimination of and violence against homosexuals has increased. In Namibia, Swaziland, Zambia, Botswana, Zimbabwe, Kenya and Uganda, presidential anti-gay invective has without exception been in direct response to the growing articulacy, confidence and profiles of gay movements in those countries.

At the core of this dialectic is the troublesome reality that that Mugabe, Museveni, Nujoma et al are right about one thing: while homosexual practise predates the colonization of the continent, the advent of a 'gay' subculture—of people taking on identities as 'gay' or 'lesbian' and demanding rights as such is without doubt a new—and Western—import, insofar as it is a consequence of urbanization and modernization in a global society. Because of their advanced economies, their large white settler populations and their histories of struggle for human rights, Zimbabwe and South Africa have become the first two sub-Saharan African countries to have to deal with the cultural trauma of acknowledging homosexuality, but the trend is developing throughout the continent. As more and more young Africans come of age in the continent's burgeoning middle class, they find the freedom, intellectually and financially, to be able to claim a gay identity, and to shift their sexuality from being a practice to being an identity. The internet, satellite TV and video rental stores are all key elements in the development of gay consciousness in Africa.

But as this happens, nerves become raw, as is clearly evidenced by the anger unleashed by African political and clerical leaders: for the first time, severely repressed societies are forced to talk about sex, a conversation which ends, logically, at a new analysis of gender, and roles that men and women play in both bedroom and society. The tension is between two very different ways of dealing with the homosexuality—the traditional approach, which finds ways of accommodating it and not talking about it (do what you like in private as long as you marry and have kids), and the Western way, which claims for homosexuals a 'gay' identity and impels them to live a 'gay' life. With the latter comes personal freedom—and extreme cultural conflict.

3

In September 1999, the International Lesbian and Gay Association, ILGA, held its biennial conference in Johannesburg; it had, consequentially, the largest ever number of African delegates at an international event of this nature: representatives from Namibia, Botswana, Uganda, Kenya, Zimbabwe, Uganda, Cote d'Ivoire, Cameroun and Zambia whose activism in the face of the opprobrium described above is nothing short of heroic.

The keynote speaker at the conference's gala banquet was the South African deputy minister of justice, Cheryl Gillwald. She reminded her audience that, in contrast with the attitudes of other African leaders, the South African president, Thabo Mbeki, had said as early as 1986 that 'the ANC is indeed very firmly committed to removing all forms of discrimination and oppression in a liberated South Africa... That commitment must surely extend to the protection of gay rights.'

How is it possible that the South African experience, in dealing with homosexuality, has been so utterly different from the rest of the continent? In marked contrast to Mugabe, Nelson Mandela made a point of mentioning the right to gay equality in his inaugural address after his election in 1994, and met with gay South African leaders a year later to reaffirm his commitment. Several senior ANC figures have called for an end to discrimination against gay people. In 1994, an outspoken gay activist, Edwin Cameron, was appointed to the Supreme Court; no one has blinked an eyelid. At a public hearing in 1995, the Independent Broadcasting Authority, tasked with deregulating the airwaves, tripped over itself to assure gay people that they would receive equity of airtime.

Opening the third South African gay and lesbian film festival in November 1996, Karl Niehaus, a senior ANC parliamentarian who is now South African ambassador to Holland, urged gay people to come out of the closet. Two years previously, opening the first festival, the minister of police for Gauteng

Province (Johannesburg), Jessie Duarte, offered herself as a patron for the local Gay and Lesbian Organization of the Witwatersrand (GLOW) and then called, loudly and publicly, for an end to discrimination against gay people. 'Not only are there legal injustices to be done away with,' she said, 'but mindsets and cultures have to be done away with too. It is one thing for you to have your rights and equality in the law, it is quite another to have them each day in the street, at work, in the bar, in public places where you socialize and where you cruise.' She then called for all homophobic police officers to be exposed.

In May 1996, when the final constitution was approved by South Africa's parliamentarians, only two legislators, belonging to the tiny fundamentalist African Christian Democratic Party (ACDP), voted against the inclusion of 'sexual orientation' in the equality clause. All the rest, from the militant black nationalist Pan-Africanist Congress(PAC) to the Afrikaner separatist Freedom Front, approved it.

Perhaps this was because they had other battles to fight, but this in itself is significant: despite voluble behind-closed-doors discomfort with gay equality within the ANC (see below), homosexuality, in post-apartheid South Africa, has by and large not been a public issue. When the leader of the the PAC, Rev. Stanley Mogoba, stated during the 1999 election campaigns that homosexuals were sick and 'needed help', the party quickly issued a statement to say that this was his personal opinion and not official policy. Not even the ACDP (which gets most of its ideology from the American Christian Coalition) deployed anti-gay invective in its election campaign. It has been, rather, in everyone's interest—particularly those representing other minorities—to accept the ANC's foundation-premise that all human rights are equal and indivisible.

The primary reason why the notion of gay equality passed so smoothly into the constitution is most likely that the ANC elite has a utopian social progressive ideology, influenced largely by the social-democratic movements in the countries that supported it during its struggle: Sweden, Holland, Britain, Canada, Australia. In exile in these countries, key South African leaders came to understand and accept—and, in the case of women, benefit from—the sexual liberation movement. Foremost among them were Frene Ginwala, now Speaker of Parliament; Albie Sachs, now a judge on the Constitutional Court; Kader Asmal, now the minister of education; and Thabo Mbeki himself, South Africa's second democratically elected president.

Very significantly, though—unlike in other African countries—those uncomfortable with gay equality could not marshal the support of a homophobic church. On the contrary, South Africa's undisputed moral leader, Archbishop Desmond Tutu, has made it an article of faith to support gay equality: he has become an international advocate for the ordination of gay priests into the Anglican church, and he has repented publicly for the church's previous discriminatory policies. Tutu has recently written that those who make gays and lesbians 'doubt that they were the children of God' commit 'the ultimate blasphemy... If the church, after the victory over apartheid, is looking for a worthy moral crusade, then this is it: the fight against homophobia and heterosexism.'

In its campaign to get the gay equality clause passed, the National Coalition for Gay and Lesbian Equality (NCGLE) managed to secure support letters from several prominent clerics, Tutu included. The NCGLE, formed in 1994, has set itself the primary task of decriminalizing homosexuality and lobbying for legislative reform. The cornerstone of its highly effective—if essentialist— strategy has been to define homosexuality as a characteristic as inherent and immutable as race: 'Every single black South African,' says Kevan Botha, the coalition's chief constitutional lobbyist, 'knows what it's like to be discriminated against because of something you have no control over. And so it was very easy for them to make the connections to what we were saying about how gay people are victimized.'

Another key element of the strategy is to view gay equality as a broad-based human rights issue rather than the narrow pleadings of a dispensable minority. This approach has taken root in neighbouring countries too—most notably, in Zimbabwe, where GALZ has aligned itself with the extra-parliamentary opposition to Mugabe's autocracy, and where the trade-unionist leaders of this movement—people like Morgan Tsvingarai who will be the next generation of the country's leaders—have made it clear that they support the notions of homosexual equality developed in South Africa.

The ground had been laid for the South African strategies of viewing gay issues as part of the struggle against apartheid by the coming out, during the struggle, of prominent gay anti-apartheid activists. Foremost among these was Simon Nkoli, who died of AIDS-related illness in early 1999. In the infamous Delmas treason trial of the mid-1980s, Nkoli disclosed his homosexuality, and eventually managed to gain the support of all his co-accused, several of whom are now senior members of the ANC government.

One of them is Patrick Lekota, the ANC national chairman and South Africa's defence minister, who said at the time of Nkoli's death that 'all of us acknowledged that [Simon's coming out] was an important learning experience... His presence made it possible for more information to be discussed, and it broadened our vision, helping us to see that society was composed of so many people whose orientations are not the same, and that one must be able to live with it.' And so, when it came to writing the constitution, 'how could we say that men and women like Simon, who had put their shoulders to the wheel to end apartheid, how could we say that they should now be discriminated against?'

Upon his release from prison in 1989, Nkoli founded GLOW, radically different from the gay organizations that preceded it in that it was a black organization. Nkoli's major contribution was thus to counter the notion, prevalent in Africa, that homosexuality is not only un-Christian, but 'un-African', a white contamination of black society.

But the work of Nkoli and other black gay South Africans is by no means over. Taking note of the extreme homophobia that exists on the continent and in South Africa, deputy minister of justice Cheryl Gillwald, in her speech to the ILGA banquet, warned South Africans not to become too complacent: her own party, the African National Congress, she admitted, 'did not come to its position [on gay equality] naturally, or by osmosis'; 'the journey to the point of [constitutional] inclusion was neither smooth nor easy.'

In January 1998—nearly two years after the constitution was passed—the ANC's newly elected governing body, the National Executive Committee (NEC), held its first meeting, behind closed doors, in Johannesburg. This was the first NEC to be elected following the ANC's 1994 victory; it represented the face of the movement, not so much in resistance, but now firmly ensconsed in power. On the agenda was a motion to adopt a resolution, proposed by progressive members of the SA Communist Party, committing the ANC to an active struggle against all forms of discrimination suffered by gay and lesbian people, and to the support of gay adoptions and marriages.

Astonishingly, given the large number of issues facing the NEC, the debate on this resolution took up an entire afternoon of the two-day meeting. The 'gay issue' became a lightning-rod for other divisions within South Africa's ruling party, a battle between social conservatives who see themselves as 'African nationalists', and the leftists aligned to the SA Communist Party. Division, too, happened along racial and gender lines—only one African man, minister for the environment and tourism Pallo Jordan, was willing to speak on behalf of gay equality; others, such as Thabo Mbeki, chose to remain silent.

Many of those who opposed the resolution were vituperative in their homophobia, re-stating the canard, most forcefully articulated by President Robert Mugabe of Zimbabwe, that homosexuality was alien to African culture, and that the battle for gay equality was anathema to an African liberation movement. The debate plunged to its nadir when the ANC's KwaZulu/Natal leader, S'bu Ndebele, a former political prisoner with Nelson Mandela on Robben Island, declared that it was outrageous for the ANC to support homosexual activity. He reminded his comrades that anybody caught doing this on 'The Island' was automatically expelled from the party, before turning to his colleague, Dumisane Makhaye, a returned exile: 'And you, Comrade?' he asked, 'how did you deal with homosexuals in the [guerrilla] camps [of the ANC]?'

'We shot them,' responded Makhaye.

Such overblown invective is (one hopes) rhetorical rather than factual; nonetheless, it is representative of the homophobia of many in the ANC. In the face of it, the party decided not to adopt the resolution, and to go no further than reaffirming 'the constitutional position on the equality clause'.

Many might say that this reaffirmation is more than enough; it reinforces the supremacy of a human-rights agenda that includes gay equality. But the message is clear: the ANC's sponsorship of constitutional equality for homosexuals came from a liberal elite within the movement, and is by no means a widely-held position of the ruling party, which was not prepared to include, in its election platform, a position perceived to be unpopular. Even if gay equality does remain, for now, in the ANC's pantheon of human rights, many of the ANC's leaders, like their constituents, remain uncomfortable about it. And so, if there is going to be full equality for gays and lesbians in South Africa, it will come from the judicial system, in its application of the constitution, and not from the ANC lawmakers in parliament.

4

It could be any Saturday afternoon football match at any migrant hostel on any South African gold mine: the 22 young men kicking a ball around on a craggy, dusty field; the speckling of spectators on the bleachers; the tarts—who congregate at mines looking for business on weekends—smoking insouciantly at the sidelines. Except the tarts are men in drag; look closely at one of the teams, too, and you'll note that the players too are wearing make-up and frilly blouses instead of sports shirts.

It is a wintry day in 1995. The girls on the sports field belong to GLOGS, Gays and Lesbians of the Goldfields. Based in the mining town of Virginia, GLOGS fields its own team. Their style is burlesque rather than sportif, and everyone is having such a good time that the spectators elect to give the winnings, about $50, to the *moffies* even though they have lost hopelessly to the 'Illiterates', a team made up of migrant labourers from Mozambique.

GLOGS's only goal was scored by the team's star striker, Pule Hlohoangwane, the organization's founder and a middle manager in the human resources department of one of the mines. I met him in 1995, when he was a personnel officer at the Harmony Gold Mine (he has since been transferred). Virginia, like all provincial South African mining towns, still follows the rigid geography of apartheid: the verdant, spread-out white town; the densely-packed, dusty township in which local black people live; the single-sex hostels set up to accommodate the thousands of migrant miners who work underground.

Pule was one of the first black people to rent a flat in the white part of town, and it had become the gathering-point, a haven, for black gay miners. In his late twenties, he was out of the closet: all the black miners under his responsibility, and the white bosses to whom he is accountable, knew that he is gay. 'I'm a very gifted soccer player,' he told me. 'In fact I am the reason why Harmony Gold is in the second division and not the third. So I am respected.'

Here is his recruiting strategy: 'When I'm walking home from a match, the young men will often follow me and say, "Pule, you are so strong and yet you walk like a lady. Why is that?" Or they'll ask, "Pule, how come you are so clean and tidy, not like the other men?" So I tell them if they want to know more, they should come to the next meeting of GLOGS in my flat. We've got about 50 members now!'

Within the single-sex compounds of the mines, there has always been much homosexual activity: men, removed from their women and families and often sequestered in near-prison-like conditions for most of the year, turned to each other for affection and relief. In fact, mine-life is traditionally organised around the *mteto*, a same-sex marriage ceremony in which novices are wedded to veterans.

Both mine administrators and labour historians have tended to write off such activity as the 'circumstantial homosexuality' akin to that which happens in prisons, or in military forces. This explanation has passed into common lore. When gay-hate hit Swaziland in early 1997, for example, a journalist calling for tolerance wrote the following in the Swazi *Times on Sunday*: 'Homosexuality began way back when men from the southern part of Africa would flock [to] the South African gold mines in pursuit for better lifestyles. Women were prohibited there and the only alternative they had was to turn to their fellow men to appease their sex drive. Upon return, these men would not only bring wealth to their families, but also homosexual tendencies, and thus the ever growing number of gays.'

The truth, as always, is a little more complex. Look, for example, at Pule Hlohoangwane: the mere fact that he, a young, relatively educated black man, lived in a flat in the middle of the white section of a conservative Afrikaner town would be astonishing enough. But he shared this flat with his 'husband', a migrant miner from the neighboring country of Lesotho.

Polygamy is very much part of traditional Southern African society, and many migrant labourers leave their first wife back home, and take a second one in the cities where they work. Pule's man, however, decided to take up with another of his own sex—and the relationship prevailed even though neither of the two men live in the single-sex hostel. When the migrant miner's wife first arrived to visit him in Virginia, Pule told me, 'she looked around and saw how neat the flat was, and said, "There must be a woman here. Where is she?" My husband pointed to me. And now I am accepted within his family as the second wife, the junior wife. His senior wife often writes to me, and she sends her children to stay with us during the holidays. And one of the kids, the eighteen-year-old boy, is very close to me. I am teaching him English, and he stays with us. Sometimes, when my husband does not return home, the boy gets very angry. He says, "You are the wife. You have rights over my father. You must not let him abuse you!"'

Pule's story is, perhaps, the exception rather than the rule, but it demonstrates a fluidity to sexual identity not uncommon in African societies. Although most township gay culture is youth culture, it is entirely wrong to suppose that homosexual activity in the townships is a recent phenomenon, imported by white activists and 'dinge queens': indeed black gay men and lesbians protest that such an analysis robs them of the agency for their own desire. Despite the recent upsurge of a township gay scene, organized homosexual activity—if not lesbian and gay organization—has existed in black communities for decades. Ronald Louw, an academic from the University of Natal, is currently doing pathbreaking work on traditional Zulu gay marriages that took place in Mkhumbane, outside Durban, up to the late 1950s, and in Cape Town, there has always been an identifiable and public black gay subculture.

There is also some evidence of rural African homosocial activity that is entrenched in traditional hierarchy. The Lovedu Rain Queen in the Northern Province is a female hereditary leader who keeps as many as forty wives. Now that some female *sangomas*—traditional healers—are now coming out as lesbians, it is being hypothesized that the institution of the *sangoma* might have developed as a way for women-identified women to find space for themselves outside of the patriarchy; at the very least, it presents to Africans the model of a respected community member who defines herself independently of men.

In African military history too there is a venerable tradition of homoeroticism. Shaka, the great king of the nineteenth-century Zulu empire, used to encourage his male soldiers to engage in *hlobongo*, thigh-sex with each other. Zulu historians have always seen this as his way of channeling the sexual urges of adolescent boys; more recently, it has become seen as a means to create tight allegiances and loyalties—love relationships, in effect—among young soldiers.

Gay Africanism, a discourse only in the very early stages of development in South Africa, maintains that it is the censure of homosexuality that is a colonial import, brought to this continent by missionaries, and that there is irony to the fact that latter-day Africanists, like Robert Mugabe, have assimilated this Judeo-Christian biblical propaganda and reconstructed it as pre-colonial African purity. But whatever the roots of homophobia, it must be conceded that homosexuality is taboo in as many African cultures as it is in Western cultures. The sometimes-violent censure of homosexuality within black cultures, however, must not be mistaken for evidence of the non-existence of homosexuality: the very fact of censure indicates that it exists.

5

'When you're gay, you're beautiful, right?' asks Pastor Tsietsi Thandekiso at the height of his sermon. When his congregation, a hundred or so young black men and women, does not answer, he volleys back, 'Has somebody got a problem here?', his voice slightly inflected, Southern-Baptist camp. 'Because if you got a problem we'll lay our hands on you and solve the problem. But you'll still be gay. No one in this church is a mistake. If you got a problem it's in your head; it's not because you are gay."

Tsietsi Thandekiso, who died in early 1998 of AIDS-related illness, founded his Hope and Unity Metropolitan Community Church (HUMCC) in April 1994, literally days after the first democratic elections. It is now the most important institution in urban South African black gay life—in fact, the cast of 'After Nines', the black gay play at the Civic Theatre, was drawn from the HUMCC's choir. The reason for the church's popularity is precisely its use of the style and the liturgy of the African Independent churches, which, fusing charismatic Christianity with local African prayer-styles and singing, are immensely powerful in black communities.

The HUMCC meets on the seventh floor of the Harrison Reef Hotel in Hillbrow, a crumbling and crime-ridden inner-city ghetto that used to be the city's gay neighborhood when it was still all-white. Downstairs is The Skyline, Johannesburg's oldest gay bar, which has changed colour along with the neighborhood: black drag queens, rent boys, professionals and township kids gather there on Friday and Saturday nights. With a jukebox and tacky modular 1970s decor, it is one of those environments that is perfectly retro without having the slightest intention of being so.

But if the Harrison Reef rebounds with the gay anthems of the '70s on Saturday nights, it gives way to a very different aural interference on Sunday afternoons: the gospel-chanting, chair-slapping, Satan-slaying, yea-saying evangelism of the church; lurid faith superimposed upon a shabby hotel room converted into a place of worship with a wooden cross wrapped in tinfoil, a keyboard, some pink tablecloths and a bouquet of flowers.

The prayer, this wintry May Sunday in 1997, is particularly fervent, because today's service is the anniversary of the marriage of two young Soweto women, Pretty Robiana and Sbongile Malaza. The couple shuffle into the room to the rhythm of an African hymn, Pretty in a military-style navy suit with gold braiding and epaulets, Sbongile in a girlish pink appliquéd dress. There is no doubt as to the gender roles in their marriage: Pretty is as burly and aggressive as any African man is meant to be; Sbongile, still in the throes of adolescent acne, is almost a caricature of the traditional African wife: she does not look you in the eye, she answers in whispers. They call each other 'husband' and 'wife'.

They grew up on the same street in Emdeni, one of Soweto's rougher neighborhoods. Sbongile is nineteen, and in her final year of high school; she has been raised by her grandparents, a domestic worker and a retired security guard. Pretty is 24 and unemployed, the daughter of a single parent, a nursing sister; she is of the 'GLOW generation', the first generation of black kids to have come out in the townships. Ostracized from her family's church because she refused to wear the women's uniform and came instead in jacket and tie, Pretty found out about the HUMCC through a magazine article. She joined the church, and decided that she wished to marry her sweetheart.

Although gay South Africans have constitutional equality, statutes that criminalize homosexuality or discriminate against gay peoples are still on the books; in its lobbying process, the NGCLE has decided to leave the marriage battle till last, fearing a backlash from an extremely conservative society that has voted the ANC in without really coming to terms with the radical implications of its social agenda.

Nonetheless, Thandekiso agreed to marry Pretty and Sbongile before God. The two were already ostracized from their families; Sbongile's grandmother, who had worked for a white lesbian couple, told the girl that it was 'Satanic' and 'un-African'. When Sbongile's grandfather turned a gun on Pretty and assaulted both of them, the young couple fled the township, spending some time in a battered women's shelter. Later, meeting her on the street, the old man fired three shots at his granddaughter's 'husband', narrowly missing her head.

Laying charges of attempted murder with the police, Pretty met with an unexpected response. The station commander, a woman, told her: 'The constitution is here now. You people have decided you want to lead this life and it comforts you, so let us call the family together and discuss it and make peace.' She convened a meeting with both families and the chairman of the local street committee who said, according to Pretty: 'This is a surprise to me. I have never seen this before, but there is nothing I can do about it.' After the meeting the station commander gave Pretty a document to sign to say that she was responsible for Sbongile, and told Sbongile's family that there was nothing illegal about the women's union.

Now that marriage has the official stamp of the station commander, the Malaza family has changed its tune: they want Pretty to pay them *lobola*, the bride-price that is at the root of African marital union. It is a startling example of how people change their ideologies to fit in with new hegemonies.

Nonetheless, the only member from either family to attend the anniversary service was one of Sbongile's sisters: 'We accept our sister,' she said in a brief and shy speech to the church, 'despite what she is.' The night before, Pretty and Sbongile held a party at the Harrison Reef, to which hundreds came: not only fellow-congregants, but neighbors from Soweto—where the couple rent a room in a yard—and even one of Sbongile's teachers, who made a speech and gave a gift.

Their story offers all the paradoxes of contemporary gay African life. 'Homophobia in the townships is superficial,' said Thandekiso before his death. 'We are living through a time where it's actually not such a big deal to be gay. Go to the township, and you will see in almost every school a group of children who are gay. There are gays on the streets, gays in the taverns. It's become a part of life.'

When I visited the HUMCC in 1996, at the height of Robert Mugabe's homophobia, I met two young Zimbabweans in the church. One, Remington Ncube, was a migrant miner working in the Johannesburg area. A deeply religious man, he had been an altar-server in his Catholic church; when his family discovered he was homosexual, he was chased out of home and church. 'I had to leave Bulawayo,' he says, 'and there was only one place to go. It is known all over the continent that Johannesburg is the freest place for black gays...'

Thoko Ndlovu comes from Bulawayo too. 'Why am I in Johannesburg?' she asked. 'Well, I picked up one of those pop black magazines in Bulawayo one day, and there was an article about all this terrible sinful activity in Jo'burg. And I said, 'Get me on the next bus! I'm going there!''

Zimbabwe and South Africa are separated by nothing more than the Limpopo river. Zimbabweans and South Africans are the same people, with similar histories and interconnected economies. How is it that their cultures have adopted so different an approach to the same issue? There are many possible explanations: the porous and hybrid nature of urban South African life, where essentialist patriarchy no longer holds much truck; the role of popular culture in South Africa, where gay issues and subjects have become immensely popular on the TV talkshow; the influence, particularly, of American ideas and styles in the country.

A lot has to do, too, with the moral authority that Nelson Mandela and the ANC carry. Shortly after the 1994 elections, GLOW organizer Polly Motene, who lives in Soweto, told me that 'attitudes have changed among those who read the newspapers, because there has been more publicity about gay people.' Motene's father, for example, is a local ANC activist, 'and he was astonished when he heard about how the ANC supports gay people.' But Motene also offered a caution: 'Most Sowetans haven't heard a thing about the gay clause in the constitution. For them, homosexuality remains a white thing, and we black gays are just freaks, *stabane* with two organs.'

Also shortly after those first elections, Beverly Ditsie, a trendy young black lesbian who writes a column in *Outright*, the gay magazine, explained the downside of ANC support for gay causes: 'Right now there is quite a lot of dissatisfaction on the ground with the government, because it is perceived to be going out of its way to reconcile with whites rather than looking after its own people. And so if you tell people that Mandela supports gay rights, they'll either get angry with you and tell you that you are lying, or they'll just say, "Oh there he goes, looking after everyone except for us again," because of course gayness for them is a white thing, so it's further proof that he is ignoring his own constituency in favour of whites.'

But while she offered a bleak picture of the persistent homophobia in township society, Ditsie did acknowledge that things had changed since 1990, when, as one of the public spokespeople of that first gay march, she found herself the victim of violent and sustained gay-bashing in her native Soweto after appearing on television. More recently, she has participated in a TV experiment called 'Livewire'; six young people from wildly differing backgrounds were thrown together in a commune and videotaped for a few months in a rather spurious sort of guinea-pig trial for integration in South Africa. The show attracted much attention, not least because Ditsie—the only black woman in the commune—made no bones about her sexuality.

'I found,' she says, 'that attitudes began to change towards me in Soweto. People began to see me as their representative on the show, because I was black, because I was strong, because I knew what I wanted.' She went onto a radio call-in show to talk about the experience, 'and people would phone in and say, "You really spoke well for us." I'd ask, "who is 'us'? The answer would sometimes be black people, sometimes women, sometimes gay people. It all become one thing, one struggle...'

6

In the early 1990s, in the sleepy township of KwaThema, east of Johannesburg, a vibrant gay subculture developed because an older woman, Thoko Khumalo, had a gay nephew and decided to open her home to his friends. Ma Thoko's place, a standard four-room apartheid-built matchbox, became a tavern and a haven for the township's gay kids, particularly for those who had been turfed out of their own homes. In townships, space is at a premium: families often sleep eight to a room, and children only leave home when they marry. Unlike in middle-class communities, there is simply no space to be gay. Ma Thoko proved that gay subculture grows around space; the fact that she was a person of standing in the community (she died in 1994) meant that if she declared herself to be 'Mama GLOW', her wards would be afforded a fair deal of respect.

In 1990, at a party at Ma Thoko's, as the township's gay kids danced and socialized and neighbors popped in for a drink and a chat, I met a sixteen-year-old schoolgirl from the township, Phumi Mthethwa. Now, seven years later, Phumi is one of the leaders of the South African gay movement—an executive member of the NCGLE, she went with Simon Nkoli and Sir Ian McKellen to discuss the issue of homosexuality with Nelson Mandela in 1995. A business student and a paralegal, she is petite, suave and soft-spokenly articulate (she chooses to dress in beautifully tailored men's suits): I will wager that, before she is 40, she will represent gay men and lesbians in parliament.

On a Friday evening in May 1997, I accompanied Phumi to Ratanda, a hardscrabble alcoholic little township in the cornfields south of Johannesburg, serving the farming centre of Heidelberg. Phumi was to be a judge in the 'Mr and Miss Gay Ratanda 1997', organized by the Ratanda Gay and Lesbian Individuals, a group of about twenty young men and women that had grown around another Ma Thoko-type personality, Flatta Mosele, a flamboyant 24-year-old woman who ran a local community arts centre and had fashioned herself as the township's 'Mama Gay'.

None of Ratanda crowd had heard of the constitution, let alone that it guaranteed them equality. Except for Flatta: 'I know,' she said, 'the constitution says everyone has the right to live, and that you can do anything you want and you have the right to be happy. So I just turn that around for me, and I say it must mean that I have the right to be a lez.' She looked surprised and somewhat incredulous, when Phumi and I told her that the constitution actually explicitly protects her 'right to be a lez'.

We met her backstage in a community hall where the show took place. The 'Mr Gays' could pass; tough-looking little sweethearts in gangster-wear, practising their swaggers backstage and spinning, menacingly, on the heels of their soft-leather shoes. The 'Miss Gays', small-town girls, had neither the attitude nor the resources of big-city snap-queens: they represented that singular township androgyny borne of scant resources and much imagination, nodding at gender inversion and conjuring fantasy with no more than a frilly blouse, a pair of palazzos, low-heeled pumps, straightened hair, a little lipstick. Nobody had shown up to watch them, but no matter. There was a grim optimism to their lives, spiked with ebullience whenever the DJ plays the Fugees' 'Killing Me Softly'.

Times are hard in Ratanda. Isaac Lebona, a domestic servant, was raped by boys who wanted to prove that they could do it; they sliced his right eye out. Japie Tshabalala, a high-school student, has been playing netball since he was six, but his dreams had been shattered: he was dropped from the Heidelberg town-wide team when it was discovered he was a boy. The gay men see them-selves as 'girls' who participate in the sexual commerce of the township by being *skesanas*—queens—who go after *injongas*, straight-acting homosexual men who play along with the charade that their 'wives' are real women.

Sex is the central, defining aspect of their identity: 'We gays are every-where now in Ratanda,' said Stephen Tsoari, who leads the group with Flatta. 'Everyone knows us. We spread the word by proposing to men in taverns. They go with us, and they see how nice it is to fuck us, then we show them what we really are and they become gay too.'

Do they practise safer sex? 'I will ask my man to wear a condom,' said Isaac. 'But if he does not, I will let him fuck me anyway. I am too scared that if I refuse him he will beat me.'

They were all 'out' and they had, they insisted, no problems with the community. Phumi Mthethwa was unconvinced: 'I know this syndrome. It's just that they have made this big thing of being open, so they need to pretend everything is okay. But it isn't, I can see. We've got a lot of work to do.'

Where black gay communities have cohered in townships, it has always been around characters like Ma Thoko Khumalo, Pule Hlohoangwane or, in the case of budding Ratanda, Flatta Mosele. As soon as these characters are no longer around, though, the subculture collapses—as it did in kwaThema once Ma Thoko died.

In Umtata, the capital of the formerly-independent homeland of the Transkei (birthplace of both Nelson Mandela and Thabo Mbeki), an official in the department of health named Vera Vimbela formed Lesbians and Gays in the Transkei (LEGIT) in the early 1990s. She tells the story of how she had been stripped naked in her rural village after having proposed, as a young woman, to another girl: when it was discovered she was not *stabane*, a hermaphrodite, and thus didn't have male organs to explain her behaviour, she was thrashed and hounded out of the community. A huge, imposing bulldyke who zoomed around town on a serious motorbike, she attracted a coterie of gay men around her. Now she is undergoing a sex change and has found the Lord; LEGIT has collapsed.

Similarly, in Soweto in the early '90s, a vibrant community developed around an older gay man, Junior, and then fell apart once he lost interest in it after some arcane romantic intrigue. Junior, in his fifties, still runs a catering company that employs gay men. In 1991, to help augment his employees' income and to provide some sort of social space, Junior also set up a 'stokvel', or revolving credit union, called the Jikaleza Boys. It worked like this: the members would take turns to hold monthly parties where they would keep the takings from the bar. While the Jikaleza Boys was up and running, there was at least one huge gay party a month in Soweto.

I once accompanied Junior's catering company on a job, to cater for a family that had just had a death, in a relatively well-to-do household in the Phiri section of Soweto. In the kitchen, the queens ruled: in demi-drag, they established a hive of activity, with all the requisite drama, attitude, and—it must be said—efficiency.

Through the swinging doors into the living room, though, one entered the entirely different world of a stolidly bourgeois township living room, with tea-drinking aunties sitting on heavy dark-wood over-upholstered furniture covered in plastic dust-cloth. When one of the aunties ventured into the kitchen, I struck up a conversation with her. What did she think of gay people, I asked her? 'Oh no,' she responded. 'We don't have that thing here.'

7

A spring Sunday evening in 1997: the sounds of a gospel band drift out across Sunnyside, a highrise suburb of Pretoria, South Africa's capital city and the heart of Afrikaner conservatism. Inside, the congregation of Deo Gloria is at prayer. A burly man with a beautiful baritone is marshalling the band through Afrikaans hymns with all the bellicose discipline of a sergeant-major. He is, in fact, an officer in the South African National Defence Force. Pretoria is a company town: most of the Deo Gloria congregants work, in one way or another, for the government: they are in the army, in the civil service, in the education system. They have the neat, buttoned-down and unstylish appearance that characterizes Pretoria. The older women wear the kind of crimplene two-piece skirt-suits that all conservative Afrikaans women wear to church; the older men have the blousoned and blow-dried look of queens of another era. Most of the men have moustaches; the younger women are in pants, brush-cuts, and lumberjack shirts. Several are with children.

Given the city's conservatism, perhaps it is unsurprising that church plays such a central role in gay life. The charismatic Deo Gloria congregation broke away from the Reform Church of Equals in Christ, which follows the liturgy of the mainstream Calvinist church to which most Afrikaners belong. The Reform Church has over 400 weekly congregants, mostly male and all white. Because of its young, willowy strawberry-blonde pastor, Sue Welman, about half of the congregants at Deo Gloria are women, and it has a smattering of black members too.

Sue Welman is, in fact, a licensed marriage officer: she earns her keep marrying heterosexual couples. She has married several couples in her congregation too, although she does not give them an official marriage license: 'As soon as the law changes,' she told me, 'they can come back and get the stamp from me.' The marriage of one of her lesbian couples was broadcast on a magazine programme on national television.

Despite the fact that both Deo Gloria and Tsietsi Thandekiso's HUMCC are charismatic, Pentecostal churches, they have little to do with each other. Welman's approach is very different from Thandekiso's, perhaps because of their different congregations. While the black pastor from Hillbrow built his congregation around being openly, assertively gay, articulating an explicitly gay theology in his sermons, you will not hear the word 'gay' at Deo Gloria—the full name of which is, in fact, the Deo Gloria Family Church. Certainly, Welman will tell anecdotes in her sermons that involve her lover Diane, and some couples will pray arm-in-arm; apart from that, though, a visitor would discern little outward evidence that this is a homosexual congregation.

In fact, there is much dissent in the church about the public role Welman now plays (she is frequently on television, specifically as a gay Christian voice to counter the African Christian Democratic Party's campaign against the equality clause in the constitution) and about whether the church should participate in Pride marches. One of the people who does not like her public profile is Hentie, the army officer: 'I disapprove of it,' he says, 'because we are here to pray, not to make politics.' He is closeted both in the military and with his family: 'I know my mother has seen Sue on the television, but she's never said anything to me about it. I think she is just so happy I'm back in church that she doesn't ask any other questions.'

After the service, I accompany a group of church regulars back to the home of Charles Steenkamp, a caterer who seems to play the role of the congregation's clucking can-do auntie. About twelve of us sit in a circle: 'Has life become any easier for you since the ANC came to power?' I ask. The answer is a resounding negative. But what about the constitution and its protection of gay rights? Sue Welman tells of how, when one of their congregants died of AIDS, the insurance company paid his lover out upon seeing the 'Holy Union' certificate that she had issued them when they were married in the church. The others don't think there has been any change at all.

I ask whether the church is actively trying to recruit black people to the church and Hentie explodes. 'Let's face it. In South Africa, the white man is under threat. We cannot get jobs, we cannot get promotions because of this affirmative action rubbish. Now this church is our sanctuary. It's the place where we pray! It's our own cultural space! Why *should* we have affirmative action here too?'

It is a fascinating insight into white South African gay consciousness. The objective reality is that the African National Congress has, legally at least, liberated gay South Africans, black and white alike. But as ever in race-obsessed South Africa, race identification overpowers everything else—class, gender and sexuality. People like Hentie have no sense of being empowered, by the new government, as gay people, because they feel so profoundly *disempowered* as white people. Hentie, an out-and-out racist, might articulate this more openly, but by failing to see how the new constitution gives them recourse to the law they never previously had, the others assent, silently, to his point of view.

Pretoria is filled with paradoxes. Despite its conservatism, it boasts a much larger gay scene than bigger, more liberal cities like Johannesburg. Lourens Smit, a gay Afrikaans man who moved to Pretoria from the small town of Lichtenburg, explains: 'You have to remember that Afrikaners come from very conservative Calvinist backgrounds. And most of us also come from the small towns. So when we come out of the closet, we really *break* from our home-cultures. We come to Pretoria and make new lives for ourselves. We've got nothing to lose. We make new families and new homes. That's why Pretoria has such a lively life, compared to a much bigger city like Jo'burg.'

The life might be lively, but the New South African spirit has not yet hit Pretoria. When Gays and Lesbians of Pretoria (GLO-P) wanted to advertise its advice hotline on municipal buses with a slogan, 'Gay is Okay, but call us anyway,' the city council turned it down. 'We were told,' says GLO-P coordinator Dawie Nel, 'that the council doesn't accept advertisements that are religious, political or offensive. Since the hotline clearly isn't religious or political, I can only assume the council finds it offensive.' GLO-P has lodged a complaint with the Human Rights Commission, and intends using the constitution to sue the council.

Perhaps not surprisingly, too, the life in Pretoria is very white. Walk through Steamers, the throbbing gay bar that spills over three floors, on a Saturday night, and you'll be hard pressed to see a black face in the crowd of thousands. Pretoria has large black townships; why, then, are there no black people at Steamers? 'We really try to encourage black people to come here,' said Christo, the manager, to me, in 1997. 'But we're dealing with the legacy of the past. Black people just aren't comfortable enough yet...'

As at Deo Gloria, the atmosphere in Steamers is *gemutlisch;* there is no heavy cruising, and the mixed male and female crowd are well-dressed and well-behaved, conducting themselves as if at a high-school dance or a small-town social. Downstairs on Thursday nights there is, quite incongruously, a raunchy strip show. Upstairs, equally incongruously, three regulars sit over their brandy-and-cokes. With their paunches, their long beards and their khaki safari-suits, they look as if they have just walked off the set of a Boer War movie.

Their names are Ben, Fanie and Gert. They are security guards. They have their own theory as to why the Pretoria scene is so vibrant: 'It's because it's white,' says Fanie. 'Why do you think all the gay people come rushing up here from Jo'burg every weekend? It's because they don't want to mix with *kaffirs* and they know they won't find any here.'

These three gay men, clearly out of kilter with both the style and the politics of the rest of the bar, are part of the small extreme who boycotted the 1994 election and even view the leader of the right wing in parliament, General Constant Viljoen, as a 'traitor to the Afrikaner people'.

They do not believe for a moment that the ANC is behind gay equality. 'It's just a vote-catching ploy,' says Ben, and, in a bizarre twist of ethnic pride, they claim that homosexuality is a solely white preserve: 'Oh come on,' scoffs Ben, 'there's no such thing as a black gay. Gay is a white thing. If a black says he's gay he's only doing it to get money.'

Strange how circles complete themselves: Ben, like those 'Africanists' who see homosexuality as a colonial depredation sullying the purity of the African continent, views sexuality in entirely racial terms. South Africa under a black government, he says, will go 'down the tubes, just like the rest of this continent, where there is no infrastructure at all—no roads, no bridges, no telephones, no gay clubs, no electricity; nothing!'

8

Thirty kilometres south of Johannesburg is Ennerdale, one of the city's 'coloured' townships. South Africa's two-million strong 'coloured' community, largely based in the Cape Province, has always been more accommodating of homosexuality, and the annual Coon Carnival—Cape Town's Mardi Gras— has long been led by a *moffie* (the word, in fact, originates in the 'coloured' community, where it specifically means 'transvestite'). Perhaps this tolerance is because of the community's hybrid, creole nature; perhaps because the strong influence of Muslim culture (which comes from Malay slaves) has always tacitly encouraged homosexuality as something preferable to heterosexual adultery.

In September 1995, the working-class citizens of Ennerdale found banners festooned all over their township: 'MISS GAY TRANSVAAL COMPETITION. CLUB STEPPING OUT. SATURDAY NITE!' Gay 'coloureds' have little to do with black gay people. And so, in the build-up to the Miss Glow drag finals, which were to take place the night before the Pride Parade, it was not surprising to find an entirely separate 'coloured' event. The girls paced their way through crudely choreographed numbers (including a Roman toga scene replete with a gladiator in shabby costume-hire), they studiously counted the beats, turning mechanically in unison; a Las Vegas extravaganza with all the self-conscious charm of a school concert. The deejay's vinyl kept on scratching, the emcee's mike was filled with static, and the crowd just loved every minute of it.

Certainly, each queen brought her gay fan club, but Stepping Out was a straight club; the gathering place of the working-class community in which it is situated. The local gangsters squatted on the floor laughing embarrassedly and pretending not to look, while the local bottle-store owner's wife, standing behind them, effused: 'God I love these *moffies!* The world needs more *moffies*. Gentle—and sweet! But when they need to, they can put their tits on the table and fight! Oh god I love these *moffies*.'

Excusing herself ('I must go backstage and give little Nadia a good-luck kiss'), she introduced me to her husband, the bottle-store owner: pot-bellied and in a maroon jersey, wielding a home videocam as if he were the proud uncle at a family wedding. How did he feel about the *moffies*? '*Ag*, I'm used to it by now.'

Outside the club there were the usual drunken Saturday-night brawls; inside, a friendly ease, even in the tiny backstage dressing-room, where the girls, clustered around a mirror, air-kissed each other good luck, helped each other out with the finishing touches of make-up, and buttoned each other's more inaccessible hooks.

Earlier, getting themselves ready, the girls talked about race. Why did the coloured and the black drag scenes have so little to do with each other? 'We want to become part of GLOW,' one says, 'but you know, it's so... nationalized.'

Another laughs apologetically. 'That's the coloured word for black,' she says. 'This New South Africa!' Sure enough: at the Miss GLOW finals a few weeks later, there was almost a brawl backstage when the winner, a black queen named Thabo resplendent in an emerald ballgown, was announced. 'That cow!' the ringleader of the 'coloured' contestants shrieks. 'She won last year, in the very same dress! We're just not bloody black enough to be queens, are we?'

Christopher, the emcee at the Club Stepping Out competition (who doubles as a primary-school teacher during the week), explained that 'in the old days whites liked coloured men. But now with the New South Africa they're all running after blacks.' Meanwhile, coloured gays are staying away from blacks, Christopher adds, 'because there's this idea that they sleep around a lot more and so it's easier to pick up the virus from them. It's a problem, this racism...'

Indeed. Given the pathologies of South African society—the logical consequences of decades of enforced racial separation—it would be unrealistic to expect instant integration within gay communities. In cities like Johannesburg and Cape Town there are, of course, a smattering of mixed-race couples; there is also a brisk trade of sexual commerce between younger black and older white men. And there is the anything-goes Gotham City in Hillbrow, a mixed gay sex club where desire seems to overpower race.

At Angels, Cape Town's major gay club until it closed in the mid-1990s, a 'straight' downstairs and a 'gay' upstairs encouraged coloured men to fraternize the club under cover and move upstairs without very much notice. But Cape Town's enormous 'coloured' gay scene is concentrated, not in the city, but in clubs out on the Cape Flats where most 'coloured' people live. Perhaps one of the most vibrant black gay organizations in the country has been ABIGALE— the Association of Bisexuals, Gays and Lesbians in Cape Town. Formed by a 'coloured' lesbian couple, Medi Achmat and Thereza Raizenberg, it managed, for many years, to bring black and coloured gay people together in Cape Town: its most successful activism, in fact, was the picketing of a large gay club in Cape Town, Strawbs, that discriminated against black patrons.

By the end of the decade, though, ABIGALE had disintegrated—evidently because of conflict between the black and the coloured members. In Pretoria, a short-lived attempt to form a union between the white members of GLO-P and a black group from Atteridgeville, one of the city's townships, led to an acrimonious split: the Atteridgeville group, called Actors, claimed they were the victims of racism; GLO-P co-ordinator Dawie Nel explains that 'there was a conflict of interest. They wanted a social club, and we were more interested in providing services, like a mental health clinic and a hotline, to the community.'

In Johannesburg, Bev Ditsie led a group of black lesbians out of GLOW to form Nkateko ('success' in Tsonga), a short-lived 'black lesbian empowerment group', because they felt that white men and women were dominating the organization. Their opening event was a Miss Sappho competition, which took place at Club Chameleon, a short-lived lesbian venue in Johannesburg, in mid-1997. On a Saturday evening, about 50 young black women gathered: students, young professionals, stylish township kids. The light was blue, the sound R&B.

Why a beauty pageant for a black lesbian empowerment group? Tebogo, Bev's younger sister, explained that 'our biggest problem among lesbians is that our butches feel they need to behave like real men, and in our African culture this means beating up their girlfriends and of course—just like any "real" African man—practising polygamy and having as many "wives" as they choose.'

And so, said Bev, 'we're trying to reach the middle ground. The whole idea behind it is to show that you don't need to be just butch or just femme to be a lesbian. You can be both.'

The Miss Sappho hopefuls were compact and shy, jaw-achingly beautiful with their fashion dreads and high cheekbones. Their butch-wear was sophisticated, meticulous in detail: they dragged like gangsters did in another era. In femme-wear some faltered endearingly. During the question session, Zanele, a magnificent femme, was asked by the emcee: 'What do you think of interracial relationships?' A white woman, one of only three or four in the audience, rushed up and kissed her. Zanele beams, somewhat defiantly. 'I think that if you love someone, you make your own world with them, doesn't matter about colour.'

Zanele was crowned first princess, I like to think, not only because of perfect bone structure and musculature, but because of the way she answered that question.

9

Veliswa is an icon of the changing South Africa: 32 years old, she is the first black female attorney at one of South Africa's largest and most venerable corporate law firms. She and her lover, Lulama, a medical student, are part of a burgeoning gay buppie scene in Johannesburg: their friends are doctors, professionals, artists, high-level bureaucrats.

Like most in South Africa's new black elite, Veliswa comes from humble beginnings: her father is a retired policeman in the rural Transkei. Because of her family's conservatism and because of the difficulties of simply being a black woman in her professional environment, she is not out of the closet. But, she insists, 'I am not a victim. That equality clause in the constitution is important to me. I'm aware of it and I know its value. I'll use it if I need to.'

For Veliswa, being free in post-apartheid South Africa is 'all rolled up in one. Under apartheid, there were so many ways I wasn't recognized: as a black person, as a woman, as a lesbian, even as a South African, because coming from the Transkei I wasn't even allowed South African identity papers. But now my country says the highest law is the constitution, so it can't discriminate against me on any of the above grounds. Finally, I feel like I can participate in my society. I used to look on with detachment and anger, but I wouldn't do anything. Now, I suddenly have opinions! If I don't like something, I say so! I can feel it happening. I'm becoming a full citizen.'

Activists feel that this sense of empowerment, of liberation, has paradoxically been something of a death-knell for the gay and lesbian movement. 'There's general euphoria,' says Nomfundo Luphondwana, a lesbian activist, 'that "We're free! We're in the constitution! So let's party!" This results in political apathy.' She says that the NCGLE 'gets daily calls from gay people asking, "Do you know someone who can marry us?" They don't even know that they're not allowed to get married yet! They think they're free and they're not!'

The NCGLE is somewhat responsible for this state of affairs. Its strategic approach, in getting the equality clause passed, was to work the backrooms of power; to slip the clause in without attracting much notice. To use the equality clause as an issue around which to mount a mass mobilization campaign would have thus been seriously counterproductive. Most gay people want marriage— a mass campaign would have inevitably focused on this demand and could have caused the backlash that the coalition justly feared.

'Our strategy,' explains Kevan Botha, 'is to have everything in place, so that gay marriage is a de facto part of South African life, even if it isn't called that. Then, when we lobby for marriage itself, we can avoid the backlash by saying, "Look, it's already there! What's the fuss?"' Strategically, this makes sense; the fallout, though, is a gay community that wants marriage now and believes it is entitled to it, and is thus somewhat alienated from national gay leadership.

It remains a conundrum why, at this moment of constitutional gay liberation, there has not been an efflorescence of gay political and cultural activity in South Africa, particularly in the black community. GLOW, the standard-bearer of gay black aspirations for nearly a decade, has collapsed and, but for the Skyline and the HUMCC, there is no formal black gay subculture in Johannesburg. White gay subculture has the usual institutions: bars, sports groups, churches, publications, a weekly radio show, a burgeoning gay sex industry— pornography was banned under apartheid, and the growth of a sex industry is, in fact, the single most visible change in urban white gay life. Perhaps the reason why there is not a flourishing gay political movement is because of 'liberation apathy'. But it also has to do with something else: in Western society, gay people put themselves into gay worlds; their homosexuality becomes their dominant identity. Gay Africans, like straight Africans, do not leave their home cultures unless they are forced to; they find, rather, ways of reconciling their differences with the values of their home-communities.

This has profound political implications for the gay and lesbian movement in South Africa. Unlike in Western Europe or North America, the call for gay equality does not have the status of the special pleading of an identifiable political minority. Gay rights in South Africa are not ghetto rights. They are, rather, general human rights, indivisible from the rights to education, housing, freedom, non-discrimination, etc. They are abstract notions that apply to all rather than concrete values that can be pinned to one particular group of people, given to them only if they behave well or wield political clout ('the gay vote'), as in the United States, and snatched away from them with equal ease. There is the tantalizing possibility that South Africa, with its fusion of individualist Western rights-politics and African communal consciousness, might show the world a far smoother way of integrating gay people into society, even if this is at the cost of the kind of robust gay subculture that dominates cities like New York and San Francisco.

There are reasons, though, why precisely such a robust, combative subculture might be necessary. For as long as Nelson Mandela led the ANC, he— together with people like Desmond Tutu, of the same generation—remained the moral authority of our society. Now that his generation has retired, there is certainly going to be a splintering of the ANC's monolithic hegemony. As was so clearly evidenced by that 1998 NEC meeting, one split could well be along 'moral' lines. There is already, within the ANC, much quiet discomfort about South Africa's very liberal abortion laws, its lax censorship regulations, its abolition of the death penalty and its acceptance of homosexuality. Christians and Africanists are already beginning to unite behind a Mugabe-type banner against the liberal, Westernized atheists who are the ANC's elite; even the constitution can be changed with a two-thirds majority. There is thus an argument for gay civil society to mobilize itself and lobby vociferously for the setting into place of as much legislative reform—and as much judicial precedent—as possible while the window of tolerance remains open.

'I'm in the constitution!' I went to that drag queen after her performance at the Pride Parade, to find out what, exactly, her new empowerment meant. She was reeking of cheap booze, but still astonishingly articulate: 'My darling, it means sweet motherfucking nothing at all. You can rape me, rob me, what am I going to do when you attack me? Wave the constitution in your face? I'm just a nobody black queen.' She paused, and her face lost its mask of both bravado and bitterness. 'But you know what? Ever since I heard about that constitution, I feel free inside.'

The astonishing possibility of the South African constitution is that its stand on gay equality has the potential of making all South Africans, gay or straight, feel this way. Albie Sachs—one of the drafters of the South African constitution and the strongest adherent for the inclusion of gay equality— explained to the September 1999 ILGA Gala Banquet that, given South Africa's diversity, 'if we become intolerant, we don't stand a chance. The only way this country can survice is by acknowledging people for who they are.' The gay equality clause in the constitution 'wasn't just for gays; it was for all of us.'

The emergence of gay identities in Southeast Asia[1]

Dennis Altman

The genesis of this chapter was my involvement in various networks of AIDS activists from Asia and the Pacific, beginning around 1989.[2] Growing out of this I developed a small research project looking at the 'emergence of gay identities and communities in archipelago Southeast Asia', and was able to do limited field work in the Philippines, Indonesia and Malaysia. Unfortunately several attempts to develop collaborative research with local gay groups and researchers were not very successful, though I have had a fair amount of informal contact with most of the groups I discuss.

I came to this research as a privileged white Australian gay intellectual, with access to considerable resources (intellectual, economic, political). But I am also very dependent on those I am researching, who have far greater cultural and linguistic knowledge than I possess, and whose explanations of phenomena reflect as much as mine a particular set of emotional and intellectual positions. In this situation I see myself as co-researcher, ultimately dependent on both the goodwill and self-interest of my informants.

The anthropologist can usually assume his or her 'otherness' from the subject of study. In my interactions with Southeast Asian gay men this assumption fails to hold up. My research builds on social interactions with people in a variety of settings ranging from sitting on the beach in Bali to meetings in air-conditioned halls at AIDS conferences in New Delhi and Chiang Mai and is predicated on my sharing a certain common ground—sexual, social, political—with those of whom I speak. I would argue that the best understandings of the gay worlds have come out of this way of work—see, for example, Edmund White's account of pre-AIDS gay America, *States of Desire*[3]—but both academically and ethically this sort of 'participant observation' poses dilemmas.

In researching the development of 'Asian' (specifically archipelago Southeast Asian) gay worlds I am both outsider and insider: indeed, I have had the experience of meeting Asian men, engaged in gay political work, who have been influenced by my own writings. Thus I am engaging with men where there is a complex power dynamic at work: I represent the power, prestige and wealth of the West, but because we are meeting on a terrain of shared sexuality where mutual desire is an acknowledged possibility, and where I depend on their goodwill, the power dynamics are not simply unidimensional. My relations with 'Asian' 'lesbians' reflect a greater distance, and so far I have not been able to make more than very superficial contacts (not least because of the ways in which international AIDS politics have opened up space for homosexual men but not women). I have constantly to balance what I seem to be seeing against an awareness that my 'informants' are both telling stories for which I am the intended audience—and, often, which fit their desires to see themselves as part of a 'modern' gay world.

These relationships are further complicated by two contradictory trends. On the one hand some Asian gay men, by stressing a universal gay identity, underline a similarity with Westerners. Against this, the desire to assert an 'Asian' identity, not unlike the rhetoric of the 'Asian way' adopted by authoritarian regimes such as those of China, Indonesia and Malaysia, may undermine this assumed solidarity. Moreover the ubiquity of Western rhetoric means that many of the informants use the language of the West to describe a rather different reality. For example the *Gay Men's Exchange*, a 'zine' (i.e. four-page roneoed newsletter) produced in Manila, includes a two page 'Gay Man's Guide to Coming Out' reproduced from a popular American publication.[4] The sort of language of this and other Western publications helps determine not only the language used in groups but also who feels comfortable in discussions and how they explain their own feelings to themselves. Some years ago in Manila I watched the film *Victor/Victoria* on local television. Although it is ostensibly set in Paris in the 1930s its characters speak of 'coming out' as 'gay'. Such politically correct historical anachronisms presumably send messages to the large audience who would have seen the film on prime-time television.

Gradually Western lesbian/gay theorists and activists are beginning to perceive the problems of claiming a universality for an identity which developed out of certain historical specificities. In his introduction to a recent book on 'queer theory', Michael Warner wrote:

> In the middle ground between the localism of 'discourse' and the generality of the subject is the problem of international—or otherwise translocal—sexual politics. As gay activists from non-Western contexts become more and more involved in setting agendas, and as the rights discourse of internationalism is extended to more and more cultural contexts, Anglo-American queer theorists will have to be more alert to the globalizing—and localizing—tendencies of our theoretical languages.[5]

Interestingly none of the contributors to this particular book take up this challenge—despite its title, *Fear of a Queer Planet*. American 'queer theory' remains as relentlessly Atlantic-centric in its view of the world as the mainstream culture it critiques. Equally interesting is the apparent lack of interest in 'queer' theory in most of the non-Western world, and the continued usage by emerging movements of the terminology 'lesbian' and 'gay'.

Sex/gender/sexuality in 'gay' Asia

In late June 1994 there was a very large demonstration in New York City to commemorate the 25th anniversary of Stonewall, the riots at a New York bar claimed as the birthplace of the modern gay/lesbian movement. The organizers went to some trouble to invite groups from the rest of the world—including the developing world—to participate, obviously believing that the events being celebrated were of universal relevance.[6] In ways which would shock many anthropologists a claim to the universality of 'gay' and 'lesbian' identities is emerging in the rhetoric of groups such as (to speak only of Asia) Bombay Dost, OCCUR in Japan, Ten Percent in Hong Kong, Pink Triangle in Malaysia, the Library Foundation in the Philippines and a number of lesbian groups such as Anjaree in Thailand.[7]

It could be objected that these groups represent only a very small part of the homosexual populations of these countries, and that their use of language and symbols derived from overseas means they will be unable to mobilize significant numbers within their own societies. But twenty years ago the gay movements of North America, Australasia and Western Europe similarly spoke for very few, and their growth was unpredictably rapid. Of course this happened where largely American symbols could be made relevant to local conditions (as with Sydney's Gay & Lesbian Mardi Gras, which has become a uniquely Australian version of what elsewhere are 'gay pride parades'). But in a world where more and more cultural styles are imported and assimilated there seems no reason why a Western-style gayness should not prove as attractive as have other Western identities.

The question is how to balance the impact of universalizing rhetoric and styles with the continuing existence of cultural and social traditions. Let me cite an encounter with a young Filipino in a bar in Quezon City, Metro Manila, early this year. Ricardo had just come from a meeting of his university gay group, and was full of excitement at the prospect of an upcoming campus gay event. He spoke with enthusiasm of a march the group was organizing in the neighbourhood, and of a play that had recently been presented in the bar where we were sitting.

The bar itself requires description: Cinecafe combines elements of a café, a bar, a porn video showroom and a backroom for sex. All this is contained in a very small three-story building hidden away in a back street far removed from the tourist hotels of Makati and Ermita, with a clientele that is almost entirely Filipino. At the same time there are certain aspects of Cinecafe that very clearly link it to a larger global gay world: the posters, the magazines, the films themselves (exclusively French and American) were the same one might find in different but similar establishments in Zurich, Montreal or Sydney. In many ways it is a Third World version of male sex-on-premises venues in such Western cities, although Cineclub is far smaller and less well appointed.

Ricardo himself (like so many middle-class Filipinos as fluent in English as in Tagalog) sounded remarkably like the young men I had known in the early 1970s in America, Australia and Western Europe, spoke indeed of gay liberation in phases that were very familiar. This encounter raised a whole set of questions about the meaning of terms like 'gay' and 'gay liberation' in very different cultural contexts. For the streets outside were the streets of an undeniably Third World country, and the men in Cinecafe, while in many ways shaped by Western influence, were themselves part of Filipino society, seeking each other out in ways similar to the ways homosexuals seek each other out in the West and not there (as some versions of the globalization of sexuality would have it) to meet Westerners or foreign tourists.

There are equivalents to Cinecafe in other parts of Asia; the past decade has seen the growth of a commercial gay world beyond its few existing bastions such as Bangkok and Tokyo to cover most of the countries of Asia where there is sufficient economic and political space. Both affluence and political liberalism seem required for a commercial gay world to appear: that it appears to be bigger in Manila than Singapore is due to a number of factors of which comparative political tolerance seems to me perhaps the most essential.

In recent years gay film festivals and magazines have appeared in Hong Kong and India; in Malaysia the HIV/AIDS group Pink Triangle is a de facto gay organization, which engages in a constant round of community development activities (and now provides some space for lesbians as well); in Indonesia the gay organization KKLGN (Working Group for Indonesian Lesbians and Gay Men) has groups in about eleven cities[8] and has held three national meetings. Films and novels with gay themes have begun appearing, especially in East Asia.[9] Thailand has the most developed gay infrastructure in Southeast Asia, including a Thai-language gay press (clearly not aimed at tourists) and several well-appointed saunas whose clientele is largely Thai.[10] It is sometimes claimed that lesbians remain almost invisible: it might be more accurate to recognize that they are less linked to gay men than in many Western countries. While the universalizing rhetoric of human rights is one which blunts gender differences, talking of both 'lesbian' and 'gay' (and sometimes of 'lesbian', 'gay', 'bisexual' and 'transgender') as if they were inherently coupled, the itinerary towards new forms of homosexual identities/behaviours/communities will not necessarily be the same for women and men. One would expect lesbian movements to develop in conjunction with the development of middle-class feminism, not necessarily to be linked to developments amongst homosexual men, which seems the case for both Thailand and the Philippines. Except in Indonesia it is my impression that only very tentative steps have been taken to establish a mutual sense of lesbian/gay cooperation. (Indonesia has had both male and female organizations, if small and largely hidden, for almost twenty years.)

Such 'modern' forms of gay life co-exist with older forms (often linked to ritualized expressions of transgender) or hybrid forms—e.g. the annual 'Miss Gay Philippines Beauty Pageant'.[11] Yet a certain blurring of the sex/gender order may not be that different from developments in the West, as revealed in ideas of the 'third sex' which were dominant in the early stages of a homosexual consciousness in Europe and more contemporary popular images such as the successful play/musical/film *La Cage aux Folles*. Western images of sex/gender in Asia often stress transgender images, as in the popularity of the play/film *M Butterfly* with its story of the French diplomat's love for a Chinese man he allegedly believed to be a woman. But to see transvestism as a particular characteristic of Asian cultures is to miss the role of drag in all its perverse and varied manifestations in Western theatre, entertainment and commercial sex.

Western fascination with these images may reflect a greater acceptance of transgendered people (more accurately, transgendered males) in many Asian countries, as suggested in a report that the Indonesian entry in the 1994 Gay Games in New York included an all-transsexual netball team—the national champions.[12] In many countries such transgendered communities are institutionalized and have won an accepted, if marginal, social status, often as providers of personal services (hairdressing, beauticians etc.) which may include prostitution. Thus in Indonesia there is a national association of *waria* whose patron is the Minister for Women's Affairs. In the Philippines local dignitaries will attend *bakla* fashion shows.

There are differences as well as similarities between groups such as Indonesian *waria* or *banci*, Filipino *babaylan* or *bac(k)la*, Malay *maknyah* or Thai *kathoeys*, which go beyond the scope of this paper. What they appear to have in common is a conceptualization of the sex/gender order which has no simple equivalent in the dominant language or social arrangements of Western societies. In translating the term *kathoey* Peter Jackson makes clear the range of concepts the word conveys: '1: originally a male or female hermaphrodite; 2: male or female transvestite, or transsexual; 3: male homosexual or (rarer) a female homosexual'.[13] And referring to similar groups in Polynesia, Niko Besnier writes: 'Sexual relations with men are seen as an optional consequence of gender liminality, rather than its determiner, prerequisite or primary attribute.'[14]

In general the new 'gay' groups reject a common identity with more traditional forms, and define themselves as contesting sexual rather than gender norms. This is not to deny the significance of gender; as Richard Parker wrote of similar developments in Brazil:

> It would be more accurate to suggest that, rather than replacing an earlier system of thought, this newer system has been superimposed on it, offering at least some members of Brazilian society another frame of reference for the construction of sexual meanings. In the emphasis on sexuality, as opposed to gender, sexual practices have taken on significance not simply as part of the construction of a hierarchy of men and women, but as a key to the nature of every individual.[15]

The existence of several 'systems of thought' leads to a certain ambivalence; thus some Filipinos who belong to gay groups might also see themselves in particular contexts as *bakla*.[16] Clearly the divisions are related to—though not identical with—those of class, much as American or Australian men who twenty years ago defined themselves as 'gay' were largely from relatively privileged backgrounds.

Often the way in which homosexuality is discussed in contemporary Asia will combine quite distinct traditional and modern discourses. Consider this sentence in a report on the first Filipino lesbian congress: 'Rep. Reynaldo

Calalay's bill seeking the appointment of a congressional representative for the third sex and Rep. Geraldo Espina's that criminalizes discrimination against gays have stirred some ripples....'[17] In these two attempts to use the power of the state one sees the ongoing confusion between those who see homosexuality as the result of gender divergence (a 'third sex') and those who see sexuality as a distinct category ('gays'). This confusion is not of course unknown in the West; indeed it is only in the past two decades that the Western understanding of homosexuality has become largely divorced from gender, that is, that lesbians are seen as other than women who want to be men, and male homosexuals as effeminate men wanting to be women. These changes were expressed in the creation of gay/lesbian communities and political movements since the 1970s in most Western countries, which tended to marginalize 'drag queens' and 'butch dykes' in favour of more mainstream styles of being homosexual, including exaggerated masculine ('macho') and feminine ('lipstick lesbians') modes.

The ambiguities between the local and the global, the traditional and the postmodern are constantly there. In my most recent trip to Manila I was half-listening to the radio in a taxi when I heard an unmistakably queeny voice proclaim: 'I'm a girl dropped in a man's body' followed by several sentences in Filipino, then: 'I'm a girl with something extra.' That same day, in *The Evening Paper*, a somewhat upmarket newspaper, I read the weekly 'Gayzette' page, where readers were asked to identify the authors of a list of twenty books ranging from *To Anaktoria* (Sappho) to *A Place I've Never Been* (David Leavitt)—only one of them (Ameng of Wu's *The Cut Sleeve*) not from the West. The quiz, headed 'Queer now, queer then' was designed to discover 'how much you know about your world. Are you a real queen? Or a mere princess? Is the baby now a fairy?'

In much of urban Southeast Asia it is easy to see parallels with the West several decades ago: existing ideas of male homosexuals as would-be women are being replaced by the assertion of new self-concepts; more men are attracted to the idea of primary homosexual relationships rather than marrying and engaging in homosex on the side; there is a development of more commercial venues (but simultaneously, perhaps, there is less public cruising as 'gay' makes homosexuality more specialized); in both organizations and media there is the emergence of a gay political consciousness. The mock-femininity of Thai or Indonesian 'queens' and the mock-macho pose of hustlers is eerily reminiscent of John Rechy's novel of the early 1960s, *City of Night*, as is the fluctuation between overt queeniness and a certain prudery, public campiness and great secrecy vis-à-vis families and workmates.[18]

There is, as well, a certain vulnerability and fragility which underlies much of the new gay life—not, of course, without its parallels elsewhere. For many of the young men who become part of the growing gay worlds of Asian cities there is a rupture with family, village, religion and social expectations which can be very painful. It is not uncommon to meet young men whose growing sense of themselves as gay has led to interruptions to study, to breaks with family, to a general feeling of being stranded between two worlds (where an older Western man will often be cast in the role of protector). Guilt, self-hatred, even suicide are not uncommon for those who feel themselves irretrievably homosexual in societies which deny open discussion of sexual difference even while allowing for certain variations much less acceptable in the West.

It is tempting to accept the Confucian and other 'Asian' discourses about the significance of the family, and forget that similar experiences are very common for homosexuals in most countries, even those in northwestern Europe that have moved furthest towards official acceptance. American research, for example, suggests the rate of suicide among adolescent homosexuals is far higher than the average. Yes, most homosexuals in Asian (and South American, Eastern European and African) cities are still likely to be more integrated into family roles and expectations than would be true in Sydney, San Francisco or Stuttgart. But we are speaking here of gradations, not absolute differences, and the growing affluence of many 'developing' countries means possibilities for more people to live away from their families, and a gradual decline in pressure to get married. One of the key questions is the ways in which gay identities will change as 'Asians' recuperate Western images and bend them to their own purposes.

To see oneself as 'gay' is to adhere to a distinctly modern invention, namely the creation of an identity and a sense of community based on (homo)sexuality. Most homosexual encounters—this is probably true even in the West—take place between men or women who do not define themselves as 'gay' or 'lesbian', and certainly do not affiliate to a community. The development of such identities and communities began in the nineteenth century, although some historians claim evidence for it at least in London, Paris and Amsterdam in the eighteenth. My focus is very clearly on those men who perceive themselves—and increasingly present themselves to others—as having a consciousness and a politics which is related to their sexuality. They may or may not be behaviourally bisexual; what matters for the purpose of this discussion is their sense of identity. Often such men appear more comfortable within an international homosexual world, which they have often encountered first hand through travel and study, than they are with the traditional sex/gender order described by anthropologists and still existing in rural areas of their countries.

What characterizes a gay community? Writing of Hungary (where the political restraints until recently were similar to those of authoritarian Asia) Laszlo Toth argued, 'There is a specific gay social institution system—from a specific non-verbal communication system to gay publications—which enable homosexuals to communicate with other gays, supporting gay community consciousness.'[19] Despite the emphasis on communication this is an institutional rather than a discursive view of community, recognizing that genuine community requires the existence of specific institutions within which a common consciousness can be expressed, which may include a community-specific language (true of many homosexual subcultures, and now apparent in the emergence of clearly defined gay slang(s) in Indonesia).

The gay worlds of Bangkok, Jakarta, Manila or Seoul are obviously different from those of Budapest, Johannesburg, Minneapolis and São Paulo, yet in all these cities—covering all continents and both 'developed' and 'developing' countries—there are similarities which seem important and which I would hypothesize have more to do with common urban and ideological pressures than they do with the cultural backgrounds of, say, Thais, Hungarians and Brazilians. There is a great temptation to 'explain' differences between homosexuality in different countries by reference to cultural tradition. What strikes me is that *within* a given country, whether Indonesia or the United States, Thailand or Italy, the *range* of constructions of homosexuality is growing, and that in the past two decades there have emerged a definable group of self-identified homosexuals—to date many more men than women—who see themselves as part of a global community, whose commonalities override—but do not deny—those of race and nationality.

This is *not* to present a new version of an inexorable march towards 'development', with the end point defined in terms of building American-style gay ghettos across the world. Stephen Murray has warned that 'there are obstacles to the globalization of an egalitarian (gay) organization of homosexuality even in the relatively industrialized and "modern" capitals of "developing" countries'.[20] But globalization, in both its cultural and economic manifestations, impinges on the very creation and experience of sexual behaviour and identities.

The reasons for these developments lie in both economic and cultural shifts which are producing sufficiently large and self-confident groups of men (and some women) who wish to live as homosexuals in the Western sense of that term, i.e. expressing their sexual identity openly, mixing with other homosexuals and able to have long term primary relations with other homosexuals. Thus the Japanese or Thai tradition that married men are reasonably free to have discrete homosexual liaisons on the side seems as oppressive to the young radicals of ProGay or Pink Triangle as it did to French or Canadian gay liberationists of the 1970s.

It is sometimes assumed that the notion of 'a homosexual identity forged through shared lifestyles' has been as Chilla Bulbeck put it 'almost exclusive to the West'.[21] In fact the evidence for homosexual identities, lifestyles and subcultures in a number of 'developing' countries, most particularly in South and Central America, dates back to the early years of the century and arguably before that, at least in Brazil. Similar historical work has yet to be done for cities like Bangkok and Manila; almost certainly there are recognizable subcultures whose history has not been recorded. (Indeed my greatest regret about my own research is that several projects for oral histories in Manila and Kuala Lumpur failed to eventuate.)

A political expression of homosexuality is far more recent. Tony Perez's collection, *Cubao*, first published in 1980, was subtitled (in Tagalog): 'The first cry of the gay liberation movement in the Philippines'. The first self-conscious gay groups appeared in Indonesia (Lambda 1982) and Japan (JILGA 1984) in the early 1980s, just before the advent of AIDS was to change the terrain for gay organizing in ways which would make it more urgent, while also opening up certain overseas sources of funding. In the past decade there has been a proliferation of gay (sometimes lesbian and gay) groups, and many other AIDS organizations do a certain amount of gay outreach or even community development.

It is clear that the language of HIV/AIDS control, surveillance and education has been a major factor in spreading 'gay identities' and facilitating the development of gay consciousness (as it has also contributed to the creation of self-conscious identities of 'sex workers' and 'people with AIDS').[22] It is impossible to know how far the dispersal of Western-style gay identities would have occurred without AIDS, which has opened up both space and resources for gay organizing and increased the influence of both Western influence and surveillance. Consider the large numbers of Western, or Western-trained, epidemiologists, anthropologists and psychologists who have used HIV/AIDS as a reason to investigate sexual behaviours across the world, and by so doing have changed the ways in which the participants themselves understand what they are doing.

The relationship is summed up in a flyer announcing a party at the 1995 AIDS in Asia Conference in Chiang Mai:

> Chaai Chuai Chaai is an NGO based in Chaing Mai. Our aim is to increase safer sex among gay and bisexual men, and male sex workers and their partners, through street outreach, bar outreach and one-on-one peer education. We are a non-profit voluntary organization staffed and run by the gay community in Chiang Mai.

Here the language of 'gay' identity and gay-defined HIV education ('outreach', 'peer education') are conflated to suggest a community which many Thais would claim is irrelevant to continuing cultural assumptions. Matthew Roberts has argued that AIDS has been the essential catalyst for these developments, although I suspect he falls into the trap of assuming a linear development towards the Western model: 'At Stonewall 50 we will likely find ourselves an open and proud community globally, efficaciously practising safe sex... and with notable advances in our civil rights across the globe.'[23]

Neocolonial 'sex wars'

A large-scale construction of a lesbian/gay identity as a central social one— what Stuart Hall calls a master identity[24]—developed in the Western world from the end of the 1960s, and clearly Asians who adopt lesbian/gay identities are conscious of and in part moulded by Western examples. In both North America and Europe gay liberation grew out of the counterculture and other radical movements, most particularly feminism. To some extent this is also true of the developing gay worlds of the South, but more significant is the global explosion of communications. A story about the opening of the 1994 Gay

Games in New York was on the front page of the *Jakarta Post,* the Sydney Gay
& Lesbian Mardi Gras is widely reported in Asia, and large numbers of young
Asians are learning about lesbian/gay/queer worlds from the proliferation of
youth-oriented television and rock videos. (Of course print media served to
disperse news of the rise of Western gay movements before the days of MTV
and CNN, though less effectively.)

Michael Tan links the rise of gay identities/organizations to Western influence and a growing 'middle class' and claims there is 'a global Sexual Revolution, involving a gradual shift in transcending the view of sex-as-reproduction
toward sex and sexuality as consent and commitment, respect and respectabil-
ity'.[25] Yet as Tan recognizes, 'modernity' in the countries under discussion is
rather different from its Western models, for it co-exists with other and sometimes actively competing forces. Tan and others have suggested that the absence of the sort of hostility towards homosexuality found in Anglo-Saxon
societies may also retard the development of gay political movements. This
argument can go overboard, as in Walter Williams's argument that 'Indonesian
values—social harmony, peacefulness and the national motto "unity in diversity"—seem to protect gays from mistreatment more completely than Western
notions of individual rights'.[26] Even if Williams's claim was right in general,
which I doubt, such protection would not extend to those whose 'gayness' took
on political forms deemed harmful to the Indonesian state.

The importation of certain concepts of sexuality is not of course new:
missionaries, anthropologists, government officials and travellers all played their
role in simultaneously interpreting and obscuring existing realities. In terms of
importing homosexual identity a significant Western influence dates from at
least the early years of this century. Western models of homosexuality have
come to Asia both through large cultural forces and through the influence of
individuals, who were often attracted to 'the East' because of its apparent
liberality. This is particularly true of Bali, which from the 1920s on was constructed by rich European homosexuals as a 'paradise' because of the seeming
beauty and availability of young Balinese men. This is most clearly expressed in
the life of Walter Spies, a German painter, who was responsible in part for the
Western discovery and fetishization of Balinese art, and who eventually fell foul
of a colonial moral drive just before World War II. Indeed Adrian Vickers
claims, 'It was not the Second World War but Bali's reputation as a homosexual
paradise which ended the golden era of European Bali.'[27]

Yet after World War II and independence there was something of a rebirth
of Bali's reputation, and a number of gay foreigners settled for a time in Bali.
Today there is a considerable expatriate gay population in Bali, as there is in
Thailand, the Philippines and Sri Lanka, drawn by the lure of 'available' young
men and 'tolerant' social mores. It is easy to condemn these men in the tones
which are increasingly being used in a blanket fashion to demonize all sex
tourists, and it is undeniable that there are some very ugly aspects to gay sex
tourism. At one level there is the same exploitation of young Asians common
in the much larger heterosexual scene[28]: beach prostitution in Kuta (Bali) or

take-out bars in Bangkok are not particularly attractive, and young men face many of the same threats to health and integrity as do young women.

Without denying the ugliness born of larger economic inequities, one has to recognize a somewhat more complex pattern of relationships at work. In many cases young men are able to use their sexual contacts with (usually older) foreigners to win entry into the Western world, through the acquisition of either money, skills, language or, most dramatically, the possibility of emigration. Some young men have made a conscious decision to use their sexuality as a means for social mobility, settling for a 'housewife' role with a richer and older Westerner out of a mixture of glamour and calculation.

Nonetheless, these relationships are inevitably shaped by colonial structures, which are almost impossible to escape. Racism and colonial scripts of super/inferiority are replicated within structures of desire, in ways which neither side is comfortable in admitting. (One reader of the manuscript assumed that I was speaking here of active/passive or top/bottom role-playing; I have something more complex in mind. As Genet showed, such roles may well be reversed in an unconscious transgression of colonial assumptions.) Ironically the assertion of 'gayness' among middle-class Asian young men is beginning to erode their willingness to play the script an older generation have used to enter the Western homosexual world.

There is a danger of both moral indignation and over-romanticization getting in the way of fully understanding the dynamics of Western/Asian homosexual contacts. This is compounded by the immaturity of many of the expatriate Westerners themselves, who import their own fractured sense of self along with their material advantages. Undoubtedly many Westerners desire in Asians (both men and women) the deference and servitude unavailable at home, and for some the colonial/racist framework of their relationships allow them to act out their own sense of self-hatred. While there is an extensive literature of the gay expatriate—from late nineteenth-century Frenchmen in North Africa to Anglo/American writers such as Angus Wilson and Francis King and, more recently, Christopher Bram, Neil Miller and Peter Jackson[29]—there is virtually nothing written from the point of view of the 'local', and there is a great need to hear those voices.[30]

But this is only part of the story: the gay men one sees in Western-style discos at Legian (Bali) or bars in Bangkok are not the only ones. There are many venues in Bangkok, Tokyo or Manila which cater almost exclusively to locals; indeed, a number of gay bars in Japan deliberately discourage foreigners, and the one gay sauna in Manila explicitly excludes them. In both cases fear of AIDS is the ostensible reason; the larger underlying motives are clearly more complex, and operate on a number of levels. Long-lasting relationships exist between Asian homosexuals, marked by a certain equality, and part of the creation of 'modern' gay identity appears to be a desire to open up the possibility of such relationships without them being framed by necessary difference of age, status or race.

'The personal is the political' for lesbian/gay politics in 'developing' countries as much as it remains the case in Western countries. But where there is a legacy of colonialism, which has infused sexual relationships as much as other interactions, that slogan takes on particular meanings. In conversations among gay activists, particularly in the Southeast Asian region, there has been some discussion of 'Asian empowerment', by which is meant a reversal of the traditional assumptions that Asian men are sexually available to Westerners. Such conversations suggest particular forms of self-assertion, and involve a rejection not only of the image of Asian men as 'available' but also of the dominant stereotype of them as 'feminine' or 'passive'.

Just as Western gay movements have asserted a certain masculinity in their constructions of male homosexuality, so Asian gays, having to counteract both indigenous and imported perceptions of them as men-who-want-to-be-women, are likely to be attracted by some variant of the Western 'macho' style. (Yes, gay men are beginning to attend gyms in the richer cities of the region.) In gay discussion groups in Manila and Kuala Lumpur there is talk of 'Asian' men learning to eroticize each other as a way of overcoming a deeply interiorized sense of inferiority vis-à-vis Europeans.

The sexual-political relations of colonialism mean that for many gay men in Asia the phallus is white and must be rejected, sometimes leading to a rejection (more in rhetoric than practice) of European men as sex partners in the belief that they inevitably bear certain racial and colonial prejudices. To quote the Filipino-American poet R. Zamora Linmark:

They like you because you eat dog, goat and pig's blood...
They like you because you kneel hard, bend over quick and spread wide...
They like you because you're a potato queen...
They like you because you take it in, all the way down
They like you because you ask for it, adore it
They like you because you're a copycat, want to be just like them
They like you because, give it a couple more years, you'll be just like them
And when that time comes, will they like you more?[31]

Linmark himself (Filipino-born but US-based) illustrates a further factor now at work, which is the development of significant communities of 'gay Asians' in the diaspora. A self-conscious Asian gay consciousness has emerged over the past decade in the United States, Canada, Australia and Britain, expressed through a burgeoning of social and political groups.[32] In this sense the image presented in the film *The Wedding Banquet* is remarkably out of date; the film opposes a (white) gay world to a traditional (Taiwanese) heterosexual one, but nowhere recognizes the existence in a city like New York of a very significant and increasingly visible East Asian gay community. Gay Asian expatriates are playing a role of some importance in the furthering of gay groups and identities 'back home', even though, as Richard Fung has warned, they often seek to 'conflate the realities of Asians in the diaspora with those living in Asian countries'.[33]

Globalizing influences on Asian sexual identities

There are three dominant scripts in which the globalization of gay identities are commonly described. The first sees Southeast Asia as possessing a 'natural' tolerance for sexual fluidity and expression before the onset of colonialism, and places great emphasis on the continuing traditions of both homosexual and transgender cultures. Thus Frederick Whitam wrote, 'The Philippines, as is generally true of Southeast Asian and Polynesian societies, has maintained a longstanding tradition of tolerance for its homosexual populations.'[34]

This view led to some parts of Asia—Thailand; Sri Lanka; Bali—being seen in the twentieth century as homosexual paradises, and the second script grows out of this, namely a strong emphasis on the impact of colonialism and tourism in creating homosexual worlds. This in turn feeds a third script, which places its emphasis on the impact of modernity, and argues for the current development of 'gay' identities, communities and organizations across Asia as part of a larger pattern of economic and cultural globalization. As two Indonesian AIDS workers wrote, 'Globalization and economic growth have allowed Indonesian youth unprecedented access to information and media about sex.'[35]

It is constantly important to find a balance between the view of globalization as a new stage of imperialism and the triumphalist discourse of globalization as the creation of a new world society, characterized by Simon During as 'magic':

> 'General magic' is an appropriate term because it catches the astonishing cross-cultural reach of the desire for broadcasting, music, camera and video products. This general desire is not 'natural'.... Desires are produced by transnational advertising campaigns, while the technologies are shaped by data gathered through ethnographic market research.[36]

While I accept the role of economic and cultural globalization as crucial to the development of new sexual identities, such explanations must build on existing sex/gender regimes and values, just as the contemporary gay worlds in the West built on pre-existing traditions and cultures. But I suspect that the emergence of gay groups and commercial worlds in modern Asia has relatively little to do with pre-colonial cultural formations, although these often continue to co-exist with newer forms. The comment of Clark Taylor that: 'Homosexual Mexicans often prefer their way of interacting to the US forms because of cherished, cultural values'[37] ignores the other factors at play.

This is not to deny the powerful symbolic and psychological reasons for exploring such connections: one of the benefits of a post-colonial approach is to unravel the ways in which colonial practices have denied cultural tradition. It is ironic that in many developing countries religious and gay interpretations present bitterly opposed views of the 'traditional' status of homosexuality. Recently Iran and China—with several thousand years of literary exploration of homosexual love—have seen bitter persecution of 'decadence'. The Malaysian prime minister has linked homosexuality with 'Western hedonism': 'Western societies', he wrote, 'Are riddled with single-parent families which foster incest, with homosexuality, with cohabitation, with unrestrained avarice... and of course with rejection of religious teachings and values.'[38] On what basis he assumes incest and homosexuality were not found in pre-colonial Asian societies is not revealed. Yet Dr Mahathir has also acknowledged, 'Wealth and success will probably undermine our morals anyhow. In the end we may decay like the others.'[39]

Sexual identity politics grow out of modernity but also show the way to postmodernity, because they both strengthen and interrogate identity as a fixed point and a central reference. The claiming of lesbian/gay identities can be as much about being Western as about sexuality, symbolized by the cooption of the word 'gay' into Thai, Indonesian etc., and the use of terms such as '*moderno*' (in Peru) and '*internacional*' (in Mexico) to describe 'gayness'. As Alison Murray wrote: 'Jakarta is now gayer than ever, and despite the dominant discourse, gay is a modern way to be. This has undoubtedly been influenced by Western trends and internationalization of gay culture, and in the process, the distinctive position of the *banci* has tended to be subsumed within the definition of gay.'[40]

Of course existing cultural and political patterns will influence the extent to which global market forces and images can shape a new sort of public sexual identity. In both Singapore and Hong Kong one feels a large gay presence about to burst forth; in both cities one meets large numbers of young men who identify as gay, but who are restrained by familial and government pressures from the lifestyle which affluence and global media increasingly hold up before them. Even in the most apparently liberal environments there will be restrictions which seem odd if we expect a wholescale replica of the Western model. Thus I once gave a couple of copies of the Australian gay magazine *Outrage* to the manger of the Kuala Lumpur sauna. This sauna is unambiguously a meeting place for gay men in K.L., and a great deal of sex routinely takes place on the premises. Nevertheless I was told firmly there could be no open display of something as overtly homosexual as these magazines—which are routinely sold in most Australian newsagents.

A new gay/lesbian politics?

The first draft of this paper was written (in 1993/94) at a time when Southeast Asia seemed set upon a pattern of rapid economic growth, which was, depending on how one saw these developments, either opening up increasing space for greater individual choice or rapidly destroying traditional kinship and communal ties. Leaders such as Mahathir have of course sought to have it both ways, regretting the decline of 'traditional values' while simultaneously pushing for a rapid economic modernization which places great stress on such values. Equally the moves to democratic regimes, most pronounced in the

Philippines and Thailand, seemed likely to expand to much of Southeast Asia along with economic affluence and liberalization.

After the crash of 1997/98 the pattern of continual growth looks far more problematic, as does any easy assumptions that affluence will offer growing opportunities for adopting 'modern' lifestyles. One concrete example: if in Kuala Lumpur I had been told that it was increasingly possible for young people to leave home and live on their own, then the economic downturn would almost certainly have cut off this option for many. At the time of writing the future of Indonesia in particular is unclear, but a rise in fundamentalism could have considerable impact on slowing the development of lesbigay life in that country. Yet in the euphoria which followed the overthrow of Suharto it was also possible to foresee a strengthened democracy which could also sweep away the restrictions in place in Malaysia and Singapore, and allow for much more overt gay organizing. Just as the student upheavals of May 1968 created the conditions for a contemporary French and Italian lesbian/gay movement, it is possible that the changes in Indonesia will create new forms of organization around sexuality.

In the short run the prospects, particularly in Malaysia, appear more bleak. In September 1998 Deputy Prime Minister Anwar Ibrahim was suddenly arrested and charged with a number of offenses, including sodomy. The attacks on Anwar were a stark reminder that in many parts of the world sexual 'misconduct' (as interpreted by those in power) remains a powerful weapon for social and political control. Ironically, by publicly accusing Anwar of sodomy, prime minister Mahathir broke the de facto ban on public discussion of homosexuality in Malaysia, despite his claimed reluctance to do so.[41] His arrest provoked considerable demonstrations in Kuala Lumpur, and a wave of anti-homosexual rhetoric, with the creation of an 'Anti-Homosexual Volunteers Movement'. At the time of writing it is impossible to know how this story will unfold.

This paper was also begun before the internet had become a major means of communication. As part of the economic growth of Southeast Asia the possibilities of computer-based communications have been grasped with enormous enthusiasm, and have created a new set of possibilities for the diffusion of information and the creation of (virtual) communities. Whereas the gay movements of the 1970s in the West depended heavily on the creation of a gay/lesbian press, in countries such as Malaysia, Thailand or Singapore the internet offers the same possibilities, with the added attraction of anonymity and instant contact with overseas, thus fostering the links with the diaspora already discussed. Work by Chris Berry and Fran Kelly has shown the enormous importance of the net in creating social bonds between young homosexuals in Taiwan and South Korea.[42]

At a more conventional level there are only occasional examples of Asian gay groups engaging in political activity of the sort associated with their counterparts in the West. While Hong Kong decriminalized homosexuality in 1990[43] and there has been some discussion of the British-derived laws in India, I am not aware of political agitation to repeal such laws in Singapore and Malaysia, though the issue has been discussed within both Pink Triangle and People Like Us (Singapore).[44] There have been several small radical gay political groups established in the Philippines in recent years, and gay demonstrations have taken place in Manila. ProGay (the Progressive Organization of Gays in the Philippines), as its name suggests, is concerned to draw links between specifically gay issues and larger questions of social justice.

The development of political movements among people whose identities are being defined in terms of their sexuality will reflect larger features of the political culture of their society. It is not surprising that there is a more politicized gay world in Manila than in Bangkok, despite the latter's huge commercial gay scene; the political history and culture of the two countries would lead us to expect this. At the same time gay politics in both Indonesia and the Philippines reflect the class structures of the countries; in both countries there are powerful upper-class figures whose homosexuality is widely known but who refuse any public identification with a 'movement'. In Indonesia in particular there is some evidence of the emergence of gay activism based among lower-middle-class people who have less to lose. My impression is that there are certain tensions between developing groups around class position, often correlated with access to the English language and the outside world, but at this stage this is only a tentative suggestion based on limited observation.

Yet because the assertion of gay identities and community in the West took a particular political form, associated with the development of gay liberation movements in the early 1970s, does not mean that groups in other parts of the world, whose sense of 'gayness' is fuelled by somewhat different sources, will necessarily follow the same itinerary. We must avoid what Michael Connors has termed the 'narcissistic transition narrative in "diffusion", whereby the trajectory of the Third World has already been traversed by the First'.[45] We must also be aware, as already suggested, that much lesbian organizing will not necessarily assume a common interest with homosexual men.

The best example of Western-style political activism has come from the Japanese group OCCUR, which has engaged in lobbying various ministries, persuaded the Japanese Society of Psychology and Neurology to declassify homosexuality as a mental illness, and succeeded in a court case against the Tokyo Metropolitan Government in winning the right to use public educational facilities. Despite these gains OCCUR has warned:

There are many obstacles to lesbian and gay organizing in Asia and the Pacific islands which do not necessarily exist elsewhere in the world. These include not only the existence of governments repressive of human rights, but also problems that stem from cultural, historical and social differences with the West. For OCCUR this has meant resisting a direct importation of models of lesbian and gay activism developed in the West and developing instead an original form of activism that reflects Japan's specific social and political context.[46]

Nonetheless OCCUR and several other lesbian/gay groups from Asia and other developing areas participate in international networks such as ILGA (International Lesbian and Gay Association) and IGLHRC (International Gay and Lesbian Human Rights Commission), thus increasing their own links to the West and furthering the idea of a universal identity with claims to civil and political rights which transcend other cultural and national boundaries. That this is highly contested was obvious in claims for lesbian inclusion at the recent international women's conference in Beijing, and in counter-claims such as that of Singapore's foreign minister at the 1994 Human Rights Conference in Vienna: 'Homosexual rights are a Western issue, and are not relevant to this conference.'[47]

I am optimistic enough to believe that these sort of arguments will lose in the long run. In the words of former UN Secretary-General Butros Butros Ghali: 'We must remember that forces of repression often cloak their wrong-doing in claims of exceptionalism. But the people themselves time and again make it clear that they seek and need universality. Human dignity within one's culture requires fundamental standards of universality across the lines of culture, faith and state.'[48] The discourses of global rights that Ghali invokes provide new weapons for groups in non-Western countries to adopt and use in international forums. The interesting development is the ways in which the new gay groups of Asia, Latin America and Africa will adapt ideas of universal discourse and Western identity politics to create something new and unpredictable.

This does not mean, however, the adoption of a Western-style lesbigay political activism. In late 1996 controversy erupted in Thailand after the governing body of the country's teacher training colleges decreed that 'sexual deviants' would be barred from entering the colleges. While there was considerable opposition to the ban (subsequently dropped), aside from Anjaree most of this came from non-gay sources. As Peter Jackson concluded: 'A dynamic gay scene has emerged... in the complete absence of a gay rights movement.'[49] When I was in Bangkok shortly after this event I visited the 'gay centre', Utopia, which appeared to be largely the creation of an expatriate American, and later that year two expatriates established an English-language gay/lesbian community newspaper.

The Thai case suggests that a political movement may be the least likely part of Western concepts of homosexual identity to be adopted in many parts of the world, even as some enthusiastically embrace the mores and imagery of Western queerdom. The particular form of identity politics which allowed for the mobilization of a lesbigay electoral pressure in countries like the United States, the Netherlands or even France may not be appropriate elsewhere, even if Western-style liberal democracy triumphs. The need of Western lesbigays to engage in identity politics as a means of enhancing self-esteem may not be felt in other societies.

If the realities of different forms of gay life require us to abandon the idea that the model for the rest of the world, whether political, cultural or intellectual, need be New York or Paris, and to recognize the emerging possibilities for such models in Bangkok and Johannesburg, we may indeed be able to speak of 'a queer planet'. We may even recognize the need to question whether the 'Anglo-American queer theorists' of whom Warner wrote are saying much of relevance to the majority of people in the world who are developing a politics out of their shared sexuality in far more difficult conditions than those within which Western lesbian and gay movements arose.

[1] This article has already appeared in several other versions, including one in *GLQ* vol. 3 no. 4 (1997); I wish to thank the editors for permission to reproduce this material. Thanks also to the Australian Research Council for financial support for the research project reported in this paper, plus a number of people who read various drafts, particularly Ben Anderson, Mark Blasius, Peter Jackson, Shivananda Khan, Suvendrini Perera, Anthony Smith and Geoffrey Woolcock.

[2] See Dennis Altman, *Defying Gravity: A Political Life,* Sydney: Allen & Unwin, 1997.

[3] Edmund White, *States of Desire,* New York: Dutton 1980.

[4] Wes Muchmore & William Hanson, *Coming Out Right: A Handbook for Gay Males,* Boston: Alyson, 1991.

[5] Michael Warner ed., *Fear of a Queer Planet,* Minneapolis: Univ. of Minnesota Press, 1993, p. xii.

[6] See Martin Manalansan IV, 'In the shadows of Stonewall', *GLQ* 1995 no. 2, pp. 425-38.

[7] See 'Anjaree: Towards lesbian visibility', *The Nation* (Bangkok), 25 Sept. 1994.

[8] KKLGN produces a monthly publication, *Gaya Nusantara* (contact: Jln Mulyosari Timur 46, Surabaya 60112).

[9] On film see Chris Berry, *A Bit on the Side,* Sydney: EM Press, 1994. The best-known novels are probably those of Mishima; few others have been translated, but see Pai Hsien-yung, *Crystal Boys,* San Francisco: Gay Sunshine, 1990 (Taiwan); Johann Lee, *Peculiar Chris,* Singapore: Cannon, 1992 and Andrew Koh, *Glass Cathedral,* Singapore: EPB, 1995; Shyam Selvaduri, *Funny Boy,* Toronto: M & S, 1994 (Sri Lanka); Neil Garcia & Danton Remoto, *Ladlad: An Anthology of Philippine Gay Writing,* Manila: Anvil 1994, all available in English.

[10] See Eric Allyn, *Trees in the Same Forest,* Bangkok/San Francisco: Bua Luang, 1991; Peter Jackson, *Dear Uncle Go: Male Homosexuality in Thailand,* Bangkok: Bua Luang Books, second ed. 1995.

[11] See Mark Johnson, *Beauty and Power: Transgendering and Cultural Transformations in the Southern Philippines,* Oxford: Berg, 1997; Danton Remoto, *Seduction and Solitude,* Manila: Anvil, 1995.

[12] Susan Wyndham, 'Out on the Streets', *Weekend Australian,* 18-19 June 1994.

[13] Jackson, *Dear Uncle Go,* p. 301. See also Jackson, '*Kathoey*><Gay><Man: The historical emergence of gay male identity in Thailand', in L. Manderson & M. Jolley eds., *Sites of Desire, Economies of Pleasure,* Chicago: Univ. of Chicago Press, 1997.

[14] Niko Besnier, 'Polynesian gender liminality through time and space', in G. Herdt ed., *Third Sex, Third Gender,* New York: Zone, 1994, p. 300.

[15] Richard Parker, *Bodies, Pleasures and Passions,* Boston: Beacon, 1991, p. 95.

[16] See J. Neil C. Garcia, *Philippine Gay Culture: The Last Thirty Years,* Quezon City:

Univ. of the Philippines Press, 1996; Martin Manalansan, 'Speaking of AIDS: language and the Filipino "gay" experience in America', in V. Rafael ed., *Discrepant Histories : Translocal Essays on Filipino Cultures*, Philadelphia: Temple Univ. Press, 1995.

[17] See Francine Medina, 'Women who love women', *Today* (Manila), 16 Dec. 1996.

[18] John Rechy, *City of Night*, New York: Grove, 1964. Compare the detailed historical discussion in George Chauncey, *Gay New York*, New York: Basic Books, 1994.

[19] Laszlo Toth, 'The development of Hungarian gay subculture and community in the last fifty years', unpublished paper, Budapest, 1994, p. 12.

[20] Stephen O. Murray, 'The "underdevelopment" of modern/gay homosexuality in Mesoamerica', in Ken Plummer ed., *Modern Homosexualities*, London: Routledge, 1992, p. 29.

[21] Chila Bulbeck, 'Exploring Western sexual identities through other sexual identities', paper presented to Australian Sociological Association Conference, Adelaide, Dec. 1992, p. 5.

[22] I have deliberately limited the discussion of AIDS in this paper as I have discussed it at length elsewhere. See Dennis Altman, *Power and Community*, London: Taylor & Francis, 1994; 'Political sexualities: meanings and identities in the time of AIDS', in J. Gagnon & R. Parker eds., *Conceiving Sexuality*, New York: Routledge, 1994, pp. 97-106.

[23] Matthew Roberts, 'Emergence of gay identity and gay social movements in developing countries: the AIDS crisis as catalyst', *Alternatives* no. 20 (1995), p. 261.

[24] Stuart Hall, 'The question of cultural identity', in S. Hall, D. Held & T. McCrew eds., *Modernity and its Discontents*, London: Polity Press, 1993, p. 280.

[25] Michael Tan, 'Introduction' to Margarita Singco-Holmes, *A Different Love*, Manila: Anvil, 1994, p. xii.

[26] Walter Williams, *Javanese Lives*, New Brunswick: Rutgers Univ. Press, 1991, p. 181.

[27] Adrian Vickers, *Bali: A Paradise Created*, Melbourne: Penguin, 1989, p. 124.

[28] See Megan Jennaway, 'Pleasuredromes and paradise', in Manderson & Jolley eds., *Sites of Desire*, Sandra Sturdevant & Brenda Stoltzfus, *Let the Good Times Roll*, New York: New Press, 1994.

[29] Christopher Bram, *Almost History*, New York: Donald Fine, 1992; Peter Jackson, *The Intrinsic Quality of Skin*, Bangkok: Floating Lotus, 1994; Francis King, 'A corner of a foreign field', in King, *One Is a Wanderer*, Harmondsworth: Penguin, 1985; Neil Miller, *Out in the World*, New York: Random House, 1992; Angus Wilson, *As if by Magic*, New York: Viking, 1973.

[30] A Western attempt to make 'the boys' central to the story is Kent Ashford, *The Singalong Tribe*, London: GMP, 1986.

[31] R. Zamora Linmark, 'They like you because you eat dog', in Jessica Hagedorn ed., *Charlie Chan Is Dead*, New York: Penguin, 1993, p. 26.

[32] See Siong-huat Chua, 'Asian-Americans, gay and lesbian', in Wayne Dynes ed., *Encyclopedia of Homosexuality*, New York: Garland, 1990, pp. 84-85; Russell Leong ed., *Asian American Sexualities*, New York: Routledge, 1996.

[33] Richard Fung, 'Looking for my penis: the eroticized Asian in gay porn video', in Leong ed., *Asian American Sexualities*, p. 126.

[34] Frederick Whitham, 'Bayot and callboy: homosexual-heterosexual relations in the Philippines', in Stephen O. Murray ed., *Oceanic Homosexualities*, New York: Garland, 1992, p. 234.

[35] See Desti Murdijana & Priyadi Prihaswan, 'AIDS prevention in Indonesia', *National*

AIDS Bulletin (Canberra), April 1994, pp. 8-11. This theme was developed in a cover story in *Asia Week*, 'Sex: How Asia is changing', 23 June 1995, and in *The Economist*, 'It's normal to be queer', 6 Jan. 1996.

[36] Simon During, 'Postcolonialism and globalization', *Meanjin* no. 2 (1992), p. 341.

[37] Clark Taylor, 'Mexican male homosexual interaction in public contexts', in Evelyn Blackwood ed., *The Many Faces of Homosexuality*, New York: Harrington Park Press, 1986, p. 117.

[38] M. Mahathir & S. Ishihara, *The Voice of Asia*, Tokyo: Kodansha, 1995, p. 80.

[39] Seth Mydans: 'Malaysia's economic ills endanger a leader who has played healer', *New York Times*, 23 Oct. 1997.

[40] Alison Murray, 'Dying for a fuck: implications for HIV/AIDS in Indonesia', paper presented at gender relations conference, Canberra, 1993, p. 6.

[41] See interview with Dr. Mahathir, *International Herald Tribune*, 23 Sept. 1998.

[42] Chris Berry & Fran Kelly: 'Queer'n'Asian on the net: syncretic sexualities in Taiwan and Korean cyberspaces', *Inqueeries* vol. 2 no. 1 (June 1998).

[43] 'After 10 years' debate, HK's gays free to love in private', *The Australian*, 13 July 1990.

[44] See Laurence Leong, 'Singapore', in Donald West & Richard Green, *Sociolegal Control of Homosexuality*, New York: Plenum Press 1997.

[45] Michael Connors, 'Disordering democracy: democratization in Thailand', unpublished paper, Melbourne University, 1995, p. 12.

[46] OCCUR, 'HIV/AIDS and gay activism', brochure, Tokyo, 6 June 1995.

[47] Quoted in Berry, op. cit., p. 73.

[48] Butros Butros Ghali, 'Democracy, development and human rights for all', *International Herald Tribune*, 10 June 1993.

[49] Peter Jackson, 'Beyond bars and boys: life in gay Bangkok', *Outrage* (Melbourne), July 1997, pp. 61-63.

'No silence please, we're Indians!'
—les-bi-gay[1] voices from India

Sherry Joseph and Pawan Dhall

'I'm a journalist, also aspiring to be a home-maker like my mother—without getting into a saree. At 27, I look quite okay. You could be slightly older and okay-looking as well. Commitments yes, but slowly and surely. If you're willing to help with the dishes, write to...'
— Personal ad in the pen pals column of an Indian les-bi-gay journal

'I came across your group's address through a newspaper. I don't remember the name but that won't matter as we are birds of same feathers. Could you please tell me what your group does for gay people? I would really like to know and at the same time like to offer my help.'
— Excerpts from a letter received by a les-bi-gay support group in India

'A gay pride march from all the directions of Calcutta to Esplanade East and somebody from the government announcing that gay rights and marriages are being legalized in India. Abolition of Section 377, Indian Penal Code.'
— A participant at a gay men's conference in eastern India expresses his hopes for the year 2000

'Who's the best role model for les-bi-gay people in India? Bachelor Prime Minister Atal Behari Vajpayee, of course!'
— Quip doing the rounds in les-bi-gay circles in India

Did anybody say 'No homosexuality please, we're Indians'? Whoever did would probably be living in a closet, most likely of colonial make. Not surprising though, in a country caught up in economic, political and cultural paradoxes.

Nuclear weapons, as against 40 per cent of the population below the poverty line. The sight of a street child finishing his day's quota of rag picking and then cooling himself with Pepsi-Cola, one of the most popular icons of India Inc. A democratic set-up striving for electoral reforms, as against dismissal of unfriendly state governments by the federal government. HIV/AIDS joining hands with tuberculosis, as against an information minister wanting a clampdown on condom advertisements. Beauty contests and modelling becoming all the rage, as against a rising trend of female infanticide and sexual abuse. Sexual behaviour surveys reveal teenagers admitting to an entire gamut of sexual experiences, while sex education in schools and colleges struggles to move beyond the reproductive systems of the toad and cockroach.

Many of these paradoxes have come into focus only in the 1990s, which have seen a sea change in the lives of Indian people. With the introduction of the New Economic Policy in 1991, the economy was opened up to multinational companies as never before. One of the areas which has been influenced the most by the wave of economic liberalization is the mass media and communications. Foreign TV channels, cable networks, email and the internet have become accessible even in smaller towns. These have been instrumental in creating significant lifestyle changes, especially in the younger generation. Community and family identity are losing ground to individual identity, with increasing recognition of personal qualities, skills and abilities.

On the political front, the nation has seen the rise and fall of several coalition governments. With constituent parties of differing ideologies, governments have been unable to make significant long-term development plans. Thus on the national level the debate on human rights has not gained much ground, even when thousands of deaths are reported due to starvation, environmental disasters, communal violence and regional insurgencies. It is only recently that the political parties have started discussing children's and women's rights. Other pressure groups working on issues like health, environment and disadvantaged classes have also managed to get the attention of the political parties. However, les-bi-gay issues have yet to figure on the agenda of any political party, including those in the present government.

Amid these paradoxes is the Indian les-bi-gay movement. Along with the sex workers' movement,[2] the les-bi-gay movement is at the forefront in calling the bluff of the essentially middle-class claim that there is no sex happening outside wedlock in India. But even as it leads a sexual glasnost in India, the les-bi-gay movement sits less than easy. It has its own paradoxes to deal with as it tries to reclaim the past and claim the future for les-bi-gay people in India.

First, let us take a look at the past. Homosexuality has an ancient history in India, extending back to some of the earliest historical records.[3] The *Kama Sutra*, a Sanskrit treatise written by Vatsyayana in the fourth or fifth century AD, is universally known as a classic pre-modern work on sexuality. Along with providing a rare insight into the urbane upper-class society of the India of those years, it presents a realistic picture of contemporary sexual mores. This includes descriptions of both female and male same-sex activity; an entire chapter is devoted solely to oral sex. Hindu festivals and sects that celebrate homosexual acts; the court customs of Babar; references to women loving women in the *Mahabharata* and *Ramayana*; and the description of Tantric initiation rites that evoked the idea of universal bisexuality in the human personality—these are all facts that counter the claim that homosexuality has no history in India.[4]

Clearly homosexual behaviour has existed in Indian cultures for centuries. However, the meaning of the behaviour is less clear. Herein lies the first paradox which the les-bi-gay movement has to deal with. While the India of the past seems to have acknowledged all kinds of sexual behaviour (apparently more frankly than today's India), did it have a concept of sexual identity as well? Was homosexual behaviour in ancient India indicative of a homosexual identity?

Social constructionists will be quick to emphasize that the framework for understanding and interpreting experiences related to same-sex behaviour as gay and lesbian identities developed only in white societies—and that not more than a few centuries ago.[5] Thus it would be illogical to interpret homosexual behaviour in ancient India in terms of homosexual identity. The fact that there is no evidence of any discourse on sexual identity in India until very recently seems to buttress this argument.

Essentialists could respond that history as it gets recorded is far from a perfect portrayal of reality. The dominant voices leave little space for dissenting voices, and popular discourse has its ways of silencing anything which sounds discordant. So it would not be too outlandish to say that even if it was never articulated clearly in the way it is today, the concept of a (homo)sexual identity could have existed in the past in India—at least at an individual level, if not at a community or social level.

The essentialist argument about dominant voices versus dissenting voices gains credence if one considers two facts: First, homosexual identity challenges the institutions of marriage and family and concepts of gender and sex only for procreation in a way that homosexual behaviour per se does not. Second, the greater the challenge to a social institution, the greater the efforts to repress the challenge. The situation in modern India illustrates this fact quite well. As long as homosexual behaviour exists 'under the blanket' and 'on the side of' or 'parallel to' marriage, procreation and the family, it does not raise very many eyebrows. Repression begins as soon as it confronts any of these institutions in the form of homosexual identity. This could have been the scenario in the past as well, explaining the lack of articulation of the concept of sexual identity at a social level.

What implications does this debate have for the Indian les-bi-gay movement's efforts to reclaim the past? The movement may not be able to make much headway in establishing the historicity of the concept of sexual identity in India purely on the basis of essentialist arguments. There is after all no visible evidence to support the essentialists' claims. This means that the movement may never be able to establish the historical validity of its own existence through the concept of sexual identity—especially in the face of arguments that it is just another example of misguided Indians aping the decadent West.

What is it therefore that the les-bi-gay movement should be trying to reclaim from the past? There is indeed much to reclaim in terms of the frankness and sense of acceptance that went into the portrayal of same-sex behaviour in ancient India. This frankness and honesty is what is needed today to overcome the hypocrisy that shrouds matters related to sex, sexuality and sexual health. The les-bi-gay movement can argue that if our ancestors could show same-sex behaviour in literature and art, why cannot the present generation do the same?

Besides, even if sexual identity was not talked about in the past in India, there is no reason why it cannot be talked about today. Does it matter so much that it is a borrowed concept? All cultures evolve over time, and some of this evolution takes place through borrowed ideas. In fact, sexual identity is not the only concept India seems to have borrowed. In the era of liberalization, some of the most welcomed imports have been consumerism, the commodification of female (and male) bodies and ideas about dating. And apart from the homegrown homophobia quite possibly generated by the rise of Vedic Brahmanism,[6] much of the homophobia in India is also an import! Judaeo-Christian values and beliefs holding that non-procreative sexual acts are a sin against nature were the ones responsible for criminalizing sodomy under the Indian Penal Code drafted by the British in 1833.

Even as the merits and demerits of borrowing concepts such as sexual identity are debated, the les-bi-gay movement in India seems to be charting its own course. If anything, the movement is evidence that a growing number of Indians too are willing to explore the concept of sexual identity, through which they are looking to move same-sex behaviour out of the realm of the clandestine. In doing so they are following in the footsteps of their forefathers, not all of whom seem to have been influenced by the tenets of Vedic Brahmanism.[7]

Sexual identity politics in India

Identity is about belonging, about what you have in common with some people and what differentiates you from others. At its most basic, it gives one a sense of personal location, a stable core for one's complex involvement with others. In the modern world these notions have become especially complex and confusing. Each one of us lives with a variety of potentially contradictory identities which battle within us for allegiance, as man or woman, upper class or *dalit*, straight or gay, able-bodied or disabled. The list is potentially infinite, and so are our possible belongings. Which of them we focus on or bring to the fore and identify with depends on a host of factors.

To understand Indian les-bi-gay identity we have to look at identity politics in a wider perspective. The racist and cultural marginalization of les-bi-gay immigrants from the Indian subcontinent in Britain and the US demanded an agenda within a racist climate different from the agenda imposed by white les-bi-gay people.[8] The impact of colonial history and concepts of orientalism on world views and perceptions has played a central role in how non-white people have been defined and perceived, and how white/non-white relations have evolved socially and on a personal level. Silenced in both South Asian patriarchal societies and the white les-bi-gay communities in America and Europe, South Asian les-bi-gay people have had to invent themselves, often with new terms of identification.

In the South Asian context, the debate over identity based on sexuality stemmed from the belief that the construction of sexual identity is not rooted in India's own history, and that the only sexuality that is relevant is that of penetrative heterosexuality.[9] This led to a quest for evidence of homosexuality in a historic perspective. Discarding the Eurocentric classification of sexuality into dichotomous categories of homosexual and heterosexual, new discourses of sexuality around a variety of experiences and desires started emerging. Thus the term 'alternate sexualities' came into vogue. Using 'alternate' as an adjective and 'sexualities' in plural, it tried to describe the meaning of sexual behaviours other than those associated with penetrative heterosexuality. This was basically an attempt to decolonize the general notion of sexuality and establish the existence of various expressions of sexualities in South Asian cultures.

From the sexual health perspective, another term, 'men who have sex with men'—later revised to 'males who have sex with males (MSM)'—evolved, as a depoliticized euphemism for 'gay men'. There has been some controversy attached to the use of the term 'MSM' to refer to gay men.[10] However, in India during the last few years this term seems to have emerged as a sexual identity—'I am an MSM but not a gay.' There seems to be more acceptance of an identity based on homosexual behaviour than around homosexual desires, emotions and feelings.

The search for new, acceptable paradigms for self-description led to the emergence of South Asian les-bi-gay groups and publications in America and Europe from the mid-1980s to the early 1990s. Prominent among the groups were Trikone (USA), Khush Khayal (Canada), Shakti (UK), Shamakami (USA), South Asian Lesbian and Gay Association (USA) and Dost (UK). Indian counterparts had their debut[11] almost simultaneously in the early 1990s, with Bombay Dost, Red Rose (New Delhi), Fun Club (Calcutta), Sakhi (New Delhi), Friends India (Lucknow) and Garden City Club (Bangalore).

While many of the initial Indian ventures did not last long or soon went into hibernation, they should be credited with making the ground fertile for future efforts. Before long a fresh wave of groups made an appearance: Sneha Sangama (Bangalore), Khush Club (Bombay), Arambh (New Delhi), Counsel Club (Calcutta), Gay Information Centre (Secunderabad), Good As You (Bangalore), Men India Movement (Cochin), Sisters (Madras), Humsafar Trust, Udaan and Stree Sangam (all Bombay). Most of these ventures started in the period 1993 to 1995, and the majority have survived.

The last two to three years have seen no let-up in the formation of new groups: Humrahi and Women's Network (both New Delhi), Expression (Hyderabad) and Sabrang (Bangalore). However, the groups which have drawn the maximum attention during this period are the ones that have sprung up in smaller cities and towns: Sahayak Gay Group (Akola), Aasra (Patna) and Saathi (Cuttack). Another two are in the initial stages in Ahmedabad and Visakhapatnam.

Some of these groups have appropriated Indian languages to express the idea of homosexuality in a culturally relevant way, while others have tried to define it in different ways. For instance, *dost* and *sakhi* in Hindi mean 'friend', *khush* in Urdu means 'ecstatic pleasure', and *sneha sangama* in Kannada would imply 'coming together of people through or for love'. 'Fun Club' sounds very much like a derivative of the 'City of Joy' sobriquet for Calcutta, while 'Good

As You' (GAY) seems to appropriate its identity from the slogan 'Gay is good.' 'Friends India', as the name suggests, provides a forum for friendship between men who like and love men.

In addition to friendship, love and fun, other themes which dominate the nomenclature of Indian les-bi-gay groups are trust and hope. Thus: *aasra*, which in Hindi means 'shelter', and *arambh*, which is the Hindi term for 'a beginning'. Interestingly, activism of the ACT-UP kind has little representation as a theme. Only the name of the Calcutta publication *Pravartak* (Hindi/Bengali for 'promoter of a cause') comes close to something in the nature of an activist assertion.

It is worth mentioning here that the first South Asian newsletter on homosexuality to be published outside South Asia was named *Anamika*, which means 'nameless' in Sanskrit.[12] It can be seen that from the state of namelessness South Asians, in particular Indian les-bi-gay people, have appropriated and subverted languages; this has been integral to their articulation of an identity.

The ambiguity of language reflects another important fact about the politics of identity of the Indian les-bi-gay movement: it is male-dominated. Lesbians have participated in the movement since the beginning,[13] but they often had the secondary role that characterizes their position as women in mainstream society. This imbalance has deep cultural and historical roots and it points to the dilemma lesbians face when they identify with the movement. Some believe that lesbianism cannot be understood alongside male homosexuality because the two are entirely different, partly because women are oppressed and men are part of the dominant culture.[14]

Thus the very notion of the co-sexual nature of the movement can be challenged. On the other hand, excluding women from an analysis would create a false impression of the movement. Though sometimes uneasily aligned, gay men and lesbians share common goals and interests as well as common enemies. Because lesbianism is rooted in both the women's movement and the gay movement, lesbian issues must be examined from both perspectives.

Some people do consider lesbianism as an integral part of the women's movement in India. Flavia Agnes, an activist of the Forum Against Oppression of Women in Bombay, remarks, 'Many women in the movement turn to lesbianism or bisexuality as a conscious political choice, for they cannot reconcile their radical understanding of themselves and other women in general with the inequality, exploitation, lack of respect and understanding and often blatant physical force that characterize typical heterosexual relationships, whether in marriage or out of it.' This point is in agreement with Shah's view on the development of lesbian identity, which describes the gradual shift from political consciousness to sexual identification.[15] Since the Fifth National Conference of the Women's Movement in 1994 lesbianism has become a regular theme of discussion.

To date there have been three groups exclusively for lesbians and bisexual women: Sakhi Lesbian Resource Centre & Research and Networking Institute in New Delhi, Women's Network, also in New Delhi, and Stree Sangam in

Bombay. New Delhi also has a helpline called Sangini for lesbians and bisexual women. Another resource centre seems to be in the making in Visakhapatnam, while the only other such group, Sisters in Madras, has closed down. Though three other groups claim to be open to both gay men and lesbians, the visibility of women in their activities is minimal. Only one has women on the editorial board of its publication. Their columns are also male-dominated. The lesbians who were members of the editorial board of *Bombay Dost* in 1990 no longer serve in that capacity.

However, serious rethinking has taken place recently, encouraging gay men to help their female counterparts confront society.[16] Thus apart from the women-only meetings which groups such as Stree Sangam have been organizing, two major conferences since 1993 have been truly les-bi-gay initiatives. The first was a seminar on 'Gender Constructions and History of Alternate Sexualities in South Asia' in 1993. It aimed at studying the alternate historical and mythological traditions around homosexuality and delved deep into diverse issues affecting les-bi-gay people.[17] The second was a workshop on 'Strategies for Furthering Les-bi-gay Rights in India' in 1997.

Politics of liberation

A starting point of les-bi-gay liberation politics is the assumption that they are a true minority. They are like a religious minority, although a religious identity differs from a sexual identity in that it is usually conferred at birth and passed on through the family. But sexual identity differs from other identities like tribe, gender and nationality in that there are no visible symbols of identification; it is hidden within a person's self. Can a group many of whose members are invisible be a minority? Minority status also seems wrongly applied to les-bi-gay people who are out of the closet, since conventional religious or ethnic minorities usually do not have to come out. Measured by the yardsticks of discrimination or social acceptance, however, les-bi-gay people are a minority. Some scholars are of the opinion that les-bi-gay people are a self-defined minority.

Discrimination, tolerance, acceptance and equality can be seen as a continuum. They can be discussed under the framework of four concepts: homophobia, heterosexism, heterocentrism and compulsory heterosexuality. Each of these concepts is relevant to the Indian context.

Homophobia refers to the irrational fear or hatred of homosexuals or homosexuality. Homophobia results partly from rigid ideas about gender. A man who appears womanly by conventional norms or a woman who appears manly threatens the sharp gender separation which most people take for granted. But research has shown that gay men can be just as masculine as straight men and that lesbians can be just as feminine as straight women.[18]

Homophobia also leads to violent attacks on les-bi-gay people, such as gay bashing by police and civilian heterosexuals. An obvious example of homophobia in 1994 was the outrage expressed by the National Federation of Indian

Women, a women's organization affiliated with the Communist Party of India, against the Humsafar Trust/Naz Project conference for South Asian gay men and MSM held in Bombay in December 1994. Describing the conference as an 'invasion of India by decadent Western cultures and a direct fall-out of our signing the GATT agreement', it urged the prime minister 'not to follow Bill Clinton's immoral approach to sexual perversions in the US' and to immediately withdraw permission to hold the conference. According to the National Federation of Indian Women, the purpose of the conference was to 'promote and legitimize homosexuality' which would 'surely start a move of sexual permissiveness among urban youth who have become vulnerable to the vulgarity of Western culture brought to them through the media'. The organizers of the conference were also issued a warning letter by Pramodh Navalkar, a legislator of the Hindu fundamentalist Shiv Sena, then the ruling party in Maharashtra state.[19]

What was ironic about the posturing of both the Communist Party of India and Shiv Sena was the inconsistencies between their statements and their own political actions on the ground. In the Communist Party of India's own backyard, the state of West Bengal, people were at that time busy setting up a British government-funded sexual health project which was supposed to address all kinds of sexual behaviours. In fact, by December 1994 the West Bengal Sexual Health Project workshops had already seen presentations from Calcutta's les-bi-gay support group Counsel Club without any brouhaha. As for Navalkar's warning, nothing came of it. The conference turned out to be a resounding success, not the least because it was opened by the Maharashtra state Director of Health Services, Dr. Subash Salunkhe!

Whatever the contradictions of political party policies, homophobia remains a serious problem at the individual, community and family level, where it is a much more immediate threat and one that can have devastating consequences. Indian les-bi-gay groups often have to deal with instances of individuals' being forced by their families to undergo 'treatment' to cure them of homosexuality.[20] There have also been instances of gay people losing their jobs, though the pretext given for firing them is never related to their sexual orientation. Newspapers often carry reports of lesbian couples committing suicide or running away from home.[21]

The AIDS pandemic has made homophobia an even more serious problem. Though AIDS in India is seen as more of a sex worker's/truck driver's/blood donor's disease, homosexuality itself has also been scapegoated for the spread of AIDS. The general perception is that homosexuality = anal intercourse = AIDS. The combination of the prejudices against homosexuality and AIDS has only served to drive male same-sex behaviour and the associated sexual health problems underground. Thus many gay and bisexual men and other MSM are wary about reporting STDs. Medical personnel are known to adopt a highly moralistic and patronizing attitude towards those who report such problems, thus driving away patients as well as losing invaluable statistical data which would have helped design appropriate health services.

While some people are only too willing to blame homosexuality and homosexuals for AIDS, many in the government are not even willing to acknowledge the existence of homosexuality in India—let alone realize the fact that unprotected same-sex behaviour can act as route for transmission of HIV and other STDs. The argument put forward is that 'our culture does not have such things'! Thus the stance adopted by government officials at public forums has often been one of silence on the subject or denial of the existence of homosexuality. An example is the remark made by the West Bengal health secretary at a West Bengal Sexual Health Project workshop in 1994: 'There are no homosexuals in West Bengal.' This was fortunately challenged outright by some of the participants, including a representative from Calcutta's Counsel Club. In response, the health secretary retreated behind a noncommittal stand on the subject.

A second important concept in connection with the politics of les-bi-gay liberation is heterosexism, the prejudice and discrimination against les-bi-gay people. Analogous to racism and sexism, heterosexism validates and strengthens the dominant group's claims to superiority and privilege. One of the ways that has been adopted to fight against it is bringing into the limelight eminent gay personalities who are open about their sexuality. India too has seen such a strategy. *Sunday* magazine carried a cover story on journalist Ashok Row Kavi, who is often considered in les-bi-gay circles to be the father of the Indian les-bi-gay movement. The *Indian Express* featured an interview with renowned gay painter Bhupen Khakkar. However, 'outing' les-bi-gay people as a tactic for battling heterosexism has not caught on in India, unlike the West. The only notable exception seems to have been *Trikone*'s speculative report on a well-known South Indian female politician's relationship with her confidante, who lived with her until about two years ago.[22]

An instance of blatant prejudice can be found in the Indian law books. Section 377 of the Indian Penal Code, 'Of unnatural offences', lumps together sodomy between males, sodomy between males and females, and bestiality. Though homosexuality per se is not an offence in India, it is often linked with sex between humans and animals, thereby illustrating both the general contempt for les-bi-gay people and gross ignorance about them.

The conventional definition of family, which includes only the traditional family, is also heterosexist. The official registration of same-sex partnerships in distant Denmark and Sweden seems to have struck a chord in India too. Les-bi-gay support groups have been unearthing and documenting instances of same-sex relationships, same-sex couples living together and even les-bi-gay people forming their own alternate families. *Bombay Dost* once carried a report on intra-gender marriage among the Kutchis in Gujarat. The tradition, as much as 150 years old, involves two men being joined ritually in marriage.[23]

Legal recognition of same-sex marriages was included in the charter of demands put forth by the Indian les-bi-gay community in *Less Than Gay: A Citizens' Report on the Status of Homosexuality in India*.[24] This report, though now somewhat dated, remains the most comprehensive account of the status of homosexuality in India. It was submitted to the Petitions Committee of parliament along with a petition for the repeal of Section 377 in 1992. The Indian lawmakers never responded to the petition or the charter of demands, but since then the subject of legal recognition of same-sex marriages has become a hotly discussed issue at a number of conferences. The first time it was discussed in depth was at the National Workshop on Drafting Gender-Just Laws in Bombay in 1996. The context for the workshop was the contentious Uniform Civil Code which was—and still is—part of the ruling Bharatiya Janata Party's (BJP) manifesto. This Code is an attempt to bring into effect the constitutional provision for a single law governing marriage, divorce, inheritance, adoption, maintenance, etc. Subsequently the Code was discussed in greater detail at the workshop on Strategies for Furthering Les-bi-gay Rights in India in November 1997 in Bombay.[25]

The present BJP federal government has not been able to push the Code through because the coalition it is heading makes its own survival the topmost issue. Les-bi-gay groups feel that the concepts of family and marriage need to be redefined in keeping with lived realities as they exist. But they fear that if and when the Code does get implemented, it will fail to recognize les-bi-gays' right to choose their partners. This is because none of the political parties (including the BJP) have ever taken cognizance of les-bi-gay rights, nor have the les-bi-gay groups been able to get their demands included in the political parties' agenda. The presence of fundamentalist, communal and sectarian parties in the national political scenario has made it difficult to put across such a liberal les-bi-gay ideology. Some of these political parties have already instigated fear in the minds of the people by, for instance, provoking the demolition of Babari Masjid,[25a] abusing artist M. F. Hussain for the nude portrayal of the mythological figure Sita, and instigating Hindu-Muslim and Hindu-Sikh communal riots, thereby narrowing the scope for a liberal, humanitarian and democratic citizenship.

Besides outright prejudice against les-bi-gay people, a more subtle form of bias can be identified in the form of heterocentrism and compulsory heterosexuality. Heterocentrism is the often unconscious attitude that heterosexuality is the norm by which all human experience is measured. It seems to have evolved from a Eurocentric definition of sexuality. Since the nineteenth century Western culture has seen a whole new discourse dividing the homosexual and heterosexual into sharply antagonistic categories. Under this discourse procreative heterosexuality became the norm. The dichotomized and hierarchical structures of what were deemed 'masculine' and 'feminine' helped frame these new concepts of homosexuality and heterosexuality. The division between sexual behaviour responding to procreative instincts and sexual behaviour responding to pleasure/lust instincts also formed the nucleus of the debate on what was deemed 'normal' or 'abnormal' and 'perverse'.[26]

The notion of compulsory heterosexuality implies that people must be pressured and coerced into heterosexual behaviour. Marriage in India determines a person's eligibility to be considered an adult. Being single, especially in the case of women, is not socially acceptable except on religious grounds, and marriage followed by procreation has become the norm. Without marriage, a person is considered irresponsible, incomplete and unsettled.[27] In a situation where neither a single life nor same-sex marriage is possible, a marriage of convenience between les-bi-gay people has become the preferred option for some. Personal ads in les-bi-gay journals are ample proof of this. Arvind Kala also mentions an attempt by a gay man to marry a lesbian to avoid the pressure from his family for conventional marriage.[28]

The last point—but a crucial one—in discussing the politics of liberation is les-bi-gays' assertion of their right 'to be treated equally, fairly and equitably as citizens of India; that respect should be given to who we are, what we are; the right to choose, the right to be unmarried and the right to our own sexual orientation'.[29] The les-bi-gay demand for freedom and equality in India was first put forth in an organized way in November 1991, in the form of a charter of demands which constituted the last chapter of the report *Less than Gay*. The significant elements in the nineteen-point charter were 'repeal of all discriminatory legislation including Section 377, IPC and the relevant Sections of the Army, Navy and Air Force Acts'; 'enactment of civil rights legislations'; 'amendment of the Constitution to include equality before law on the basis of sex and sexual orientation'; 'establishing of a commission to deal with the human rights abuse faced by les-bi-gay people'; and 'amendment of the Special Marriage Act to allow same-sex marriages'.[30]

Almost a year later, on 11 August 1992, a demonstration was held in New Delhi to protest atrocities against homosexuals. Carrying placards with slogans like 'Gay is normal', 'Down with Section 377', 'Why is it a sin if a woman loves a woman?', 'Homosexuality is neither a crime nor a disease', 'Arrest AIDS not gays', the protesters articulated central les-bi-gay concerns. Another poster which read 'Gays of the world unite, you have nothing to lose but your chains' might have caused Karl Marx to turn over in his grave.[31] Songs sung during the protest like '*Woh hamara geet rokana chahatey hain / khamoshi todo waqt aa gaya*' ('They want to stifle our song / The time has come to break the silence') show the spirit of the movement.

In 1994, following a medical team's visit to the Tihar jail in New Delhi, a controversy arose over reports of homosexual activity in the male wards of the jail. While the survey report of the World Health Organization on 55 prisons in 31 countries says that there is a higher rate of HIV transmission among prisoners than in the general population, Tihar jail authorities responded by denying that there is any homosexual activity in the prison. Seeing this as an opportune moment, AIDS Bhedbhav Virodhi Andolan (ABVA), a human rights activist group, filed public interest litigation (ABVA vs. Union of India and Others) in Delhi High Court in April 1994. The petition urged that Section 377 be struck down as being unconstitutional on the grounds of violating the right of privacy, which is part of the fundamental rights of life and liberty guaranteed under article 21 of the constitution and recognized by the 1948 International Convention on Human Rights. The petition argued that Section

377 also violates article 14 of the constitution, as it discriminates against persons on the basis of their sexual orientation; and that having been drafted in 1833 by the British (who enacted the section in all their colonies, including India), it is archaic and absurd.

Advocate Janak Raj Jai filed a reverse petition seeking a ban on the move to supply condoms to Tihar jail inmates, on the grounds that it would be a violation of Section 377. He went on record as saying that the 'immoral act of homosexuality' was not half as widespread in the jail as was being said and that moral instruction, rather than condoms, was the crying need of the hour.[32] About two years ago the National AIDS Control Organization and Indian Council of Medical Research, respondents to the petition, filed a reply to the Delhi High Court saying that condoms should be made available to inmates of prisons as a safety measure. However, they did not comment on the constitutional validity of Section 377, leaving it to the judiciary to make up its mind on the issue. Since the petition was filed in 1994, a number of hearings have taken place, but expectations of further hearings have been frustrated.

For their part, les-bi-gay support groups have been making small but significant efforts, such as discussions, write-ups in their publications and media interaction, to generate mass support in favour of repeal of the law. ABVA organized a meeting in April 1995 to develop strategies for action.[33] In December 1995, in an open session of the International Conference on AIDS, Humanity and Law, the constitutional validity of India's Victorian sodomy law was questioned before an international audience in the context of HIV transmission. A nationwide signature campaign has also been initiated by the support groups. Support is being solicited from members of the groups, NGOs, civil rights groups, medical practitioners, lawyers, media workers, educators and the public at large. The signature campaign was thought up at the Strategies for Les-bi-gay Rights workshop in Bombay in November 1997. But at the same meeting, none of the support groups could muster the courage to take the lead in the legal battle for decriminalization of sodomy!

Creating visibility

Les-bi-gay visibility in India is not narrowly limited to marches or parades, but includes representation in other forums also. The most remarkable event in the Indian les-bi-gay movement was the August 1992 protest in New Delhi. The demonstration, held in front of police headquarters, was in protest against the unwarranted and illegal arrest of eighteen people suspected of being homosexual.[34] The demonstration was organized by social workers and human rights activists working with ABVA, but les-bi-gay people also participated in significant numbers in the protest. The protest received wide publicity in the media. However mild and even ineffectual it was in comparison to the more aggressive and provocative tactics of groups in Western countries, it marked a turning point for the Indian les-bi-gay community. In the tradition of the Stonewall rebellion, a small band of men and women decided that they had had enough of victimization and decided to take a stand.[35]

Apart from a few individuals, the most visible face of the les-bi-gay move-ment in India today is provided by les-bi-gay publications. To date nine pub-lications have emerged in Calcutta, Bombay, Gulbarga, Lucknow, New Delhi, Patna and Bangalore. The earliest of these was the short-lived *Gay Scene,* which was published in Calcutta in the late 1970s. However, the current trend began in 1990 with the publication of *Bombay Dost.* Today seven of these publica-tions survive. Some come out periodically while others are less regular. Apart from *Bombay Dost,* all the publications are for private circulation only. How-ever, besides *Bombay Dost,* which is available from as many as four bookshops in three cities, a few copies of *Naya Pravartak* also get circulated through two outlets in Calcutta and New Delhi. Keeping pace with the Internet era, at least one of the publications (*Darpan* in New Delhi) has developed its own website.

Many of the publications have adopted a multilingual format in order to reach a wider audience. *Bombay Dost* started off being bilingual in English and Hindi but now has discontinued the Hindi section. *Sacred Love* is bilingual in English and Hindi, while the newborn *Sanghamitra* (Bangalore) is bilingual in English and Kannada. *Naya Pravartak* has more or less retained its English-Bengali-Hindi format from the start. To supplement these publications, there are a number of journals from abroad available to Indian readers, usually free of charge. *Trikone* magazine (USA) changed its marketing strategy for India in 1996 and started distribution through the Humsafar Trust and Counsel Club with the idea of providing financial assistance to these groups by allowing them to keep the proceeds from selling the magazine. However, Counsel Club had to discontinue the arrangement when the Customs Department seized a consign-ment of the magazine addressed to the group—on the grounds that the maga-zine dealt with les-bi-gay issues which were 'derogatory to the morality and social system of our nation'. The colonial masters of yesteryear would have been pleased at the Customs Department's sense of duty!

Mainstream Indian print and audio-visual media have exhibited a mixed response, with the English press being the most les-bi-gay-friendly. In fact, magazines like *India Today* and *Sunday* played an important role in drawing attention to les-bi-gay issues in India through their coverage in the late 1980s of the South Asian les-bi-gay movement in the West. The magazine *Savvy* scored a first for the Indian media when it published Ashok Row Kavi's coming-out interview in 1986. The 1990s have seen a flood of articles on homosexuality in publications of almost all kinds—film glossies, newspapers, general interest magazines, research-based journals and even business publica-tions.[36] Among English dailies, *Indian Express, The Times of India, The Tele-graph* and *The Statesman* have covered the issue fairly regularly and objectively. In the last two to three years their regional-language counterparts have also started writing about the subject, which is generally considered a positive de-velopment by the les-bi-gay community.

The tone of most of the articles has been progressive, though not always free of bias and sensationalization. The nature of the articles has ranged from personal interviews to social analyses and articles written from a medical research perspective. Some of the articles have carried the names and addresses of support groups, which has helped them reach out to a large number of isolated les-bi-gay people.[37] Sensational snippets about les-bi-gay people seem to have given way to more constructive coverage of the issue of homosexuality in the Indian print media.

As a strategy for campaigning for visibility, les-bi-gay support groups ask their members to write protest letters to the editors whenever offensive and negative coverage is given to the issue, stating clearly what les-bi-gay people are and what they stand for. There have also been calls for more les-bi-gay people to take up careers in journalism, as the mass media are the most powerful means to increase visibility and combat the silence imposed by society.[38]

The English theatre in Bombay has been one arena where les-bi-gay themes and characters have been portrayed quite openly. From 1950 to 1990 there were 32 such theatre performances.[39] In 1995 Delhi's Theatre Action Group staged performances of Shantanu Nagpal's *O Come Bulky Stomach*, which dealt with the issue of AIDS quite sensitively. For the record, neither of the two male gay characters in the play had AIDS, though it is not clear if the playwright decided on this with the intention of combatting myths. In 1994, Rajesh Talwar, a member of ABVA, published *Inside Gay Land*, a satirical play about sexuality and the law criminalizing homosexuality in India.

In Calcutta music and dance is being used to talk about homosexuality. In June 1996 Sapphire Creations Dance Workshop staged what was billed as the 'first ballet on homosexuality in India', which has since been performed at a number of dance festivals all over India. In April 1999 a gay troupe called Sarani staged *Coming Out With Music*, which included a number of Bengali songs and a dance performance. Contemporary fiction has also tried to portray homosexual characters.[40]

Les-bi-gay themes have been visible on the silver screen as well. Every year on January 25th, an informal group called Friends of Siddhartha Gautam screen a number of les-bi-gay films as part of a day-long event in New Delhi. This annual event is held in memory of the late lawyer and activist Siddhartha Gautam, one of the most active members of ABVA and the inspiration behind the Red Rose les-bi-gay meetings in New Delhi. Some of the films shown this year included Riyad Wadia's *BOMgAY* and Pratibha Parmar's *Jodie*.

International film festivals held every year in the metropolitan cities screen a number of les-bi-gay films. Indian film makers too have produced a number of films on the subject. *BOMgAY, Tamanna, Darmiyaan, Dayra* and *Fire* have set the screen alight with hopes and expectations for Indian les-bi-gay people. What is refreshing about these films is that the les-bi-gay or transgendered characters have not been shown in the usual stereotyped manner for which Bollywood is notorious. Not surprisingly, however, most of the films mentioned above have run into trouble with the censors. *Fire*, which portrays a lesbian relationship, generated the most controversy and was ultimately driven out of circulation by Hindu fundamentalist attacks on theatres where it was showing. In what is really a sad irony, *Adhura*, the first ever Hindi gay feature film, never saw the light of day—*Adhura* means 'incomplete' in Hindi.

While on the subject of films, it should be mentioned that Indian les-bi-gay people are just as fond of the Bollywood stars as other Indians. For many Indian gay men, Hindi film actors like Akshay Kumar and Amir Khan are the stuff that dreams and fantasies are made of. None of the stars has spoken openly about his sexual orientation. But gay circles in Bombay and Delhi claim that a number of actors—not to mention fashion designers and even politicians—frequent their parties and get-togethers.

Besides the cinema, television and radio too have started dealing with homosexuality quite candidly. Apart from a number of talk shows and interviews with les-bi-gay people and support groups, Hindi serials like *Tara* have been featuring gay characters. However, the Hindi serials are still where the Indian print media was at one time. The portrayal of gay characters often has an underlying element of pathology that is yet another form of subtle stereotyping.

Les-bi-gay support groups in Calcutta, New Delhi and Bangalore have made their own efforts to educate and entertain their members through films and plays. In early 1995, Counsel Club and Arambh organized a series of video film shows in collaboration with Trikone members who were visiting India. Some of the films shown included *Double the Trouble, Twice the Fun* and *Destiny, Desire, Devotion*. Good As You in Bangalore sometimes organizes film shows during its weekly meetings. In December 1993, Arambh staged a play called *Varun* which was written and acted by the group members.

Community, culture and social networks

Indian les-bi-gay people define a community symbolically rather than geographically à la the Castro district in San Francisco. Community means common unities, as defined by a working group at the Humsafar-Naz Conference in Bombay.[41] The charter of Bombay Dost clearly speaks of this: 'To provide a framework whereby all such people, both male and female, from the Indian subcontinent can come together and support each other so as to show solidarity and a sense of identity of an alternate sexuality'. All the Indian les-bi-gay publications carry pen pal ads and the addresses of other support groups in India and abroad. These serve as invaluable tools for national and international networking, which in its turn gives rise to a sense of sharing and community. The publications also provide space for individuals to articulate and ventilate their feelings and to develop a sense of identity and the 'we' feeling.

All the support groups provide a variety of support systems. Regular meetings—monthly, weekly or biweekly—provide the forum through which the sense of community is strengthened. The venues for the meetings change from public cafeterias to public open spaces to residences of individual members. Lack of availability of safe social spaces is a concern often expressed by the les-bi-gay community. Most groups, especially those with publications, have a good collection of literature on les-bi-gay issues.

Parties and social gatherings form another part of the les-bi-gay culture, as do celebrations of festivals and special occasions. Large-scale gatherings are not rare. Sneha Sangama and Friends India are famous for organizing such extravaganzas, often at places of tourist interest like Goa and Jaipur in Rajasthan. New Year's Eve bashes in Bombay and New Delhi attract huge numbers from all over the country. Calcutta has its own Christmas and New Year's Eve parties, though the more popular event is the Counsel Club birthday bash on August 15th, which is also the country's Independence Day!

Social networks also include networking at the international level. In 1995, when *Trikone* organized Pride Utsav in San Francisco, members of Bombay Dost also participated with much fanfare. The event, with its theme of 'Affirming Our Culture, Celebrating Our Sexuality', was held on the occasion of *Trikone's* completing a decade of existence as the oldest surviving South Asian les-bi-gay initiative in the world. A number of Indian les-bi-gays also participated in the Gay Games in 1994 and 1998.

In October 1995, the International Gay and Lesbian Human Rights Commission presented a tribunal in New York on human rights violations against sexual minorities to coincide with the 50th anniversary of the United Nations. Among those testifying was civil rights and anti-AIDS activist Anuja Gupta from India, who talked about the rights abuses Indian les-bi-gay people and people living with HIV and AIDS face at the hands of the police and other agents of the state.[42]

Other support systems provided by the support groups are related to sexual health, counselling, accommodation, employment and legal issues. With the targeting of so-called 'high risk groups' with regard to STD/HIV/AIDS intervention, the stigma associated with les-bi-gay people has increased. This has stopped many of them from coming out of the closet. Peer group training and counselling have evolved as an effective strategy to address this situation. The Humsafar Trust, an NGO linked to Bombay Dost, came into existence because Bombay Dost recognized that almost no work was being done in terms of AIDS education, prevention and support for gay identified men and other MSM. Similarly, Friends India has started the Bharosa Project to provide sexual health services to gay men in Lucknow. In Calcutta an NGO called Praajak (funded by none other than the West Bengal Sexual Health Project) is conducting a similar sexual health programme, while in the capital city the Naz Foundation (India) Trust is running a sexual health programme for les-bi-gay people, apart from helping a gay group called Humrahi in terms of space and other resources. In Madras, much of the STD/HIV/AIDS intervention work in the context of male same-sex behaviour was initiated in 1993-94 when Shekhar, a volunteer with the Community AIDS Network, came out publicly about being gay and HIV-positive. This was a first of sorts for India. Later Shekhar set up a support group for HIV-positive people called Anbu Alayam (Temple of Love).[43]

Les-bi-gay publications provide information on various facts of HIV transmission and condom use. Condom promotion programmes are also undertaken through social networks and advertisements. Testing facilities for HIV, with pre- and post-test counselling, are provided as well. The groups have been particular about involving only les-bi-gay-friendly doctors and counsellors in their sexual health programmes. Tele-counselling has also caught on in a big way, with four support groups providing this service. Some psychologists, social workers and psychiatrists have also extended their services to sexuality-oriented distress counselling on behalf of the support groups. A conference in Bombay in December 1994 for South Asian gay men and MSM, called 'Emerging Gay Identities in South Asia: Implications for HIV/AIDS & Sexual Health', was attended by about 60 participants from India, Sri Lanka and the South Asian diaspora. In addition to generating discussions on emerging gay identities among the participants, it dealt with the implications of their sexual behaviour for their sexual health.

The les-bi-gay community has clearly decided to adopt a self-help approach to AIDS rather than wait for the government to act. In fact, AIDS has given les-bi-gay people the leverage to talk about same-sex behaviour and relationships much more openly than ever before in modern India. Though the National AIDS Control Organization does not shy away from talking about same-sex behaviour in its AIDS awareness and prevention programmes, visual depiction of same-sex behaviour is still rare in the safer-sex educational material in circulation, like leaflets, posters and hoardings. Besides, government-sponsored efforts fail to address the larger social, legal and economic issues around same-sex behaviour. As a result all the NGOs mentioned earlier have gone in for designing their own communication material.

Accommodation becomes a problem when the family ostracizes a person after coming to know his/her sexual orientation.[44] *Sacred Love,* the Friends India publication, sometimes carries notices from gay men who are willing to share accommodation with other gay men. A similar effort is being made by Sakhi for lesbians in New Delhi. Moreover, it is quite common for les-bi-gay people to extend hospitality to those who are travelling. This trend can be seen as a tool for building a community.

Claiming the future

Ongoing historical changes have led to the emergence of a variety of discourses individuals employ in order to construct their sexual identities. Prior to the 19th century a person's sexual self was not defined in terms of the sex of his/her partners. The rise of les-bi-gay people transformed 'doing' into 'being', and homosexual behaviour became a basis for their identities.

In any society, there are dominant modes of expression generated by dominant structures. It is these articulations that are heard and listened to, especially by outsiders. Minority groups, if they wish to communicate, must express themselves through the same dominant modes. However, there is a lack of congruence and compatibility between the ideas and experiences of minority groups like les-bi-gay people and the modes of public communication available. This enforces a characteristic inarticulateness or muteness. This is true with regard to alternate sexual practices as well, which are seen as 'the other' of the accepted and approved—heterosexual—practices. In a system of binary opposition—good-bad, right-wrong, black-white, constructive-destructive—'the other' is seen as inferior or bad, the opposite of the dominant entity.

The dominant entity, through the discourses it is capable of generating, constantly strengthens and perpetuates itself by self-definition in opposition to 'the other'. Discourses function as ways of legitimating, authorizing or validating some modes against some others in order to silence, control or domesticate certain elements seen as threats to the existence of the dominant entity. However, resistance to the power generated by the discourse—and hence counter-discourse—are inherent in the very nature of discourse. All the activities and issues related to the Indian les-bi-gay movement we have mentioned can be seen as the shaping of a counter-discourse.

Many of the visible les-bi-gay liberation efforts on the legal front are made by the activist group ABVA, which does not have a gay identity. This path seems to be the same as in Britain, where the early law reforms were initiated by non-les-bi-gay groups like Albany Trust. However, one can now see a slow awakening among les-bi-gay people in India, who are beginning to carry forward the legal struggle themselves.

This awakening, however, is far from uniform and is riddled with resistance and paradoxes. Not all les-bi-gay people identify with the movement and its objectives. Les-bi-gay activists are often seen as an elite who can afford to indulge in activism because they don't have to worry about earning a salary. Not all the people that the movement reaches are willing to redefine the concepts of family and marriage. Often unwillingness to join a support group stems from the fear that being part of the group would mean coming out to the whole world. In other words, many les-bi-gay people fear that visibility may well mean too heavy a price to pay. So why move out of the cozy secrecy offered by the homosocial environment of our cultures? The right to choose is not a felt priority; marriage and procreation are considered as givens.

In fact, the les-bi-gay movement has been questioned from within the emerging community as to how it could appropriate the right to break the silence and speak on behalf of all others in the larger community, which remains invisible. The stand taken by the support groups has been that they are there to offer an option to those who want to break the silence, and that their intention is not to coerce anyone into joining them or coming out to the world.[45]

Another paradox is in the making with regard to possible shifts in the les-bi-gay movement's priorities. While in the past priority was given to the effort to remove the act of sodomy from the category of crimes, now there is a trend whereby les-bi-gay groups are widening their horizons of operation in search of financial support. This may lead to a situation whereby aid-giving organizations, whether governmental or non-governmental, will dictate terms and conditions according to their policies. This could in its turn lead to shifts in priority from liberation to sexual health. While some of the support groups, like Arambh and Friends India, are already funded by aid-giving organizations, others have so far resisted the idea of relying on aid-giving organizations. Groups like Counsel Club are not willing to give up their self-funded status.

It is through this maze of paradoxes and conflicts of interest that the Indian les-bi-gay movement needs to go about claiming the future. There is much at stake. The les-bi-gay network provides for its members what other communities do: a training ground for norms and values and a milieu in which they can live from day to day. It provides social support and functions as a source of information for its members. The movement offers not just alternate identities, but also prospects for social reconstruction.

In spite of its marginality, the movement rejects the monolith and the mass. It is a reminder that if forced conformity is to be resisted, it must be by representing human lives as multiple, selfhood as several, communities as voluntary and various. A new definition of political pluralism would be one that judges a society not only by the plurality of groups it tolerates, but also by the plurality of identities it allows individuals to assume.

[1] In the term 'les-bi-gay' (lesbian, bisexual and gay), the use of 'bisexual' is in the sense of a sexual orientation rather than a sexual behaviour. In India 'bisexual' may often be used to refer to heterosexually married gay men and lesbians, many of whom may also self-identify as bisexual. However, such (self) identification is in the sexual behaviour sense. That is not to say that bisexuality as a sexual orientation does not exist in India. In fact, there is a growing identification with the term 'bisexual' in the sexual orientation sense among people who feel that 'gay' and 'lesbian' do not explain their sexuality completely. Hence the use of the term in a sexual identity sense here.

[2] In 1995 sex workers in the red-light areas of West Bengal came together to set up the first ever sex workers' forum in India, the Durbar Mahila Samanwaya Committee. Since 1996 the forum has organized a number of national and international conferences in Calcutta, which have generated a lot of public interest—in the form of both empathy and condemnation. The forum is at the forefront of the demand for decriminalization of prostitution and also conducts an STD/HIV/AIDS intervention programme. Recently some male sex workers have also joined the forum. Some members of Counsel Club, Calcutta's les-bi-gay support group, have also established links with the forum by helping organize their events.

[3] AIDS Bhedbhav Virodhi Andolan (ABVA), *Less Than Gay: A Citizens' Report on the Status of Homosexuality in India*, New Delhi: ABVA, 1991.

[4] Subodh Mukherjee, 'Homosexuality in India: a personal quest for the historical perspective', *Trikone* vol. 5 no. 1 (1990).

[5] Nayan Shah, 'Sexuality, identity and the use of history', in Rakesh Ratti ed., *A Lotus of Another Colour: An Unfolding of the South Asian Gay and Lesbian Experience*, Boston: Alyson, 1993, p. 17.

[6] According to Giti Thadani, independent lesbian researcher and founding member of the Sakhi Collective, same-sex experiences enjoyed much greater acceptance in the days before the advent of Vedic Brahmanism. Texts like the *Rig Veda*, which dates back to around 1500 BC, and temple sculptures and reliefs depict sexual acts between women

as revelations of a feminine world where sexuality was based on pleasure and fertility. However, with the rise of Vedic Brahmanism the increasingly dominant patriarchy started suppressing homosexuality. In the *Manusmriti* there are references to punishments like loss of caste, heavy monetary fines and strokes of the whip for same-sex behaviour, both male and female. Compulsory heterosexuality thus started emerging as the norm. (Interview with Thadani by *Lesbia* magazine, reprinted in *Shakti Khabar* no. 14, 1991.)

[7] Even after Vedic Brahmanism made its presence felt, homosexuality seems to have co-existed with compulsory heterosexuality in Indian culture. Male homosexuality seems to have had the official patronage of the Mughal rulers, as is evident from the harems of young boys kept by Muslim nawabs and Hindu aristocrats. However, with British colonization, the destruction of images of homosexual expression and sexual expression in general became more systematic and blatant. The British had strong assumptions about sexuality: any sexual activity which was non-procreative in nature was dubbed 'unnatural'. In time the Indian psyche also absorbed Western ideas about homosexuality as being something 'pathological'.

[8] Editor's response to a letter by LN in *Shakti Khabar,* Dec. 1990-Jan. 1991.

[9] Shivananda Khan, 'Report of the Seminar on Gender Construction and History of Alternate Sexualities in South Asia (New Delhi, December 1993)', London: Naz Project, 1994, p. 10.

[10] R. Duffin, 'People with HIV and the National Conference', *National AIDS Bulletin,* Dec. 1992-Jan. 1993; M. Pollak, 'AIDS: a problem for sociological research', *Current Sociology* vol. 40 no. 3 (1992).

[11] Though the Indian les-bi-gay movement is generally considered to have started in the early 1990s, sporadic attempts had been made at les-bi-gay action since as far back as the late 1970s. The earliest and most significant of all these attempts seems to have been a journal called *Gay Scene* which was published by a few individuals in Calcutta in the late 1970s and early 1980s. Only a few issues of the journal seem to have been published. (Reported in *Shakti Khabar* no. 12 (1991)).

[12] Arvind Kumar, '*Bombay Dost* and *Shamakami*: two new publications make their debut', *Trikone* vol. 10 no. 4 (1990).

[13] Amita Kar and Bombay Lesbians, 'Country report: 1992', *Bombay Dost* vol. 1 nos. 5 & 6 (1992).

[14] S. Kulkarni & P. Jagannathan, 'Lesbianism as a political act', *Shakti Khabar* no. 10 (Oct.-Nov. 1990).

[15] Shah, 'Sexuality, identity and the use of history', pp. 115-16. Not everybody in the women's movement seems to think like Agnes. The Sakhi Collective writes, 'We... have not received one letter of acknowledgment or support from any Indian feminist organisation. Statements to this effect ['There are no lesbians in India'] have been made by Madhu Kishwar of *Manushi* and Urvashi Butalia of Kali for Women. Sakhi has never been invited to any feminist events.' Kishwar later denied having made the statements attributed to her by Sakhi.

[16] Shivananda Khan, 'Emerging gay identities in South Asia: implications for HIV/ AIDS & sexual health, Humsafar-Naz Conference Report (Bombay, December 1994)', London: Naz Project, 1995, p. 51.

[17] Ashwini, 'Anirudda Bhumi?', *Pravartak* no. 2 (Apr.-June 1994).

[18] Michael Storm, 'Theories of sexual orientation', *Journal of Personality and Social Psychology* vol. 38 (1980). Rigid ideas about gender may not be limited only to the appearance of a man or a woman but also to his or her sexual orientation. One of the

reasons why Arvind Kala's work on Indian gay men (*Invisible Minority: The Unknown World of the Indian Homosexual,* New Delhi: Dynamic Books, 1992) was criticized and rejected by the gay community was that it contained such stereotyping remarks about masculinity and femininity (see the critiques in Ashok Row Kavi, 'Gay abandoned', *The Sunday Times,* 5 Aug. 1992, and Parwaiz, 'Of homophobia and Kala', *Pravartak* no. 1 (1993)). Although a number of books have been published on homosexuality in India, few would count as notable works. Shakuntala Devi's *The World of Homosexuals,* New Delhi: Vikas, 1978, was the first book of its kind; given the time of its publication, it was surprisingly much better researched than Kala's *Invisible Minority,* which was written during the upsurge of les-bi-gay movement.

[19] *Times of India,* 9 Nov. 1994 and later in Nov. 1994.

[20] Ritesh, 'They want to make me a man', *Pravartak* no. 1 (1993); Andrade A. Chitra et al., 'Behavior therapy for transsexualism', *Indian Journal of Psychiatry* vol. 37 no. 3 (1995).

[21] 'Trying time for "odd" couple', *The Telegraph,* 15 Apr. 1995; 'The two who got away', *Sunday Mail,* 25-31 Mar. 1990.

[22] The politician in question was Jayalalitha Jayaram, then (in 1995) chief minister of Tamil Nadu state. Her confidante and roommate was Sasikala Natarajan, whose political clout is said to have grown phenomenally over the years, thanks to Jayaram. The two separated about two years ago when Jayaram became embroiled in a controversy generated by corruption charges against her. Rajani Kumar, 'Jayalalitha and Sasikala: Tamil Nadu's "First Roomies"', *Trikone* vol. 10 no. 4 (1995).

[23] Rakesh, 'A strange wedding', *Bombay Dost* vol. 2 no. 2 (1995).

[24] See footnote 3, above.

[25] Stree Sangam and Forum Against Oppression of Women, 'Lesbian and gay rights in India: background paper for the Workshop on Strategies for Furthering Les-bi-gay Rights in India (Bombay, November 1997)', Bombay, 1997.

[25a] Babari Masjid: during the Mughal invasion of India, a temple believed to be built at the birthplace of the Hindu god Rama was converted into a mosque by Babar, the first of the Mughal rulers. However, the idol of Rama was retained in the mosque. This mosque, located at Ayodhya in Uttar Pradesh state, is what is referred to as the Babari Masjid. In 1992, the Hindu fundamentalists with their Hindutva ideology decided to set right what they saw as an 'historical wrong' and managed to demolish Babari Masjid on 6 December 1992. The fundamentalists were supposed to have had the tacit support of the ruling BJP state government in Uttar Pradesh, and the Congress government in New Delhi also failed to prevent the destruction.

[26] See Shivananda Khan, 'Cultural construction of male sexualities in India', paper presented at the 10th World Congress on Sexology (Yokohama, Aug. 1995).

[27] Khan, *Emerging Gay Identities in South Asia,* p. 30.

[28] Kala, *Invisible Minority,* p. 189.

[29] Khan, *Emerging Gay Identities in South Asia,* p. 60.

[30] ABVA, *Less Than Gay,* pp. 92-93.

[31] 'Gay protest Against police crackdown', *The Indian Express,* 12 Aug. 1992.

[32] Modhumita Mojumdar, 'Sex in the prison', *The Hindustan Times,* 27 May 1994.

[33] Sherry Joseph, 'Report of the meeting on the legal struggle: repeal of Section 377, IPC', New Delhi: ABVA (mimeo), 1995.

[34] The police claimed that all eighteen people were arrested 'for attempting sodomy in a public park'. Most sections of the press dutifully reported the police version of the

story. However, ABVA asserted that no one was having sex in the park. This, it said, was proven by the fact that the police themselves had later charged the people under Sections 92, 93 and 97 of the Delhi Police Act, which did not cover homosexuality and sodomy. ABVA also questioned the legality and ethics of the modus operandi adopted by the police in acting as decoys and entrapping gay and bisexual men. It alleged that the policemen were misusing Section 377 to harass homosexuals found in public places and extort money from them, a complaint common to gay and bisexual men almost all over India. Les-bi-gay people joined ABVA in asserting that two consenting adults of the same sex should be within their rights to meet in a public place and become friendly, which may or may not culminate in sexual activity in a non-public place later. ABVA also said that the police action had amounted to contempt of parliament since a petition for the repeal of Section 377 was already pending with the Lok Sabha (lower house).

[35] John Burbidge, 'Lifting the veil: Gay India revisited', *Campaign*, Nov. 1994.

[36] *Business India* (Mar. 1992) published '*Bombay Dost*: gay voice', an article on the potential of the les-bi-gay community as a market segment.

[37] Parvez Sharma, 'Emerging from the shadows', *The Statesman*, 3 July 1994, and Chitralekha Dhamija, 'Loving women', *Sunday*, 17-23 May 1998, are two such examples.

[38] Rantim Bhattacharya, 'Out in the media', *Trikone* vol. 9 no. 1 (1994). Detailed reviews of visibility in the media can be found in Sultan Khan, 'Media watch', *Bombay Dost* vol. 2 no. 3 (1993); Debjyoti, 'Omitting acts of commission', *Pravartak* no. 2 (Apr.-June 1994); and Pawan, 'Out on the stands, under the open skies', *Naya Pravartak* no. 5 (May-Dec.) 1995.

[39] Editor's response to a letter by LN in *Shakti Khabar*, Dec. 1990-Jan. 1991.

[40] *Starry Nights* and *Strange Obsession* by Shobha De; *One Day I Locked My Flat in Soul City* by R. Raj Rao; and *The Conversations of Cow* by Suniti Namjoshi. Partha, 'Prejudice mightier than pen', *Pravartak* no. 3 (July-Dec. 1994), examines the treatment of male homosexuality in Bengali literature.

[41] Khan, *Emerging Gay Identities in South Asia*, p. 29.

[42] Anuja Gupta, 'A testimony', *Trikone* vol. 11 no. 1 (1996).

[43] ACTIONAID/British Council/UNDP, 'Broadening the front: NGO responses to HIV and AIDS in India', *Strategies for Hope* no. 11 (1996).

[44] PD, 'Homosexuality, homelessness and guts', *Pravartak* no. 3 (Feb.-Mar. 1992).

[45] See Pawan, 'Offering a choice', *Pravartak* no. 2 (Apr.-June 1994).

Awakenings: dreams and delusions of an incipient lesbian and gay movement in Kenya

John Mburu[1]

To raise issues of gay rights in Kenya is to ask for trouble, in a country and time where trouble frequently comes to gays unasked. In the course of the 1990s they have faced recurrent diatribes from President Moi; anathemas from Christian clerics and university lecturers; sensationalist scandal-mongering in the press; government charges of devil worship; and attacks by the immigration authorities, on top of the usual corruption and brutality of the police and officially approved repression by tribal authorities. These onslaughts have taken a major toll on the few gay and lesbian activists who, almost invisibly, have been taking part in the rise of non-governmental organizations and the democratic opposition's efforts at reform.

The backlash against the 'spread' of homosexuality in Africa has never been so loud and so heated as in the last few years. Evidently the movement towards reform and tolerance in South Africa, as well as pioneering efforts by gay and lesbian groups such as Gays and Lesbians of Zimbabwe, has elicited a sharp and critical response. Will more widespread information about the existence of homosexuality in pre-colonial Africa increase tolerance and respect? Can the sincere efforts of gay and lesbian anthropologists, historians, or even political activists in Europe and America bring about the liberation of gays and lesbians in Africa?

My contention is that while studies being undertaken by anthropologists and historians may finally disprove the notion that homosexuality is 'un-African', this in itself will not bring change. What is at stake is a pervasive ideology that stills portrays the supremacy of individual rights—women's, gays', or others'—as un-African and deleterious. Only the awareness and the willingness to create greater acceptance of universal standards of human rights can bring about momentous change in the future. Any gay and lesbian movement in Kenya must articulate a new political agenda, including but not exclusively focused on gay rights.

Same-sex identities in sub-Saharan Africa

Kenya, an East African nation with a population of about 30 million, is split almost in half by the equator. To its north, Kenya is bordered by Sudan and Ethiopia; to the northeast lies Somalia, to the south Tanzania, and to the west Uganda. Kenya's present-day population is mainly Bantu, a group of African peoples who are said to have originated in western Africa and slowly migrated eastwards by about 300 AD. The Nilotes, of whom the Maasai are the

most famous, originated in southern Sudan, traversed Uganda and finally set-
tled along Lake Victoria and in the eastern and western regions of Kenya. The
Cushites—so called because of their origins in Ethiopia and Somalia—the
smallest of Kenya's native African inhabitants, are found along the borders with
Somalia and Ethopia. About 5 per cent of Kenya's population is made up of
Swahili peoples originating from the intermarriage of migrating Arabs from
Persia and the Arabian peninsula with African peoples; Indian immigrants; and
British settlers. Kenya gained its independence from Britain in 1963.

It is widely held that despite their wide geographic spread, most ethnic
groups in Africa still share many common religious beliefs and practices, family
and kinship relationships, and linguistic traditions. Common traditions amongst
various African groups indicate the dynamism of belief systems, precipitated by
cultural assimilation and the interaction of peoples from different ethnic backgrounds. An example of this is the adoption of various Maasai customs by the
Kikuyu, Kamba and Nandi peoples in Kenya.

The near uniform condemnation of homosexuality by leaders throughout
Africa arises from this notion of a shared group of beliefs and customs. But in
fact the pervasive notion of homosexuality as 'un-African' harks back to late
eighteenth-century Europe. In one of the earliest instances of this opinion,
Edward Gibbon, author of *The Decline and Fall of the Roman Empire*, wrote, 'I
believe and hope that Negroes in their own country were exempt from [homo-
sexuality]'. In a similar vein, nineteenth-century British explorer and writer
Richard Burton sought to draw an arbitrary line below the Sahara desert,
suggesting the furthest reaches of the practice of homosexuality in Africa.[2]

More recently African leaders, politicians and church officials have made
trenchant speeches assailing homosexuality as yet another example of the vestiges of colonialism. While Zimbabwean president Robert Mugabe's vitriolic
ranting has received the most press coverage, a chorus of other African leaders
have joined in. The February 1997 issue of the *Mail and Guardian Reporter*
quoted Namibian president Sam Nujoma describing gay groups supporting
local Namibian organizations as '[European] perverts who imagine themselves
to be the bulwark of civilization and enlightenment'. In Kenya the *Daily Nation* reported President Moi repeatedly warning of the menace of homosexuality and lesbianism, saying that 'words like lesbianism and homosexuality do not
exist in African languages'.[3] African leaders have argued that the apparent lack
of homosexual identity in sub-Saharan Africa shows that homosexuality is only
a recent phenomenon.

But could the rarity of homosexual identity in sub-Saharan Africa today
instead be evidence of an ideology that has stifled Africa's same-sex traditions?
In fact, the work of noted anthropologists and historians testifies to the existence of same-sex relationships in Africa prior to the colonial invasion. This
evidence of homosexual behaviour amongst certain African peoples could lend
weight to the hypothesis that it was a widespread practice, precisely because of
the common traditions, cross-pollination of cultural beliefs, and assimilation
of cultural practices between different African peoples.

Some of the earliest evidence for the existence of same-sex relationships dates back to the early twentieth century. In his studies amongst the Fang people of Ghana, German anthropologist Gunter Tessman found that homosexual intercourse was considered an omen of prosperity.[4] Interestingly, in the proceedings of the criminal case brought against former Zimbabwean president Canaan Banana, a security officer for the former president alleged that Banana claimed that homosexuality was an omen of prosperity.[5]

The Nandi of Kenya and the Lovedu of South Africa had traditions of woman-woman marriage, widespread throughout Africa. The practice involved an widowed elderly woman taking a younger wife, who helped with household chores and bore children as a surrogate for the older woman. While a controversy exists as to whether these relationships were sexual, among the Azande women formed lesbian relationships amongst themselves that were kept secret from their husbands. Thomas George Barton also notes in his comprehensive anthology that there was great apprehension about these relationships among Azande men, since they feared that women would 'relish the sense of personal control and making it last as long as they wanted'. Similar relationships were also fairly common among the Nupe and Hausa of West Africa.[6]

Along the east coast of Africa, Africans and Arab migrants from Oman and other parts of Arabia contributed to the Swahili culture that developed a thriving Indian Ocean trade based on ivory, cloves and slaves. In Zanzibar, the capital of the Omani empire after 1840, as well as in Mombasa, Malindi and Kilwa, male homosexuality had become a conspicuous example of the influence of Omani traditions and cultures. Lamenting the habit of male homosexuals wearing female dress in Zanzibar, General Rigby, an American living on the island, stated, 'Numbers of sodomites have come from Muscat (Oman), and these degraded wretches openly walk about dressed in female attire with veils on their faces.'[7] It is highly likely that similar practices were in evidence all along the Swahili coast from Mogadishu in Somalia south to Mozambique.

Another method of tracing early same-sex practices in Africa has been to identify African traditions among slave communities in the Americas. Author James Sweet demonstrates effectively not only the 'tenacity of core beliefs and practices' retained from Africa but that such evidence 'may be used to fill in the silences created by the lack of documentation on the specific practices of Bantu-speaking peoples'.[8]

Tracing the saga of Joane, a slave from 'Guinea' charged by Portuguese authorities in Brazil in 1591 with sodomy, Sweet demonstrates that male homosexuals were considered to be powerful religious figures according to African customs. The testimony against Joane seemed to indicate that he compelled his partner to have sex. Sweet points out, however, that 'given their numerous encounters, [his partners] probably welcomed Joane's invitations'.[9] This leads the author to question why these African slaves would choose to flout Portuguese laws. His answer lies in the west-central African institution of *jin bandaa*, a medicine man who was seen as a medium between the spiritual world and the world of the living. Drawing on the writings of a Portuguese captain familiar with the tradition, Sweet suggests that Joane may have been revered as *jin bandaa*.

Gloria Wekker's work among Surinamese women similarly helps to establish the case for same-sex identities and traditions in Africa. By focusing on Afro-Surinamese traditions, Wekker's research on the tradition of *mati*-ism, 'women who have sexual relations with other women', confirms Sweet's findings of the continuity of African traditions in the black populations of South America.[10]

It is evident that the notion of exclusive heterosexuality in pre-colonial sub-Saharan Africa is not borne out by the evidence. Though same-sex practises were not met with social approval in all African societies, it is clear that in many communities same-sex relations were closely interwoven in the social fabric. In some cases, as with the institution of *jin bandaa,* transvestite homosexuals played a significant role in the community. We can hope that in the coming years more information will 'fill the silence' that has resulted from the pervasive ideology that refuses to accept notions of same-sex relations in sub-Saharan Africa.

Obstacles to gay and lesbian rights in Kenya

In the words of Amos Alcott, 'To be ignorant of one's own ignorance is the curse of the ignorant.' No truer words could be spoken about the general level of ignorance of Africa's traditional same-sex practices. This ignorance results from a pervasive ideology that homosexuality is 'un-African'. The effect of decades of evangelizing colonization and several more of post-colonial, nationalistic fervour, along with a schizophrenic reaction to urbanization and westernization, has contributed enormously to fanning homophobic rhetoric.

With the one of the fastest growing church populations in the world, Africa is pervaded by the influence of Christian doctrine opposed to homosexuality. Early evangelizing missions surreptitiously meshed traditional African customary belief systems with biblical scripture. One result was that early missionaries adopted traditional symbols. For example, traditional names of the Supreme Being were co-opted by missionaries. Sacrificial rites and initiation ceremonies that were not considered 'pagan' or 'heathen', such as male circumcision, were left intact. However African practices that were considered an abomination—such as levirate, a practice in which widows would marry their deceased husband's brother; female circumcision; woman-woman marriage; and homosexuality—were stamped out or driven underground.

Nothing illustrates this better than the case of Kabaka (King) Mwanga, who ruled over the Baganda people of modern-day Uganda at the turn of the nineteenth century. His rule unfortunately coincided with the spread of Christianity in his kingdom. In keeping with Baganda tradition, the Kabaka often had page-boys betrothed to him as 'boy-wives'. Mwanga's pages Kizito, Mwafu and Denis Sebuggawo, among others, were however converted to Christianity and forbidden to have sex with the king by Charles Lwanga, an African convert who was evangelizing in the king's court. Such was Mwanga's ire that he immediately banned missionary work in Buganda and ordered the execution of Lwanga and seventeen Christian converts, included his 'boy-wives'. While Mwanga's intent was to destroy the growing influence of Christianity in his kingdom, his actions led directly to his overthrow at the insistence of the Anglican church, and ultimately the colonization of Uganda by Britain.[11]

Evangelizing by these Christian missions has been so effective as to border on brainwashing. Often *wananchi* (citizens) who condemn homosexuality as 'un-African' call upon biblical denunciations of homosexuality in support of this claim. This curious phenomenon is not restricted to ordinary citizens but appears among highly educated people. At the meeting of World Council of Churches held in South Africa in 1996, despite the call for 'deep and dispassionate' debate on the matter of homosexuality, Kenyan clerics in the Anglican church displayed a remarkable ignorance of African's traditional practices. While South African Archbishop Desmond Tutu likened discrimination against gays and lesbians to South Africa's former apartheid system, Douglas Waruta, a senior lecturer in religious studies at the University of Nairobi, cautioned about 'accepting lectures from the Western church'. He went on to add that homosexuality was a taboo in Africa, equating the practice with bestiality. 'African culture', he would claim in his revisionist sermon, 'rejects such behaviour outright and the Church in Africa can build on this tradition to maintain the natural sexual orientation acceptable to Africans.'[12]

Sadly, such ignorance is not restricted solely to members of the clergy. While in most other nations institutions of higher learning have played a significant role in propagating new ideas and shedding light on past traditions, African scholars remain tight-lipped if not blatantly homophobic about Africa's multifarious sexual traditions. African scholars have shown themselves unable to accept the diversity of Africa's own sexual practices, and instead have sought to perpetuate the myth of Africa's exclusive heterosexuality. The fact that few African historians or anthropologists would broach such topics gives further credence to a state-sanctioned or imposed mandate that shuns intellectual inquiry into the existence of Africa's 'less savoury' traditions.

Chris Dunton, a professor of African literature in South Africa, provides an illuminating insight into the post-colonial rhetoric in the works of some of Africa's foremost writers. He finds that in the great majority of texts homosexuality plays a political role in defining nationalist and anti-colonial ideology. In the following passage, Dunton describes the role homosexuality plays in the mindset of the African writer:

> In a number of different contexts—the colonial situation; the neo-colonial state ruled through collusion with Western advisers; the prison system under apartheid; the situation of the African student living in the West—homosexuality is identified with exploitation, being enabled by money or power relations, and understood to be all the more disturbing because alien to African society.[13]

Homosexuality is used in literature as a tool to portray the baseness of the foreigner, Arab or European; to denigrate the dictator or puppet-king; or to describe the hapless African in the midst of oppression.

The result of these diatribes by politicians, clergy and intellectuals is the construction of a powerful mechanism for social control and imposition of a heterosexist ideology. This machine is deployed in various ways, but most powerfully when attacking external and internal threats to the status quo. When the media joins in spewing this xenophobic rhetoric, the result is an explosion of hatred. For example, the *East African Standard* newspaper ran a story with the highly inflammatory heading, 'Schoolgirls in Lesbian Sex Trap'. The exposé purported to have uncovered a syndicate led by a madam, the ex-wife of a former cabinet minister, with a taste for young schoolgirls. Her largesse, the story alleged, had led unsuspecting schoolgirls into debauchery and immorality. The sordid tale received instant media attention. No names were revealed, neither the ex-minister's wife's nor those of her cohorts, two European expatriates. Not even the names of the newspaper's correspondents covering the story were revealed. Yet the ensuing debate led to motions in parliament demanding immediate action to rout out the vice of lesbianism before it contaminated society.

In another example, as the president and ruling party stalwarts were under intense pressure from the public and the IMF to probe allegations of government corruption, President Moi issued a proclamation forming a commission to look into the growing cult of devil worship in the country. Amongst the supposed practices of the cult followers were human sacrifice, drinking human blood, homosexuality, bestiality and lesbianism. The telltale sign of practitioners was the numbers '666' emblazoned on their foreheads. As Paul Muite, an attorney and opposition activist, commented to a journalist, 'Moi won't release the reports, but it won't be long before he says it names his enemies as devil worshippers. I know from statements of those around the president that I am one of the people he would like to use the report to destroy.'[14] While these incidents may seem farcical, the results have been harassment, persecution, and murder of gays and lesbians.

Kenya's archaic penal code dates back to the era of British colonial rule. While in Britain penalties against 'crimes against nature' were repealed in 1967, these vestiges of Kenya's colonial past still remain intact. Sections 162-165 of the Penal Code[15] deal generally with 'unnatural offences', but in practice the laws are used exclusively against gay men.[16] Further evidence of persecution of gays and lesbians is to be found in the words of the Kenyan ambassador to the US. Justifying the use of the penal code against homosexuals, he states:

Homosexualism (sic) itself is outlawed in Kenya and as such homosexuals have no protection from the government regarding their practice... Homosexuals in Kenya, and in the majority of countries in Africa for that matter, are social outcasts and have no respectable place to practice their trade...

When homosexuals are caught, they are arrested and charged for contra-
vention of 'natural law'... Government does not offer any protection to
those engaged in homosexual acts.[17]

These statements pale in comparison to the macabre details of the daily
lives of gays and lesbians living in Nairobi. In the following passage a young
man, whose name will remain undisclosed for fear of retribution, recounts his
experience as a gay male living in Nairobi. It is a chilling reminder of the effect
of the rulers' political ideology:

[Nairobi's] social [gay] life [is] completely underground. There are no
bars, associations, or formal meeting places. Everyone tried to keep their
homosexuality hidden from heterosexual society. When people discovered their sexual orientation, they were persecuted. I felt I could not be
safe anywhere. When I left home, I was raped; when I returned, I was
insulted and beaten.

The young man goes on to describe how his homosexuality led him into
the underbelly of Kenya's corrupt and violent penal system.

In April 1996, I went out dancing with five gay friends... At around
midnight or so, we took a walk for fresh air. The police stopped us and
demanded our identification cards... [Kenya's national identification cards
list each person's name and province, which easily identifies people's tribes.]
In Kenya, the police take people to jail if they catch them without their
identification cards. I had lost mine a while ago and my replacement
application was still pending. I did not have my card and the police wanted
to take me to jail. The officers asked me whether I was male or female, and
I flippantly told them none of the above. They told me I was rude and I
responded that they wanted to make fun of me... I recognized that the
policemen were the same tribe as the president. The rest of my friends all
had their cards and were all identifiable as Kikuyus. In addition, the
officers assumed we were gay. They insulted us by saying we were from
Sodom and Gomorrah. The police threatened to take all of us to jail... We
began to plead to let us go. I was particularly panicked, afraid that my
mother would never come for me. The officers struck a deal and proposed
that if we did not want to go to jail, we must let the officers 'fuck' us...
They threatened it would only be worse if we went to jail. I knew we could
not run because they had guns and clubs. Our lives were in danger. We
did not run away, and we were brutally raped. The officers gang-raped all
of us.

It was with foresight that a former commissioner of prisons in Tanzania in
the early nineteenth century, Mr Rugimbana, decried the imposition of colonial laws in East Africa. Though his comments refer to Kenya's southern neighbor,

they still provide a cautionary note about the blanket application of colonial laws on African peoples: "In a nation of different tribes, with different social values and ethics, the application of such common codes and sanctions creates a class of law breakers with no real criminal tendencies or intentions who, nevertheless, are herded along with, and branded as, criminals in their generality."[18]

Rugimbana's cautionary words find are brought into relief by Marc Epprecht's legal research into homosexual crime in early colonial Zimbabwe (then Southern Rhodesia). Epprecht's research shows how British prudery led to the needless incarceration of hundreds of African men. He first debunks the myth that homosexuality in precolonial Zimbabwe resulted from exposure to corrupting foreign white males or migrant workers from Mozambique. On the contrary, 90 per cent of all cases that were tried involved 'African men "assaulting" other African men or boys'. Homosexual activity was not confined to mines or prisons, or generally to men who were unable to have sex with women. The 'criminals' from mines or jails only slightly outnumbered those from farms or 'black townships', where some of the criminals could easily have sated their sexual appetites with women. Furthermore if economic hardship were the only motivating factor one would expect a general increase in criminal activity, which was not the case.

While these relations between men often involved monetary exchange, the money mostly functioned as a 'dowry', which provided the semblance of a long-term relationship with rights and responsibilities. As a result most cases brought forward involved the plaintiff complaining that the defendant had not kept his promise to make monetary gifts. Epprecht is lead to the conclusion that these 'criminals' were actually victims of 'reciprocal, relatively long-term, and apparently loving relationships... in an atmosphere that so utterly militated against them'.[19]

In a curious twist of fate, these laws have even been used by African lawmakers and judges to persecute non-Africans. In jail in Kenya during the 1960s for whipping a local poacher, itinerant American writer and photographer Peter Beard had as his cellmate a 'white policeman in on a trumped-up charge of "being seen on the same bed as an African", a thinly masked charge of homosexual behaviour'.[20] In December 1994 immigration officials deported an Australian man under suspicions that he was working in concert with other foreigners to foment a gay and lesbian movement. The officials said the man was a menace to the 'people of Lamu'. Immigration spokesman Frank Kwinga stated, 'Homosexuality is prohibited under our country's laws and is morally unacceptable in our society.'[21]

The application of 'customary' law purportedly based on traditional legal mechanisms for dealing with social deviance also plays a role in the persecution of gays and lesbians. Anthropologist Mary Porter reports on a conversation with a Kenyan on native customs dealing with homosexuality. Among the Samburu, Turkana, Rendille and Boran homosexuality 'is considered an abomination. If anyone is ever found to have done "it", they dig a hole, light a fire in it, lay stones in it, put the offender in on top of the stones and then bury him alive'. Among the Luo, homosexuals are forced out of the community.[22] As customary law only requires that the punishment, in this case for homosexuality, not be repugnant to justice and morality, such laws can pose grave dangers to gays and lesbians in Kenya, especially given the government's stance against homosexuality and the general ignorance of African traditional customs.

Undoubtedly any further excavation of the past practices of Africans would be revealing to Africans, given our ignorance of our sexual customs. However there are a number of factors that might mitigate against the success of such an enterprise. First, the fact that such research would be undertaken under the auspices of foreign institutions would mean that little of the information would actually flow back to Africans agitating for their rights. Second, while a cross-cultural perspective can be useful in combatting homophobia in American society', drawing parallels between same-sex practises in pre-colonial Africa with Western homosexuality requires great care. Finally, in addition to these scholarly pitfalls, the government's censorship in institutions of higher learning in Kenya makes it doubtful that such material would make it into the public arena. Scholars and professors who tried to publish it would no doubt come under intense scrutiny, if not outright harassment.

An emerging lesbian and gay movement in Kenya?

Nevertheless, literature about gay and lesbians Africans is becoming increasingly available. This trend has lead to some to over-exuberance about the prospects for gay and lesbian movements in Kenya. Yet some Kenyan gays and lesbians, both at home and abroad, are slowly coming to terms with the notion of a gay and lesbian movement. Activists have begun contemplating creating political groups and, given the political change afoot in Kenya, a new political agenda. They have also begun articulating a distinctive outlook for Kenyan gays and lesbians.

Gay and lesbian activists have made their presence felt in Kenya, in particular in their response to the AIDS epidemic. Such was the goal of the recently disbanded Forum for Positive Generation on AIDS Prevention. The group was formed by homosexual men from Kisumu, the third largest town in Kenya, on the shores of Lake Victoria. Its purpose was to increase social awareness and sensitivity towards people with AIDS, and more specifically to highlight and relieve the plight of marginalized groups such as homosexuals with AIDS. Despite their laudable goals of reaching out to an invisible community with few resources to handle the AIDS emergency, the group ran afoul of politicians and opened themselves to attacks alleging that they were 'recruiting' homosexuals.[23]

It should not be surprising that in the wake of the AIDS epidemic in Kenya gay activists would raise issues about the appropriateness of 'conventional labels' of human sexuality. An editorial in the *Lancet* argued recently that current labels identifying human sexual behaviour can be misleading. Drawing an analogy to the US, the article argues that some men described as homo-sexual were either married, homosexual men with recent heterosexual experi-ences, or heterosexual men with homosexual experiences.[24] While the spread of AIDS in Kenya, as in the rest of Africa, has been predominantly a result of heterosexual intercourse, research suggests that heteronormative assumptions underlie current research into AIDS awareness. In prisons, for example, where AIDS is rampant, little is mentioned about the risks of unsafe anal intercourse. Furthermore, inconclusive studies suggest that homosexual behaviour among the general populace is being ignored. One study of public awareness of AIDS in Rwanda concludes that sex occurs 'frequently between some European and Rwandese men, and occasionally between Rwandese men themselves'. It fur-ther reports that homosexuality was traditionally practiced among adult Tutsi males, despite the fact that 'all male Tutsi informants denied knowledge of this practice in either their present or past'.[25] Though the above research was con-ducted in Rwanda, it sheds light on the situation in Kenya, where as yet little research has been done on the spread of AIDS through homosexual contact.

In the case of Forum for Positive Generation on AIDS Prevention, the catalyst for the group was the threat of AIDS; one of Africa's best-known gay and lesbian groups, Gays and Lesbians of Zimbabwe, was also founded as a response to the AIDS epidemic, and began by offering safe-sex workshops.[26] In other African countries the development of gay and lesbian groups has gone beyond AIDS advocacy to include demands for gay, lesbian and transsexual rights. As South Africa's National Coalition fans the winds of change north-wards, gay and lesbian rights advocacy has become the calling of emergent groups in Namibia, Zimbabwe, Zambia, Bostwana, Lesotho and Swaziland. The film *Woubi Cheri* shows organizing led by activist transvestites in Ivory Coast, under the 'pre-op' transsexual Barbara, who hope to increase the trans-vestites' visibility and sensitize Ivorians to their plight. In Gambia, the film *Dankan* portrays the love of two boys in high school, who endure societal demands, Christian and pagan exorcisms and parental rebuke in order to stay together. The dream of a transnational umbrella organization may even have been ushered in at an AIDS conference in Kampala, Uganda, organized in 1996 by South African ANC veteran Simon Nkoli, which brought together lesbians and gays from about twenty African countries.[27]

Gay and lesbian concerns go hand-in-hand with other social movements that are afoot in Kenya. The strategies being applied differ significantly from those in the West. A few gays and lesbians have began to play an instrumental, albeit quiet, role in the process of constitutional reform. Reform resulted in multi-party elections in Kenya in 1992, renewed press freedoms, and trans-formed the country's political debates, amounting to what has been termed a 'second birth' of Kenyan politics. This process followed an earlier rise of social movements: the women's movement in particular was given a significant boost by Nairobi's hosting the 1985 Non-Governmental Organization Conference as well as the Third Annual World Conference on Women. Since then numerous women's groups and non-governmental organizations have emerged in Nairobi and more strikingly in smaller towns and rural areas. Despite the rancour that still characterizes debate in parliament, the opposition parties have made significant headway in exposing corruption and arguing for greater political freedoms.

By placing gay and lesbian rights on the political back burner, gay and lesbian activists hope to create alliances with women's groups and non-governmental organizations, which will in turn lead to a greater openness to universal human rights. Fabian (a pseudonym), who sees himself as a gay activist, nonetheless asks whether 'in a country where basic, acknowledged human rights are still not respected, where women's rights aren't guaranteed, the idea of gay rights is going too far'. While the fear of retribution or the prematurity of a gay rights platform is certainly echoed in Fabian's rhetorical question, Muthoni Wanyeki attributes the reluctance of gay and lesbian activists to self-identify as a process of creating a unique 'queer' African identity. Wanyeki's interview with Mumbi (also a pseudonym), a lesbian activist in Nairobi, also provides insights into this reticence. A 'hierarchy of rights', explains Mumbi, 'implies that as a lesbian I'm not affected by being a woman and I'm not affected by the political situation in this country'. 'The fact is', she continues, 'all these things affect my life at the same time.'[28]

Mumbi's argument carries more weight in the context of women's rights and the precarious situation of the poor. Mumbi's apprehension about being pigeonholed is a deep concern of many Kenyan gays and lesbians who want to advocate for change. Mumbi's explanation of her approach to contending with other crucial social and political problems in the country concludes, 'I don't want to risk my sexuality becoming the be-all-and-end-all of what I am.'[29] In Mumbi's case lesbian activism combines with feminist theory to shape an approach influenced by and at the same time distant from western notions of same-sex identity. In Katie King's analysis of local and global formations of lesbian and gay identities, Mumbi's apprehension about an all-encompassing lesbian identity could be described as 'cultural feminism': 'a sometimes essentialist and sometimes anti-essentialist synthesis of identity politics'. Mumbi accepts her global heritage as a lesbian and a feminist, but is also simultaneously troubled by their implications in her local setting.[30]

Kenyan gays and lesbians both at home and abroad are trying to envision a new direction for the civil rights debate in Kenya. By claiming a multifaceted and multilayered identity, as Africans and as gays and lesbians, we hope to confront the formidable challenges before us. The pervasive ideology that still portrays homosexuality as un-African and Western can only be neutralized by an ideal that embraces Africa's various traditions and customs as well as the Western influences that are now an indelible part of Africa's traditions as well. This ideal aspires to universal standards of human rights, weaves together the struggles of the *wanaichi,* and articulates a new political agenda including but not exclusively focused on gay rights.

[1] I would like to acknowledge all the contributions of my friends, colleagues, and loved ones. Suffice it to say, I could never have completed this article without their insight, encouragement and faith. I dedicate this paper to D.A., whose strength, encouragement and friendship has seen me through it all. This article has also been informed by Walter L. Williams, 'Being gay and doing research on homosexuality in non-Western cultures', *The Journal of Sex Research* vol. 30 no. 2, pp. 115-120 (May 1993).

[2] Stephen Murray, 'Africa', in Wayne R. Dynes ed., *Encyclopedia of Homosexuality*, New York: Garland Publishing, 1990, p. 22.

[3] *The Daily Nation,* 24 Sept. 1995.

[4] Murray, 'Africa', p. 22.

[5] An article describing the details of the Canaan Banana scandal appeared in the *Mail and Guardian* newspaper, 28 Feb. 1997.

[6] Evelyn Blackwood ed., *The Many Faces of Homosexuality: Anthropological Approaches to Homosexual Behavior,* New York: Harrington Park Press, 1986, p. 11; Thomas George Barton, *Sexuality and Health in Sub-Saharan Africa: An Annotated Bibliography,* Nairobi: African Medical and Research Foundation, 1991, p. 188.

[7] Quoted in Gill Shepherd, 'Rank, gender, and homosexuality: Mombasa as a key to understanding sexual options', in Pat Caplan ed., *The Cultural Construction of Homosexuality,* New York: Tavistock Publications, 1987, p. 259.

[8] James H. Sweet, 'Male homosexuality and spiritism in the African diaspora: The legacies of a link', *Journal of the History of Sexuality* vol. 7 no. 21 (1996), pp. 187-88.

[9] Ibid., p. 188.

[10] Gloria Wekker, 'Mati-ism and Black lesbianism: two ideal typical expressions of female homosexuality in Black communities of the diaspora, *Journal of Homosexuality* vol. 24 no. 3-4 (1993).

[11] The information on Kabaka Mwanga is in large part supplied by Ken Davis and Deborah Amory. My own study of Bagandan history while in high school provided supplementary information.

[12] Osman Njuguna, 'Africa-at-large churches examine homosexuality', *All Africa Press Service,* 6 Apr. 1996.

[13] Chris Dunton, 'Whetying be dat?', in *The Treatment of Homosexuality in African Literature, Research in African Literature* vol. 20 no. 3 (fall 1989), p. 424.

[14] Chris McGreal, 'Kenya commission has a devil of a time', *Mail & Guardian* (Johannesburg), 11 Oct. 1996.

[15] *Laws of Kenya, The Penal Code,* chapter 63:
162) Any person who—
　　has carnal knowledge of any person against the order of nature; or
　　has carnal knowledge of an animal; or
　　permits a male person to have carnal knowledge of him or her against the order of nature, is guilty of a felony and is liable to imprisonment for fourteen years, with or without corporal punishment.
163) Any person who attempts to commit any of the offences specified in section 162 of the Code is guilty of a felony and is liable to imprisonment for seven years, with or without corporal punishment.
164) Any person who is unlawfully and indecently assaults a boy under the age of fourteen is guilty of a felony and is liable to imprisonment for seven years, with or without corporal punishment.

[16] L. Muthoni Wanyeki, 'Human rights: Gay rights still a long way off', *Inter Press Service*, 26 Apr. 1996.

[17] Kenyan ambassador to the US responding to questions posed to him regarding the status of homosexuals in Kenya, 7 Dec. 1994.

[18] Leonard Clayton Kercher, *The Kenya Penal System: Past, Present and Prospect*, Washington: University Press of America, 1981, p. 9.

[19] Marc Epprecht, 'Good God almighty, what's this!': Homosexual "crime" in early colonial Zimbabwe', in Stephen Murray and Will Roscoe eds., *Boy-Wives and Female Husbands: Studies of African Homosexualities*, New York: St. Martin's Press, 1998, pp. 206-08.

[20] Jon Bowmaster, *The Adventures and Misadventures of Peter Beard in Africa*, 1993, p. 115.

[21] *Outlines*, 2 Nov. 1994.

[22] Mary A. Porter, 'Talking at the margins: Kenyan discourses on homosexuality', in William L. Leap ed., *Beyond the Lavender Lexicon*, Amsterdam: Gordon Breach, 1995, p. 147.

[23] Wanjiru Kiama, 'Homosexuality and AIDS: A double-edged sword', Wednesday Magazine: Special Report, *The Daily Nation*, 24 June 1998.

[24] *The Lancet* no. 31 (Jan. 1998).

[25] Douglas A. Feldman, S.R. Friedman & D.C. Des Jarlais, 'Public awareness of AIDS in Rwanda', *Social Science and Medicine* vol. 24 no. 2, pp. 97-100 (1987), p. 99.

[26] Matthew Roberts notes that organizing around AIDS prevention has been the foundation of many emergent gay organizations in the developing world: 'Emergence of gay identity and gay social movements in developing countries: The AIDS crisis as catalyst', *Alternatives* no. 20 (1995), pp. 254, 256.

[27] I am thankful to Ken Davis of the Australian AIDS Council for information about the meeting adjourned in Kampala, Uganda. I had heard of this or a similar meeting from a friend who lives in Uganda, though I am unsure of the exact date.

[28] Wanyeki, 'Human rights'.

[29] Ibid.

[30] Katie King, 'Local and global: AIDS activism and feminist theory', *Camera Obscura* vol. 28 (1992), pp. 81-87.

Individual strategies for *tongzhi* empowerment in China

Chou Wah-shan

In this article I explore the possibilities of mainland Chinese *tongzhi* empowerment through not antagonizing but rather queering the mainstream, and through not segregating same-sex relationships but rather appropriating categories of family and kin into *tongzhi* discourses.

'*Tongzhi*' is the most popular contemporary Chinese word for lesbians, bisexuals and gay people. The word, which has very positive historical connotations, was a Chinese translation of the Soviet communist term 'comrade', which referred to revolutionaries who share a common cause. The term was first adopted by Chinese in Republican China and then taken up by both Nationalists (Guomindang members) and Communists to refer to comrades struggling for a nationalist or socialist revolution. '*Tong*' literally means 'same' or 'homo-'—it is the Chinese word used in translating 'homosexual'—and the word '*zhi*' means goal, spirit or orientation.

The recent emergence of *tongzhi* discourses is evidence of an endeavour to integrate the sexual into the social and cultural. In a cultural tradition which has never felt the need to divide people by the gender of their erotic object choice, *tongzhi* may find the identity 'gay' or 'homosexual' alienating, not necessarily because of homophobia but because they do not feel the need to segregate themselves from those who love the opposite sex. Chinese culture has a cosmology in which sexuality is not a separable category of behaviour and existence but an integral force of life. Chinese *tongzhi* who have resisted adopting the category 'lesbian' or 'gay' have often been criticized as being closeted, dishonest and self-denying. There may be some truth in this, but their resistance may also be an attempt to resist the imposition of a homo-hetero binarism onto a Chinese relational and fluid conception of sexuality.

In 1995 I stayed in Beijing for three months to conduct research on same-sex eroticism. I was first referred to two *tongzhi* activists in Beijing, who then introduced me to various friends of theirs. I also went to the parks, bars and discos where *tongzhi* meet one another. Formal interviews were impossible. I chatted with about two hundred people for an average of an hour each. Most of the people I spoke to were young people in their twenties and thirties, not because they are more representative but because they felt freer to express themselves and to come to cruising areas in the first place.

Not a single one of my informants referred to him- or herself as a *tongxinglian zhe* (homosexual). They used the Chinese term *tongxinglian* (homosexual) not as a noun for a distinctive kind of person (i.e. *tongxinglian zhe*), but as an adjective referring to a practice. They would refer to themselves as *wo men zhe zhong ren* ('we, this kind of people') or *na zhong ren* ('that kind of people') or say *ta shi gao tongxinglian* ('s/he is playing around with homosexuality'). In the book *Women Houzhou* [We Are Alive], in which 22 mainland Chinese wrote their own *tongzhi* stories, the term *tongxinglian* was used more than 30 times, but never to form the noun *tongxinglian zhe* and refer to a type of person.[1] Similarly in the movie *East Palace, West Palace* (1998), considered the first *tongzhi* movie in China, when the main male character first discloses his sexual identity, instead of saying *wo shi tongxinglian zhe* ('I am a homosexual'), he says *wo shi tongxinglian* ('I am homosexual'). This continues the traditional Chinese discourse in which there is simply no linguistic and cultural equivalent to the concepts 'homosexual', 'lesbian', 'gay' or 'bisexual'.

The only exception is some young males who use the English word 'gay' in their otherwise completely Chinese speech, for instance using use mix-coded language to say: *wo shi gay, ta shi gay, jan men dou shi gay* ('I am gay, s/he is gay, we are all gay'). When this new generation adopts the Western notion of sexual identity, they find no cultural equivalent in Chinese language or thought and have to resort to Western language and use the English term 'gay' in a Chinese sentence. They are actually integrating two very different cultural traditions by 'inserting' the concept of homo-hetero binarism into Chinese language and culture. Bilingual language becomes a necessary way of wording new experiences when no native term exists for a Western concept.

The resistance to taking up a 'homosexual identity' among people who are erotically attracted to the same sex should not necessarily be seen as a product of homophobia. Many Chinese *tongzhi* stress that sexuality is only one integral part of life and does not mark them as categorically different people. Traditional Chinese culture treats homosexuality behaviourally as an option that most people can experience, rather than as something psychologically restricted to a sexual minority having fixed, inherent traits.

However, with the advent and popularization of romantic love in the twentieth century, marriage has become a personal pursuit of (sexual) happiness. Instead of pleasing one's parents and parents-in-law, one also has to please one's partner, emotionally and sexually. Post-Mao Chinese are supposed to date before they get married and to choose their own partners instead of having their marriages arranged by their parents. During courtship they are supposed to be intimate, passionate, seductive, playful, sexual, physical and even jealous. This arrival of courtship culture has inflicted much pain on *tongzhi*, who now have to pretend to be aroused by a person of the opposite sex. The marital bond has become an important social relationship in which husband and wife must be very intimate. Therefore marriage has become the most oppressive and torturous institution imaginable for people who love people of the same sex in a way it never was before.

A cause of yet more pain for *tongzhi* is their romanticization of the Western lesbigay world, which is perceived as non-homophobic, carefree and liberating. Few Chinese can get a visa to the West, so the only images and knowledge they have about the Western lesbigay world are the images of lesbigay marriages and parades where thousands of lesbigay people march in a relaxed and proud manner. They tend to romanticize the Western world as a lesbigay haven, and are shocked to be informed about the extent of gay-bashing and homophobia in the US and Europe. Some simply find it unbelievable.

What is also new in postwar China—and also Taiwan and Hong Kong— is the intervention of the state apparatus, specifically the police, courts and legal system, to prosecute men for their same-sex activities. This state intervention, together with the 'scientific basis' of medicalization and pathologization of same-sex eroticism, has been another crucial factor accounting for the pain felt by contemporary *tongzhi* in China as well as Taiwan and Hong Kong, especially in the 1970s and '80s.

Yet my research showed that despite the oppressive environment, Chinese *tongzhi* manage to manipulate their indigenous cultural resources so as to expand and reclaim their personal and social space. Here I discuss four specific *tongzhi* stories, not because they are typical or representative of mainland Chinese *tongzhi*, but because the stories elucidate certain unique features of the mainland Chinese *tongzhi* struggle.

1

James (27) has lived with his boyfriend Xiaoliu (29) in Beijing for three years. They live together with James's parents, brother and brother's wife.

When I first met James in a private *tongzhi* gathering, James was not at all interested in sharing his *tongzhi* story with me. He was keener to talk about money, money and money, together with information about all sorts of fashion brand names and video entertainment. Consumerism, economics and class seem to be much more his concern than sexuality. Several times, when I talked about sexuality, he smoothly changed the subject. At first, I suspected that he might be hiding something. Then I realized that my suspicion was overdetermined by my own obsession with sexuality. James said:

> Why always ask about my sexuality? I know you are doing research, and want to ask about my sexual experiences with men. I don't care. I enjoy my life. Sex is not that important to me. I don't want to stress that I am gay, not because I'm scared, but there are other things in this world that I care for, like my parents, environmental issues and the economy. I don't see my relationship with Xiaoliu as homosexual, we are just lovers like everybody else. I don't want to hang around only with gay people in gay bars and gay cruising areas. I have more straight friends than *tongzhi* ones.

At a time when I was pursuing my research on mainland Chinese sexuality James's statement was the best critique of imposing a homo-hetero binarism on all people having sex with people of the same sex. It was during our second encounter that James shared his story. James is the eldest son in the family. He experienced his first same-sex love with his best friend at school when they were both seventeen. After graduation James went to university and his lover went to work in a factory. Their relationship started to turn sour and they finally split up. James was very hurt and thought that there was no future in loving a man. Four months later James received a letter from his ex-lover saying that he now had a girlfriend and was planning to get married. Towards the end of the letter he said, 'Our previous relation was *biantai* [perverted]; I have now been converted to normality by the real love of my girlfriend. You should try to enjoy loving women. Or maybe you should see a doctor.'

Clearly the letter was devastating to James, especially at a time when he was still fantasizing about getting back together with this classmate. That night he drank two bottles of dishwashing liquid together with 50 pills. He was unconscious for two days. James's best friend thought that James might die and decided to tell James's parents the full story after being pressed by them desperately. James has survived, but he still has serious stomach aches and kidney problems as a result of his attempted suicide.

Since then James's parents have been very kind to him. They never mention a word about *tongxinglian*. Even in recent years they have rarely urged him to get married, which by Chinese standards is incredible; most Chinese in their twenties would be pressured to get married. James said:

> My parents seriously worry and care about my health. They prefer our family members to stay together so that we can take care of each other. I think my previous suicide attempt really scared them, and they would do everything to avoid its happening again. So when they feel that I really love Xiaoliu, who is such a nice guy, they are quite happy. From their point of view Xiaoliu is mature enough to take care of me, which is preferable to my getting married and having to take care of a wife and family. Another thing is that Xiaoliu works as a professional, is very mature, and he is rich...
>
> At first I only introduced Xiaoliu as a good friend of mine. Then he often came to visit me and have dinner together with my parents. He gets along very well with my parents. They invite him to stay overnight if it is too late, I mean in the same bed with me. *He gradually attended all our family dinners and became part of my family*. Finally, two years ago when he changed to a new job where there is no housing allocation for him, my mother simply invited him to move in! Isn't that cool! *My parents treat him as their son, and never say a word about sex.* I think it is better to come out in deeds than with words or arguments. I can't expect my parents to understand the concepts of *tongxinglian*. The terms 'gay' and *tongxinglian* could be very scary for my parents, since they would be associated with perversity and Western corruption. *But they understand intimate* ganqing [sentiment] *and* guanxi [relationship]; *they accept Xiaoliu fully, not as a gay man, but as my intimate friend.* [Author's emphases.]

James has used food as a cultural marker to bring Xiaoliu into his family. As James said, 'He gradually attended all our family dinners and became part of my family.' James also uses quasi-kin categories to describe his relationship with Xiaoliu ('My parents treat him as their son, and never say a word about sex.').

James also shared a fascinating experience with me which well illustrates the public's insensitivity—bordering on indifference—towards *tongxinglian*. On the last day of university James and his classmates had a wild party. They sang, danced and drank. At midnight James's roommate took his girlfriend into their room and had sex. When James came back to the room with his boyfriend at about 4 a.m., this opposite-sex couple was already asleep and naked. About an hour later several policemen suddenly came in and turned on the light. They arrested and took away this opposite-sex couple, saying that someone from the opposite building had reported seeing some 'obscene behaviour' between a naked man and woman. Interestingly, James was also sleeping naked together with his boyfriend. But the police did not say a word about them. They simply did not 'see' *tongxinglian*; they had no such concept. They thought James and his boyfriend were just close friends, whereas this opposite-sex couple was obscene. James remarked in the end, 'That was seven years ago. I am afraid if it happened now, we might be caught and charged with *liumang* [hooliganism].'

2

Song and Jenny are another *tongzhi* couple who live together. I interviewed Song (33) in early 1998 when she was attending a business conference in Hong Kong. When Song was 23, her parents arranged for her to marry the son of a Communist Party member. Song resisted, but her parents insisted that they desperately needed this party member's help. The marriage proved to be a total failure. Although Song's parents at first rejected the possibility of divorce, they agreed to let Song go to Beijing to study. It was at Beijing University that she met her present lover Jenny (29), who was a student majoring in economics.

Song and Jenny were each other's first girlfriend, and neither had much difficulty in accepting their relationship. Song said, 'It is just beautiful!' They have been together for five years. All their best friends know and accept their relationship. Song explained:

Beijing is changing very fast; people are now very pragmatic and care less about ideological debates. Our friends are all university graduates. They are only concerned about two things: whether our love is genuine, and whether we can manage the practical arrangements like divorce, housing allocation, and a plan for our old age.

Song stressed several times that their relationship is one of *tong-zhi*—they share the same (*tong*) goal or spirit (*zhi*) of life:

> *Tongzhi* is not just about sex but about sharing a worldview and a goal in life. For our generation of mainland Chinese who have come through the Cultural Revolution, the appropriation of the identity *tongzhi* is a fantastic integration of a sexual minority with the revolutionary struggle. It is now the sexual minority who ironically take up the most sacred political label of the mainstream world. It's really great!

After coming to Beijing to study, Song was separated from her husband for seven years. She initiated the divorce and now lives and works in Beijing for the government. Although she is allocated a house in the work unit, she prefers to live in Jenny's apartment, which was allocated by Jenny's American firm in Beijing. Song lies to her workmates, saying that Jenny is her nephew. She admitted that she gained much freedom and space by moving away from her work unit. She also warned me:

> If you want to find *nu tongzhi*, don't just approach the ones who have 'come out'—there are only a handful of those—go chat with married women. I have been working as a volunteer counsellor for a woman's hotline in Beijing for half a year, and I've come across several married women who have little interest in having sex with men. Their sex lives are a mess and they feel like whores. One even flirted with me during the phone chat. I am not saying that they are *nu tongzhi*. That is not the point. These categories may be meaningless for them. Chinese women simply have little choice in their lives, especially in terms of sexuality. Women's sexuality has been buried in marriage and domestic responsibility.

Song and I also had a serious talk about women's issues in China:

> I never thought of myself as belonging to the 'second sex'. Since I was born, I have been accustomed to the idea that 'women hold up half the sky'. For us equality of the sexes is natural, not something achieved through the feminist struggle. My mother worked on the farm; she did all the ploughing, raking, seed mixing and harvesting, with no sense of treating work as liberation, and my father cooks very well. Western feminists see women as individuals with inalienable rights. But in the Chinese world, the family rather than the individual is seen as the basic unit of society. I have been asked by white feminists and lesbians about my views on the one-child policy. Of course I support it. The policy stops the most populous country in this world from suffering the human disaster of having billions of people starve to death. A foreigner criticized me for denying the child's right to survive and the woman's

right to have as many children as she likes. As a person who has lived through the Cultural Revolution and all kinds of human disasters, of course I understand human rights. But precisely because I understand them, I support the policy that creates a better social environment for the next generation. We simply have different priorities from women in the white world.

3

The rapid development of *tongzhi* venues in big cities has drawn many female and male *tongzhi* from smaller cities and towns. A common problem facing young *tongzhi* who migrate to big cities is that, unable to find a proper job that enables them to keep up with the high cost of living, some of them become prostitutes. Peter (25) is a good example. He grew up in a poor village in Wunan where he finished his primary school education. He went to Guangzhou at age fourteen with his uncle. In his five years in Guangzhou he worked as a waiter, hawker, gardener, cleaner and, most of the time, prostitute. At age nineteen he was brought to Shanghai by a Hong Kong businessman. Peter worked in his factory for three months, until they split up. Peter then lived with an American gay man forty years older than he for nine months. Then he changed jobs several times; since last year he has worked as a waiter in a bar where there are many white customers. Although Peter did not really love this American gay man, he is very grateful to him. He said:

When I moved into his place, I was really fascinated by his collection of gay videos and magazines. It was very empowering to know about the Western gay world. I grew up in a society where 'gay' means 'pervert' and is supposed to be cured by electric shock. When I watched all these videos, or when he translated the articles in *OUT* or the *Advocate* for me, I felt that I was born again. I decided to be a happy gay.

When I first met Peter in Shanghai, he was wearing a tight mini-T-shirt, stylish blue jeans and a baseball cap. When a friend introduced me as a university lecturer from Hong Kong, Peter immediately changed from Mandarin to English, though his English was not at all fluent. It was unclear whether he just seized every chance to practise English, or if he thought speaking English was superior, or whether English represents a Western fantasy and space that he desperately needed. During our conversation he asked me seriously about the possibility of emigrating to Hong Kong. He is desperate to leave China. 'I will do whatever I can to leave this country—marry a white man, buy a fake visa, whatever. There is little hope for gay men in China; I have to get out.' He told me that some male prostitutes are not gay but use sexuality as a tool for social mobility and economic advancement.

Peter is very positive about his prostitution: 'I am young and good-looking, what's wrong with that? Everyone sells something about himself; I sell my body. And you need a lot of talent and skill to cruise your patrons; otherwise no one picks you up. I work only part-time. I choose my working hours and clients.' He has earned a lot of money. He has even stolen:

Once I stole 7000 yuan from a Taiwanese businessman. Well, don't condemn me; it is only a few pennies for him. I spent 4000 to buy a fake residence and work permit and gave the rest to my parents. That is my tactic to please them and delay my marriage. Money is the best tool in the world. My brother and sister in Wunan earn only 300 dollars a month. But every New Year when I go home, I give my parents several thousand! That's why my parents are not that keen to push me into marriage. I only see them once a year; it's easy to entertain them. I won't get married. I'm gay and I want my freedom.

Peter is very critical of Chinese culture. He prefers whites, as he thinks they are more creative and romantic. This racial and cultural fantasy about 'Western modernity' enchants the new generation. Public morality and attitudes among young people are changing rapidly. Individuality and mutual happiness have become the main values cherished by the urban young generation. Peter admitted that China is now much more open than before:

As long as you do it in private, the police will not disturb you. But if I cannot tell my parents about my sexuality, how open is it? In recent years, there are more gay people who are willing to come out of the closet and be visible. The driving force behind the growing openness in socialist China is ironically capitalist economic growth and the concomitant convenience of tele-communication. People are now busy earning money and don't bother about your private life. So I think we should talk about pink dollars. It's stupid to drone on about gay rights. I think we should follow the market economy and open up gay consumption and lifestyles. Money is the best tool for gay rights.

Once when I was chatting with two of Peter's friends about Chinese and English names, they both said that they did not know his Chinese name at all, though they have known him for two years. Until recently it was rare for a Chinese to introduce her- or himself only by an English name. This shows once more that it is Peter's strategy to enmesh himself in a Westernized discourse and take his distance from his birthplace in Wunan, which for him only represents poverty, suffering and oppression. A Western given name also symbolizes egalitarian relationships and culture, rarely found in Chinese culture, which has a hierarchy of human relationships and forms of address.[2]

Peter is also using the Western discourse of romantic love to bargain with his parents. He emphasizes the need for 'true love' in a happy marriage and uses the notion of romantic love to put off marrying, saying that '*yuan fan*' (a sort of romantic coincidence) has not come yet. While his parents still pressure him to get married, his Western lifestyle and handsome income have ironically given his parents good reasons for accepting his resistance to marriage.

Peter is an example of a Chinese *tongzhi* who manipulates the space of economic development, urban migration and Western gay discourse to develop a new form of sexual and social identity and subjectivity. Western gay discourse provides some contemporary Chinese a ready-made array of weapons that they can use to counteract indigenous traditions, values and customs that they find oppressive. In Peter's words, 'The Western world has its own problems, but I don't care. It provides me with the best tools for self-liberation.'

4

While Song won her *tongzhi* space partly through divorce, there are some women who choose to stay married while having same-sex relationships. Ning (36) has been married for ten years and has no intention of getting divorced. Instead of coming out and being a visible *tongzhi*, she argues that such visibility would only destroy the relationship that she is presently enjoying with the married woman next door. She told me:

> There are no lesbians here! How can one be a lesbian in this country? In my case I was married ten years ago when I was 26; now I have a nine-year-old child. What can I do? If I 'came out' to my husband and parents I would become a devil in people's minds, not so much because of my *tongxinglian,* but for failing in my obligation and responsibility as a wife, daughter and mother. I accept my homoerotic desire, but why should I make a big fuss and destroy the harmonious family order I have in my life? Why should I become a different person just because I have sex with a person of the same sex?... When two men or two women sleep together, it is acceptable when you are friends, relatives or classmates. Of course, if you have sex, it cannot be publicized. But what constitutes sex? If sex has to be penetrative, then I don't want it. If sex is the most intimate expression of our love, then our relationship is very sexual. I prefer to emotionalize sexuality rather than sexualizing all emotions like some Americans do.

I took her words seriously. She is comfortable with her sexuality and has no feelings of guilt or shame about her sexual desire and behaviour. So why should her sexual desire, rather than her class, ethnicity, family or any other social category, determine her personal identity? In other words, why should her sexual desire be her primary identity? And why is the gender of someone's erotic object choice singled out to determine her sexual identity? What kinds of social hierarchy are we establishing in prioritizing the gender of someone's erotic object choice at the expense of all other social and sexual categories?

Ning's story does not end here. She had a marvellous relationship with a partner before she came to Beijing. Later she missed the relationship deeply.

She said:

> We loved each other very much. We slept together; we shared every-
> thing; we talked every day. We were a couple. But at the time I simply
> did not have the language of same-sex love to interpret or even compre-
> hend our relationship in that way. You know, my perception of
> *tongxinglian* was very derogatory; I associated it with broken families,
> casual sex and AIDS. We loved each other of course. If I had stayed in
> my old village and had not moved to Beijing, our relationship would
> have continued even if I had married a man. I can love my girlfriend
> while maintaining a harmonious relationship with my husband,
> without serious conflict. It is easier to camouflage a relationship
> between women than a heterosexual one. *Tongxinglian* is more invisible
> and less threatening than extramarital heterosexuality. I brought my
> previous girlfriend back home; she stayed and slept with me. No one
> suspected anything. Basically if you don't have sex in front of them, no
> one associates intimacy between women with *tongxinglian*. It would
> give me a lot of trouble if I came out as a 'lesbian', a Westernized
> category that challenges the basic family-kinship structure and my
> cultural identity as a Chinese. What benefits could coming out in
> public bring me?

Tongzhi, lesbian, gay or queer is a subject position that has to be constructed and claimed. Same-sex eroticism does not necessarily contradict one's
marital status. It is only when someone asserts a lesbigay identity and con-
structs her or his experiences and lifestyle around this sexual identity that
sexuality and marital status come into conflict. The tension is most acute when
someone wants to proclaim a sexual identity as a public statement about her or
his body. Ning treasures her social role as a wife, daughter and mother so much
that she finds a lesbian identity threatening rather than empowering. As she
said, 'It would give me a lot of trouble if I came out as a "lesbian"'.

To classify Ning as a lesbian is to impose an imagined binarism based on
the gender of her erotic object choice and to fix and inscribe such differences
onto her body, asserting that this identity is her natural and core self. Ning's
experiences expose the considerable problems of universalizing the homo-hetero
binarism to all cultural practices of same-sex eroticism.

*   *   *

The above four cases are neither ideal nor without pain. All four people
live in very difficult situations. Yet all four of them have manipulated their own
unique circumstances to claim their personal space.

James has integrated his sexuality into his family life, not by confronting
his parents, but by integrating Xiaoliu into his family's life. He has used the
cultural marker of food and the category of kin to draw Xiaoliu in as a quasi-

member of his family. James has also protected his parents' cultural innocence and developed their tolerance towards same-sex eroticism. Instead of provoking a debate on the status of *tongxinglian*, Xiaoliu has established an intimate relationship with James's parents and literally lives with them. Song and Jenny used their middle-class economic space and the divorce law to secure an independent life of their own. Peter, despite his limitations as a rural young man with only a primary-school education living in a big modern city, manages to identify positively with the Western gay discourse, which became a major source of empowerment and liberation for him. The Western discourse on romantic love, a carefree lifestyle and individualism are strategic tools for Peter to negotiate with his parents' expectations of marriage. Ning takes advantage of the traditional space in Chinese culture for intimacy between women while rejecting the Western strategy of coming out.

Tongzhi do not have a monolithic discourse. Even in the big cities of mainland China, different *tongzhi* of varying genders, ages, classes, education, marital status and economic power resort to different resources to protect their space as *tongzhi*. James lives with his boyfriend, redefining the meaning of marriage and male intimacy without openly challenging the marital institution; Song divorced her husband in order to stay with Jenny; Peter firmly resists marriage by increasing his economic assets and Western ties; Ning adopts a non-confrontational model to take advantage of the cultural space for intimacy between women. It is the complexity and diversity of their strategies that enrich the scenario of *tongzhi* resistance. What we need is not a single monolithic discourse on 'The Chinese *Tongzhi* Strategy', which is impossible and undesirable. Instead, differences and diversities among *tongzhi* should be explored and celebrated in order to further and invigorate each individual *tongzhi*'s struggle.

While some *tongzhi*, like Peter, have to exile themselves from their families to attain personal freedom, for other *tongzhi* like James and Ning the mainstream categories of family relations, filial piety and marriage actually help them attain personal happiness and protect themselves from social mistreatment, more effectively than the categories of coming out and human rights would. This strategy of carving out space for same-sex eroticism has in fact been commonly adopted in traditional China.

Homosexual practices are well documented in Chinese historical records. The classic work on the subject is the book *History of Homosexuality in China*, in which Xiaomingxiong discusses in detail emperors, kings, princes, intellectuals, peasants, men and women who have had homosexual practices. Another authority was able to list 55 Chinese emperors, kings and princes who were involved in homosexual acts. The classic novel by Cao Xueqin, *The Dream of the Red Chamber*, openly refers to same-sex eroticism among women and men. Another novel called *Outlaws of the Marsh* vividly depicts male bonding among characters who live on the fringes of society, most of whom come from the lowest social strata. Stephen Likosky states plainly that 'China, through much of its long history, has had a rich and varied tradition of same-sex love. It was only with the arrival of British colonialism in recent times that the stigmatization of homosexuality appeared and prudery began to reign.'[3]

The notion of *qing* (an indigenous word for deep sentiment or passion) is central in understanding the Chinese conception of sexuality.[4] For example, the late Ming novel *Bian er chai* [Caps and Hairpins] powerfully articulates the discourse of *qing* in the context of same-sex eroticism.[5] *Bian er chai* is composed of four long stories, each named after a different kind of *qing*: 'Qing Fidelity', 'Qing Chivalry', 'Qing Sacrifice' and 'Qing Marvel'. All four stories have similar plots about a (male) intellectual who meets another kind-hearted male, with whom he shares an intimate and genuine *qing*. The couple then experiences various social misfortunes but still manages to climb up the social ladder; all four stories have happy endings.

At the beginning of the first story, 'Qing Fidelity', the male protagonist says, 'We are the people who really appreciate *qing*. Although our [same-sex] relationship has deviated from the norm (*li*), it flows with *qing*... a discourse that confines itself to the life and death of a female-male relationship is not really *qing*.'[6] This story is about the love of a fifteen-year-old student, Chao, who is pretty, elegant and bright, and the young scholar Lin who is spontaneously attracted to Chao. Chao is finally touched by Lin's sincerity, and they decide to live together. Thanks to Lin's academic enlightenment and guidance, Chao passes the examination to become a scholar and official. Yet Lin is later in danger of execution because of his insistence on justice, which irritates a powerful rich person. The powerless Chao takes the risk of rescuing Lin, and in the end they leave officialdom behind to live a very peaceful life. Chao and Lin's families also become very close for many generations.

The (unknown) author of *Bain er chai* takes a non-confrontational strategy of using one of the most profound mainstream categories, *qing*, to describe a same-sex relationship which is congruent with the social morality of *qing* and *yi* (righteousness). Instead of oppressing people having sex with people of the same sex, mainstream social values like fidelity, loyalty, intellectual scholarship and social justice are deployed to become key elements in a same-sex relationship.

In the third story, 'Qing Sacrifice', the male protagonist Wen is imprisoned because he is set up by a rich man who refuses to let his daughter marry Wen. A prison guard is disturbed by the framing and lets Wen escape. Wen is then homeless and jobless, becomes an actor in the theatre, and is admired there by the scholar Han. Han and Wen gradually become intimate friends. Unfortunately a wealthy villain wants to possess Wen and kidnaps him. Out of his *qing* for Han, Wen sells himself to this wealthy villain for a considerable sum of money, which enables Han to prepare for the scholarly examination. Wen then commits suicide to show his fidelity to Han. Wen's action is so touching that the heavenly spirit decides to intervene and let Wen return from the afterlife to continue his love with Han. Han passes the examination and takes revenge on the wealthy villain. In the end Wen returns to the spirit world to become a sea god. In this story, Wen and Han are portrayed as brave, righteous and noble not only in their true love but also in fighting against social oppression. Wen's fidelity, loyalty and *qing* are so profound that he is rescued twice—first by the prison guard, then by the spirit that brings him back from the afterlife.

Instead of portraying same-sex relationships as confronting the mainstream culture, *Bian er chai* shows social ideals like nobility, love, self-sacrifice and fidelity as constitutive of same-sex relationships. More importantly, these stories do not replicate mainstream culture but are highly subversive of the heterosexist presuppositions of notions of love, sacrifice and long-term relationship. They use a strategy of resistance in which same-sex relationships are legitimated not by rejecting the mainstream but by 'queering' it.

East Palace, West Palace, the so-called first *tongzhi* movie in China, is a vivid illustration of this strategy of queering the mainstream. East Palace and West Palace are *tongxinglian* slang names for the public toilets on either side of Tiananmen Square. The movie presents two male characters: one young male *tongxinglian* (A-lan) and a straight policeman who hauls him in for an overnight interrogation. This cop not only represents the straight world but is a powerful symbol of dictatorial control in China. The political implications are sharpened by the fact that the filmmaker, Zhang Yuan, had been warned by the Chinese authorities about his five previous 'illegal' movies. In the movie, A-lan is trapped by his own childhood experiences and desperately yearns to be caught and punished. He actually entices the cop to catch him and bring him to the police station for questioning. The movie can be read as proposing the strategy of 'queering the straight' in which A-lan keeps on flirting and seducing the cop and successfully evokes the cop's desire for sadomasochism, transvestism and homoeroticism. A-lan is portrayed as a charming storyteller in sharing his personal story of homoeroticism, which determines the mood of the cop and of the movie itself. While the movie elaborates in detail the socio-psychological basis for A-lan's sadomasochistic desires, it is actually the policeman who asks A-lan to cross-dress, who enjoys the sadomasochistic 'torture' of A-lan, and finally falls prey to A-lan's seduction by kissing A-lan passionately. The closing scene portrays the puzzled cop 'escaping' from the police station, followed by a closing shot in which A-lan leaves the station in the most serene and self-contained elegance. One of the last lines in the movie is a question thrown by A-lan back to the cop: 'You always ask me what I want, but do you know what you want?!'

While the straight world, as represented by this policeman, is being seduced and challenged by a *tongxinglian,* the film clearly goes beyond identity politics. When A-lan first 'comes out' after he is caught, he proclaims firmly: *wo shi tongxinglian* ('I am homosexual'), instead of *wo shi tongxinglian zhe* ('I am a homosexual'). And though the cop unconsciously exhibits his own desire for and pleasure in sadomasochism, cross-dressing and homoeroticism, the movie never intends to define his sexual identity. The cop's homoerotic desire is actually rather ambiguous: when he kisses A-lan, A-lan is wearing women's clothes at his request. It is unclear whether the cop treats A-lan as a man, woman, transvestite, gay or straight. Indeed, the sadomasochism, transvestism and same-sex eroticism which appear to be associated with the *tongxinglian* character A-lan are fully present in the straight world represented by the cop.

If same-sex eroticism (and sadomasochism and transvestism) are something anyone could experience, then homo-hetero binarism and rigid identity politics turn out to be counterproductive—not only in understanding the *tongzhi* world but also in understanding the so-called straight world. The straight world is itself never immune to the seduction of homoerotic desire.

[1] Gary Wu & Chou Wah-shan eds., *Women Houzhou* [We Are Alive], Hong Kong: Hong Kong Queer Studies Forum, 1996.

[2] In contemporary China, people tend to address each other as either *xiao* (little) or *lao* (old), rarely as equals in the way Westerners do when they use first names.

[3] Samshasha (Xiaomingxiong), *Zhongguo Tongxinglian Shilu*, Hong Kong: Pink Triangle Press, 1997—earlier version available in English as Xiaomingxiong, *History of Homosexuality in China*, Hong Kong: Pink Triangle Press, 1984; M.P. Lau & M.L. Ng, 'Sexual attitudes in the Chinese', *Archives of Sexual Behaviour* vol. 19 no. 4 (1990); Cao Xueqin, *Hung Lou Meng* [The Dream of the Red Chamber], Qi Yong et al. eds., Taipei: Sunrise Press, 1984—available in English as *The Story of the Stone*, David Hawkes & John Minford trans. (5 vols.), Harmondsworth: Penguin, 1973-86; Robert van Gulik, *Sexual Life in Ancient China*, Leiden: E.J. Brill, 1961; Stephen Likosky, *Coming Out*, New York: Pantheon Books, 1994, p. 24.

[4] Adolf Tsang, *Sexuality: The Chinese and Judeo-Christian Tradition*, paper presented at Conference of the Hong Kong Psychology Society, 1986.

[5] Keith McMahon, *Causality and Containment in Seventeenth-Century Chinese Fictions*, London: Leiden, 1988, pp. 76-77.

[6] Samshasha, *Zhongguo Tongxinglian Shilu*, p. 390.

Reinventing liberation: strategic questions for lesbian/gay movements

Peter Drucker

Same-sex sexualities in the Third World are not identical to those in advanced capitalist countries, as the articles in this book make clear. Lesbian/gay/bisexual/transgendered (LGBT) people in the Third World are often very aware of lesbian/gay subcultures in North America and Western Europe, are often consciously influenced by them, are in some ways unconsciously coverging with them. Yet men in the Third World who have sex with men and women who have sex with women have their own more or less distinct traditions, realities, sexualities and identities, which neither they nor outside observers always even see as 'lesbian' or 'gay'.

In my introduction I tried to give an overview of how Third World same-sex patterns are like and unlike those in the US, Australia or Holland. While many people involved in same-sex sexualities in the Third World do not have same-sex identities, I said, many others do. More and more of them are speaking openly about their identities, coming together and acting openly as communities, and forming public lesbian/gay movements. Now I want to raise some questions about strategic issues facing these Third World lesbian/gay movements, which are often wrestling with somewhat distinctive issues in somewhat distinctive ways.

The title of this conclusion, 'Reinventing Liberation', itself raises questions. 'Liberation' is a word that harks back to the 1960s and '70s. It was adopted in Paris, New York, Mexico City and Buenos Aires by lesbians and gays who wanted to identify with women's liberation and Black liberation and with national liberation movements in places like Vietnam, Palestine and South Africa. Before the late 1960s and again since the 1980s, people have used words like 'rights', 'emancipation' or 'integration' more than 'liberation', including lately in the Third World. As Max Mejía says in his article, the time for general denunciations of oppression is past; now it is time to focus concretely on 'every abuse, outrage and form of discrimination'. Many activists would probably agree with Mejía's idea of a necessary shift from liberation to civil rights. To the extent that the word 'liberation' is used at all nowadays, it seems to be not much more than a vaguely radical-sounding, rough equivalent for 'rights'.

What then is the point of resurrecting the word 'liberation' now when discussing strategy in São Paulo, Johannesburg or Manila? I suggest three reasons why it may make sense in the Third World to talk not just about 'rights' but about 'liberation'. More or less following the categories Norma Mogrovejo uses in her article, we can talk about liberation in three different senses: in the sense of *achieving full equality*, in the sense of *expressing one's identity in every part of one's society,* and in the sense of *transforming a whole culture's sexuality.*

Increasingly in Western Europe in particular, these three aspects of liberation have gradually seemed less crucial—at least to many of those at the head of mainstream lesbian/gay organizations. Many European LGB people have secure enough jobs and lives to make legal equality seem like a reasonable approximation of full social equality. Even if there are still churches, bars, families and neighbourhoods that are not about to welcome an open lesbian/gay presence, that still leaves space elsewhere to live open lesbian/gay lives, both inside 'gay ghettos' and in many relatively tolerant workplaces and neighbourhoods in the secular society outside them. And even if drag queens, sado-masochists or people in intergenerational relationships are denied the tolerance granted to homosexuality as such, some lesbian/gay people seem able to live with that—particularly those who are trying to fashion an image of the lesbian/gay community that will be palatable to the officials they are lobbying.

I wonder myself whether most LGBT people will be happy in the long run with the model of emancipation that has been taking hold in Western Europe and North America in the last thirty years. Many are rebelling against it even now. In any event, it seems unlikely that it can succeed to the same extent in the Third World. While there are people and organizations in the Third World too who are attracted to this model, it is difficult there to avoid questions about its limits.

* First, not many Third World LGBTs have much chance of getting jobs at wages high enough that they can afford to go often to bars and discos, let alone live away from their parents. Legal equal rights to employment, housing and accommodation mean less to LGBTs who cannot afford them. So particularly in the Third World the question needs to be asked: how can LGBTs win substantive economic and social equality?

* Second, it is harder for economic reasons for large gay ghettos to maintain themselves in the Third World; and intolerance, in many cases based on institutionalized religion or communal divisions, is often pervasive outside the commercial scenes that do exist. So it becomes even more important to ask: can LGBT people be fully accepted and integrated into the families and communities they come from?

* Third, the Third World's same-sex identities are extraordinarily diverse. It seems like less of a victory there to win acceptance for that part of the same-sex spectrum that consists of gay 'real men' and lesbian 'real women', particularly if this implies marginalizing transgendered people and others. This makes it more important to ask: can the broad range of existing same-sex sexualities in the Third World win public visibility and acceptance?

In the following remarks I look at each of these questions about liberation in turn.

* On issues of *equality,* I discuss what democratic breakthroughs like the end of apartheid in South Africa can mean for sexual emancipation, and I raise the issue of whether full LGBT equality in most dependent countries will require even deeper-going economic and social changes that put an end to

poverty and underdevelopment.

* On issues of *identity*, I discuss the thorny problems of building autonomous LGBT movements while seeking necessary alliances, and developing LGBT identities and subcultures while trying to survive within and change existing families and communities.

* On issues of *sexuality*, I look at the implications that the diversity of sexualities included in their ranks, particularly the prominence of transgendered people, has for the demands and strategies of lesbian/gay movements in the Third World.

What kind of equality?

Victories for lesbian/gay rights in advanced capitalist countries have usually gone together with other changes in sexual culture—particularly the spread of contraception, abortion rights, and tolerance for pre- and extramarital sex in general. But the backdrop to these changes has been a relatively stable democratic capitalist order. In the Third World, by contrast, the backdrop has more often been emergence from dictatorship, accompanied by some degree of social upheaval.

Even in Third World countries that have multiple parties, elections and other trappings of constitutional democracy, it is often difficult or virtually impossible for independent social movements to have an impact on decision-making. In Mexico, for example, where a single party has in practice monopolized political power and dominated social movements for 70 years, Mejía describes the consequences for LGBT people: 'the corruption of the authorities, the dead letter' of the law, and police abuse. Mogrovejo points out that there are similar problems in other Latin American countries too—'police abuses, extortion, murder and even torture', charges of 'corruption of minors' and 'immoral and indecent behaviour'—including in countries where dictatorships are a thing of the past and different parties are routinely voted in and out of office.

In many Third World countries today many of the most important policy decisions are not made by elected governments at all, but by unelected officials of the International Monetary Fund and World Bank. This does not necessarily mean that politics is unimportant to people. On the contrary, particularly when unemployment is very high, getting a government job or official favour can make an enormous difference. Whole towns, ethnic groups, regions and extended families can line up behind particular parties and fight fiercely to put 'their' parties in office. But this kind of politics, even when it is formally democratic, often leaves little room for individuals to decide their loyalty on the basis of their personal beliefs, social positions or sexual identities. People may be able to change one government for another but be powerless to bring about any kind of structural or social change. Politicians faced with multi-party elections for the first time may even end up catering more to entrenched elites and communal prejudices than they did when they headed liberation movements or single-party regimes, particularly where multi-ethnic grassroots movements are weak.

Organizing LGBTs in the Third World is easier when there is a minimal democratic space in which to form an organization, hold a demonstration or hand out a leaflet. But winning victories usually seems to require a deeper kind of democracy than that: not just a free press and elections, but also a political culture in which there is room for individual, active citizenship and a lively civil society. Even a difference only in degree can make a big difference for gay organizing. The Philippines is a poor country where parties are often led by rival landowning families, but as Dennis Altman points out, 'there is a more politicized gay world in Manila than in Bangkok, despite the latter's huge commercial gay scene', thanks to differences in political history and culture. Turkey is a country that has emerged only recently and incompletely from military dictatorship, but as I mentioned in the introduction, that still leaves room for gay organizing that does not exist in Egypt or Pakistan, which also have multi-party elections.

Wherever a minimal democratic space and lively civil society develop in the Third World, there is reason for optimism about the chances of lesbian/gay movements. This can be true even when poverty and underdevelopment persist and deepen. The gay commercial worlds that were growing up until 1982 in Latin America and until 1997 in Southeast Asia have been set back by economic crises. For individual LGBT people, this has often had tragic consequences. But lesbian/gay organizing has often bounced back in the wake of these crises and sometimes even been stimulated as rigid political and social orders have been shaken.

The one country in the Third World where the widest range of lesbian/gay rights has been won, South Africa, experienced a deep economic and social crisis in the 1980s that is not yet over. Partly as a result, it went through a far-reaching process of democratic transformation with the end of apartheid in the 1990s. Vast sectors of South African society were mobilized in the process, including black LGBTs. It has not always been easy after the end of apartheid to keep the lesbian/gay organizations going that were built during the struggle. The mobilization has nonetheless resulted in gains for LGBTs that are unique in Africa, and one of the two national constitutions in the world (Ecuador has the second) that explicitly bans discrimination based on sexual orientation.

Mark Gevisser quotes a drag queen who sums up the constitution's importance: 'You can rape me, rob me, what am I going to do when you attack me? Wave the constitution in your face? I'm just a nobody black queen... But you know what? Ever since I heard about that constitution, I feel free inside.' Discriminatory laws, including the sodomy law, have been struck down, and same-sex relationships are now recognized for immigration purposes. Resistance to lesbian/gay rights and the danger of backsliding still exist, of course; Gevisser describes the bigotry and intransigence present at the highest levels of the ANC and in many parts of society. Nonetheless, South Africa's legislative record is one that lesbians and gays in the United States should envy.

Wherever lesbian/gay movements have emerged in the Third World, they are fighting for the same equal rights that South Africans have fought for. The fight against sodomy laws continues in Nicaragua and Puerto Rico (the only countries in Latin America that still have them), in India and Sri Lanka. In some cases these discriminatory laws can probably be repealed through lobbying and organizing without major upheavals. Other demands will be harder to win. So far efforts to win national constitutional bans against discrimination have failed in Brazil, despite the breakthroughs for lesbian/gay movements as the dictatorship was dismantled, and been fiercely resisted in Fiji. The kinds of partnership rights that have been won in several Western European countries have not yet been achieved in South Africa despite the constitutional promise of equality, in Brazil despite the Workers Party's support, or in India despite the movement's call for them in its 1991 charter of demands.

Furthermore, even the kinds of breakthroughs for lesbian/gay liberation won in South Africa fall short of full lesbian/gay equality. There are after all limits to the lesbian/gay equality that can be won in countries marked in general by deep social and economic inequality, as almost all countries in the Third World are.

Even the South African lesbian/gay movement now finds itself wrestling with questions about the meaning and content of their newly won equality, because South Africans in general are struggling with such issues. The democratic transformation that the ANC called for from the 1950s to the 1980s included more than an end to formal apartheid: it included land for blacks whom apartheid had made landless and a more just division of the economic power concentrated in white hands. Democratic transformation on this scale has still not taken place in South Africa. This constrains the lives of most LGBT people. Gevisser notes that in black townships, for example, where families often sleep eight to a room, 'there is simply no space to be gay'.

Full lesbian/gay equality requires Third World liberation in a broader social sense: liberation from poverty and dependency. LGBT people need housing to give them physical room for their relationships, for example, and jobs that can save transgendered and young people from dependence on the sex trade. How can gay men deal with AIDS, in those countries where male-male sex is a major factor in the epidemic, without challenging structural adjustment programmes that decimate health care? How can LGBT people hope to escape from or remould their families without the protection of a genuine welfare state? At the dawn of the twenty-first century, however, 'the resurgence of market dominance once again threatens to pull away a wide range of social supports and rights', including whatever fragile welfare states had been won in the Third World.[1]

Freedom and equality for lesbians in particular in the Third World means women's emancipation, so that women have other options than marriage and economic dependence on men. All these concerns help explain the links described by Mogrovejo that Latin American lesbian/gay activists made in the 1970s between lesbian/gay liberation, socialism and feminism.

There are many countries in the Third World that have the potential to build advanced economies. Brazil, South Africa and Indonesia certainly have the land mass, population, natural resources, know-how and industrial base to be economic powerhouses. Whatever the different factors holding back their very different economies, there are clearly structural reasons why not one dependent nation broke through into the closed circle of advanced capitalist countries in the whole of the twentieth century. Those Third World countries that achieved the fastest growth rates and most dramatic gains—like Latin America in the 1950s and '60s and Southeast Asia in the 1970s and '80s—have seen their gains undone by the logic of the world market as it is now structured. For this reason the idea of breaking with the world market as it is now structured—breaking with capitalism—will undoubtedly continue to be raised in these countries, including in their lesbian/gay movements. The idea will be more credible to the extent that the left understands that Marxist categories on their own are not adequate to deal with women's and sexual oppression—they must be enriched by the analyses of feminist and lesbian/gay theorists—and that socialist parties need to respect the autonomy of lesbian/gay movements.

Autonomy and alliances

LGBTs have experienced again and again their exclusion from democracy on virtually every level: from supposed democratic institutions, from minimal democratic rights, even from movements fighting for democracy. Even when constitutions guarantee everyone's right to demonstrate and organize, LGBTs have often found that police attack their demonstrations with impunity and officials refuse to register their organizations.

This means that LGBT people feel the need to organize themselves to insist on their inclusion in democracy, autonomously from the existing institutions that are supposed to embody it. This sense of the word 'autonomy', as Mogrovejo mentions, has been the subject of major debates among Latin American feminists in general and lesbians in particular. Since existing institutions make a difference to LGBT people's lives, it is inevitable that LGBT people will respond to them, confront them, negotiate with them and even sometimes take part in them. This raises a host of problems and dangers.

When LGBT people negotiate with or take part in institutions, they ought to be defending LGBT people against them, not representing the institutions to LGBT people. When the World Bank, Dutch or Scandinavian governments or development agencies fund social movements, there is a danger, as Sherry Joseph and Pawan Dhall say, that 'aid-giving organizations, whether governmental or non-governmental, will dictate terms and conditions'. The temptations and need for vigilance are great. But refusing to engage at all with institutions, trying to build LGBT communities while ignoring institutions' existence, is not a solution. It does not respond to reality or to the urgency and scope of LGBT people's needs.

The ultimate goal can be to transform institutions rather than be coopted by them, to create institutions that are not just formally democratic but substantively and genuinely democratic. But lesbian/gay movements usually do not have the social weight to bring about such large-scale social and cultural change on their own. This makes it a matter of basic self-interest for them to ally with broader and more powerful democratic and radical movements, which as in South Africa can win lesbian/gay rights as part of more sweeping political and social changes. In Mexico, for example, breakthroughs for lesbian/gay rights seem unlikely while the 70-year-old party-state regime remains in power. Radical democratic forces fighting against the regime, by contrast, have expressed support for lesbian/gay rights. Mejía notes LGBT participation in the Zapatistas' Aguascalientes Convention and the fact that Cuauthémoc Cárdenas' Democratic Revolutionary Party is Mexico's only major electoral party to come out in support of LGBT rights.

Similarly in Indonesia, gay leader Dédé Oetomo has turned to the radical People's Democratic Party for changes that the Suharto regime did not deliver despite its tolerance of LGBT groups. Joseph and Dhall note the obstacle posed to LGBT rights in India by the strength of 'fundamentalist, communal and sectarian parties': if lesbian/gay rights are ever won in India, the odds are that it will be as a result of radical democratic movements against these forces. In Muslim countries like Pakistan or Egypt, Islamic fundamentalism will have to be confronted in a radical and democratic way. In all these countries true democratization will require mobilizing and organizing the poor majority, which in turn can set in motion fundamental social change.

Lesbian/gay liberation in the Third World thus means not only legal rights achieved through the normal mechanisms of constitutional democracy, but transformations achieved together with other social forces fighting against dictatorship, clientelism, racism, fundamentalism and poverty. Even when LGBT activists see the need to join in these battles, however, it does not follow at all that other democratic and radical forces will welcome LGBT allies. This implies a second kind of autonomy alongside autonomy from state institutions: autonomy from other movements. Independent lesbian/gay organizations, initiatives and thinking are indispensable. Very little organizing for LGBT rights happens if LGBTs do not organize themselves. Occasionally there are exceptions—ABVA in India is one broad human rights group that has advocated lesbian/gay rights, and early law reform efforts in some advanced capitalist countries provide other examples—but generally they occur in relatively brief take-off periods, before LGBTs have succeeded in organizing and taking control of their own movements.

Lesbians in particular feel the need to organize their own lesbian groups. Otherwise they end up too often being subordinated in broader movements in at least three different ways: as gay people in left, democratic and human rights movements; as lesbians in mixed gay organizations dominated by gay men and their sometimes blatant, sometimes subtle misogyny; and as lesbians in feminist groups, facing what Mogrovejo calls 'internalized lesbophobia, as much from heterosexual feminists as from closet lesbians'.

Building autonomous communities and organizations should be combined with working in broader movements that have the social weight to bring about change. As James Green says, autonomy and alliance can be combined. Mogrovejo gives the example of lesbians who as 'loyal daughters to their mothers' have 'continued to fight for space as women and feminists within the feminist movement'. There are many other examples of a persistent, increasingly visible and vocal LGBT presence inside radical movements in South Africa, Brazil, Indonesia and other parts of the Third World. The gains made through working with the Sandinistas and ANC, to mention only two examples, show that visibility and vocalness can pay off. Admittedly, LGBT radicals run occupational risks: a double burden of activism and a tendency towards split personalities. Only as their numbers grow and understanding grows in both LGBT and other movements will the burdens and pressures on them ease.

Dialectics of identity

Along with autonomy from institutions and autonomy from other movements, there is the issue of autonomy from the families and communities that LGBT people are themselves born into. This kind of autonomy means the development of distinctive LGBT identities and subcultures. The obstacles to this in the Third World are particularly great. Many LGBT people even doubt the practicality or desirability of this kind of separate cultural identity, at least if it reaches the point of ghettoization.

Gloria Wekker has argued that 'the notion of a sexual identity in itself carries deep strands of permanency, stability, fixity, and near-impermeability to change'.[2] The identification of sexuality with core selfhood that she describes, drawing on Michel Foucault's work, has come to be deeply rooted in European cultures. But it is not unique to Europe. Transgendered *kathoeys* in traditional Thai culture were also perceived as having natural, unchanging identities, to the point that changing *kathoeys* to men or men to *kathoeys* was forbidden in Buddhist scriptures as a form of witchcraft. There are thousands of transgendered people on every continent who have little choice about developing a separate identity, since a separate identity is thrust upon them from a very young age.

On the other hand, where lesbian and gay communities do emerge, membership in them does not necessarily imply a one-sided, unchanging sexual orientation. Many people who consider themselves bisexual live partly in and partly out of lesbian/gay communities. Others continue to identify as lesbian or gay and take part in lesbian/gay communities even while having long-term— even primary—heterosexual relationships, a choice accepted by some and viewed suspiciously by others in their communities.

One could imagine Third World lesbian/gay communities and movements continuing to emerge and thrive, even while sharing much of the Afro-Caribbean conception of selfhood that Wekker describes: 'multiple, malleable, dynamic, and possessing male and female elements'.[3] LGBT communities could be defined by identities that are allowed to be fluid rather than required to be fixed. Lesbian/gay movements could be defined as embracing everyone who wants to fight for greater sexual freedom, rather than as proclaiming and defending ghettos. Existing same-sex identities could be treated neither by repudiating them—as queer theorists sometimes seem to do—or fetishizing them, but by respecting them and building on them, as stepping stones towards liberation.

This dialectical approach to identity would have different dynamics in the Third World than in the First, and different dynamics in different parts of the Third World. The dynamics would be different where transgender identities are deeply rooted from where lesbian and gay identities have gained ground, and different again in cultures where same-sex eroticism is more or less tolerated without necessarily implying distinctive identities. But the key to the dialectics of identity everywhere would be accepting that change and variability are inevitable and legitimate.

The possibility of communities that are not ghettos and liberation that does not imply segregation comes up in several articles in this book. It often goes together with the idea of a lesbian/gay community that discards much of the economic and cultural baggage of consumer capitalism which often accompanies lesbian/gay life in advanced capitalist countries. Gevisser speaks of 'the tantalizing possibility that South Africa, with its fusion of individualist Western rights-politics and African communal consciousness, might show the world a far smoother way of integrating gay people into society, even if this is at the cost of the kind of robust gay subculture that dominates cities like New York and San Francisco'. In Margaret Randall's interview, Ana V., a Costa Rican living in Nicaragua, contrasts the society that Nicaraguan LGBTs want with the kind of gay ghetto they see emerging in Costa Rica: 'we've wanted to push society, so it will make a place for us, not carve a place out which is only for lesbians and gay men'. Also in this book, John Mburu speaks of an 'agenda including though not exclusively focused on gay rights'.

A vision of liberation without ghettoization can go together with different choices in people's personal lives. It is not always clear to LGBTs in the Third World that 'coming out' as lesbian or gay is a key moment in winning their liberation, as many people in the US seem to believe. In some cases they have never been 'in the closet': the Afro-Surinamese women in sexual relationships with women whom Wekker describes 'are not singled out or stigmatized in a working-class environment nor do they feel the necessity to fight for their liberation or to "come out".'[4] In other cases LGBTs feel that discretion is a reasonable way of sustaining a way of life in which same-sex relationships are only one part, and not necessarily the most important part. The Chinese woman Ning interviewed by Chou Wah-shan says, 'It would give me a lot of trouble if I came out as a "lesbian", a Westernized category that challenges the basic family-kinship structure and my cultural identity as a Chinese. What benefits could coming out in public bring me?' In either case people can be understandably skeptical of the notion that coming out in itself decreases prejudice. After all, women, blacks and Jews have almost always been 'out', and it is questionable whether this has limited prejudice against them.

In the Netherlands, interestingly, LGBT immigrants from the Islamic world have spoken of a 'powerful double life', a life in which they can be open about and celebrate their sexualities at some times and places while remaining discreet in their original families and ethnic communities so as to preserve those important ties.[5] This idea of a double life may make it possible to respect the tactical decisions people make without glossing over the oppression that often contributes to their choices. The Afro-Surinamese women Wekker describes may not be stigmatized as women loving women, for example, but their choice to continue to have sex with men, who are sometimes abusive, seems in some cases to be largely determined by their poverty and economic dependency as women. Ning says that being open about her sexuality would make her 'a devil in people's minds' and be seen as 'failing in my obligation and responsibility as a wife, daughter and mother', suggesting that the 'harmonious family order' she seeks to preserve is based in part on her own sacrifices.

Altman even says that the tradition of married men's having 'discreet homosexual liaisons on the side seems as oppressive to the young [Asian] radicals of ProGay or Pink Triangle as it did to French or Canadian gay liberationists of the 1970s'. None of this means that the choice to announce or emphasize different identities in different spheres of life is wrong, just that this choice is the product of circumstances that are sometimes oppressive and always subject to change.

In general in the Third World, where there are fewer possibilities for living entirely apart from existing family structures, LGBTs are challenged more to find ways to cope with them and change them without surrendering their own needs and identities. In the absence of welfare states, family is more important in the Third World for simple survival. Marriage and children are the only form of old-age or health insurance in many poor countries. This has meant that even when extramarital sexuality is tacitly tolerated it is important that it not be mentioned, so as not to put parenthood and family order in question.[6]

Sometimes refraining from blurting out awkward facts can help make surprisingly flexible solutions possible. Chou gives the example of Chinese parents who invited their son's male lover to eat with the family and eventually even move in. I have run across similar stories of lovers moving in with the family in South African black townships and Brazilian *favelas*. Arguably, arrangements like these can do more to change the society's sexual culture than moving away to some other city with a lover would, even if that were an option. There may well be tensions and constraints in such a situation. As Indonesian gay leader Dédé Oetomo has said, it may be necessary for LGBT people to have 'a safe space for people to gather' so as to make up for 'what is lacking in the heterosexist family'.[7] Openly naming what is happening and discussing it with the family and the whole neighbourhood would be still another step towards liberation. But where is it laid down that the naming has to happen first?

Perhaps the disproportionate influence of US gay culture on the rest of the world has helped foster a model of coming out that in some ways is quite

US-specific. The idea of picking up and moving on to another town is after all a commonplace of US culture. So is coming home to the folks years later, visibly changed by experiences on the frontier. Not all of this imagery is easily transferable even to Western Europe. In a smaller European country like the Netherlands, a lesbian or gay child who comes out will have a hard time moving very far from the parental home, since no place in the country is more than three or four hours away. This seems to imply, at least for Dutch lesbian/gay people whose parents do not belong to the fundamentalist Christian minority, that a gay lifestyle involving great emotional distance from existing families is less common, and forms of integration into existing families more common, than in the US. Perhaps most LGBT people in the world live somewhere in the middle of a continuum between the man who comes out and moves to a big city far away, on the one hand, and the woman who lives with her husband and children and his parents and has a secret female lover, on the other.

As Altman says, 'we are speaking here of gradations, not absolute differences, and the growing affluence of many "developing" countries means possibilities for more people to live away from their families'. But the economic crisis since 1997 puts a limit on these possibilities for the great majority in Asia, as Altman himself acknowledges at the end of his article. The levels of prosperity in East and Southeast Asia until 1997 were exceptional by Third World standards anyway. The objective difficulties of separating from family and community will thus probably continue to make it necessary for most LGBT people in the Third World to develop identities that are multiple and nuanced rather than categorical and all-embracing.

Getting radical about sex

Multiple and nuanced LGBT identities have consequences for lesbian/gay movements. In the introduction I suggested some reasons why 'queer' rhetoric and politics have not caught on much in the Third World: queer theorists' one-sided emphasis on cultural issues, their lack of attention to economics and basic survival issues, and a diffuse conception of power that is not necessarily convincing to women, poor people and others on the bottom rungs of Third World societies. But the queer rejection of a homogenized, assimilationist lesbian/gay sexuality may well be convincing to many Third World LGBTs. Third World LGBT communities are unlikely to become homogenous, and there are too many diverse subcultures to marginalize them all.

Issues of transgendered people and sex workers in particular are important in the Third World. The great diversity of identities gives substance to the idea of an *alliance* of all the sexually oppressed, rather than a movement around a single lesbian/gay sexual identity. To the extent that broad communities do come to identify as lesbian and gay, the words tend in the Third World to be defined politically rather than in terms of a sexual model. As Chou says, the extent of diversity does not allow for a single strategy or 'a single monolithic discourse'.

Lesbian/gay communities in Europe and North America are sexually diverse as well, of course. There has been a profileration of sub-subcultures in the 1980s and '90s. Transgendered people remain one of those sub-subcultures. But there has been a strong tendency to emphasize the most 'normal' images and keep the more 'extreme' ones under wraps as lesbian/gay organizations have pushed their away into the mainstream in advanced capitalist countries. Undermining gender differences, one of the original goals of lesbian/gay liberation in the 1970s and promoted by forms of 'gender fuck' in the 1980s, has been increasingly neglected as a goal by LGB movements. Third World movements can re-raise this dimension, and are in fact doing so, sometimes in the face of resistance from moderate leaderships and disproportionately middle-class gays who prefer to mimic European and North American imagery. Challenging gender roles may help in the future to preserve Third World movements from a reformist, assimilationist politics, which always seems to leave transgendered people behind.

Transgender organizing has a long history in the Third World, as well as a growing presence today. Pakistani transgendered *hijras* organized successfully in the early 1960s against a ban on their activities by the Pakistani government. Indonesian *waria* were also organized in the 1960s, before there was any attempt to organize a gay movement as such, in fact before there was much gay organizing in Europe or North America.[8] Although *hijra* organizing seems rare today either within or outside South Asian lesbian/gay movements, one *hijra* ran for office in Pakistan in 1990, while another was even elected to the city council in the northern Indian city of Hissar in 1995. One of the most prominent leaders of the lesbian/gay movement in Turkey, Demet Demir, is a transsexual who has also played an important role in sex workers' organizing, the feminist movement, and HIV/AIDS advocacy; in 1991 Demir was the first person in history recognized as an Amnesty International prisoner of conscience due to persecution on account of sexual orientation. Since 1993 Brazilian transvestites have both organized themselves and forced the lesbian/gay movement to open up to them.[9]

Transgendered people put forward specific demands when they mobilize. The lists of demands that have come out of transgender organizing in Argentina have been particularly comprehensive; some of the demands have been won. In 1998, for example, the city of Buenos Aires adopted a measure against police harassment of transvestites and sex workers. Other demands have been to reduce the number of documents and occasions when people are classified as male or female, since such classifications often serve no particular purpose, and to fund sex change operations by public health services.

The growth of organizing by transgendered people does not mean that they are monopolizing same-sex politics. 'Masculine' gay men and 'feminine' lesbians are organizing in increasing numbers as well. In the right political circumstances, transgendered people can even become politically active along with their non-transgendered, 'non-gay' partners. The transgendered *skesanas'* 'non-gay' *injonga* partners who led the 1992 Johannesburg Pride parade, whom

I mentioned in the introduction, are a striking example. *Injongas* are exceptional in having a distinctive identity and a traditional word they use to refer to themselves; Latin American men who have sex with *locas* have neither, for example. But perhaps macho men or femme women who have sex with transgendered people in Latin America or Asia could one day play a visible role in lesbian/gay organizing, if and when lesbian/gay movements become strong and popular enough.[10]

Transgendered people's sexual partners, who sometimes have heterosexual relationships at the same time, can be seen in some ways as a Third World equivalent of First World bisexuals, who have also been organizing and demanding more recognition in recent years. But the dynamics of their organizing, and their special role in some Third World lesbian/gay movements, are in other ways quite different from those of First World bisexuals; in many ways they are unique. It is bound to be an enormous step for men and women in the Third World who are married and have families to acknowledge openly their own same-sex relationships. Until that step is taken, the potential base for LGBT organizing is divided and weakened by suspicions, tensions and sometimes even contempt between transgendered people and the non-transgendered people who have sex with them—all the more when class differences are at work. Replacing these suspicions with respect and solidarity is a crucial step towards liberation.[11]

The implications of a broad alliance of varied same-sex identities go beyond adjustments of terminology or this or that subgroup's specific demands. For lesbians, Mogrovejo says, it can mean 're-evaluating the masculine figure—seen no longer solely as an opponent, but rather as a potential ally: gay men, transvestites, transexuals and the transgendered'. It can also mean a redefinition of lesbian/gay movements' goals.

European lesbian/gay movements seem increasingly to demand a recognition of same-sex love enshrined ultimately in the right to marry. The ideal of romantic love has a specific European history, from medieval chivalry to Protestant ideals of domesticity to nineteenth-century romantic novels; and European ideals of marriage are one product of that history. These ideals have been spread by global media, and they influence LGBTs as well, including in the Third World. But in the Third World as elsewhere, many sexual relationships have at least as much to do with satisfying desire or holding together family and community as with romantic love. As they formulate their demands, Third World lesbian/gay movements do not have to privilege relationships based on romantic love as the universal prism through which all struggles must be refracted.

Altman suggests that whatever country we look at, 'whether Indonesia or the United States, Thailand or Italy, the *range* of constructions of homosexuality is growing', and that this broad range will be characteristic of an emerging 'global community'. If so, the Third World may be playing a pioneering role in defining this global community now, as the US played a pioneering role in the first decades after Stonewall. The Third World can pioneer the return of lesbian/gay movements to a broad vision of sexual and cultural transformation. It can raise again the objective of universal sexual liberation, including as Chou says that of the 'so-called straight world', which 'is itself never immune to the seduction of homoerotic desire'.

[1] Barry Adam, Jan Willem Duyvendak & André Krouwel, 'Gay and lesbian movements beyond borders?: national imprints of a worldwide movement', in Adam, Duyvendak & Krouwel eds., *The Global Emergence of Gay and Lesbian Politics: National Imprints of a Worldwide Movement,* Philadelphia: Temple Univ. Press, 1999, p. 356.

[2] Gloria Wekker, '"What's identity got to do with it?": rethinking identity in light of the *mati* work in Suriname', in Evelyn Blackwood & Saskia E. Wieringa eds., *Female Desires: Same-Sex Relations and Transgender Practices across Cultures,* New York: Columbia Univ. Press, 1999, p. 132.

[3] Wekker, '"What's identity got to do with it?"', p. 132.

[4] Wekker, '"What's identity got to do with it?"', p. 131.

[5] 'Een krachtig dubbelleven', *Grenzeloos* (Amsterdam) no. 18 (16 June 1994).

[6] Marc Epprecht, 'Outing the gay debate', *Southern Africa Report* (July 1996), p. 15.

[7] Dédé Oetomo (interviewed by Jill Hickson), 'The struggle for lesbian and gay rights', *Green Left Weekly* no. 351 (3 Mar. 1999).

[8] Nauman Naqvi & Hasan Mujtaba, 'Two Baluchi *buggas,* a Sindhi *zenana,* and the status of *hijras* in contemporary Pakistan', in Stephen Murray & Will Roscoe eds., *Islamic Homosexualities: Culture, History and Literature,* New York, New York Univ. Press, 1997, p. 265; Dédé Oetomo & Bruce Emond, *Homosexuality in Indonesia,* [n.p., 1992], p. 23.

[9] James N. Green, '"More love and more desire": the building of a Brazilian movement', in Adam et al., *Global Emergence,* p. 104.

[10] Neil Garcia is skeptical, arguing that 'gay organizing in the urban centers of the Philippines will most likely always gravitate around inversion', while masculine gays 'will persist in their actively pursued silence: closetedness' (*Philippine Gay Culture: The Last Thirty Years,* Diliman: Univ. of the Philippines Press, 1996, pp. 214). Adam, Duyvendak and Krouwel argue along similar lines that '*activo* men, in a gender-defined system of homosexuality... are not likely to feel a commonality with *pasivos,* thereby inhibiting solidarity and political organization' ('Gay and lesbian movements beyond borders?', p. 351).

[11] The workshop on Algeria and Morocco at the 1999 Euromediterranean Summer University on Homosexualities in Luminy, France, helped me get more of a sense of these dynamics.

Notes on the contributors

Dennis Altman is professor of politics at LaTrobe University, Melbourne, and author of nine books, including *Homosexual: Oppression and Liberation; Power and Community;* and *Defying Gravity: A Political Life.* He has long been involved in international AIDS work, and is on the executive of the AIDS Society of Asia and the Pacific.

Dr. Chou Wah-shan taught at Hong Kong Polytechnic University (1988-91) and the University of Hong Kong (1994-98). He has published twenty Chinese books, eight of them on *tongzhi* issues. He now works at the gender training programme of the United Nations Development Programme in Beijing.

Pawan Dhall has always had les-bi-gay community building as a parallel career while working in the fields of newspaper journalism and development communication. His enduring passions are editing *Naya Pravartak* (Calcutta's Counsel Club's house journal), communing with nature and finding the right relationship. He hopes to build bridges between the Indian green and les-bi-gay movements.

Peter Drucker, trained as a political scientist, has been an activist and writer on lesbian/gay issues and international affairs for twenty-odd years. In 1993 he began researching Third World same-sex politics in order to prepare a lecture on the topic for a Third World activists' seminar at the International Institute for Research and Education in Amsterdam, where he had just begun work as co-director. The lecture led to a 'working paper', the working paper to an article in *New Left Review,* and the article to being asked to edit *Different Rainbows.* He continues to lecture on sexual politics at the IIRE and to be active in the Dutch lesbian/gay left. He is also an advisory editor of the US socialist magazine *Against the Current* and on the editorial board of the Dutch socialist newspaper *Grenzeloos.*

Mark Gevisser is a South African political journalist, author and filmmaker, with a particular interest in the history of sexuality in Southern Africa. He was the co-editor of *Defiant Desire: Gay and Lesbian Lives in South Africa* (1994), and recently wrote and produced *The Man who Drove with Mandela,* a documentary about Cecil Williams, a gay man in the South African liberation movement, which has won awards at the Berlin and Milan film festivals. He is also the Southern Africa correspondent for *The Nation* (New York), and the author of *Portraits of Power: Profiles in a Changing South Africa* (1996). He is currently working on a biography of South African president Thabo Mbeki.

James N. Green is assistant professor of Latin American history at California State University, Long Beach, and a member of the editorial board of *Latin American Perspectives.* A co-founder of the Brazilian gay and lesbian movement in São Paulo in 1978, Green recently completed a social history of male same-sex eroticism in Brazil entitled, *Beyond Carnival: Male Homosexuality in Twentieth-Century Brazil,* published by the University of Chicago Press.

Sherry Joseph is a social worker by profession, now teaching at Visva Bharati University. An assertive les-bi-gay researcher, activist and practitioner, he is currently doing research for his doctoral degree on identity, sexuality and survival strategies of males having sex with males.

John Mburu was born in Nairobi and raised on a farm on the outskirts of the city. He completed a B.A. degree in rhetoric and a B.S. degree in business administration from the University of California, Berkeley. He works as a financial planner with Merrill Lynch, specializing in financial and estate planning for gay and lesbian couples. He lives and works in Oakland, California.

Max Mejía studied social anthropology at the Escuela Nacional de Antropología e Historia in Mexico City. He was a founder of Mexico's gay and lesbian liberation movement and a founding member of the Grupo Lambda de Liberación Homosexual (Lambda Gay Liberation Group) of Mexico City (1978-84). Since 1991 he has been director of the monthly newspaper *Frontera Gay*, based in Tijuana, Mexico. He is also a founder of the Tijuana group Red de Cultura Civil (Civil Rights Cultural Network) and of the Tijuana Gay Arts Festival.

Norma Mogrovejo is a Peruvian lesbian feminist living in Mexico who has been a pioneer in several diferent fields. She founded the first feminist group in her native city, Arequipa, 19 years ago. Once a lawyer, she is now a sociologist and researcher in Latin American Studies, having obtained her doctorate with the thesis, *A Love that Dares to Speak Its Name: The Lesbian Struggle and its Relationship to the Feminist and Gay Movements*. She says that she immigrated to Mexico not only for her studies but for political reasons, so that she could live out her sexual and affectional choice freely. She is studying Latin American history and will continue to think, contribute to and stimulate collective development of a lesbian theory of the region.

Margaret Randall is a writer, photographer and political activist living with her partner, the teacher and painter Barbara Byers, in the foothills of the mountains outside Albuquerque, New Mexico. Recent titles include: *The Price You Pay: The Hidden Cost of Women's Relationship to Money* and *Hunger's Table: Women, Food and Politics*. She is currently working on a memoir, and thinking a lot about the need to develop a new theory of power.